T0104462

Quiet Savage

Marlene Collins

iUniverse LLC
Bloomington

QUIET SAVAGE

This is a work of fiction. All of the characters, names, incidents, organizations, and dialogue in this novel are either the products of the author's imagination or are used fictitiously.

iUniverse books may be ordered through booksellers or by contacting:

iUniverse LLC
1663 Liberty Drive
Bloomington, IN 47403
www.iuniverse.com
1-800-Authors (1-800-288-4677)

ISBN: 978-1-4917-1819-3 (sc)
ISBN: 978-1-4917-1821-6 (hc)
ISBN: 978-1-4917-1820-9 (e)

Library of Congress Control Number: 2013923007

Printed in the United States of America.

iUniverse rev. date: 03/20/2014

CHAPTER 1

April 11, 1948

Marty Toliver inched down the Grumman Goose airplane's isle, holding her squirming daughter, Amy. Her husband, Eddie, ducking to clear the low ceiling, was ahead of her. His son, Ted, giggling playfully, clung to Eddie's flight jacket so the boy was towed, half-dangling, behind his father. Marty smiled tenderly at their obvious affection when Eddie grinned broadly over a shoulder at the boy.

Moving felt good after five hours of flight from LA to Boise, the stop to refuel and eat.

She watched Eddie open the door's curved top onto the roof then swing the door bottom to the right, under the wing. He manhandled the stairs down into place, stepped over the high sill to hop down then reached a thin, bony hand up to help Ted and Marty down from the blocky, low-bellied plane.

Straight white teeth gleamed in an impish grin as Eddie wrapped an arm around Marty, slipping his other hand under her jacket. She squirmed in embarrassed delight while he groped her shirt pocket for the cigarettes and matchbox he'd put there earlier.

Edward Toliver Senior's bulk filled the doorway as he high-stepped through it, eyes twinkling in amusement at Eddie and Marty.

After a quick restroom stop they followed dish clinks to the café. Marty's mouth watered as coffee was poured. Amy fussed on her lap, whining, "Hunry, Mama. Wanna eat." Marty patted and quietly shushed the girl.

She saw Ted peer across the table at Eddie with big brown owl-eyes from a chair between Grampa and Marty, fingertips in his mouth. His wink at Daddy squinched up the whole side of his face. He giggled when Daddy winked back and looked away like he hadn't done that.

Marty watched Eddie fidget impatiently, chain smoking and gulping coffee, so hungry his stomach rumbled. Ted giggled at the noise; Edward grinned at his grandson. Embarrassed, Marty was amazed a mature man like Edward encouraged such rude behavior. She knew Edward enjoyed every moment he spent with his grandson, and that Edward had fought the boy's mother until he got custody for Eddie, who was just returning from the War.

When bowls of thick pea soup and a plate of ham sandwiches was served, Amy laughed in glee, then quietly ate what Marty fed her. Marty ate occasional bites and listened to the men.

"You've never caught a real trout 'til you've caught a big hungry Brown." Edward waved his soup spoon for emphasis. "Now, they're so hungry they'll even bite on a clean, shiny hook." He winked at Marty, who suppressed a grin.

"You go fishing then, Dad. I'll bag us a deer." Eddie grinned. "With all the choice spring sprouts to eat they'll be melt-in-your-mouth tender by now." He smacked his lips. "I can already taste venison steak. Should be herds of 'em I can just take my pick of." Eddie aimed an imaginary rifle, winked at Ted then jerked his head back toward his father, struggling not to smile. Ted giggled in delight.

"That lake you picked for vacation is so remote the game's surely never been hunted." Eddie nodded at Edward, his mouth curling into a half-smile. "But you'll never tell how you got hunting and fishing permits for us in Canada, will you?"

Edward grinned, silently, busy with his food.

"Won't take long to reach the lake, once we leave Calgary, not like this first hop, Babe." Eddie smiled at Marty. "Course, here to Calgary is nearly four more hours."

Edward had construction bids to make in Calgary before they went on to the lake, but that would take less than two days. The rest of the two week trip was vacation—an overdue celebration of Eddie's return from the Air Force and his abrupt marriage to Marty, his war buddy's widow. With Eddie's war-taught flying skills, the mobility of an airplane meant that Toliver and Son Construction, Edward's business, could expand to capitalize on the continent-wide post-war building boom.

Amy tugged at her blond curls. Recognizing the girl's signal, Marty took her to the restroom.

The café's wooden chairs were even less comfortable than the plane's lightly padded ones, so standing felt good. Marty's wiry frame had scant padding, but enough curves to make Eddie whistle when he'd come to express his regret over her loss. He'd blurted out, "You are beautiful. I thought Frank was just sh . . . um, bragging when he said you were."

They'd talked about Frank and what the men had done together, then how Frank died. Marty had thought all her tears were dried up, but she'd cried again and Eddie had comforted her. A deep and immediate bond had formed; they'd both loved Frank.

Eddie was gone when she returned. She glanced around uncertainly.

"He's checking weather and refueling." Edward waved a hand at her unfinished food. "You have time to finish lunch." He chuckled, jiggling the delighted boy on one knee.

The plane's engines coughed to life and roared as it taxied to the refueling area. The youngsters squirmed impatiently as Edward and Marty drained cool dregs of coffee. Struggling to control Amy, Marty found it hard not to spill any.

"Want down! Wanna go play!" Amy thrashed her feet, trying to slide out from under Marty's restraining arm.

"Let's stretch our legs and let these tykes run off that steam." Edward suggested, to Marty's relief, as she ate a last bite.

They stood near the door to watch the youngsters scamper around a small rock garden.

"They'll get dirty." Marty fussed, but hoped playing would wear them out enough to sleep through the rest of today's flight. She sniffed and stretched, enjoying the wet aroma of brimming irrigation canals whose faint gurgles were suddenly audible as the plane's engines were cut for fueling. She saw bright greens of new grass and tender leaves, and dusky purple Lilac buds swelling toward bursting on bushes lined precisely along the building.

Giggles and squeals of delight sounded as Ted first chased Amy, growling, his hands bent into open-fingered claws, then ran from her with big brown eyes flashing mock terror. He went just fast enough she couldn't quite catch him, but her gray eyes glinted with determination as her short legs pumped frantically after him.

Striding quickly on long, stilt-thin legs, Eddie called, "We'd best get going. Might have a bit of weather catch up before we get past the Divide." His lean frame conveyed tension along with his usual impatient abruptness.

At Marty's frown he said, "Shouldn't be dangerous, Babe, but might get a bit bouncy." He flashed that wide, toothy grin that made her knees weak and her heart flutter.

Reassured by that grin, Marty took the dirt-smudged, rumpled youngsters to the restroom to clean up.

Amy balked and howled, "Wanna play! Don' wanna go!"

Marty firmly took her anyway, then ushered the clean, subdued children toward the plane, eyeing it with wonder at modern ingenuity.

The 1937 Grumman Goose could carry a crew of two and six passengers, but was filled with camping gear and food to generously last five people two weeks. It sat on wheels that could retract into side indentations to belly-slide smoothly across water. Attached under each wing was a long, narrow float to keep the plane upright on water.

Boarding with Eddie's help, Marty caught a glimpse through the bulkhead door of Edward buckling into the copilot's seat. Herding the children, she edged past wooden crates, fat, musty smelling canvas duffel bags and tied-down piles of camping supplies heaped in careful spacing inside the cramped fuselage. The reek of aviation fuel mixed with odors of oil and hydraulic fluid seemed to permeate everything and stung her nose.

Eddie had spent hours rearranging inside the newly acquired plane to get ready for this trip. Only two seats remained. Her seat was back-to-back with Eddie's, through the bulkhead wall and over a bin filled with small items. The other seat was through the bulkhead from Edward's seat and over a crate of emergency survival gear that was displaced from the nose compartment to make room for bulky, folding camp cots Marty considered a luxury. Edward insisted they were necessary because the ground might still be frozen where they'd be camping and he didn't want little grandbabies to get cold.

Marty tucked a wool blanket around the youngsters, clipped their seatbelt, and then settled in her own seat.

Eddie muscled in the steps, secured the door and inched by, slipping his cigarettes and matchbox into her pocket, rubbing her nipple for a fleeting second. Marty grinned, momentarily distracted from uneasiness over the flight—but she knew he did it to divert her. His lectures on what to do in an emergency, meant as reassurance, had increased her nervousness. Today was the first time she'd flown and didn't care much for it, even with Eddie piloting. Anxiety goose bumps crinkled across her arms.

The engines chugged to life and wound up to a roar as the plane inched along. Eddie's muffled voice sounded faintly over engine noise as he conversed with the tower operator. Marty's stomach fluttered with butterflies as the plane taxied onto the runway, its twin, wing-mounted engines roaring smoothly. The roar grew louder and rose in pitch as the plane lurched forward, moving heavily down the strip.

As they climbed Marty swallowed and flexed her jaw so her ears popped to accommodate changing air pressure. A sensation of heaviness told her they were climbing, though looking out her window past the wing-mounted pontoon, it seemed more like the world below was shrinking. A momentary feeling of lightness signaled when they leveled out at cruising elevation.

The steady engine drone soon lulled the children to sleep. Marty tucked the other wool blanket around them to shield from the altitude's chill. They didn't flinch when she tucked the corners under drooping heads to keep their necks from getting stiff.

Through cloud gaps, rolling hills below gave way to steeper, more rugged crags with snow-capped peaks that plummeted into yawning ravines and deep, shaded valleys studded with ponds and laced with frothy, racing streams with banks overflowing in spring snow-melt.

The engine drone made Marty sleepy. She drowsed, soothed by the steady buzz.

Bumpiness roused her. Thicker clouds streamed past the wingtips. The air was cold, the ride no longer smooth and soothing. Jagged, precipitous mountains loomed close as the engines labored loudly against load and elevation.

The whole plane seemed to drop suddenly, then slide sideways before steadying again. Wide-awake now and queasy, she regretted eating so recently. The din of laboring engines changed, straining harder as shuddering turbulence grew and icy mountain peaks hulked closer below. A stab of fear took her breath as the plane plummeted through another air pocket.

Eddie revved the engines until their roar became a piercing scream, struggling in cold, thin air to clear the peaks. The plane's nose surged upward behind her, pitching Marty forward, as Eddie fought to gain precious altitude. Alarmed by a sensation of the plane hanging suspended and unmoving in midair, she was shocked to hear Eddie curse vehemently, realizing with a stab of fright she'd never before heard him use such profanity.

Fearfully glancing down out of her window, she saw icy rocks surge up so fast through thin veils of cloud she knew they couldn't avoid hitting them, and froze in utter panic, feeling totally helpless. For brief seconds it looked like the plane might, just barely, clear the icy rocks despite the treacherous downdraft. Twisting to see out better, she strained against her seatbelt, trying to will the aircraft to rise another foot as she watched the ice-crusted peak slip past inches below the wing's pontoon, toward the tail.

A bone-jarring jolt snapped the right side of her face solidly against the metal wall backing her seat, made colored sparks explode behind clenched eyelids. Gusting from in front of her, near the tail, icy air stung her skin and sucked at her breath as she lurched powerlessly forward against her seatbelt, feeling weightless as the plane's nose plunged downward, thrown off its rising course by the glancing blow of solid rock under its tail. The motor roared at full-throttled frenzy as Eddie fought to bring the nose back up before they plummeted into the trees.

Eddie's desperate cursing grew shriller, became a horrifying scream . . . another violent, slamming jolt, an ear-shattering screech of wood-on-metal, a twisting, bending SLAM!

. . . Marty was falling . . . drifting through a soft swirl of darkness that deepened . . . cushioned . . .

Far, far away, a young child was screaming. The strident noise shot pulses of piercing agony through her head like a vicious, living demon. What's wrong with that child? She wondered drowsily.

The stinging reek of gasoline jerked her abruptly back to awareness, disoriented, nauseated. She knew that piercing cry! "Amy!" She croaked.

Desperately she forced her eyes open, but the dim world exploded into hurtful pinpoints of flashing light. She wiped both hands across her face, trying to erase the agony. A shock of memory froze her, but the reek of gas fumes and her daughter's outraged screams were goading alarms to ACT! DO SOMETHING!

"Amy! Teddy!" She couldn't hear him. Why wasn't he crying, too? She struggled to look around, saw only chaos through an unfocused blur. Confused and uncoordinated, she fumbled with her seatbelt, struggling desperately to get it undone.

"Eddie! I can't get loose! Help me!" She screamed, then cringed at new agony in her head.

No answer. Only Amy's enraged screams, now getting hoarse. In desperation, with eyes squeezed shut against the pain in her head, she mindlessly clawed at the buckle until it fell slack, loose at last.

Shaky and dizzy, she struggled up, swayed on rubbery legs, trying to see the screaming child. Groping, fumbling, she felt her way to where the children had been, stumbled and fell, forced to crawl over displaced, yielding piles and sharp-edged crates until she felt a patch of warm skin that moved. She grabbed it in one trembling hand, rubbing the other across her eyes, trying to clear the haziness away.

Teeth gritted, she forced her heavy, shaky body to move, struggled to get the children unfastened and untangled from their seatbelt. Raw gas fumes choked her and stung her eyes—but there was no heat or smoke, the gas hadn't ignited. Yet.

Amy was hoarse, hiccupping. Teddy sniffled and clutched his step-sister tightly, protectively, shaking all over. She had to get them away from danger! A fire could start and cause an explosion—Eddie had warned those were the worst dangers after any crash.

Where is Eddie? He'll know what to do, she thought desperately as she scrambled toward the light, dragging both blanket-wrapped youngsters, painfully cutting her palm on jagged metal at the edge of the light as she reached for something, anything, to help her move faster. She forced herself out of the plane and away, struggling past sharp, tangled scraps of trees, scattered bags and smashed crates. She plunged blindly past face-whipping branches, staggered and fell over slick, tilting rocks hidden treacherously under clumpy, rotten snow, struggled to her feet and ran on. She fell again, gasping, starved for air, and realized the gas smell was only faint now. She sagged, sobbing each ragged breath, and tried to think what to do next as she clutched her precious blanket-wrapped burden.

The children had quieted to sniffling hiccups; both stared wide-eyed at her when she opened bleary eyes. They're safe. I got them out. We're alive. She drooped in relief, gasping for air. Why can't I see?

When she sat up to tug her jacket open and pull out a flannel shirttail to wipe her eyes a rush of cold air hit her exposed skin. Gasping, she peered at the snow they sat on, felt its chill seeping through heavy corduroy pants. I have to get them warm, she thought, glancing at solemn, tear-streaked faces to be sure they were safe, then around at twig-littered snow under ancient, massive trees. Fire. Have to build a fire for warmth—her stomach lurched with fear.

She looked down, trying to understand why that was so frightening, saw her blood-smeared shirttail. A hand went to the sore side of her face, and felt a slick wetness—she'd been hurt!

Unable to focus on that, she shivered violently and stood up, nearly falling as dizziness made the world dim and fuzzy. Colored sparks danced in her vision as agony spiked through her head and her stomach churned. She paused with eyes clenched until the pain and dizziness eased, then looked toward the plane. She gasped in disbelief.

Thick chunks of glossy ice clung to the front edge of a silvery wing fragment leaning crazily against a huge, newly-scarred tree trunk. The snow below was shrunken, compacted by gas from the ruptured wing tank. Twists of jagged metal lay scattered between tilted crates and khaki duffel bags. The warped tail section was yards away from the yawning end of the fuselage. The plane's crumpled front was wedged under a broad, sharply canted snag that had scraped end-first along the nose and rammed through the front windows and cockpit, had stopped partway through the distorted roof.

"Oh, no. Please, no." Marty sagged to her knees, moaning softly, shaking her head, unwilling to accept what had to be true.

An awesome silence pressed in on her.

Numbly she rose, moving jerkily over slippery rocks to the plane, crawling over sharp, torn metal into the dim fuselage and across the canted, jumbled floor, toward traceries of light from the arched cockpit door. There, she hesitated, not wanting to look, unable to keep from it. She had to know!

She took a deep breath, leaned through the door and abruptly fell backwards, gagging from the stench and sight of bloody, mangled bodies crushed between the twisted metal wall and jagged splinters of the snag's end. She screamed and screamed until the horror became numbness, the effort sending stab after stab of blinding agony through her ravaged head as if in punishment for being horrified.

High wails of distress jerked her back to awareness. She forced her leaden body to move. Her screams had terrified the children, they needed her to calm and reassure them.

There was no one else to do it.

She had never felt so alone in her life.

She had never BEEN so alone in her life.

A sharp wind sliced at Marty as she crawled from the tilted wreckage. "Get these babies out of this cold!" She chided herself aloud. "Where to? How long 'til we're found? What should I do?" She desperately needed someone—anyone—to tell her what to do. Hearing a voice, even her own, helped a little. Both men were dead. She was the only adult alive. Never in her life had she experienced anything to prepare her for such a catastrophe.

"Never go anywhere without taking something that needs to be put away where you're going." Mother's stern voice admonished from deep memory, as Marty's subconscious fed her incentive her conscious mind could not. Absently, she grabbed a duffel bag in each hand, cringing at renewed agony from bending over to get them, and moved woodenly toward the wailing children.

Dropping the bags nearby, she secured the blankets around the shaky youngsters and patted them gently, making soft shooshing and crooning sounds. This she knew how to do, its familiarity as soothing to her as to the distressed children. Still, she strained to overcome confusion and the awful pounding in her head, desperately searching for any familiar thing to focus on so she could recognize what to do next.

She shivered from the cold breeze. Cold. That was familiar. She knew what to do about cold. Shelter and fire were needed for cold. She had to do those first—little ones could get sick in such cold. She couldn't let them get sick. They might die and then she would be utterly alone in the world.

Seeing blood on her palm, she thought, I need the first aid kit, too. Nursing cuts was another thing she knew well how to do.

Marty hurried unsteadily back through the towering trees, across the slippery incline to the plane, resolutely shutting mind and emotions away from the death there. The dead would have to wait while she did what she could for the living.

She found most of what was needed quickly, her whole being focused on what she'd come for. The first aid kit, from under her seat, fit in a pocket. She searched and searched for paper to start a fire but found nothing. Some was in the cockpit, Eddied kept maps there. She was horrified at reaching in there but they absolutely had to have a fire. Jaw clenched, she took a deep breath and forced herself to reach in and grab a thin sheaf of folded aviation maps, shaking violently as she jerked back. Shuddering in revulsion, she scrambled away, huffing out her in-held breath.

Trembling, gasping thin, cold air to catch her breath and gulp back nausea, she paused near the wreck to look past broken, tangled trees for a clearing far enough from spilled gas that starting a fire would be safe. She saw almost level ground bordered by low, thick brush and went there, ducking to push through dense branches of towering, aromatic cedars to avoid wading through a trickling spring.

The scanty clearing had been made by a giant tree falling. Its huge, rotting trunk made a good windbreak. She brushed wet snow from littered evergreen needles along the mossy, fern-dotted trunk. Then, teeth clenched against agony pulsing through her head at the effort, she struggled to move the children, who now felt like they out-weighed her. She sat on bare, wet duff, clutching her head with icy fingers, trying to ease the throbbing torment.

Hunting firewood, she realized she had to cut some. Plenty of dead limbs were scattered everywhere, but most were too long to use. Marty sighed wearily.

"Teddy, I have to go find the ax. Will you watch Amy while I'm gone?"

Ted nodded, his dark eyes wide in his thin face. Did she forget he'd been watching Amy?

She puffed back up to the wreck, adrenalin still feeding her energy.

Ted felt important to be assigned to watch Amy. He felt grown up, almost. It was good to help Marty. She was hurt. Her face was all fat and purply and smeared with blood on one side, and a drop of blood dripped from her chin. It made her look kind of funny, made him feel like giggling, but he knew it wasn't really funny. The smeared blood looked almost like a Halloween mask he saw during Trick-or-Treat last year. At first, that mask scared him, too; but then it was only pretend.

He was scared now. He didn't know why Marty swayed and stumbled like her feet were asleep and she kept looking around. She never did that before. Where's Daddy? And Grandpa? They could help her. I can help, too. I can take care of the baby, he nodded.

Marty couldn't find either axe or hatchet but did find the tent, partly broken open but with stakes, poles and ropes still rolled inside. It was crucial for keeping warm tonight. Nudging the bulky roll showed it was very heavy. Teeth clenched and using every ounce of strength, she struggled to carry it across the littered, snow-slippery incline.

She dropped it near the children and stood gasping, her throat so dry every breath stung. Her body ached and her head pounded with nearly blinding pain, but she forced herself to gather dry limbs. Out of desperation, she resorted to smashing them against tree trunks to break them shorter, each wood-on-wood jolt causing flashes of agony in her head and dancing black sparks in her vision.

She groped for dry tinder under dense branches against tree trunks. With wood and tinder handy, she crumpled the maps and heaped on dry evergreen needles and twigs. Puffs of cold wind tugged at the precarious heap. Marty was shaky and uncoordinated, using match after match before flames began to blacken the paper, then the duff. Slipping the matchbox back into the shirt pocket, reminded of Eddie's caress when he put them there, she choked back a sob. That promise would never be fulfilled.

She nursed the fire, concentrating on what to find next, gulping at the lump in her throat. Rescue could not come yet so they had to spend at least one or two nights here. Narrow shafts of sunlight glinting between crowded branches placed the sun low—the day was nearly gone!

Marty hung her aching head. So much to do before dark! And she was the only one left alive to do it, but the life-saving fire couldn't be left yet. She had to force herself to think; head pain and unfamiliar surroundings made her world strange. Nothing was familiar. Nothing was as it should be. And there was absolutely no one to tell her what to do or how to do it, only the helpless children and this stark, cold silence.

Nursing the fire, she realized the silence was not total. Wind whispered through high treetops, mosquitoes hummed, fire hissed, snapped and crackled, the children sniffled and hiccupped. Wood smoke tang blended with sharp conifer pitch and wet, moldy humus. Nearby, water dripped and trickled. She was suddenly acutely thirsty. She had to find the water bag.

When the fire could be left she stumbled back to get more of what they needed. Starting the fire took long enough for adrenaline levels to drop, so now she had to use sheer willpower to drive her heavy, shaky body up the slope.

Swatting absently at biting deer flies, she found a few essentials scattered near the wreck and returned to the fireside. She fed the fire, welcoming its warmth, and squatted by it to rest and warm icy hands, eyes squeezed shut against the harsh head pain.

Following the sound a short ways, she filled the water bag with fresh, cold snowmelt where a trickle spilled over a mossy rock. She helped the youngsters drink from its uncorked spout, then gulped icy liquid. Its cold took her breath away, but soothed and numbed her raw throat.

She warmed a pan of water against the fire while searching bags for a washcloth. Finding nothing, she tore a chunk of cotton from the first aid kit's roll. Very tenderly she wiped tear-stained faces and applied first aid crème to a few mosquito bites on both children, Amy first.

"Where's Daddy and Grampa? Should we fix them, too?" Ted asked softly, his dark eyes filled with concern.

Marty flinched. What can I tell him? Is he old enough to know what death is? She took a deep breath and answered in a soft, quivery voice, "Your Daddy and Grampa got hurt too much to fix. They're dead. We can't do anything to help them." A thick, hurting lump filled her throat, kept her from saying another word.

Ted stared toward the wreck, remembering a tiny yellow bird his Mama used to have that he'd found stiff and cold in its cage. That was dead. Daddy and Grampa were dead like that. It made Marty feel so bad she'd screamed and cried. It made him feel bad, too. Empty inside. Like when Mama left him with Grampa and walked away with her head hung down.

Ted knelt and took the cotton she'd cleaned them with. He rinsed it and gently swabbed dried blood off her face. Marty was surprised to feel raw sore spots. Squinting, he rubbed harder at a crusty place on her forehead, softer on her cheek and split lip. He rinsed the cotton, squeezed just like she had, and washed her hands, being very careful by the slash across her palm. Then he smeared ointment on her hurts, like she'd done.

Touched by Ted's tenderness, Marty gave him a snuggly embrace. The kneeling boy collapsed against her, clutching her and sobbing uncontrollably. She cradled him, her own tears welling as she remembered that not only had he just lost his father and grandfather, but it had been scant weeks since he'd been taken from his mother. He had every right to cry. Holding him, forgetful of her own anguish, Marty rocked side-to-side and hummed softly until he was cried out.

Embarrassed now and sniffling, Ted pulled back to sit by Amy, who'd watched in silent fascination.

Swallowing at that stubborn lump, Marty searched nearby supplies and found a can of Spam. She used its key to twist off the top, stirred the fire, then realized she'd found no utensils. She broke the meat apart with her fingers, mindful of the can's sharp lip. They nibbled the cold meat and drank deeply from the water bag.

Amy tugged at her hair soon after eating.

"No bathrooms out here." She said. "You'll have to go in the bushes, just not close to food or camp, or near water." She took Amy one way and Ted went to other.

Ted helped Marty clear snow, rocks and twigs from the clearing for the tent. They'd practiced setting up the large Army Surplus wall tent at home, and with Ted's help she managed to do it, but it was a hard job without Eddie.

Amy tried to help too, but only managed to get underfoot and tangle the ropes.

The floor tarp was missing so Marty used the small saw that had been under her seat to cut evergreen boughs to pile along the tent's upper side to pad sleeping bags from cold, wet ground.

After she lugged them to camp, both children helped her pull three down-filled bags from their denim stuff-bags. Ted tucked flannel liners into them, nearly crawling out of sight to do so. One bag was a small one Edward had special-ordered for the children; Amy would sleep in that.

Without the children's help, Marty would have been too exhausted to drag the other salvaged items inside. And Amy actually did help gather wood. Ted handed her a small armload of light pieces, and she gloated all the way over to dump them in the pile by the tent. She was so obviously pleased with herself that Ted and Marty both grinned. Marty realized rather sadly that her little girl was not a baby anymore.

Marty lugged in larger broken pieces while Ted brought small ones. She smashed long ones shorter, the jarring effort making her painful head swim and her ears ring.

Setting another chunk on the fire, Marty realized predators would be drawn by the carnage at the wreck. A chill rippled along her spine—she needed a weapon for protection. Where had the men packed the guns? She had to go look now, before full dark.

Darkness crept out almost perceptibly from deep shadows under primitive conifers. A furtive scuffle and barely audible growl issued from brush near the plane. Marty's heart thumped madly as she froze, peering intently into deepening shadows for the growl's source. Darkness intensified quickly, but she heard nothing more. Energized by fear-induced adrenaline, she rushed on, searching frantically, glancing over a shoulder every minute or so.

She couldn't find the guns and her attention refused to stay on the search. The day was gone and other things still had to be done—things didn't do themselves, they had to be done—and no matter how terrified she was, she was the only one to do them. She grabbed more duffel bags so the nerve-wracking trip wasn't wasted. She dared not leave the children alone any longer.

With sunset the air chilled quickly so she pulled another layer of clothes from the bags to dress them warmer and found the new knitted caps and mittens Edward insisted on for 'just in case'.

Prickling neck hair goaded her to find a stout stick for defense. She fervently hoped fire would keep nasty beasts away—she doubted she had enough energy to use the club.

They huddled together on a duffle bag by the fire's light and warmth in unfamiliar stillness, wrapped in a wool blanket for at least the illusion of protection. When two heads started to droop, she put the children to bed in the musty smelling tent, removing only their shoes and coats to tuck them in.

She sat by the fire a while longer, staring at shimmery flames. Pungent smoke and soothing heat soon made her sleepy. She fervently hoped rescue would come soon. Eddie had warned her that if a plane went down in a rugged area it could take several days to find. Nearly always everyone had died in the wreck, so rescue efforts were stopped after about a week. But they would come. It was only a matter of which day. They'd come. She scraped up dirt to bank the fire, to save matches and the bother of lighting another one. And there was no more paper.

She crawled into the thick mummy bag, the stout club handy, and let comforting sleep drift like shadows through her awareness, finding at last an easing of the pulsing pain in her head and the awful, hurting weariness of her body.

She was still very afraid. And so terribly alone.

Again.

CHAPTER 2

Marty was startled awake by birds chirping and was briefly confused by the noise and by odors of new tent, damp humus and wood smoke residue. Camping out. That's what the smells and sounds meant. Something was wrong with that.

Remembering where she was, and why, her throat tightened and tears welled. Shutting away that memory and its emotion, afraid of being helpless from it, she rolled over, thinking, we're alive, I have to focus on what keeps us alive and nothing else.

Faint gray lit the tent roof. Her warm bed was comforting, but she was so thirsty her throat felt like it would stick shut if she swallowed. She glanced at shadowy lumps of nearby sleeping bags, relieved by deep breathing within them. Struggling out of the mummy bag, trying not to wake the children, she stood up—and instantly swayed from intense dizziness that made the world dim.

In shivery haste in faint dawn light, breath wisping white around her, she coaxed fire from glowing coals and dry tinder. She refilled the burlap covered canvas water bag in thicker dimness, drinking deeply while squatting by the trickling spring. The water was so cold it took her breath away, but tasted pure and clean. She pressed its woody cork into the metal-rimmed, top corner opening.

In camp, she pushed a pan of water against the growing fire to heat. She was hungry, but wanted coffee first; for years, she'd sipped a cup each morning while planning her day. Searching the few supplies in the tent, she grimaced. No coffee. No breakfast food. No utensils. Not even a coffee cup. That meant another trip to the wreck before the children awoke. She had to force herself to face that grim place again. Emotions threatened to burst from her tight control. But the youngsters would be hungry and feeding them was a familiar routine she needed to follow, even here. Anything familiar was reassuring. She was desperate for any reassurance.

Marty ducked between door flaps to check the kids and spotted the empty stuff sacks. Squinting through fresh headache from bending over, she took them to gather scattered items.

Spotty fog hung knee-deep between towering trees as she plodded up to the crash site. Nearing, she smelled stale gas fumes, overlaid by the odor of death. Clenching her teeth, she forced herself on, determined to do what she must to keep her children alive.

She was met at the wreck by striped deer flies that darted among a humming swarm of mosquitoes. She absently swatted at them, then jerked and gasped in fright at a sudden furtive scurry in nearby underbrush. Finally realizing the sound was of a tiny creature, too small to be a threat, she patted her fluttering heart.

"I need guns and shells." She spoke softly for the reassurance of a human voice in unfamiliar silence. Feeling so alone and frightened, the sound of any human voice, even her own, helped sooth raw nerves.

She wished Eddie had lived. Even hurt, he could tell her what to do. But he was dead. Her heart thumped and a hot tear slid down her cheek. She should do something for the men, but couldn't think of what was possible.

"I can't bury them." She mumbled apologetically. "I'd can't even get them out." Guilt for not giving them a decent burial spiked a flood of tears and a pang of sorrow.

A startled jerk in the brush jarred Marty back, hands sweaty and heart thumping, to the urgency of her situation. The odor of death had surely drawn scavengers and predators by now.

She was in danger here. If anything happened to her the children would die.

They were alive now.

They needed her now.

She was the only person in the world who could keep them alive.

With all her soul she needed to keep someone she loved alive.

They would soon be awake.

Repeatedly glancing around, she grabbed items strewn nearby, stuffing them in a sack. It was hard to decide what to get when she was so scared and her head hurt so much. Rescue should come soon, but food and warmth mattered now. How long could she get near before the reek of death made approach intolerable? Her hands trembled. Her nape hair prickled from fear. She could feel malevolent predator eyes on her, waiting.

She paused to be sure she had all she came for after quickly filling the other two bags, time and again glancing into indistinct dimness. The first step away, back turned to hidden dangers in the undergrowth, her nerves failed and Marty rushed headlong through the forest toward camp, spurred by terror, stumbling, nearly running down the jumbled rocks of the steep incline despite the bulk and weight of her load. Impetus carried her further downhill than across, took her below camp's level while still many yards to the side. But she was now far enough from the wreck that she dared to pause.

Gazing anxiously back to be sure no beast pursued, panting, she chided herself for giving in to such childish fear. Of course nothing was chasing her!

Gasping, she plunked the heavy bags down on sloped, uneven forest duff. The last bag sagged solidly against the first and toppled it downhill. Cans and packages erupted from the bag's mouth, rolling, bumping, and sliding down the steep, broken slope. Marty wailed in dismay and frantically chased scattering containers, grimacing at new agony in her head. But, for every item caught, more bumped further away, some rolling out of sight under trees and bushes, or worse, far on down the grade.

She finally collapsed, gasping hoarsely, near hysteria over the scattered food. At last she realized the errant items had stopped rolling. She peered into shadows, trying to spot where everything was. One last glance up the slope proved nothing stalked her.

Finally, gathering what she could see, she refilling the bag, dragging it downhill as she went. She moaned aloud at how far she had to struggle back up with the heavy bag.

Reaching for the big coffee can, the last item she could see to reclaim, Marty's attention was drawn to a luminous wedge between huge trees. Curious, she tucked in the coffee and tied the bulging bag shut and walked the few steps further down to the bright opening, at the edge of the deep conifer forest. Here, it gave way to winter-barren willow, aspen, birch and alder, revealing the valley that sloped gradually away below.

Awed by the view, she stared. Sunlight fell on most of the valley though it was still early. She stood in dim shade. The crash site was in deep shade on the north side of the steep incline behind her. Camp was slightly east and downhill from that, also in shade, and would be until hours after the sun cleared the valley's high, rugged eastern rim. Even then, only a few narrow shafts of sunlight would penetrate those high, thick trees.

Fascinated by such unspoiled wilderness, she studied the valley. As far as she could see, craggy, snowy mountains surrounded it. Precipitous slopes were laced with rock slides that cut through conifers forming the forest's upper edge, leaving irregular intervals of treeless swathes down nearly vertical sides. Faint snow patches glinted through dense evergreens below snow-capped, rocky crests. Below the conifers were stands of large barren trees, then down further, wide expanses of brush edged a grassy meadow, still drab and brown from winter. No snow remained where evergreens ended and the sun could reach open ground beneath leafless trees.

Closer than the meadow and slightly west was a large pond, its edges marked by naked trees and brush that jutted above mangled cattail leaves poking through wisps of ground fog. Near the meadow's northeast edge rose a wide, grassy knoll. East from that, barren deciduous trees and bushes formed a dense grove that continued up the valley center as far east as she could see, gradually rising higher in the distance.

The sun lit both the pond and the meadow.

"I have to move us down into sunshine, out of the snow. Then rescuers can see us. They'll never find us where we are." She mumbled, looking up into shadowy dimness.

Back in camp, panting from the strenuous climb, she stoked the fire with shaky hands and put desperately needed coffee on to boil. She had to dump one whole sack to reach the new bag of oatmeal, then put a pan of it on to cook.

Sorting out the food she brought, she wondered what all had been packed. The men had done the actual selection and packing. The coffee suddenly boiled over. She pulled the pan off the fire and poured a cup of fragrant brew, too eager for it to allow time to brew properly, or for the grounds to settle.

Wood smoke tang accented the coffee flavor and aroma. A few blissful sips of steaming liquid made her feel more alert and clear-headed and eased the constant, throbbing headache.

Startled, Marty realized it was just one day since she left LA. The last coffee she had was at the Boise airport, with Eddie. He couldn't share that with her today. He was dead. Too. Tears left cold trails down her cheeks.

Not now, I have too much to do! She brusquely wiped tears with a coat sleeve. The children would be up soon and she refused to show weakness in front of them. It would upset them. She swallowed hard at a throat lump. Sorting again, she found only a few of the eating and cooking utensils she did remember packing.

A forlorn wail startled her. Marty ducked into the tent, grimacing at new shards of agony in her head, and picked Amy up, brushing tangled curls from her face to kiss her cheek.

Ted popped his head up, fisted sleep from his eyes, and yawned deeply. In one quick move he rolled over and bounced out of his sleeping bag, smiling and ready for the day. Marty envied his energy.

They only needed coats and shoes to be dressed. Marty stirred burbling oatmeal, then washed hands and faces with water warming beside the fire, thinking wistfully of how much easier it was to turn on a faucet for warm water. But this was camping out.

Searching for a brush produced nothing, and the comb she had in Boise was gone, so she finger-combed the girl's worst tangles. It would have to do for now.

"Eat, Mama! Wanna eat!" Amy insisted.

Marty had to serve breakfast in metal cups because she hadn't found bowls, but at least they had spoons.

"You'll have to eat this with just sugar on it. I haven't found the canned milk yet."

As Marty fed her daughter, Amy kept trying to grab the spoon, wanting to feed herself. Marty could imagine how messy that would be with sticky oatmeal and resisted her attempts. After both children were full she absently ate the remaining cereal while considering what to get next.

"Teddy, will you watch Amy again? I need to get more from the plane."

Flashing a toothy grin so much like his father's it made Marty's heart ache, Ted said, "I can do that. I like to take care of the baby."

Marty smiled tenderly and went uphill, pausing briefly to scan the few meager patches of sky between towering treetops and listen intently for rescue planes. Not this soon, she chided herself, frowning. They won't even know were in trouble yet.

When Marty left, Ted gathered twigs and showed Amy how to build stick houses like Grampa had with lollipop sticks. They scraped out rivers in the clearing's cold, wet soil. Excited about this new game, Amy danced around and giggled, stomping the twig house and smashing it flat.

"Humph." Ted snorted, both fists on his hips. He started building another one.

They used bark chips for pretend boats in dirt rivers, and rocks for cars that drove on roads paved with conifer needles.

More rustles came from brush at the crash site. Crows, blackbirds and magpies flapped away at Marty's nervous approach, noisily resentful of her intrusion on their scavenging.

"Where are those guns?" She wondered aloud. Searching every nook and cranny in the plane—except beyond the cockpit wall—she grabbed every usable thing she saw and dragged it, huffing and puffing, clear of the wreck.

The last item she toppled from the wreck was a heavy wooden crate. It was hard to drag so she looked inside. It was crammed with food. Unable to handle the bulky weight, she emptied some of the canned goods out into a dip that kept them in place.

Searching quickly for other salvage, she saw the tail section. It lay across the slope yards from the main body, torn off in front of the rear bulkhead wall. It took prying with a broken branch to open the warped door. She sighed in relief when it popped loose—the guns were here! Plus the camp shovel, hatchet, axe, and both galvanized metal buckets.

"I still need shells." She reminded herself, absently noting broken fishing poles. She left those as useless. Shouldering both rifle straps, she grabbed the dented tackle box containing both leather-sheathed skinning knives.

Fear prickled as she looked far up through trees to skimpy sky patches. What if we're not found? Her stomach clenched. Compulsively she grabbed all she could imagine as possibly useful and moved it over to the rest.

Ted paused in play to watch Marty awkwardly approach with her arms full, but she went on by and out of sight downhill. He was puzzled and afraid. What was she doing? Why did she go by? She did a lot of strange things. Sometimes grownups did that, he shrugged, turning back to entertaining Amy. He tried hard not to be afraid.

After a second trip down to the new camp, Marty puffed slowly up to move the children and some of that camp down into the sunshine.

Ted helped take down and fold the tent and stuff sleeping bags in their emptied sacks, wondering why she was doing this. He looked at her bruised face and didn't ask.

Marty carried all she could at once while Ted led Amy by the hand, guiding, sometimes struggling to pull her over obstacles on rough, litter-strewn ground along the winding, well-worn game trail. When they finally reached the sunlit clearing Marty's arms were shaky and nearly numb with fatigue.

Down out of snow and among trees starting to bud leaves on branches festooned with dangling brownish catkins, this campsite was warmer. And now it could be seen from the air.

Amy sat quietly watching her mother and Ted move things. Entirely worn out from the long walk after playing so hard, she soon fell asleep.

Ted watched Marty trudge back up into the shady woods. Amy was sleeping. Marty needed help. What else could he do? Grinning in anticipation of her surprise, he looked nearby for firewood, piling all he could move at the clearing's edge.

Camping out was fun. He could do so many new things. If only he could show Daddy and Grampa how good he could help. But they weren't here. They got dead.

Panting, Marty dropped the tent in the clearing and sat on it, her aching head resting on arms crossed over her knees.

"See what I did?" Ted proudly pointed at the jumbled pile of scrap wood.

"Oh! Thank you." Marty said, hugging him and resting her aching head briefly on his shoulder. She straightened. "Are you kids okay? I still have so much more to bring."

"Yup. Baby's sleeping." He smiled bravely.

After she left, he struggled with the tent, trying to unroll it. But it was too heavy, and he was tired. He usually took a nap with Amy but he was watching her today. He was getting too big for naps. Naps were for babies, and babies didn't take care of someone else like we was.

Marty returned with a load that included the dangling three-gallon bucket holding hot coals. She was desperate for the break required to start this new fire. Wafting smoke reminded her of the wood stove at her childhood farm. Home. She fought tears, nearly overwhelmed by homesickness, fear and uncertainty.

Amy woke and needed attention so Marty shut her feelings tightly away. She had missed fixing lunch and now dinner was late. But the most urgent things had to be done first and she was the only one to do it. She still felt guilty for not feeding them on time.

Dismayed at the random jumble of supplies, she settled for fixing cheese and crackers and opening a can of peaches with the prong-tipped can opener. They sat on a fat duffel bag near the fire to eat. She let Amy feed herself—no floor to clean up, here.

The sun was nearly down when they set up the tent. Ted was obviously almost as tired as Marty. They lacked energy to cut boughs to lay on, but the ground here was warmer and dryer.

From the fireside, Marty held a child on each knee and sipped morning's coffee dregs, watching darkness fill the surrounding valley. The crystal clear sky was nearly solid with bright stars. It was comforting to cuddle the children, to hold someone she loved, someone alive.

Putting the youngsters to bed left cold empty places on her lap; still, it was nice to just sit and look at the billions of miniscule stars that lit the moonless sky.

Far, far off a cougar screeched its eerie, hair-raising cry, causing a jolt of terror and a violent shiver. Marty fumbled in flickering firelight to find and load the pistol from the survival kit. Snapped into its holster, she held it until she was ready to bank the fire with dirt and ashes and crawl into bed. She tucked the pistol under the edge of her sleeping bag where it would be handy if she needed it.

She cuddled very, very close to the children all night.

CHAPTER 3

A squabbling flock of gray jays woke Marty at daybreak. Cheered by the sociable fuss, she slipped on boots and coat and stepped out to stretch and yawn. A flash of headache and dizziness staggered her, so she quietly waited for the world to stop wavering. Squinting past the ache, she watched flitting, cheerful birds in chilly, misty light.

A new moon crescent glowed in the gray sky, its disc silvery transparent, one side lined by a thin wedge of glowing brightness. It was beautiful.

This campsite gave a new perspective, made the sky seem larger, craggy mountains taller, more precipitous and impossibly high above incredibly steep slopes. Marty felt dwarfed and insignificant in such immensity. The squeaks, tiny scurries and rustles from nearby brush and the scolding of gray jays flitting through frosty branches were comforting, made by creatures too small to harm her or the children, from creatures unafraid for their own safety. The frightening sounds by the wreck had been from larger, dangerous beasts. Marty shuddered at remembering those furtive, menacing sounds.

A few sprouts showed pale green through forest litter, reminding her of greens she'd seen in Boise. But there, grass was obvious, the leaves well grown. Here, few things had begun to green up; high elevation delayed the new growth. The drabness revived her grief.

By the gurgling spring, getting a bucket of water, dense bushes of willow catkins made the world less bleak. She'd seen bouquets of Pussy Willows in grade school. Gram had been right when she said that even the worst times have blessings you only have to open your eyes to see. She blinked back tears.

Stoking the fire, she set coffee on to boil, this time in the coffee pot. She wondered if anyone realized they'd never reached Calgary, where they were due yesterday. They were scheduled to be gone for two weeks. How long would it be until anyone searched this area?

Sipping fresh, aromatic coffee, she reminded herself that rescue can take a few days. The ritual of brewing and drinking and the smell and taste of her morning coffee was comfortingly familiar. It kept alive a link to the rest of the world, a link she desperately needed to maintain any sense of reality.

She was frightened of being so alone and of unknown, unfamiliar dangers, felt inadequate to cope with this unexpected situation. Someone else had always taken care of things and made decisions. Now, for the first time, she was totally on her own, responsible for herself and two small children. She felt lost and empty.

Abruptly she felt an urgent need to get done what she did know how to do. Sitting idle left too much time to think.

Surveying jumbled supplies, now damp with frost, she decided to put camp in order—she was good at cleaning up. She sorted random piles into some semblance of order: clothes here, food there, dishes and utensils over there, all the rest in that pile. She set the men's two rucksacks and a custom-made backpack for carrying Amy in the last pile. Rescue would come before those were needed.

Opening the crammed tackle box, she removed a leather-sheathed hunting knife to put on her belt opposite the holstered pistol. She left the whetstone and the other knife under the lift-out tray. Now she felt less vulnerable or defenseless; but still felt insignificant in such vast, primeval wilderness.

Checking the sleeping children, she decided to move more supplies before they woke. Hopefully, she could do it all in one trip. It was a long, steep distance up and back.

Despite the chill, a strong, distinctly offensive odor surrounded the wreck. Raucously noisy, flapping, squabbling birds already crowded around the fuselage. Marty's stomach churned at what they were after. She clenched her teeth and shut away all emotion. Immediate, urgent things needed to be done. Things she could do something about. No room was left for sorrow or regret over things she could do nothing about.

She told herself that over and over, and over.

Sunshine brightened camp when Ted and Amy poked their heads out the tent door, awakened by the aroma of cooking cornmeal. The sun's warmth melted frost into tendrils of mist with a crisp odor, leaving only shady places shiny white.

Dishing up steaming mush, Marty smiled. "Good morning. Are you hungry? You even get milk on your cereal today. I finally found it." She said in strained cheerfulness as she added canned milk and spooned sugar from the slightly dented metal canister.

Both children were so hungry they bolted their food down, giggling at each other even though the hot mush brought a hint of tears.

After eating, Marty took them to the first camp, where clothes and food remained. But, finally, that was the last she had to move.

Marty held Amy's hand to help her over tangled roots and forest debris. Once Ted had to take her other hand so he and Marty could swing the girl over a rotting log in the trail.

Amy giggled in delight. "Do 'gin, Mama. Wanna do 'gin."

Marty smiled and shook her head. "Not now. We have to go this way now."

Ted glanced wistfully over a shoulder at the log. That looked like fun. But he was too big for that now. Anyway, Amy was too small to help Marty swing him like that.

They finally reached the old camp. It would be hard to get it all at once, but it was a waste to make a trip for a few items. As it was, she had to repack and condense everything. A shirt bulged from the gaping top as she cinched the last bag shut.

Tying the drawstrings of two bags together, she slung them over a shoulder, then grabbed the last bags, one in each hand.

She couldn't help Ted with Amy, this was all she could handle. Ted was so much help, she thought, shifting the bulky load into better balance. He was a good kid, always taking care of Amy and getting wood, usually without being asked.

Turning to leave, she saw their empty cans and wondered what to do with garbage, the bulky, swinging bags nearly tipping her over. Camping as a child, she was always upset at someone else's trash and she dreaded leaving any. But no rescuer would haul garbage. She'd have to leave most of what they had, as it was. No rescue plane could hold much more than the three of them.

"Why am I doing all this?" She carefully picked her way down the trail. "I'll have to leave most of it when we go." A pang of fear reminded her they might not be found, this was 'just in case'. Besides, staying busy kept her from thinking about things she couldn't yet stand to face.

Gratefully dumping her load by the tent, Marty sagged down and let achy arms dangle until they stopped throbbing, squinting against the ever-present headache.

For lunch, she spread peanut butter on graham crackers and thinned canned milk to wash it down. Amy was so tired she hardly ate. Arms quivering with effort, Marty put the child to bed.

Sorting gear and supplies, she mentally tallied how much of what they had. Some items were missing but she could think of nowhere else to look for them. Some things would never be found, like a whole slab of bacon from a smashed crate—something had a real feast on that! One skimpy chunk of another slab remained, only because it had been tucked into another crate.

Reminders of the two men were everywhere: Edward's hard candies; their sleeping bags; their shaving gear. It was hard to sort through things, constantly reminded of men no longer here; but Marty set her jaw and did what she could do something about.

Beds lined one side of the tent and clothes went along the other, the men's against the canvas. Three unbroken crates, arranged upright like cupboards along the end wall, steadied by sticks wedged under to balance them, held food and cooking gear. The hinged lids opened easily that way. The slowly dripping water bag hung by its thick rope handle from a branch stub on an alder near the door, staying cool in the breeze.

Amy slept through the rearranging. Without the girl to play with, Ted became bored and sleepy. It was a long, hard trek for him, too. He tried to stay awake, but at four-and-a-half, hadn't entirely outgrown the need for a nap. Aching with fatigue, Marty wished she could nap. But someone had to be awake to signal the rescuers when they came.

She settled for a coffee break, unfastening her jacket to cool off. Blowing a cool breath down the neck of her shirt, she glimpsed the flattened cigarette pack in her pocket. She'd forgotten it, but recalled Eddie's grin when he put it there . . . tears clouded her vision.

Fumbling the cigarettes and matches out, she wiped them away. Never, never would she fall in love with another pilot, she vowed bitterly.

The wooden matches were priceless but Marty had never smoked. She briefly considered giving the cigarettes to a rescuer, but the idea of doing it made her suddenly furious.

"No!" She snarled, jabbing the rumpled pack into the flames with a wood stub. She glared at the bleak forest, fighting to overcome the unexpected anger. She couldn't change what was. But until now she'd been unaware of being angry about it. Mother would've scolded her for not quietly making the best of her situation and reminded her that life wasn't always fair, that everyone experienced situations of testing and you had to make the best of them.

Marty's chin sagged onto her chest as she sought strength and courage to endure. This wouldn't last forever. Life would return to normal. She only had to do what needed to be done until then. Staring into the smoldering fire, she considered what would happen if she got hurt; the children were too young to take care of themselves. If they were not found, how would she get them home? It had taken so many trips to move what they had, she'd be unable to take but a small portion if she tried to walk out. Amy couldn't walk very far, had only taken her first step eighteen months ago. Ted was too small to carry much. So they couldn't carry enough food to walk out, even if that was all they took.

How long would this food last? They'd planned to get eggs and meat in Calgary, but packed plenty of everything else for two weeks, allowing for bigger appetites while out camping. Together, the three of them ate about what either man would. But some food had been lost or was not salvageable, like part of the canister of sugar that had spilled. What would happen when all that ran out?

Anxiously, Marty resorted food, now counting how many meals they had. Thoroughly discouraged, throbbing head clenched between both hands, she sat down. They had enough for a month if she let absolutely nothing go to waste, but meat would be long gone by then. Surely, by that time, even if they were not found, she could come up with some kind of solution.

Rescue would come. It had to!

Drooping through neglected chores, often searching the empty sky for a plane, she unconsciously tried to will one into being. She hauled water in the smaller bucket, trying to keep it from slopping down her leg. But she was tired and icy water soaked one corduroy pant leg.

She put the stewpot over smoking coals to heat water then found the hairbrush, perched the small polished-metal mirror on a branch stub, and began untangling her hair. She was startled to feel a sore knot on the back of her head. Peering into the mirror, her reflected image shocked her. Vivid purple bruises covered the right side of her face and a wide scab coated her right temple and brow. Her upper lip was also scabbed, with flecks of dried blood smeared nearby.

Marty's knees suddenly gave. She sat down hard near the fire, automatically grabbing the familiar coffee cup for reassurance. She curled over the cup, ashamed of looking so horrible—what would the rescuers think? No wonder the kids had stared so strangely at her that first day. No wonder her head hurt so much.

How close had she come to dying? She saw several possible, horrible fates for the children if she'd also died. All three of them had been inordinately lucky.

Finally, using the hunting knife, she shaved slivers off the bar of Fels Naphtha soap into the enamel washbasin of hot water and whisked it into suds with her fingers, the sharp pungency smelling like home. She washed accumulated crusty dishes. The stewpot held rinse water. She used the sturdy iron grill, brought to set over a fire for a stable, even cooking surface, to drain dishes. Both children woke from their naps as she dried the last dish.

Marty and Ted rolled the biggest rocks they could move in to surround the fire and support the grill. Marty adjusted them level and stable so no food spilled into the fire. She couldn't waste food, but also didn't want to start another fire in a pit of wet ashes.

Ted dragged in more wood as she fed the fire and started a stewpot of fresh potatoes, carrots and onions, adding a few strips of jerky. The jerky had been meant for a few light snacks. Some cans of Spam had been salvaged and the bacon remnant was only enough to flavor a meal or two; the meat wouldn't last long.

Sighing in resignation, she checked the empty sky. They'll come when they get here, she shrugged, trying not to worry.

She searched nearby until she found a debris-coated log about the right size, rubbed off the duff, then struggled with it to the fireside, rolling and pulling it laboriously along. It was well-seasoned wood, light for its size, but still a challenge to move. She dropped one end by the fire. When the log hit the ground it broke in half.

"Now we have two consarned logs! Why couldn't it do that before I moved it?" She grumbled, stamping a foot.

A jay's coarse squawk reminded her of last night's eerie cougar scream, made her nape hair prickle again. So, while stew simmered and the children played a boisterous game of tag around the clearing, she sat on the new log seat and cleaned both rifles and the pistol.

The pistol was a Smith and Wesson .38 revolver that held six shells. She cleaned, oiled and reloaded it, then snapped it back into the holster, comforted by its weight at her hip. Its box of fifty shells was missing the six that filled it.

She frowned at the weight of the bolt-action 30.06 Springfield rifle Eddie had brought back as a war memento. He's said it was a sniper rifle with an extended barrel for long range accuracy. The hardest part of learning to shoot it was the struggle to hold it steady enough to sight and shoot, in spite of using its sturdy leather sling for bracing. It was too muzzle-heavy for her to always hit the target, but sometimes she had. It had a full box of long, lethal-looking shells. She decided to keep it unloaded because of the children. And she couldn't picture needing a gun that size for protection.

The other rifle, a new lever-action 30.30, was shorter, its weight half that of the 30.06. Its recoil bothered her less. She even consistently hit in the target rings with it, but not often the bull's-eye. It had two boxes of shells so it could be sighted in accurately. She also left it unloaded, the pistol was enough protection.

There had to be room on the rescue planes for the rifles, they were far too valuable to leave behind.

Marty was glad she'd learned to shoot and care for the guns. Now, with them ready to be loaded, and camp further from the crash site, she and the children were safer from lurking predators—comforting to know.

She gave each child a soft, transparent bag of the new-fangled oleomargarine to mix up. In a corner of each bag was a small yellow button of flavored oil that she popped into the pasty white grease, then showed them how to knead in the oil. They loved that.

With them occupied, Marty set the foldout reflector oven on the grill, mixed a batch of soda biscuits and slipped a mess kit lid full in to bake. She would have preferred to walk to a corner grocery to buy a loaf of bread.

Then, with soap this time, she washed the children's hands and faces and brushed Amy's tangled hair. The children returned to their new fun while she washed her own hands, staring at forming calluses and broken fingernails. But that was part of camping out. This wouldn't last forever. Camping never did. She'd groom herself better after they got home.

The biscuits were done and cool before the stew was ready but the oleomargarine tasted good on the biscuits even if it didn't melt in. Marty had canned butter, another of Edward's luxuries, but it was safer from nosy animals than plastic-wrapped margarine so she'd save it for later.

At sunset she mixed and heated a pan of hot cocoa, sipping it with the children, cuddling them by the fire as darkness oozed from the shadows. Both cuddling and cocoa were soothing. She was bone-tired but satisfied with all she'd done that day. Still, there'd been no hint of a plane, not even faint sounds. No rescue today. Surely they'd come tomorrow.

The children had napped late and resisted going to bed, so she told them the fairy tale of the Three Billy Goats Gruff. Two pairs of eyes grew wide when she got to the part about the mean old Troll under the bridge. Both begged for another story but Marty was too tired to think of one. They giggled and squirmed, but finally settled down to sleep, each in a small sleeping bag with the two spare ones under them for insulation.

Marty was so tired that sleep came quickly, swooping her gently away from aching weariness, and from worry.

She dreamed something sad—couldn't remember what—and woke from tears scalding her temples, feeling terribly alone. The children's deep breathing proved she was not entirely alone. She'd die in this strange place without them; keeping them alive gave her a reason to stay alive, to struggle on like she was. But if we're not found soon we'll run out of food, she fretted. If I can't keep them fed, they'll die. Hopeless dismay filled her eyes with tears again.

What all did we do on the farm? Mother and Dad took care of so much. How did they do everything?

She strained to remember but her thoughts drifted to one of her talks with Gram. Gram had been teaching her to knit but talked steadily about her own childhood, back before there were easy, modern ways to do things. She'd told about wiping soot from kerosene lamp chimneys every day, boiling clothes so they came clean with less scrubbing on the washboard, dipping tallow candles—no end of fascinating things. She'd even shown Marty what weeds in the garden were good to eat and, on camping trips, other wild foods.

Unexpected pitter-patters of little feet raced across the sloped tent roof, startling Marty wide awake, set her heart thumping madly. She heard small squeaks and faint rustles and rattles as tiny creatures prowled in the unwashed coca pan and metal cups.

Somebody's hungry, she thought, smiling, reassured she and the children were not in danger if tiny creatures felt safe to be out foraging. She drifted back to sleep.

This time she dreamed of childhood on the farm, of food she'd helped with, baking, gardening, harvesting, canning . . . and butchering. Her last half-conscious thought was: we need fresh meat.

Morning was chilly and cloudy. The cheerful gray jay flock could not be seen or heard, their absence a huge disappointment. Rekindling the fire in the unnatural hush, she heard faint deer snorts and rustles in thick brush toward the pond. A vision of venison steak made her mouth water and her heart thump in excitement.

"The kids are asleep and we need meat." She whispered aloud, then hissed, "I'm going hunting."

Quietly loading the 30.30, she remembered how long it had been since her first hunt with Robert, the brother nearest her in age. The biggest thing she'd ever shot was rabbits and that was with Robert's .22, his varmint gun, he'd called it.

Making sure both pistol and knife were on her belt, she crept stealthily toward the snorts and rustles. Tense with adrenaline, she stalked intently, her mouth dry, her heart pounding wildly, each sense acutely sharp and her hands sweaty despite the chilly air.

Glimpsing a grayish, big-eared doe, she raised the rifle and stepped forward—on a brittle twig. At its loud snap, deer scattered everywhere, swiftly bounding in springing leaps through the brush. She couldn't even draw a bead on one.

Trudging back, Marty seethed at her carelessness. She knew how to hunt better than that! She was hungry, scared of letting the kids down by not getting fresh meat. Adrenaline letdown left her shaky and weak-kneed. Only after making and drinking coffee could she calm down.

"Maybe a whole deer was too much." She grumbled.

"How could I keep so much meat from spoiling before we ate it? We won't be here long, anyway. They'll come any time." Worry knotted her stomach as she fruitlessly scanned the brightening sky.

The children were up early and, though quite hungry, she barely ate, focusing on how to get fresh meat. They had fishing tackle. The poles were broken but she could always cut a pole, and could take Ted and Amy to go fishing. She hated leaving them alone so much, but fishing wasn't dangerous like taking them to the wreck had been. It was fun. Ted would love it.

Filling both coat pockets with raisins and graham crackers, she put Amy in the baby carrier, but Ted had to help get it up onto her back. Amy was getting heavy, not a baby anymore—she'd even helped gather wood. Marty smiled, remembering Amy's gloating satisfaction at collecting the small armful of twigs.

Ted proudly carried the dented tackle box, net and fishing creel, grinning broadly as he followed Marty along a winding game tail leading toward the pond. He held Marty's hand to hop across a narrow brook to keep from getting wet.

She paused under a barren tree to wonder about patches of missing bark far above her reach. Tooth marks showed in the darkening wood—some big animal had made those holes. She'd heard of deer and elk eating bark in winter but was stunned that any could reach so high. Then she remembered the winter before last had been so severe it had produced nearly double the normal snowpack. How deep did snow get here?

Continuing on, she kept searching the sky. Why was rescue taking so long?

A reddish-gray squirrel chattered and scolded as it whipped around its tree to hide, then cautiously peeked out to scold more. Grinning, Ted edged around the tree to see it better. It scampered up higher and scolded louder from the safety of its perch. Amy pointed at it, giggling, and tried to imitate the sound. Marty puckered up and sucked like a wet, noisy kiss that sounded almost like it. Ted practiced the kissing sound as they walked, further enraging the squirrel until they were out of sight. Marty chuckled over the outraged protests, wondering what Ted was saying in squirrel language.

Passing out of sunlight, Marty felt the shade's coolness. A soft breeze carried faint goose honks and the odor of decaying leaves. Narrow vegetation breaks ahead showed glimmering pond water, while a brisk stream gurgled to her right, behind a solid wall of willows. She clucked her tongue in annoyance—how could they fish if they couldn't reach the water?

Marty worked back upstream, looking for thinner brush they could squeeze through. After yards of struggle she found where a narrow, gravelly gap gave access to the strong current.

Sighing relief, she said, "Amy, you have to walk on own your more." She slid the carrier down and rubbed aching shoulders. "You're getting too big for me to carry."

Amy chortled in pleasure, clapping her hands and gloating, "Yeah. I big, Mama!"

Marty grinned, rolling her eyes.

"Now we need a fishing pole." Four wide eyes focused on her. "I went fishing a lot when I was a kid." She said, hunting for a tough, flexible sapling. "We never caught much, but we had fun trying."

Using the skinning knife to cut down and trim branches from the chosen sapling, she told them about learning to fish. Both giggled at faces she made describing the first time she baited her own hook with a slimy, wiggly worm.

Ted watched every move as she untangled line, secured one end to the pole's tip and then tied a hook on the other end.

"Now we need bait . . . should be something where it's damp." Ted helped Marty turn over rocks and scrap wood, hunting worms or grubs for bait, while Amy stared at wet, root-laced dents under each piece they moved.

When several fat white grubs were in the rusty bait container, Marty said, "I heard you could eat these." She shivered in disgust. "I'd rather fish with 'em and eat the fish!"

Ted guffawed, nodding so hard it shook his whole body. "Me too!"

Amy laughed, too, but wasn't sure what was funny.

Patiently fishing, Marty looked at the valley's craggy, snow-capped rims and noticed how fast dark, high clouds sped by. A slight breeze reached the valley floor, barely swaying brush tops. She was glad for the wind protection those high crests provided.

Dark water swirled around rocks and projecting roots that created foaming pools. The stream spilled over its sharply cut banks from spring snowmelt, washing dark debris over scattered barriers as it tumble noisily along. Tiny animals scurried through thick willows and birds flitted among bare branches. The children played quietly with small heaps of colored rocks by her feet. Ted built a stick fort between the pebble hills.

From the corner of an eye, Ted watched Marty's every move. Soon he could fish and he'd do it exactly like she did.

Feeling peaceful, Marty wished her constant headache would go away. Willow, she thought, aspirin was made from willow. But which part? And how do I get it out? Gram could have told her. Maybe chewing a twig would help.

When she laid the pole down and stepped away to break off a twig, it jerked and slid toward the water. With a yell, Ted dived sideways to grab the pole an instant before it disappeared into the roiling water. Frozen in astonishment, Marty watched.

"It's a fish! I'm catchin' a real fish!" He yelled, voice cracking in excitement as he scrambled to his feet and clung to the whipping pole, leaning back and struggling to land it. With a whoop of pure delight, he jerked back with all his weight. A big spotted trout erupted from the water and slapped to the gravelly bank near his feet.

Ted hopped and danced around his thick-bodied, foot-long, thrashing prize, shrieking, "I caught a fish! A really really really big fish!"

Marty and Amy covered their ears. In blind panic, every bird and tiny hidden creature scattered to safety. In a scant second the whole area was utterly silent except for the stream. Marty and Ted gaped at each other. Then they started to laugh at the panic Ted's boisterous enthusiasm had caused, laughed so hard they nearly cried. Amy danced around looking puzzled but laughing, too, and they laughed all the harder. Near hysteria, both doubled over and held their sides, laughing until tears streamed.

Finally it wasn't funny anymore. Laughing hurt too much. And surely more fish waited to be caught. But a deep tension between Marty and Ted—that neither had been aware of—was broken by the shared laughter.

Ted jiggled with excitement as Marty held his fish down with a waffle-soled boot to work the hook free.

"Ooh. My poor fishy! His mouth is bleeding, and, and it's hurt." He was near tears. "Don't hurt my fishy!" He pleaded, his bottom lip quivering.

Marty's heart melted. She gently patted his shoulder. "It's only a fish, and fish don't feel hurts the same way we do." She soothed. Then, trying to cheer him up, she teased, "Now that you caught the biggest fish in the stream it's my turn."

Marty soon caught a much smaller trout. She added new bait and tossed it back out, then laid the pole down and stepped on it firmly. She showed Ted how to clean his fish, using hers for example, nervously watching him handle the sharp knife, so big in his small hands. It was hard to keep from doing this herself, but he had to learn skills like this some time, it might as well be now. Camping was time to learn these things, and they might be gone tomorrow.

Amy squatted to watch. One tentative touch on a fish's cold slime made her say "Aaakk" and wipe the finger on a pant leg. Marty smirked and Ted giggled.

With both fish cleaned, Marty handed the pole to Ted. He was so excited he couldn't make his legs hold still, softly giggling in anticipation every few seconds. Smiling, Marty gathered a few small willow twigs, started to stuff them in a pocket and discovered their forgotten lunch.

After they ate she showed them how to cup their hands to get a drink from the stream. Ted barely took his eye off the pole when she held it so his hands were free to drink. Amy loved dipping and scooping, loved any water, even when it was icy cold.

By early afternoon the clouds were dark and thick. A cold buffeting wind picked up. Marty noticed a tinge of rotting flesh in one gust. A lump hardened in her throat and she looked away until she could hide her distress from small eyes.

Ted soon caught two more fish, the last biting as bait hit the foamy water. Enough. Time to get back to camp. The brisk wind and darkening clouds worried Marty.

Ted helped with the baby carrier then followed, proudly carrying the stringer of fish, his big one at the top nearly dragging the ground.

Marty snagged the hook in the pole's bark and stored it by the guns. Stoking the fire, she fretted about a storm delaying rescue. How long would a spring storm last here? Already she couldn't remember how long they'd been here. Blurry memories of finding supplies and endlessly moving them seemed like several days, but she wasn't sure. Tears stung, but she refused to let the kids see her cry. If they knew she was afraid they would be, too, and she didn't know how reassuring she could be.

Turning the sizzling fish, small bits of forest debris blew in her eyes and blowing sparks stung her face. They had plenty of fish, but it was too nasty out to fix anything else. Retreating inside with the cooked fish, she picked out bones and let the children eat all the flaky meat they wanted, allowing Amy to feed herself again.

Ted ate his whole big fish by himself. It was hard to get down the last swallow of his very own fish, but it was so good!

"We did this. We went out and got this meal by ourselves." Marty proudly said.

Ted flashed that dazzling grin, knowing he'd caught all but one fish.

Understanding, Marty smiled as she ate her share of tender, delicious meat, feeling a deep sense of accomplishment.

Escalating winds became gustier, icier. Ted and Marty went to gather several armloads of wood in case it got really cold. Amy wasn't interested in going out. She was full, but it was fun to smear around the last flakes on her plate, on her bed, on her clothes.

Straightening from grabbing a chunk of wood, Marty saw a flash from the corner of an eye, jerked a hand up by her face in reflex. A broken fir branch jabbed its needles into the back of the shielding hand making her gasp in shock at instant, staggering pain like a hundred hot needles were stabbing it. The branch thunked down, bounced and rolled, propelled by the gust that broke it loose, its smell sharply pungent and its wrist-thick broken end raw and jagged. She stared at it in horror, thankful it had missed her head.

The next gust brought death fetor, underscoring how lucky she was to be alive, and how easy it could be to die. This was enough wood, it was dangerous out here.

When sprays of hot sparks stung her face and hands and singed her hair with a biting stench, she gave up trying to heat dishwater.

Huddled together inside, protected from fine, hard granules of snow and most of the growling wind, Marty frowned at the flapping, billowing tent. Their breath puffed white in the frigid air.

Neither child resisted crawling into bed and nestling down deep. Marty tried to bank the fire, then crawled into her own bed in barely-controlled panic, her injured hand stinging fiercely. Haunted by the whistling, howling wind, she worried about mountain storms. When the children's deep breathing signaled they were asleep, she allowed herself to cry, softly gasping away some of her fear and frustration, and the sorrow that hovered always at the edge of her awareness.

Chapter 4

Awareness of the world crept in gradually, crowding out a vague dream. A cloud of white vapor formed at Marty's every breath, ghostly in the dimness. She slid from her bag to peek out the narrow door gap, and groaned. Snow had swirled into drifts nearly knee-deep in places, flanking shallower spots. The air was briskly cold and, though the wind was hushed, she remembered it moaning and whistling most of the night. The layer of puffy snow on the tent's sagging roof limited the meager light from outside.

Was this a brief spring storm or was it a lull in a blizzard that might go on for days? Numb with despair, Marty shivered into dank clothes. Tucking in her wool shirt, her needle-punctured hand scraped across the waistband's rough corduroy ridges. Searing pain made her gasp and jerk the hand free. In dim dawn light she saw the back of that hand was swollen and covered with tiny, fiery blisters where the needles had pierced the skin. Surprised at the inflammation, lightly rubbing it, she reminded herself it could have been worse, the branch could have hit her head.

White fluff dusted the grill's flat metal edges, but the center was dry so some live coals remained. She groped through snow at the woodpile and tapped clinging snow off thin limbs to stoke the fire, but retreated inside to blow feeling back into stiff fingers while the fire took hold. Before going back out, she donned her fur-lined leather gloves, wincing at the pressure on her blistered hand.

Ted and Amy were delighted with the snow. Amy, born in southern California, had never seen snow, so going out meant repeated stops to gape at this new white world.

It felt too cold to stay out long enough to cook, even by the blazing fire, so Marty passed out dried apple rings, raisins and shelled peanuts.

It was not a proper breakfast, but it would do for now. Both children were ecstatic.

Marty hurried out to start a belated pot of coffee, hoping a cup would make this cold, bleak day seem better. It usually did.

The snow-laden, sagging tent roof made the space seem smaller, more confining, so she slapped up from inside to knock it off in clumps that fell on drifts around the tent sides. That accumulation helped cut off draftiness but inside was still so cold every puff of breath could be seen. To get heat inside she had to move the fire in. Warmth was important or they might get sick, but she dreaded the increased fire danger, the soot and the smoke. Light snow still fell, so the storm wasn't over yet.

Marty bundled the youngsters in a second layer of clothes, adding knitted caps and mittens so they could go play outside. Both were so well rested she worried they might tear the tent down if they didn't burn off some energy. Shooing them out, she thought of Edward insisting on emergency cold weather clothes—just in case—because spring storms were common as far north as they were headed; she thanked his soul he had.

But they hadn't reached Calgary so how far north were they? Had they gotten off course? Was that why no search planes had come over yet?

Now, this storm meant no one could search until the weather cleared. Would they look at all? She sternly reminded herself she had chores to do. Now.

She brushed flammable litter away from just inside the door and brought rocks from the outside fire pit then used the hatchet to shave kindling shreds on the cleared spot. She scooped glowing coals into the frying pan with the spatula and poured them over the shavings, covering that with fine twigs. Blowing on the coals gave her a headache so she fanned them with a dishtowel until flames licked through the shavings.

Wiping tears from smoke irritation, she asked Ted to knock snow off the wood they'd gathered and bring it in to dry. She dragged in the log seats. Though resinous smoke from pitchy wood filled the tent's peak, heat already radiated into their living area. Glancing up, she saw smoke starting to seep out through the inverted v-shaped gaps at the peak ends, where the roof support hole went.

She fretted about something catching fire, but was reminded of smelling wood smoke as a child. The odor was comforting, familiar, reminiscent of when life was safe and dependable. It helped ease the panic she was so near giving in to.

With new coals established, she brought the grill in, again struggling to get the supporting rocks level. Having it in place made her feel safer from fire, even if she wasn't actually. She let the outside fire die, bringing the coffee inside to finish brewing and took both buckets to fill at the shallow creek. Using the bigger one, she scraped the creek bed deep enough to fill a pail with one scoop. Shivering, she waited for the water to clear of stirred-up debris before filling the pails. A thin margin of lacy ice lined the creek's shallow edges, but the moving water wasn't cold enough to freeze. Running water has to be much colder than standing water to freeze. From that, she guessed the air must be in the middle twenties. Still shivering, she struggled with the heavy buckets, but splashes of icy liquid made her blistered hand sting like fire.

Setting the smaller bucket on to heat, she applied ointment to her hand then tidied up the beds and tent. Using a corner of the grill, she heated a can of chicken noodle soup for lunch. Saltines, soft and soggy from moisture, wilted instead of snapping, but tasted great in the soup.

Thinking of the mess, she tried to feed Amy. But the girl insisted on feeding herself, clenching her teeth, her lips stubbornly puckering each time Marty offered another bite. Marty sighed resignation and handed the bowl and spoon to the instantly delighted girl.

Amy ate with more enthusiasm than skill, spilling soup down her fuzzy jacket front. Her grey eyes glinted in pride as she grinned triumph at her exasperated mother.

Marty glumly watched the girl eat, but her heart melted at the self-satisfied grin that lit her daughter's face. Maybe cleaning up the mess wasn't so bad. She had nothing better to do.

After cleaning up the lunch mess and washing dishes, she looked for something else to keep her busy. She fed the fire, shifted things around a bit, and then fussed with her hair. Finally she poured a whole pound of split peas into the soup kettle, adding hot water, minced onions and carrots. She diced a can of Spam in, then could think of nothing more to do. Fear gnawed at her when she was idle.

The children had slept late and were having so much fun throwing soft, lumpy snowballs and playing tag around snow drifts, that it seemed a shame to interrupt them for a nap. They didn't act sleepy, and no one else would know they hadn't taken one.

Marty puttered around trying to keep busy, even knocking snow off the roof again, though hardly any had fallen. Dismal clouds still formed a blotchy, unbroken ceiling.

When day faded to cold dimness, the kids finally came in, worn out. She wondered where they got the energy to play so hard as they dived ravenously into their meal. Smiling, she realized they'd eaten the whole pot—how could so much rich soup fit in those little tummies?

After checking supplies, she put a pot of beans to soak.

Once they sat still, fatigue quickly quieted the children. They climbed onto Marty's lap, each straddling a leg. She rocked side-to-side, humming to break intense, snowy silence. She soon had to struggle with Amy's limp arms to remove her clothes and put on pajamas.

Ted changed his own clothes and was in bed before she turned around. He could do it himself. He was big now.

Marty took their clothes out to shake off beaded moisture from caked, melted snow and spread them on crates, hoping they'd dry overnight.

The snow's thick blanket muted the woods into stark silence. Not even the wind blew.

When she sat back by the fire she suddenly felt too exhausted to move. Or maybe she was just bored. It didn't matter which. She wanted sleep more than anything right then.

Immobile, removed and isolated from time that swirled and spiraled past in rainbow colors beyond her reach, Marty stood frozen, horrified at her powerlessness, helplessly watching her precious children waste away to fleshless skeletons. Two larger, heavier skeletons—Eddie's and his father's, crushed, lopsided and broken but still somehow intact—loomed up out of deep, wooded darkness in oppressive silence to join the children's small, frail skeletons at the fringe of shimmering firelight. Side by side in a row, all four skeletons glowered at her accusingly from eyeless orbs of inky blackness in pearly white glistening skulls that grinned in toothy mockery at her helpless immobility.

She struggled and fought to move, to escape—could not!

She struggled and fought to scream—COULD NOT!

She jerked awake precipitously, sucking icy air, her whole body drenched with cold, clammy sweat from the vivid, horrifying nightmare. She sobbed in deep, silent gasps. Her heart pounded and her hands shook violently. It wasn't real, she thought, over and over. It was just a dream. Only a bad dream.

She struggled free of the tangled sleeping bag, her whole body shaking. Dazed, still sobbing soundlessly, she crawled and groped through inky blackness, touching things that lay where she remembered them being when she went to bed, struggling desperately to gain a sense of reality, to find assurance that the world was as it had been when she fell asleep; that it was not actually worse than the terrible reality of her situation.

Finally able to regain some emotional control, she crawled back into bed, shifted closer to the children and stretched a protective arm over them. The arm was cold, but she left it, desperate for any contact that proved she was not entirely, irrevocable alone in this isolated wilderness.

She grimly swore to find some way to feed them, no matter how long they were stranded in this barbaric situation.

She would not let them starve like that!

She would not be helpless!

She would die trying before she let her precious babies starve!

Marty was nearly overwhelmed with relief to find the morning sky clear and the air warmer. Cheerfully noisy, the flock of squabbling birds were back from wherever they'd been. She hoped their return meant the weather would remain clear, but she wasn't sure. This storm seemed to be over.

She'd slept later than usual, though she didn't feel more rested. She coated healing blisters with ointment, then started cooking powdered eggs and pancakes. The sun was melting the snow by the time they finished eating. Trickles and drips fell, forming winding tracks of rivulets that undermined the mounds and created telltale sags and dips.

Stormy weather had caught her unprepared once but, birds or no birds, she was going to be sure they had enough wood for a few days, in the tent where it would stay dry. But, blindly groping through wet snow, the only wood she found was so wet it would take days to dry enough to burn.

Then she remembered what Gram said about squaw wood. Under live branches on most evergreens were always several limbs that shading from above had killed. They were dry and easier to break loose than live boughs. They were still not effortless to get, but the hatchet helped. Scanning the sky now and then, she chopped off dead wood and piled it on a layer of green boughs to stay dry.

Ted made trip after trip to move it inside the tent. Amy tagged behind him, also carrying a small branch or two, sometimes.

After a dozen trees were done, Marty's aching arms and shoulders forced her to take a break and see how much they had.

Ted piled all he could in the allotted space, then had to put more out into the floor. With gear and beds around the outside edges, the ten-by-twelve wall tent had been nearly half clear—before adding wood. She could barely get in the door, unless she stepped on beds or wood. Shocked, Marty inched to the fire, poured coffee, and sat to survey the jumbled heaps of wood.

Ted watched from the doorway, not understanding her expression.

The boy's worried look made Marty giggle uncontrollably. Ted jumped at its suddenness. She laughed so hard she nearly spilled her coffee. Nothing was funny to him.

"You did fine, Teddy." Marty finally managed to say. "I didn't realize I cut so much wood. Guess I wasn't paying attention."

Ted flashed that whole-face grin in relief. She wasn't mad at him.

"But some of this has to go back out so we can move around."

"I can do that." He grinned.

"Only move what's in the middle. The rest can stay in."

Straightening beds, she noticed snowmelt seeping under the tent sides, so she grabbed the hatchet and went to cut densely-needled bough tips to keep the beds up and dry.

The sky was clear now, without a cloud. But no search planes, either.

Putting the padding under the beds, she switched them to the back, so cooking gear was closer to the fire. The back was also less drafty, so they'd sleep warmer there.

Amy came in rubbing her eyes, ready for a nap. Marty winced with guilt, the girl hadn't had lunch yet. Amy wanted her bed but it was not where it had been. She wailed forlornly. Marty hugged her, patting her and whispering *shoosh*. When she quieted, Marty slipped off snowy shoes and tucked her in bed. She tiptoed quietly out, though the ground was too soft to make any noise—old habits were hard to break.

She took the pot of soaked beans to rinse off at the brook, glancing at the sky on the way. Frowning, she mumbled aloud, "Where are they?"

Ted was playing when she returned. He didn't look sleepy and this was supposed to be vacation, so she told him, "Amy is taking a nap but you don't have to if you don't want. You aren't tired, are you?"

"Nope." He chirped. "I'm havin' fun."

Marty smiled warmly and put the beans to cook, straightening up some more.

When the beans began to soften she slivered half the bacon into them. Surveying the dwindling food, she mixed more biscuits. Hazy nightmare images of starved skeletons returned, bringing a shiver of fear that made her hands shake. She squeezed her eyes shut. "That was only a dream. Just a bad dream." She mumbled. "It wasn't real. They'll come before the food is gone. They'll take us home and all this will be over."

But the fearsome images persisted, reminded Marty what Gram had said about starving as a child. Gram said it was late spring of an extremely hard winter. Her father couldn't ride the horse into town for supplies and they ran out of food. Gram's mother, of the Nez Perce tribe, had gone out and gathered up old beef leg bones the dogs had abandoned. She washed dirt off and broke the thick, hollow bones open with the hammer, smashing them into small pieces. She boiled them until all the greasy marrow was stewed out, removed bone fragments and thickened the weak, oily broth with the meager remnants of flour and cornmeal. The family of five ate that for two days, a scant ladle full each, every few hours.

Gram said, when that was gone, Great Grandma had used an axe to strip bark from the maple tree by the front door so she could strip out the inner bark. She diced that into tiny shreds and boiled it until it thickened. They ate that sweet gruel for nearly a week before Great Grandpa could get the horse into town through melting snow for regular supplies.

Gram said that was the hardest winter she'd lived through. But every time she passed it, she paused to thank that dead tree for giving its life to keep the five of them alive.

Marty was not the least reassured by that memory.

"Nothing is ever so bad that someone else hasn't had it worse." She admonished herself, but her hands still shook as she stoked the fire to bake the biscuits.

For once she cooked more than they could eat in one meal. She went to bed feeling slightly more hopeful than she had since it snowed. The sky was clear and the snow was melting. Sleep came easily, and if she had any dreams, she was too tired to notice.

CHAPTER 5

Noisy birds greeted Marty when she went for water. She envied their camaraderie within the flock, missed having anyone to talk to except two children. The birds showed no fear of her. One flitted to a nearby perch—just out of arm's reach—and seemed to try to communicate with her. That's only my imagination because I'm lonely, she thought. Birds are dumb creatures.

No clouds marred the azure sky. Marty was amazed how much snow had melted overnight, though the air was still chilly. A profusion of animal tracks rumpled shrunken snow out past the clearing's edge. Why didn't I notice the tracks yesterday? Simply concentrating too much, she thought. Maybe the creatures had come out since then.

She examined several lines of tracks. Some were rabbit prints. Birds, mostly about chicken size, made the rest. She clicked her tongue, fresh meat all around and she didn't notice. But what would she have done if she had noticed? Any gun bigger than a .22 would blow game this size to wasted, unusable shreds.

Marty shaded her eyes from sun glare to search the sky; with a clear sky rescue operations could resume. They could come any time. Then she wouldn't have to worry about getting meat.

Restlessness drove her to look around before they had to leave this beautiful virgin wilderness. Once gone she'd never, ever return.

She wandered east from camp with the children, along the slope where brush was thin. She held Amy's hand since they were not going very far. In the shade, slush was slippery and made travel hard so Marty maneuvered down to the leafless trees where the ground was bare and more level—and less reminiscent of the crash site. The muddy soil showed numerous deer tracks and a profusion of other tracks she couldn't identify, most from animals with paws. Some were so tiny they had to be from mice, others quite large. One set was bigger than her palm.

Heart pounding, Marty stared at those. Was this a predator she needed to guard against? Were the children small enough to make good prey? She peered around tensely to be sure it didn't lurk nearby.

Slush soaking into their clothes quickly chilled them. Amy's lips turned blue and she whimpered so Marty carried her the short ways back to camp.

Marty dug through clothes to find dry ones but had to dress the children in lightly soiled ones because the rest were filthy. How had they used so many already? A lunch of hot soup and damp soda crackers warmed their chilled bodies.

Amy crawled into bed and fell asleep. Marty was weary, too. But since the soiled clothes were handy she got out the sewing kit to mend before washing them because washing them first made any rips harder to fix. The familiar activity, even here, was comforting.

Ted wasn't tired so he went out. He soon grew bored with playing alone and wandered down the mucky trail they'd followed to go fishing, grinning anticipation at seeing the squirrel. He wanted to see if it would come when he called it. He'd practiced the scolding sound until he was sure it was right.

The spring he couldn't cross by himself stopped him. He didn't want to get wet again. He climbed on a nearby log and sat quietly in warm sun to wait but he didn't see or hear the squirrel, so he made the sucking sound, hoping it would come or scold back.

Between willows he could see a narrow strip of the pond and grassy meadow from his perch. Part of the meadow had scattered clumps of thin snow and more was covered by floodwater. He squinted at little white patches in the unflooded part. Each spot would jerk a time or two, then not move. The white spots looked like snowballs, almost.

But snowballs didn't move unless somebody threw them and nobody was over there. So they couldn't be snowballs. He frowned in concentration. They must be some kind of animal. He nodded, feeling smug at figuring that out.

Movement high up caught his attention, a dark, quickly growing spot plummeting straight at the meadow. He gaped—it was a bird! It was falling! His heart pounded. It would get hurt or dead! It would break like Grandpa's airplane!

At the last second the bird's wings spread wide and it swooped right onto one of the snowball animals. It flopped and fluttered with wings outstretched for several seconds before rising slowly back into the sky with a snowball creature drooping from its feet. It flapped in a widening, ascending spiral, then flew east.

Ted gaped in awe until it disappeared beyond distant trees, then slumped in relief and started to breathe again, his heart hammering. He had to tell Marty about this.

A loud, quick TAP-tap-tap startled him. He cringed and craned his neck to see what it was—would something swoop down and get him like that? But he wasn't some kind of animal, he was a People. He squared his shoulders, then slumped again. Did people get swooped up like that?

The staccato tapping continued. Ted peered around. Where was it from? Then he heard the squirrel chatter. He bounced with excitement to hear his squirrel friend, grinning in anticipation.

A mahogany streak with a long fuzzy tail raced through branches, followed by another just like it. Chattering and scolding, they whipped through branches, down the trunk, through bushes and up another tree.

Ted was so excited he nearly fell off his log—two of them! And they knew how to play tag. When he puckered up and sucked both squirrels instantly popped their heads out of separate places to look straight at him with alert, sparkly eyes, scolding zealously. He giggled in delight. His friend had brought another friend to play with him.

Eating reheated beans and fresh cornbread for supper, Marty noticed Ted was quieter than usual. She finally asked, "Ted, is anything wrong?"

"I saw a big bird fall out of the sky today. I was scared it would get dead." He leaned forward, brown eyes wide. "It made its wings go out and landed on a thing like a snowball, but it wasn't, and it didn't get dead." Ted bounced with excitement, nearly spilling his beans. "Do you know what that snowball thing was?" He squinted, his head tilted sideways.

Marty struggled to keep a straight face—how could any child bounce up and down with his legs straight out in front? "Be careful not to spill your food. That white thing was probably just a rabbit. Some of them get white like snow." She smiled. "And the bird must have been an eagle or a hawk. Those birds swoop down real fast to catch game."

Grimacing, the boy straightened. "Can they get a People?"

"No." Marty chuckled. "Only small animals like rabbits. People are much too big for them to carry."

His brown eyes bulged. "A BUNNY RABBIT?" Tears welled. "The big bird got a BUNNY?"

"No, these are not tame Bunnies. They're wild rabbits. That's different." Marty's heart melted in sympathy.

"Oh." He wiped his tears away. "What do they do with 'em?"

"Why, they eat them, of course."

"Can birds make a fire?" Ted asked doubtfully.

"No." Marty chuckled. "They don't eat cooked food. They eat everything raw."

"Raw!" Ted wrinkled his nose.

"Of course. We eat vegetables and fruit raw sometimes. Nothing wrong with that."

"Oh." Ted stared blankly at his beans. Then he brightened. "I saw my friend squirrel today." He bounced with excitement again. "And he brought his friend to play with me." He beamed his father's whole-face grin. "They even know how to play tag and I didn't have to show 'em how."

Marty could picture that.

"Are there doors in the woods?" He was serious again.

"Doors?"

"Yeah. Doors are for knockin' on and somebody knocked on a door. Or . . . somethin'."

Marty tried to stay serious. "That must have been a woodpecker. I thought the same thing when I was young. They're pecking a hole in a tree."

"Oh." Ted was finally satisfied.

Shivering in her dank bed later, Marty smiled about the questions. They reminded her of asking some when she was young. Robert, her youngest brother, often answered with "I don't know." But he'd explain when he did know. He'd been her best pal and had taken time to show her how to hunt and fish, and even how to set simple snares. After Ted's questions she could appreciate Robert's patience with her.

She dreamed of setting snares with her brother, of the triumph she'd felt when one of hers finally caught a small brush rabbit.

Cleaning up the next morning, Marty felt the scabs on her cheek and brow coming loose. Underneath, rose-colored spots were surrounded by fading bruises that were now a sickly yellow-green. She tried to pry off the lip scab but it stuck and hurt to peel. Beads of clear serum seeped from the raw scar that would form another, smaller scab. Sadly, she realized the lip scar would last the rest of her life. Tears welled but she reminded herself it could have been worse, at least she was alive and able-bodied. Wiping tears, she turned—chores had to be done.

In the sunshine the snow was gone, the ground thawed but muddy, the air quite warm. She decided to put the sleeping bags out to air and dry. They'd gotten uncomfortably damp and musty. Inside-out, she draped them over bushes where the sun would shine for several hours.

Inside, a strong moldy odor stung her nose. Between the indoor fire and sunlight heating the tent roof, it was damp and toasty enough inside to grow mold. Elbows out, knuckles on hips, she surveyed the clothes bags. It all needs to be aired, she thought, good thing lots of bushes are nearby. But she'd prefer a clothesline and wooden pins.

Drinking tepid coffee, she wondered what to do next to keep busy. She thought of last night's dream of snaring that rabbit and sat bolt upright. Rabbit snares! Of course! Lots of rabbits are nearby! She needed to get meat, but not so much any would be wasted, like a whole deer.

"Cord. What can I use for cord?" She mumbled, turning to search. All she found was too coarse and obvious or too soft and binding to slip tight easy enough.

Dismayed, she grumbled, "Well, we could always go fishing again." She rolled her eyes at an image of untangling more fishing line to make Ted his own pole.

Fish line! The green-and-gray speckled line would be hard to see, would slip tight easily, and she had plenty of it.

Marty set five snares, loops of line propped on twig ends over faint traces, betrayed by muddy footprints where game traveled, the other end secured on the sturdy base of the nearest bush. The loop tops were high enough to clear what she guessed were the highest their heads would reach, the bottoms a couple inches above the ground. The loops would slip off the twigs at the slightest pressure, hopefully around something's neck.

Marty worried the snares wouldn't work, most of her early ones hadn't. Glancing at the sky, she saw it was only late morning. Maybe they should fish again. Just in case.

She opened the new, two pound brick of cheese for a take-along lunch, trying not to break the waxed coating too much to reseal over its stringy cheesecloth. Cheese and crackers lunch, wrapped in a dishtowel, barely fit in her coat pocket. She called the children, grabbed the sapling pole, net, tackle box and creel, and made sure both pistol and knife were on her belt. She was so accustomed to them being there she was seldom aware of them. She decided to see what kind of fish the pond held, this time.

She let Amy walk since there was no hurry but held her hand as they strolled down the meandering trail.

Off in the woods courting grouse sounded hoot-hoot and drummed a whirring-thrumming noise like an engine reluctant to start. Both sounds reverberated among tangled trees until it was impossible to tell where they came from but Marty craned her neck to look, glancing at the sky for search planes as they went.

Before they reached the pond the trail dwindled into a maze of faint traces that disappeared into dense marsh growth. Water seeped past the roots yards away from the pond's edge and so many plants crowded the shallow fringes that they had to skirt the sloshy border for half a city block before they could approach the still water.

As she guided Amy between clumps of bur reeds and bulrushes, a pair of huge Canada Geese thunderously erupted in heart-stopping, honking alarm. Marty cringed back and grabbed her shrieking, terrified daughter, knocking Ted over as she recoiled.

The frantic geese flapped vigorously as they ran over the water to get airborne and away from the strange intruders. Each rapid wing beat smacked the water and flung spray yards out from their noisy escape route.

"I hate geese!" Marty fumed, patting her thumping heart. She calmed Amy and helped Ted back up, relieved he wasn't hurt. At least she hadn't stepped on him in her panic.

She edged through vegetation to the slight rise along the shore. A small area of plant-free water showed it was too deep here for aquatic plants. Some kind of big fish should lurk there.

They probed roots and half-buried rocks for bait. Ted hunted with youthful eagerness. This was as much fun as hunting Easter Eggs. At last they located a few slimy worms that squirmed to escape when Marty baited the hook. The worm's twisting efforts sent both children into fits of giggles when Marty wondered aloud if worms were ticklish.

After one glance at the jiggling boy she handed him the pole. Smiling at his beaming delight and holding Amy's hand, Marty maneuvered past round-stemmed reeds to examine cattails that lined most of the pond's shallows.

Just past broken stubs of last year's drab cattail leaves, a large Blue Heron stood motionless, staring intently into shimmery water. Its long, thin neck was curved back in an S-shape like a snake while it waited for a flit of shadow to betray a fish of frog.

The bulky, stilt-legged bird, standing so patiently in wait for prey, and the tangled masses of cattails were familiar from childhood. They reassured Marty that this place was not so different from what she'd known, after all.

The first time she ate the cattail shoots Gram cooked she'd loved the taste, a sort of celery-cucumber or celery-cabbage flavor. These cattails had green shoots, tightly overlapped bundles of forming leaves as thick as her thumb, showing at the bottom of the old, dead ones.

Amy tried to throw rocks and debris in the water but most fell behind her or near her. When she finally hit the water with a pebble, the prehistoric-looking heron silently stalked away, its dignified movement so smooth and unhurried not a single ripple formed in the glassy water.

Smirking over the girl's attempts at throwing, Marty gathered every cattail shoot within easy reach, stepping in shallow overflow to twist and snap them off thick, gnarled roots anchored in muck just underwater. When no more would fit in one hand she realized she'd brought nothing to carry them in.

Shivering from icy water seeping into her boots, she made several trips back and forth with the girl, piling the shoots near the tackle box. If they came again, she needed to bring a bag, she fussed. And dry socks. Her feet stung with cold wetness.

Ted looked so mournful about not getting a bite yet that Marty checked his bait. It was gone. She showed how to hook on another worm.

Before all the shoots were moved Ted caught two long, white suckers. They weren't much fun to catch, didn't fight like trout, and were unexciting despite their size. Cleaning them, Marty was repulsed by their toothless, puckered, down-turned mouths, but cleaned them anyway. Food is food, and at least we don't have to eat the worms or grubs we use for bait, she smiled.

Ready to head back, she realized the empty creel could hold the shoots if she carried the fish on the stringer. She's just have to rinse off stale fish odor before using them. On impulse, she plucked one of last year's old, battered cattail heads and added it to the creel.

Slowly strolling home, she was surprised to see how many plants had sprouted since the snow melted. Busy searching the sky and listening to the grouse earlier, she hadn't noticed.

Worn out from the long walk, Amy started crying. Marty carried her back and put her to bed, upset at having to lay her on bare boughs because the beds were still out airing. She tucked the dishtowel that had held lunch under her head. After stoking the fire, she eagerly went out to check the snares.

They worked!

The first held a big, plump grouse that looked like a dove-pigeon cross, only bigger. The two snares closest together each held a hefty snowshoe hare. Their white winter coat was shedding badly and new brownish summer fur showed through. The other two snares were not sprung.

"Now we have plenty of meat." She gloated, resetting the emptied snares.

Not wanting to attract scavengers, she called Ted and carried the game away from camp to clean. If he could learn to fish, he could also see how game was cleaned. But his coordination was too poor to let him actually try it.

Ted was fascinated. The cuddly, flop-eared Bunny he'd seen before wasn't like these. These weren't fat and fuzzy. Maybe they weren't the same. And this bird wasn't like a chicken but almost as big. He was content to watch what Marty did to the game.

Because the bird was already cold, the feathers would be hard to pluck without first scalding the bird to loosen them. That entailed heating and hauling water, so she decided to skin it just before cooking it.

She cut a shallow slit from the bird's ribs to its vent then cut across and peeled back the skin. She poked her fingers under the flaps and loosened around the gut sack, cut off the head, feeling up into the cavity to loosen the windpipe, then grabbed it to pull out the gut sack. Slicing the heart and liver free, she made sure the bird was well cleaned then dropped those organs back in for easier carrying.

Ted watched every move, smelling the distinct odor of the gut pile. Marty's hands were smeared with blood but it didn't seem to bother her. He wondered why.

Setting the bird aside, she looked for a thin, sturdy stick, bending several to test their strength. She cut a two-foot section of one and whittled both ends sharp. With the knife tip, she made a short slit in all the hind leg hocks, and positioned the sharpened stick through the slits on both hind legs of one rabbit so its legs were spread.

"You gonna hurt the Bunnies?"

"No." Marty smiled. "They're dead. Nothing feels pain when it's dead."

Ted frowned, unsure how that could be true.

Marty cut through the hide around both legs next to the stick then along the back of the legs from hock to behind the tail and to the other hock. She cut a circle around the tail and genitals so they stayed connected together. She cut off the head behind the ears and the front feet at the ankle, and hooked the stick over a branch stub with the belly towards her. She peeled enough hide loose to get a good grip and jerked down hard to strip the hide off in a tube. Like peeling off a tight glove, the pelt ended up inside-out.

The naked body hung slack, every muscle showing clearly. Fur was left only on the straddled hind feet, like woolly socks, and the puffy tail. She sliced the tail base at the joint then cut between leg muscles and anus while pulling the attached tail, careful not to nick the intestines. Then she sliced down to the ribs, split the ribs and on along the throat to the end and pulled out the gut sack.

She removed the stick, laid that carcass on its inverted skin and did the other rabbit, saving nothing but the heart from either.

Dad always kept the hides when he butchered, but she was unsure what he did with them. Collecting the game and pelts, she wondered about that.

As Ted followed her, carrying the bird, he asked, "How come you kept some of the, um, that stuff, and not the rest?" Wide pumpkin pie-colored eyes glanced sideways up at this woman who was starting to seem like a mother, or at least a friend.

"My Daddy told me never to eat the liver of a wild rabbit, it can make you sick. But the heart and liver of birds is good. And their gizzards, but I forgot to look for those." Marty answered patiently.

"I don't know what those are." Ted stared downward, ashamed.

"Those what?"

"Those . . . stuff you took out." He didn't know how to say it.

Marty hadn't realized the boy had never seen an animal cleaned; it had been familiar all her life. "That 'stuff' was their insides, their guts. Like when we cleaned the fish, you throw away most of the guts because they're no good to eat. But these," she pointed, "the bird liver, and all the hearts, are very good."

Ted looked carefully, then asked, "Whatcha gonna do with the Bunnies?"

"Cook them. We have to have meat to eat."

"Bunnies are for eating?" Ted's voice was thick with sadness.

"These aren't Bunnies, Teddy Bear. They're wild rabbits, Snowshoe Hares, actually. They're very good eating. You'll see."

"Oh." Ted looked doubtful.

After a while, he went back to the gut piles, curious. Guts, insides, he thought. He could tell which were from the bird because they were different, even smelled different.

Swarms of biting flies had gathered, so he left.

Using fish line, Marty tied the bird and a rabbit to the tent ceiling pole where thin smoke kept flies away. The meat might draw dangerous creatures if hung outside and would be eaten before they could spoil from the inside heat.

She made willow hoops by bending flexible withes—long thin branches—into a loop and winding the thinner end around the thicker base end until they stayed in place. Then she pushed those hoops inside the reversed skins to hold them open to dry out properly.

Dad would approve, she thought, hooking both hoops onto the highest branches in reach near the tent. The childhood familiarity of drying rabbit hides was reassuring. But what would she do with them when they were dry? What could they be used for? At least, she shrugged, she could take them back for souvenirs. They were fuzzy, like Amy's cute fur jacket.

But she couldn't take them back until the rescuers got here. The afternoon sky held no planes, again. When would they come? She wiped away a brimming tear.

She busied herself with bringing in clothes, pleased that they smelled so much better. Then she gathered bedding, wondering what to cook for dinner.

Dinner! She had to get it cooking, it was getting late.

Upset at losing track of time, she tried to stuff the whole rabbit into the heavy cast iron Dutch oven. It had to be cut into several pieces to fit. She tucked cattail shoots in every tiny space, then minced the last chunk of bacon to sprinkle over and add fat and flavor to the lean meat.

She struggled to get the beds together and back in place. The rabbit seemed to take forever to get tender, though the fire under it was built as hot as she dared make it. The children got cranky with hunger before the rabbit was tender enough to get a fork into, so she scooted it aside to fry the suckers, relieved the fish looked less repulsive without their fat-lipped heads.

Both children stuffed their mouths with fish as she doled it out. It didn't taste as good as trout and was full of branched bones that were difficult to separate from the flesh. Marty nibbled a tiny bit and vowed to fish for trout from now on. The suckers, with their stagnant-mud flavor, were hardly worth carrying home. But it held the children until the rabbit was cooked. Bacon and cattails added just the right seasoning so the meat was delicious, but still quite chewy. They all ate it with enthusiasm.

Both children soon went to bed, not even cuddling very long. Ted was still sad at eating a Bunny, but it did taste very good.

Marty sat by the fire holding the ratty-looking old cattail spike. Soft and velvety, it brought many childhood memories of when life was so simple, so easy. You did what Mother said, then what Dad asked. In school, you obeyed the teacher. Then you could do anything you wanted, even just nothing.

Now there was no one to tell her what to do or if what she did was right or wrong. She had only herself. Was she doing her best? Frustrated, she twisted the thick, fuzzy spike. It came apart easily, a segment breaking away in one piece, almost like very thick wool. Looking closely in pale firelight, she saw a layer of fine seeds on the fluff's inner surface.

Gram said parts of some plants were edible while other parts on the same plants were toxic, like potato plants, whose tubers were the only nontoxic part, though most simply tasted terrible or were too tough to chew. Cattails were never poisonous, but some parts got very tough.

Marty nibbled a tiny seed and was delighted at the taste. She'd used celery seed for flavoring, and this was similar. Excited, she rubbed the tiny seeds off into a clean dishcloth. Standing to get a container for them, loose fuzz wafted around her. With the seeds in an empty can, she gathered stray fuzz, tucking it into a fist, then tossed the wad in the fire. Flames flared hotly for a second, the fluff glowed a few more seconds, then crumbled into fine ash. Marty welcomed knowing what good tinder it made. She stored the rest of the fluff in another saved can. She'd get lots more of both if she had a chance.

For the first time since the crash Marty went to bed without worrying about food. Drifting off with a smug smile, she dreamed of the tent sides bulging from too much food. So much was packed in no room was left for her and the children. The smile faded when she had to fight off an army of flies and other bugs that tried to get to their precious food.

CHAPTER 6

Scattered cloud streaks veiled the mountaintops and the air was warm when Marty dumped breakfast dishwater. She heard no aircraft drone, only sporadic courting bird sounds. She sighed in disappointment and began to put away the clothes aired yesterday, laying the dirtiest aside.

Depressed at handling the men's clothes, she repacked them separately. She wouldn't take them back when they were rescued. But where were the search planes?

She scratched her itchy scalp, frustrated at being so dirty. Her once beautiful nails were ragged. At least brushing her hair didn't make the back of her head hurt now, that lump was only tender, not painful, and her punctured hand had only a few faint red spots.

In case they went fishing again, she decided to ready the daypacks for use. After adjusting one to fit her, she called Ted in. The other pack, made for an adult, had to be altered for him.

Worried about getting poked, Ted held as still as possible as she sewed the straps shorter. Now he had his own pack. He hated to take it off when she finished, but Marty let him put it at the head of his bed and promised he could wear it next time they went fishing.

Amy sat playing with a jumble of sticks that had been a house when he went in. He didn't want to make houses with her, she always ruined them. He didn't want to be alone, though.

"Let's go see the squirrels." He held out a hand to help her up.

"Kay!" She grinned and popped up without his help but held his hand as they walked.

Ted went to the log where the two squirrels had come to play with him. But it was too high for Amy to get up on, even with his help, so he found a low rock they could sit on. Each made their own version of the kissing sound, but no squirrels came that day.

Marty bound a handful of twiggy branches together with a pajama drawstring for a makeshift broom to sweep the tent's dirt floor. It worked, but not very well. She used the soup ladle to scoop excess ashes from the fire pit into the small bucket, pushing aside hot coals, then sat with a cup of coffee, wondering where it was safe to dump them. Gram had said wet ashes were caustic from lye that could damage your skin, and laughed about how her mother's homemade lye soap turned skin red with irritation that she called 'the flush of good health'.

Gram had also explained how they made the harsh soap by soaking wood ash, pouring off the leach water into a huge pot and boiling it with rendered animal fats until it thickened. They ladled that into bar-shaped wooden molds to cool and cure. The crude yellow-gray soap worked for all cleaning from scrubbing floors to washing dishes, clothes, or bodies.

Gram had told Marty about different kinds of ashes, which woods made the most or least ash, the most or least smoke, uses for different types of smoke, and the virtues of green versus seasoned wood. Cool smoke from slow burning hardwoods, like ash, maple and oak, was used to cure meat or fish. Softer, hotter burning wood, like alder, aspen and evergreens, was best for cooking. It produced comparatively little smoke, a lot of ash for soap, and caught fire easily. To keep a winter fire going all night, they used hardwood on a bed of softwood coals because hardwood required hot coals to get it burning. Once started, relatively few logs burned long and hot. Whether hard or soft, the more seasoned it was the less smoke it produced.

Marty finally dumped the ashes down into a rock pile so the children couldn't reach it.

She floured chunks of rabbit to fry in lard and made gravy from the drippings. Though terribly chewy, the rabbit was delicious with boiled rice covered in gravy, and fresh cornbread covered in maple syrup from the gallon can. Marty couldn't help wondering how honey would taste instead of syrup, and if any honeybees were nearby; but they wouldn't be here long enough for it to matter, even if there were any.

Morning air felt warm and the sky was clear when she went out. Rank body odor made her wish she could get away from herself.

They'd gone far too long without a bath, even for camping out. She circled to check the snares, found one sprung and all empty; she took them down. The grouse was for dinner today so she didn't even have to go fishing. Plenty of time for everyone to have a sponge bath, at least.

While a bucket of water was on heating she fried pancakes, heaping them on a mess plate. The last was browning when the children wobbled out of bed, wiping sleep from their eyes.

They ate pancakes with margarine and syrup. Marty put leftover pancakes in the food crate and secured the door against bugs. They'd make good sandwiches for lunch.

When heating water steamed and the tent was toasty warm she called the children in, set the stew pot on the floor and mixed hot and cold water to a good temperature.

When the children burst in the door, she cheerfully announced, "We're going to have a bath today. But just a sponge bath, we don't have a tub for a real bath."

She undressed Amy and stood her in the stewpot, then used the soup ladle to pour water over the girl's hair. Amy grinned. She liked a bath and water never scared her. She squeezed down into the enamel pot and splashed in delight.

Marty groaned—no room was left to dip water. Mixing more in the washbasin, she thought wistfully about merely turning on faucets to fill a tub. But this was better than nothing, she shrugged, sudsing Amy's dirty hair with the aromatic bar of Ivory soap. Her hair was so dirty the first rinse turned the bath water gray and scummy. Ashamed, Marty soaped the hair again, almost running the pot over with the second rinse water.

"When you have a bath," Marty lathered a washcloth and scrubbed the girl's dirty face, "you start at the top and wash as far down as possible." Marty washed to her waist, "then you wash up as far as possible." She washed one foot, then the other, and had Amy stand up. "Then you wash possible." She grinned, scrubbing her daughter's bottom.

Ted watched, fascinated. He'd stripped to his undershorts but refused to take them off.

Marty vigorously dried Amy and dressed her in her cleanest clothes, then dumped the scummy water, ashamed of how dirty the girl had been. She mixed fresh water.

"Now it's your turn." She motioned for Ted to step into the pot.

He froze, ready to bolt out the door if she made a move toward him. When they lived at Grandpa's house she always let him bathe himself. He could do it himself!

Instinctively understanding, Marty said, "Okay. If you'll kneel down here I'll wash your hair."

He hesitated, then knelt down with his head over the warm water, glancing sideways up at Marty. She had to scrub his hair twice, too. It was even dirtier than Amy's.

Amy tried to help. She still wanted to play in the water. Exasperated, Marty handed Amy the hairbrush and sat her on a bed. That satisfied Amy for a while, but the brush tangled in her curls and had to be untangled, again and again.

Marty stood Ted up and scrubbed his face and neck with a soapy rag. She rinsed them and scrubbed him to his waist then rinsed and started to dry him.

Ted fidgeted nervously, accusing, "You said you was just gonna wash my hair."

Smiling, Marty said, "There. Now you're washed down as far as possible. I'll take Amy out so you can wash up as far as possible, and wash possible, while we're gone. You be sure to get between your toes." She shook a finger at him.

Ted was so relieved he flashed Eddie's whole-face grin. Marty's heart lurched with new ache, but it was the best 'thank you' possible.

Outside, she sat on a log near camp to untangle Amy's dark blond, curly hair. The Ivory soap aroma reminded her of bathing Amy as a baby. Tears of homesickness threatened, so she took the girl for a stroll around camp for distraction, pausing now and then to study the sky and listen.

It was empty. Still no rescuers.

They were sitting by the old fire pit when Ted came out with his clothes rumpled like he'd dressed in a hurry. With a shy smile, he said, "I'm ALL clean. Can we go play?"

Marty laughed and nodded. Ted nearly dragged Amy after him.

The dirty clothes pile was bigger and they'd used all the hot water so her bath had to wait at least two hours for more to heat. Glancing up to scan the sky, she saw it was only midmorning, enough time to wash a few clothes, though they might not dry today. Their little brook was full of easily stirred-up debris, but she could dip water out to wash these few dirtiest clothes. The Ivory was for skin, the Fels Naphtha for dishes, though it worked fine for laundry. She decided that just a good rinsing would get out enough dirt to last until she could get home to her wringer washer and lots of hot water. After all, this was only temporary.

The water was very cold despite the sun's warmth and soon her hands began to ache. Still, she dipped and squeezed until no more dirt came out, doing each piece as well as the first. The last item was impossible to squeeze with cold-numbed fingers, and her arms ached fiercely from using new muscles.

The bushes she hung clothes over had leafed out noticeably since last time she'd used them—how long had that been? Surely no more than a couple days. Unease haunted her as she stepped inside. Amy was sound asleep and Ted was laying quietly, awake.

While dish water heated she rummaged in the rifle corner for the spit bar to roast the grouse on, then realized using the bar would require the outside fire and two pronged sticks to hold it. The inside fire would be needed to cook supper and heat water. Fluff burned too fast to ignite twigs without wood shavings, so she whittled some to start the outside fire.

She cut forked branches two feet long, sharpened the bottoms to points and used the hatchet back to pound them into the packed dirt beside the fire until the notches were about a foot high. But the props were too far apart so, after testing the length of the metal bar, she pulled one up and pounded it back in closer. She hadn't seen a spit bar set-up since early childhood and only remembered the general idea, not the details; others had taken care of that.

While the outside fire grew she mixed biscuits and set up the oven inside by the heating water, wishing it was a loaf of bread. She'd helped Mother bake lots of it. Nothing tasted better than hot homemade bread with home-churned sweet cream butter. Marty's mouth watered wistfully.

She spitted the freshly skinned bird as Amy came out rubbing her eyes, awake. Ted was not nearby. Marty felt guilty for not keeping track of him better.

He popped out of the bushes nearby, startling her and Amy. Amy giggled and rushed to tickle him but he tickled her instead. They laughed and tussled in fun.

Marty grinned, rubbing weary arms, and showed them the spit. "Someone has to turn this handle slowly, like so, while this cooks, so no place will burn. You can take turns doing it."

They were both so eager to be first they held the handle together. Sometimes they cranked too fast and burst out laughing. Struggling not to laugh, Marty reminded them to go slow.

When they settled down she went in to cut a pan of potatoes but had to push it against the outside fire since it wouldn't fit on the grill inside.

Without the fatty, moisture-saving skin, the bird was chewy and dry, but so tasty they ate it all, stuffing themselves. They even left some biscuits uneaten.

Just before dark, she set the snares up in a different area, reasoning that catching the others had depleted the first place. Gathering the clothes on her return, she folded and put the dry ones away, though it was too dark to tell if they were cleaner. She draped damp ones over crates.

Marty gave the children diluted canned milk to drink while she cuddled them by the outside fire. The air was cool, not cold. When they were asleep she started her bath. She was ashamed of letting them all get so dirty and stinky. What would rescuers have thought if they'd come yesterday? She huffed.

After she washed, dressed and dumped the scummy water, she rolled up her sleeves and tucked the collar under to wash her hair. Hers had to be soaped twice, too. It didn't get squeaky clean with this soap but smelled so good she really didn't care. She used the last of the heated water to rinse her hair. Maybe she didn't need so much, but the warm water felt so self-indulgent she kept dipping and pouring it until it was all gone.

With a towel around her head, she took the brush out to sit by the smoldering fire, wide awake now. Bathing had perked her up. Brushing her hair in the light breeze by the fire helped dry it.

The pleasantly cool night was very bright. Lush trees and bushes stood out clearly in shades of browns and grays. A light breeze brew strands of hair across her face so she kept tucking it behind her ears.

A full head of wavy, light brown hair fell to just below her shoulders. It hadn't blown in her face when it was greasy dirty. She clucked her tongue—hers was as dirty as the children's. She smiled at remembering how Amy's clean hair glowed golden in the sunlight.

A vagrant breeze carried a heavy odor of rotten meat. Suddenly sad, she remembered Eddie's hair had been dark brown, straight, and trimmed military short. Edward had had a full bush of dark hair with gray temples that made him look dignified.

Marty reared back. Why did I think about that? Her head sagged to her knees as she blinked back tears and tried to escape the images. Sniffing, she looked around and tried to think of something else.

Several dark shadows darted erratically past. Marty caught enough of a glimpse to know bats were eating their fill of night bugs. She was glad to know something ate mosquitoes.

Looking beyond to the nearly solid star mass, she recognized the three stars of Orion's Belt. A nearly Full moon was so bright it dimmed any stars near it.

The moon! Marty gasped. It's full! But it couldn't be! It was New when we crashed! It couldn't be that long ago! Marty's whole body quivered in panic: Eddie said rescue efforts were stopped after about a week, but it took two weeks for the moon to go from New to Full.

It couldn't possibly have been two weeks—could it? Could time so thoroughly get away from her? Did they give up? Are we stuck out here forever?

Shaking violently in panic, she jumped up and paced back and forth by the fire.

Her mind raced from one possible solution to another, discarding each as she thought of it. Finally aware of what she was doing, Marty forced a deep breath through gritted teeth. Gram had said, "Nothing is ever as bad when you're calm as it seems when you're afraid." She forced herself to sit still and breathe slowly, fists clenched to keep her hands from shaking.

"It's up to me to get these babies out of this place . . . back home. I'll find a way! I will take care of them!"

What if you can't? Mocked her. She had only the vaguest idea where they were. How far was Out? Which way would take them to the nearest people? Any people.

Her heart hammered against her ribs. Maybe this wasn't temporary after all. Maybe she couldn't figure out how to get them back home. A throat lump choked her as hot tears scalded down her face. Sorrow overwhelmed her, too much to control any longer.

Marty clamped both hands over her mouth to stifle sobs and ran into the darkness, blindly stumbling over bumps and dark tangled things in the night, until she was well away from camp.

Something unseen tripped her. Instinctively she put both hands out to catch herself as she fell. Without her hands over her mouth, the racking sobs they'd held back were released. Sprawled on cold, rough ground she sobbed away all the grief and anger and fear and frustration she'd refused to express all those days since the crash.

It was so unfair! She'd loved Frank so much. Then they said he was dead, but she hadn't believed it until his flag-draped casket arrived. She sobbed forlornly. Then Eddie had come in sympathy and she'd fallen in love with him. Now he was dead, too. Why did everyone she loved have to die? Even gram had gone and left her feeling so alone, so incomplete. Deserted.

Fresh pain stabbed her soul and she abandoned her whole self to grief, sobbing her heart out, washing away the agony with salty, purging tears.

At long last her gulping sobs eased. Her face against the cold ground was smeared with tears and plastered with dirt and debris, her nose stuffy and running. She reminded herself that not everyone she loved had died. Her precious daughter had survived the crash unhurt. And Teddy was also unhurt. He was so sweet she loved him, too.

Trying to wipe off her face only smeared it worse. Hiccupping, Marty was totally drained of emotion. She looked around for water to wash her smeared face and soothe her burning eyes—and realized she didn't know where she was. Or which was camp was. Suddenly afraid, she struggled to her feet, trying not to give way to fresh panic.

"Everything looks different at night." She said in a thick, hoarse voice. Wiping fresh tears from swollen eyes, she told herself camp couldn't be far away. She could find it.

She searched the moonlit valley slope, trying to spot a recognizable feature. Finally, with a sigh of relief, she realized she'd run blindly down the path to the pond, and now stood near it.

Step by step she forced herself to move to where she dipped drinking water from the creek. Kneeling by the pool, she scooped icy water on her face until she no longer gasped at each splash.

She tossed and turned in bed. What would happen when they did get back? She'd come to love her little Teddy Bear. Would he have to go back to his mother? Marty knew she could take good care of him, and was now. If he went back to his mother would she ever see him again?

That would be almost as bad as if Teddy had died, too.

She finally drifted off into the deep black sleep of emotional release and exhaustion. Tears continued to slip softly down into her hair long after she could feel them.

CHAPTER 7

Drying tears pulled Marty's cheeks to puckered itchiness, rousing her from distressed sleep. She scratched, realized what caused the itch, and felt the burning puffiness of her eyes. She dragged out of the snug bed. If the children saw her eyes now they'd ask questions she had no answers for. She dressed to go out into predawn's thin blackness.

Kneeling by the spring, she splashed icy water over her face until her eyes felt less swollen. With filled water buckets she checked the snares. All were empty. Her trembling made tiny waves in the water on the way back.

This was not just a tragic vacation. Now everything was a matter of sheer survival.

As much by feel as by sight in dim light, she checked the depleted food, fighting new tears. Staple foods, rice, split peas, beans, flour, sugar, canned milk, margarine and lard, oatmeal and cornmeal would last a couple of weeks. Only a meal or two of others remained, like canned fruit, soups, and Spam, fresh carrots, onions and potatoes, plus the cheese and oddments like syrup, cocoa and peanut butter.

Plenty of coffee was left but, for the first time since the crash, she didn't make any, instead she stepped out and scanned the brightening sky from habit, unaware of doing so, then looked critically at camp. This was fine for temporary, but not for long-term, not past summer—if she could find enough food to keep them alive that long. What about winter, when food was unavailable and temperatures fell far below freezing? What if she didn't get them to safety before then?

She HAD to find a way to get back to the rest of the world!

But which way was that? Out camping as a child, Dad said if she got lost to follow water downstream. She'd find people eventually, and they'd help her get home.

With sudden determination Marty ducked back inside. She would find a way out of this situation.

When cornmeal was cooked she woke the children. While they yawned and ate she made cheese sandwiches from leftover biscuits.

It was near full daylight when they left. Marty slipped the strap of the leather-cased binoculars around her neck and made sure both pistol and knife were on her belt. She went toward the pond, holding Amy's hand. Ted strutted ahead wearing his knapsack holding their lunch. Marty wore the baby carrier but wouldn't use it until necessary.

They reached the pond soon after the sun cleared the eastern crags. The valley on this side was much narrower than across the stream, and narrowed more as they went west, downstream. This side was also brushier. Dense willows bordered the flooding stream, but back from the water the brush thinned, leaving a few small park-like glades.

Marty went along a maze of faint animal traces, looking for the outlet stream to follow, often detouring around overflow. Once, a foot broke through debris, drenched in a hidden pool when she sank where the lightweight youngsters didn't.

They saw red squirrels, more than once. Ted grinned and made the kiss-call to each one, setting off enraged chatters. Several tiny, striped chipmunks darted about in one area, then a pair of grouse erupted explosively from almost underfoot, making them all cringe.

Marsh cattails were replaced by a dense willow hedge, the change showing where water moved swiftly again. She followed as near the edge as possible, carrying Amy through the thickest brush and glancing back often to see how Ted was doing. He lagged behind, looking distressed, so she took the next trail upslope to a dry place to rest.

While resting, all Marty could see of the valley's edges were steep bluffs footing rocky cliffs capped by evergreens. Such rugged steepness worried her, but so much water had to drain from the valley somehow. She soon felt pressured to hurry on.

The left slope forced them closer to the water until they had to push through brush along the slanted edge to keep from wading in the stream's overflow. Marty carried Amy in her left arm, twisted to keep her right hand between Ted and the roiling flood. Brush was so thick they heard a waterfall's deep rumbling roar before they could see it. Marty's heart thumped harder.

Pushing into an opening on the gravel bank, they finally saw the whirling stream's outlet. Marty was stunned. Her knees buckled. She collapsed onto cold rocks. Open-mouthed, she let Amy slide down beside her. The world felt unreal, like a bad dream.

An ancient rockslide filled the narrow cut between left and right cliffs. Though nearly dammed by the massive jumble of boulders, murky water sucked treacherously down through the few narrow gaps in writhing whirlpools. Its roar echoed through the narrow wedge of canyon with a thunderous sound so intense the rock under Marty vibrated. Cold mist floated from the chasm's depths to coat all the surfaces with wet, sunlit radiance.

They couldn't leave this way. They couldn't find people through here—not alive.

Marty's head drooped as she fought tears. Amy leaned against her mother and hugged her, patting Marty's shoulder. Ted edged closer and laid an arm across Marty's back. He didn't know why they came or why she was so upset, only that her upset had something to do with the water. The youngsters' sympathy made it harder not to cry, but also fed Marty's determination to get them to safety. She looked up at the sky. Noon. Time to go back. No time to look elsewhere today and still reach camp before dark.

She forced herself to rise and start back. Away from the roar and cold mist, she found a place to rest and eat, though she had no appetite. The children were ravenous.

At every brush gap on the way back she paused to scan across the valley through binoculars for a way to scale the sides into another valley, one with water she could follow to safety. She hadn't seen any she could climb, even without the children, by the time they reached the pond.

She could now see much of the valley's length, and studied the contours of her new, confining world. She recalled the view of mountains from the air, their rugged steepness. How would this look on an aerial map?

The maps! She'd burned ALL the maps! Near panic she wondered, where are we?

But it didn't matter where they were. They were still Here, alone, no matter where Here was. She still had to keep them alive in this wilderness valley with only what it held.

How? This couldn't be permanent! She'd get them Home! Somehow. She swore on her life to get them Home.

She had to feed them between now and then, though without refrigeration nothing stayed fresh more than a few hours. With the weather warming each day, she'd have to gather what she could every day or two or it would spoil. Startled, she realized she could do that while seeking a way out. So many plants here were familiar the valley seemed like one huge garden, almost, just not all in one handy place and everything ready only in its own time.

Vivid memory of the skeleton nightmare made her heart race. She clenched her jaw—she would do what she must to feed them!

Across the pond a hawk pursued a frantically quacking teal to the sanctuary of tangled cattail leaves. An instant before colliding with the matted wall of leaves the hawk veered up, screeching, as the teal disappeared with a rattle into the jumble, then was silent.

She gaped. Ducks. How can I catch ducks to eat? If they were migrating in they'd soon lay eggs she could gather. She'd eaten them while growing up and liked both the big duck and the huge goose eggs.

She continued on, looking for edible plants she recognized. Between old battered cattails she saw new Arrowhead leaves, but could see no way to reach them to get their starchy, potato-like tubers. Beyond the cattails floated huge, heart-shaped Yellow Water Lily leaves. In late summer those would bear seeds she'd never tried; Gram said they could be shelled and eaten or popped like popcorn but were hard to get free of their thick pods full of mucilage unless it was allowed to rot off. Their distended stem bases and bulbs were edible but grew in mud up to five feet under very cold water.

Back toward the trees she saw a bunch of lacy leaves up just enough to notice. They looked like carrots, but Gram had warned emphatically that some plants similar to carrots were deadly poison. Marty plucked a leaf to smell, was suddenly shaky with relief from the familiar odor. She tried to pull one up but the leaves broke off so she used the knife tip to pry up one, then a clump of a dozen thin roots.

"Teddy!" She called, "Look. Isn't this great?" She tucked the spindly roots into his pack.

He grinned and looked at and sniffed the plants. These made her happy, they were something good. He was taking them back for her.

She hunted under dead bracken ferns for new shoots Gram called Fiddleheads. When she had a big handful she rubbed off the coarse, russet fuzz by pulling them through her hand from the bottom up. She grinned while adding them to Ted's pack.

He watched carefully. These also made her happy.

Along the trail she added young dandelion leaves and flower buds to his pack, then Miner's Lettuce, easy to recognize by the leaves growing unbroken around its stem.

Ted's pack was getting heavy and he was very tired. But he didn't like Marty to be upset and these made her happy, so he was glad to carry them. He vaguely remembered his mother being upset and then going away. He was afraid Marty would go away, too. He watched Amy bob along in the carrier, half asleep and nodding against Marty's head at every step. Maybe it was from the waterfall, it was so loud it hurt his ears, too.

Death odor grew strong as they neared camp, and was so strong there that Marty felt nauseated, and terribly depressed again.

"What stinks?" Ted grimaced.

Marty flinched. "That's . . . something dead." She evaded.

While dinner cooked she reset the empty snares in new places. Asparagus-looking fern shoots that tasted like meaty green beans simmered gently. She made a salad of slivered wild carrots, dandelion greens and buds, and Miner's Lettuce that tasted like tame lettuce. She sliced and fried a can of Spam, the only item she had to use from her stores.

Dawn was cloudy when Marty went for water. She felt tired from yesterday's long walk, most of it carrying Amy. Her achy body was so stiff she had to force herself to get water and check the snares but she was determined to look for a way out again, anyway.

She was relieved to find a snared snowshoe hare. So far, she was able to get as much food as they had time to eat. Loosening the speckled line and resetting that snare, she noted this one was fatter, with a smooth brown coat. She took it aside to clean so the odor wouldn't scare other game away then hung it in the tent peak. She nodded, the snares did have to be moved often to stay effective.

She hung the hoop-stretched skin near the others, wondering what to do with them. "I can't worry about it." She sighed. "I have to find a way out more than anything except keeping us fed. Everything else has to wait."

She woke and dressed the children while oatmeal bubbled. She grabbed the last jerky sticks, dried apple slices and raisins for lunch. The mush, and knowing she had meat for tonight, renewed her jaded energy.

Almost before it was light enough to see well they set out again, this time east, up the valley. Once away from streamside brush, Marty could see the upper end was further so she walked faster, with Amy in the carrier. She soon puffed with exertion. Ted lagged behind, wondering what she was doing today.

This way seemed less flooded and brush was thin enough she could often glimpse water. Fishing spots would be easier to find here. Water-smoothed rock cobbled the trail and where it lay thickest was a barren area half a city block long. Marty stopped there to catch her breath.

Just ahead the valley floor's gradual uplift was sharply split by a steep wall. It looked like the lower part of the valley had broken off and sunk down a few yards from the top part. This fracture extended across the valley as far as she could see, breached only where the stream cascaded over the drop-off in a series of low waterfalls.

To the right, another landslide lay at the bottom of the precipitous cliff forming the valley's southern boundary. It was an old slide, broken off where the stream had undermined the steep face deep enough for the rock to fracture. The slide rubble extended twenty feet to the water and up out of sight above the drop-off.

The slip-fault scarp wasn't high, maybe twenty feet, but seemed awfully tall when looked at from below. How to get over it with two small children presented a problem. Comparing the cliff with the roiling water, she assessed each as a possible route.

She WOULD find a way out!

The falls created a wide, deep pool of churning vortexes that swirled between huge scattered boulders from the rockslide. The pool's lower end was less turbulent but remained wide and looked shallower because several smaller boulders protruded, then the pool narrowed and water again became swift and turbulent. She didn't want to cross that. It looked easier to climb the broken scarp face, though she couldn't see beyond the top.

Marty showed Ted a route up so he could go first and she could catch him if he fell or boost him higher if needed.

From the scarp top she could see past the slide. The south cliff continued east unbroken then curved gradually north, out of sight beyond trees. Straight ahead the stream curved sharply to slightly undercut the towering cliff a short ways before angling back to slide across the scarp and down its face.

She sighed in disappointment. Can't go this way. They had to cross the stream.

She tried to return by backing down but couldn't see where to step. Turning to face out brought a wave of vertigo that shocked her—she'd become intensely afraid of heights since the crash! Gritting her teeth with determination, carefully looking only where she had to step next, she worked her way down, pausing to help Ted down every few feet. Going up sure was faster than coming down, she fumed.

Whenever Amy's feet or knees bumped the rocks behind her Marty became unbalanced, nearly sending the terrified woman and child plummeting down. One hard lurch made the world flare bright then dim from panic as she desperately twisted aside to cling to rough rock with splayed fingers, eyes clenched shut until she could quit shaking enough to continue. Chiding herself it was not far enough down to panic so much, she took slow, deep breaths to regain self-control. This was not like on the plane when she'd helplessly watched rocks rushing up . . . She shook her head to clear the images.

When only five feet remained she decided to risk sliding the rest of the way. This was too slow.

"Stay here until I'm down, then I'll get you." She told Ted as she sat on a smooth boulder. She leaned forward to avoid scraping Amy's feet and pushed off over the rounded edge to slide raggedly down. She landed with a solid thud on her rump.

Ted slipped down beside her, grinning from ear to ear. "That was fun." He crowed.

Marty didn't think so as she stood up, legs quivering, rubbing her friction-hot, achy bottom, feeling to see if she'd ripped her pants.

"I told you to wait for me to get you down!" She snapped. Sudden tears threatened and a lump in her throat tightened her voice as she said, more softly, "You could have been hurt. I wanted you to wait so you wouldn't get hurt."

Ted was alarmed. He did a bad thing. He made Marty very upset. She was almost crying and the scars on her face were bright red. Would she go away now? There was no Grandpa to stay with anymore. He got dead. Almost in tears, his bottom lip quivering uncontrollably, he could only say, "I'm sorry."

Marty's heart melted. She hugged him. "When I tell you to do something, or not to, I have a good reason. Even if I don't remember to tell you what the reason is."

Ted nodded silently, afraid he'd cry like a baby if he talked. The quiver in his bottom lip spread to his upper lip.

Marty turned back to how to safely cross the stream. Pacing restlessly along the rocky edge, she studied the protruding rocks in the lower part of the pool. It would take less than a dozen long steps to cross the slower area and enough rocks were available to step from one to another without having to jump. But how could she get both children safely across?

Sitting on a driftwood chunk, she gave the children dried apple slices and munched a couple herself. She'd have to make a trip for each child. It would be safe, they'd still be in sight.

"Ted, I'm going to take Amy across, then I'll come back for you. Will you wait here?"

Ted nodded soberly, his brown-black eyes intent. He would do exactly as she said.

He sat quietly and watched her step hesitantly from one protruding rock to the next as she worked across the swift, churning water. He held his breath when she wobbled dangerously and swung both arms wide to regain precarious balance on the longest step. He exhaled explosively when she reached the far shore and walked to the brushy edge, then struggled to get the carrier off. He stood with knotted fists, frustrated he couldn't help her take it off, as he usually did.

She finally managed to slide the straps off—too fast. She barely caught Amy before the girl's head hit packed rocks. He saw Marty squat down and talk to Amy, patting her, but he couldn't hear what she said over the swift water's noise.

Leaving Amy in the carrier by the brush, Marty went to the water and took two steps on protruding rocks before Amy screeched in enraged terror so loud even Ted could hear.

Marty stopped and turned back, arms flailing for balance, unsure what to do.

When Amy screamed again Marty went back to pick her up, swaying to calm the child. She finally got the pack back on, straightened it, and then stepped back across, now more sure-footed and confident. Puffing, she strode to where Ted stood with knotted fists, frustrated he couldn't help her. When she plunked down on the log he sat next to her, waiting to see what she did next. He jumped when she finally spoke.

"I'll have to carry both of you over at once. Those rocks are too far apart to get you across any other way. Can you hang on real tight, all the way?"

Wide-eyed, Ted stared without focus while he pictured that in his mind. He flashed his dazzling grin. "I can do that."

With Amy in the carrier and Ted wrapped in one arm, his legs clenched around her waist, Marty balanced with her free arm as she crossed again. It was tricky and spooky with water swirling so rapidly past rocks she had to step on, made her queasy and lightheaded. She focused only on each rock's top, not allowing her attention to shift to the moving water.

Some rocks were not very stable and others a bit slippery, but she'd already found them when she crossed with less weight, and this time adjusted her balance before reaching them. She'd never have made it safely across if she'd taken both children the first time.

Though feeling pressed for time, Marty had Ted help her off with the carrier, to rest and catch her breath. Amy first clung to Marty, then Ted, still terrified of being left alone in this strange, noisy place. They took long drinks of hand-dipped water and chewed on raisins until Marty's legs stopped quivering enough to continue.

The escarpment was much less steep on this side and only a few feet higher than Marty could stretch up to reach. Its unevenness was more filled in with debris and dirt, giving hand-and-toe holds Ted could use to pull his way up and onto flat ground past the verge.

Marty was already so tired she had to force herself to climb. Safely beyond the drop-off, on level ground, she looked back down the valley and sagged: was that all the farther they'd come today?

Up here she saw that the slip-fault cut the whole valley in half from one mountainous side to the other, giving it a two-story effect. The upper half was drier, the brush less dense. From top to bottom, the valley gradually dropped a few hundred feet in elevation, making a distinct change in vegetation, providing a rich variety of herbs, bushes and trees. More snow remained under the trees up here. Open areas up here had more severe weather extremes. The lower end was protected by being a deep, sheltered cup of dense vegetation.

The drop-off looked highest at this end. She'd return on the north side, where it seemed lowest—enough sliding down steep rocks!

Marty continued up the undulating slope near the stream. Near a maple grove a familiar odor stopped her. She found what seemed to be Cow Parsnips nearby, setting off a memory alarm—Gram had shown how to be sure this was not Poison Hemlock. She dug up a huge branched root that looked like a hefty parsnip and halved it lengthwise. This flesh was solid—she sagged in relief—while the deadly Hemlock had hollow chambers inside, though they looked similar outside.

She found several of the plants whose umbrella-size leaves would soon reach her shoulder. She trimmed away unopened leaves for the thick, succulent, hollow stems. She kept only that root, one was plenty for a meal.

Ted looked around, patiently waiting. He saw the huge, dark brown eagle carry game up from the lower valley. Fascinated, he saw it swoop toward a high tree topped with a wide mass of sticks. He nudged Marty and pointed as the bird glided onto the nest's edge. She looked in time to see the female eagle raise up to snatch the prey from the male and hungrily start tearing it to shreds.

They craned necks to watch the male drop off the aerie's side and flap in a growing spiral up toward gray clouds, so small he was hard to see.

Moving at a brisk walk with her mouth open soon made Marty thirsty so she veered to the stream for a drink. She squatted so Ted could hand-dip water for Amy to drink.

Sipping water, she saw plants underwater, in the shallows. Tearing out a handful she sniffed, frowning. Watercress! She pulled up a double handful of the pungent herb, squeezed out water, and showed it to Ted. She had him try a nibble then added it to his quickly filling pack.

Ted frowned at the peppery taste, but it must be good because it made her happy.

Returning to the game trail, she stopped suddenly at a faint aroma. A green plant poked through remnants of dead grass. She sniffed a leaf and recognized Lemon Balm. She and Gram had made tea from some—there was more to eat here than she'd have guessed. She plucked enough for a small pan of tea.

They stepped up on the trail and went east at a fast walk. Raucous, irate squawking began as they appeared over the bank. "Blue Jays always squawk at everything." She mumbled, then stopped so suddenly Ted bumped into her then backed away, confused. She smelled onions. Hunting for the familiar hollow leaves, she backtracked a short ways until she saw them.

Ted sat on a hump to catch his breath. He was getting tired. He was accustomed to running in play half the day, but not so continuously.

None of the small, highly scented onions would come up without being dug, so Marty pried up the half-dozen she found with the knife.

They finally, wearily reached the stream's upper end. Marty plopped down on a deadfall a few yards short of a deep, crystal clear pool beneath a misty falls that sprayed down thirty feet of sheer rock cliff. At its top she could barely see the lower edge of snow bank that filled the depression between two towering, snowy, cloud-shrouded peaks—the stream's source.

A slate gray, stubby-tailed Dipper flitted around in the falls' spray, singing merrily. Marty shivered to think how cold that mist was.

No way out at this end, either. But there HAD to be one somewhere!

She had to get them out of this trap of precipitous cliffs and soaring mountains. She sneered at recalling being glad for the protection of high rims the day of the snowstorm. Some protection! It was a trap! One she WOULD find a way out of!

Looking up at the rims she was startled to see it was mid-afternoon. She jumped up—they had to hurry or it would be dark before they got home!

Marty fought to stay calm, reminding herself how much time was lost getting across the stream and the whole way had been uphill. Going down would be faster.

She couldn't see the slip-fault from here, or any of the lower valley. Clouds had thickened and grown dark—would there be another snowstorm? Fear tightened her chest. The brisk wind was cold, but not distinctly so, and smelled wet. She hadn't even thought to watch the weather. How could she be so careless? Again.

Marty went as straight down the north side as she could find trails to follow, hurrying as fast as she could expect Ted to go. Not looking for food, she concentrated only on getting to camp, grimly refusing to acknowledge the terror threatening to overwhelm her.

Ted was afraid, too. Marty was going so fast he had to run several times to keep up. Was she mad? Would she go off and leave him? Fear spurred him on but he was so tired his whole body ached and his pack was heavier than it had ever been.

Marty got further and further ahead until, rounding a corner, he couldn't see her. He stopped and looked around with his breath caught in his throat—which way did she go? He edged down the widest trail, hoping she hadn't taken one of the smaller ones that branched off every few feet. Did she mean to leave him? He'd been bad at that rock. Burning tears made it hard to see.

Blurry but recognizable, Marty popped her head around a Blue Spruce by the wider trail, gray with worry and fatigue. Ted gulped back his tears and ran to catch up.

"I couldn't see you." He said, his voice breaking. He swallowed hard. "I didn't know where you went."

Marty heaved a sigh of relief that he was safe. "I'm sorry. I'll slow down. I was trying to hurry so we can get to camp before dark."

Ted gulped relief. She hadn't meant to leave him after all.

Marty repeatedly looked back to be sure she didn't leave him behind again, but had to keep slowing down for him.

At the fault's north end, several rough but well used game trails laced diagonally down the side, easing the descent, but it was still quite steep.

Raindrops began to splatter off exposed rocks beside them. Going left, Marty followed the escarpment toward the stream, head ducked against the rain. Icy, pelting rain soon saturated their bowed heads.

Despite the forced pace, Ted ached with cold wetness. He was so exhausted only his fear of being left behind kept him from dropping where he was.

Amy started to cry from the startling coldness. Marty stopped and squatted long enough for Ted to wearily wrestle the girl from her carrier. Wrapping Amy inside her jacket, Marty hurried on over slippery mud.

Ted envied Amy's warm security, but she was the baby and babies had to be taken care of. He wished he was small enough to be taken care of like that. But he was big now, big enough to carry dinner in his pack. Sometimes it was very hard to be big.

Gasping at the rain's shocking cold, Marty felt vulnerable to everything outside her control—especially this miserable weather—and her failure, again, to find a way out. Her wet hair dribbled cold rain down under her collar and stole her breath by soaking through her heavy flannel-lined corduroy jacket. Cold wetness saturated her heavy boots and soaked her sore, nearly blistered feet.

Ted was so miserable he had to struggle as hard against crying as against the slippery muck and heavy pack to keep from losing sight of Marty again. His teeth chattered from the cold, despite his exertion. She'd said why she had to hurry, so the boy toiled along after his step-mother, trusting that what the omnipotent adult said was absolute Truth, that she knew everything.

Through the noisy gray dimness of pouring rain, Marty saw a huge dark shadow beside the scarp. Nearer, she saw it was two enormous cedars growing side by side. Their old, interwoven branches hung protectively over a needle-carpeted dry spot. On knees and one hand, she crawled under the droopy branches, gasping from the fast pace.

Shaking with cold and fatigue, Ted plopped breathlessly down and huddled against a huge, scaly trunk, his teeth clattering loudly. Scattered raindrops managed to drip past lacy branches and the chilly wind, though considerably weakened, made them shiver miserably. Marty crouched by Ted to wrap an arm around him to share warmth. He sagged against her, tears of relief slipping unnoticed down his rain-drenched cheeks.

Marty vaguely recalled seeing huge twin trees from where they'd climbed the cliff earlier, so they were near the middle falls. Now she knew how far camp was. She peered out, wondering when the rain might let up. In front of the scarp she saw a few gnarled cedar roots had grown out of the soil and onto the domed edge of a partly buried rock. Past that, in the scarp face, she was startled to see the dark shadow of a deep overhang partly hidden by the rock dome.

Excitedly pointing it out to Ted, she motioned for him to follow and, half crawling, carried Amy to the cavelet. As her eyes adapted to the dimness, she studied the structure to see how safe it was to be there. It was not cracked or shaley like most of the scarp face, but the solid granite of the mountains. The huge chunk of shale had fractured away from the stable granite eons ago and now lay half buried in front of the overhang.

Looking out from the overhang's center, she estimated the highest point was nine feet up to her left, tapering to her right down to five feet high. The ends were about fifteen feet apart. Behind her, the rear wall sloped down to eight feet behind the overhang's lip. The back wall stayed that deep most of its length, angling gradually out to the right, but angled abruptly out at the very end on the left. About a foot above the rubble-strewn floor, a ledge of fractured shale ran across the back, wide enough to sit on and lean back. Marty sank down in relief. They were now out of the rain and most of the wind.

But she fretted about possibly being unable to get to camp before dark. It was late afternoon and rain still poured. Her whole body ached with fatigue and cold.

Ted sprawled alongside, leaning against her. Only shivering kept him awake. Amy sat quietly under her mother's coat, content to peek out. Marty roused Ted to share the jerky and raisins.

Like a faucet being shut off, the rain abruptly stopped. With Amy back in the carrier, Marty and Ted wearily slipped and slid through mud under drippy trees the gloomy half-mile to the stream.

So much sudden rain had raised the water level and Marty's cleated soles were clogged with mud so her feet slipped unpredictably on the abbreviated rocks, making it terrifying to carry both children back across.

Marty shook violently from cold, fatigue and panic by the time she reached the far bank. She paused to let Ted slip down beside her and partly catch her breath. It was getting dark, no time to rest, so she clenched her teeth and forced herself to hurry on. Dim shafts of sunlight briefly lit the undersides of the western clouds, fading as she watched. Humid air grew frigid in a brisk breeze that swayed treetops.

With a lurch of her heart and a searing pang of fear, Marty cringed at a sound in dark shadowed brush to her left, a furtive rustle of some large stealthy creature stalking just out of sight—she was sure the beast could hear the thunder of her pounding heart. It trailed alongside them the last, seemingly endless half-mile to camp. Marty kept a tight protective hold on Ted's hand while he walked on her right. Both shivered violently. The warm hand contact was as reassuring to her as to the exhausted boy.

It was dark when they reached camp, nearly impossible to see the way. Only because it was familiar and the gray tent was vaguely visible, did they reach it. It was impossible to see anything inside the tent, which was nearly as cold as outside, the smoke stale and old. Marty knew the fire was out. She hadn't banked it enough to be gone this long.

Fumbling blindly, she cut shavings with the hatchet, jumping at every tiny sound and reaching for the pistol as she peered at the barely perceptible doorway. A fire would keep the beasts away, but would whatever followed them here brave coming in after them without one? She shuddered in fear but forced herself to arrange wood chips she couldn't see and nearly sobbed when she found the matchbox. Striking the last match was a trauma, but there was no choice. Her hand shook uncontrollably as she crouched to shield the tiny flame long enough to ignite the tinder and flare brightly. Marty nearly collapsed in relief as the fire grew and began to throw welcome, dancing light on the tent sides. Smoke, then precious heat radiated from the growing flames.

Three sets of teeth chattered as they shivered out of wet clothes and into dry pajamas while the fire stabilized. Marty was too exhausted to fix any food they'd gathered the last two days, so they ate a late but warming dinner of the last can of soup piping hot and steamy, and the last can of peaches.

After the children were tucked into bed, Marty brewed the Lemon Balm into tea. She sipped aromatic tea by the comforting fire, and though she felt guilty for not sharing it, she drank all of the soothing, calming brew.

When enough coals had formed she banked the fire and dragged into bed. Thinking about again failing to find a way out, she started to cry softly, struggling to keep from waking the children. She didn't dare go outside for a real cry, not with some hulking brute out there. The guns wouldn't help now—she couldn't hit what she couldn't see.

If only she could talk to someone.

Anyone.

CHAPTER 8

Marty had made and drank coffee first thing every morning for years; not observing that ritual the past two mornings was a measure of her desperation to find a way out. This morning she would.

She carefully stoked the fire, frightened that all the matches were gone. What can I use if it goes out again? She wondered, feeding bigger pieces of wood to growing flames. She'd heard Indians could start a fire by rubbing sticks together, but seriously doubted she could figure out exactly how that worked.

Finally she dared leave to get water and check the snares, limping on sore, blistered feet. One snare was gone; the heavy shaft it had been tied to was broken at the ground. Spatters of dry blood and loose feathers dotted the grass where the snare had been set—the predator following them last night had taken game from the snare!

Heart pounding, she looked around. Is it still near? Still hungry? She rushed back to make sure the children were safe—and to hide in the sanctuary of the tent.

As the fire formed a good bed of coals and coffee boiled, she thought about how important fire was. Not having one could mean death, even in summer, if not from predators, then from starvation or illness from bad or raw meat; she grimaced at the image. They would surely freeze to death in winter without fire.

Feeling more alone than ever, she drank cup after cup of coffee and thought about nearby dangerous beasts and how bad the stench of death that first drew the creatures had become. She scrubbed at her nose, trying to get rid of the putrid smell that always lingered near camp. She needed to move away from the stench, the swarms of flies and lurking scavengers from the crash site—camp was only a scant half-mile from there.

But where? Closer to the pond? Almost every trip from camp had been to it, or near it. This side of the stream was steep or muddy there, but most foods she'd found had been near the pond.

As important as safety, she wanted to avoid reminders of all she couldn't change—constantly depressing, distracting things. Her full attention was needed for what helped them survive.

To guess the valley's size, she recalled that, strolling in a straight uninterrupted line in the city, it took nearly an hour to go a mile, counting time waiting to cross busy streets. It took half a day of fast walking to reach either end of the valley, though that was never in a straight line and they'd backtracked now and then. This time of year half a day was just under six hours, so the valley was somewhat less than six miles long by about a third that wide. Not very big.

How big would that be on a map of the northern Rockies? Would it even be marked?

Would anyone ever happen across this place?

Would she ever find a way out?

The children waking broke her discouraging thoughts. They'd slept unusually late. Poor things must be as worn out as she was.

Cooking breakfast, she decided to keep looking for an exit, and simply had to find a new campsite, across the stream, if possible. But she wanted to find a shorter, safer route to get there. She shuddered at remembering how spooky the trips carrying both children over had been.

Limping slowly, Marty let the children set the pace, searching for a new way across, often squeezing through thick brush. Now and then she absently glanced up to search the sky, unaware of still doing so. The only place possible to cross was the leaky remnant of beaver dam at the pond's lower end—nothing was further downstream.

Ted and Amy sat together on a dry knoll to watch as she pushed through brush to the dam; she would try it alone first.

Arms out for balance, she carefully stepped onto the old wood. On the third step, a foot broke through surface wood and plunged into the rotted understory, so deep icy water ran into her boot to soak her foot. Wobbling dangerously, arms waving, mouth dry with terror, she finally managed to free the foot and retreat.

No crossing here, even without the children. Marty was terrified of getting hurt. What would happen to the children if even a minor injury kept her from getting food?

Safely on the bank, she looked wistfully over at the meadow's broad, nearly flat slope. Water glinted between matted grasses—its whole lower end was in shallow flood. She couldn't move anywhere it flooded! This part of the year was good for learning that.

Enough looking for today. To make this trip worthwhile, she gathered several cattail shoots, amazed at how fast they'd grown, picked a few intensely aromatic Spearmint sprigs from boggy, wooded shade, and lots of Dandelion buds and leaves along the path.

Both children took a long nap as soon as they returned, despite sleeping so late. Marty rested a while but was too anxious to sit for long. She cleaned the neglected camp and did dishes, then moved the snares further from camp, remembering that lurking predator. Each time she looked for places to set snares it was easier to spot the faint brush-lined trails grouse and hares made.

She cooked the rabbit snared two days ago with the wild onions and braised watercress, and peeled the raw Cow Parsnip stems they gathered yesterday. It was a pungent, spicy meal, but all of it had been gathered, none was from the depleted stores; she'd rather carry that packaged food almost anywhere than be without it. But moving everything would be a formidable task, despite the reduced bulk and weight from the food they'd consumed.

Determined to move camp as soon as possible, it occurred to her that if she must to use the same crossing they already had, there might be a way to make moving camp safer and easier.

Moving the snares worked again, one held a plump grouse the next morning. Marty took time to build a good bed of coals to bank for several hours, and to bake cornbread and scramble powdered eggs for breakfast and lunch before leaving camp, thinking wistfully about duck eggs she could soon find and gather. Tame ducks faithfully nested only in select spots. Where would wild ducks nest? How could she find them? Tangled cattail leaves seemed worth checking; she'd do that while they were out looking for an exit and a new campsite today.

She grabbed a carrying bag at the last moment, in case she found any eggs.

Adding rocks across the swift water was a harder job than Marty thought. From the stepping stones near the bank, she tossed out rocks that looked big enough to stick up out of the water, only to see them sink from sight or be swept away by the water's irresistible force. The rocks were far heavier than she imagined, and it took unexpectedly big ones to fill any gap, even near shore. This water was far deeper than it looked.

Ted tried to help, laboring to roll the biggest he could move over near her. They were too small to help much but, reluctant to discourage the boy, Marty used each one, stepping further and further out as the accumulation finally made a difference. She worked back from the far side, too, but the center was the hardest part. Each rock had to be lugged out, then tossed as far upstream as possible before the current washed it downstream, hopefully to sink about where she wanted it. But adding stones near the side diverted water to the center, making that swifter than ever.

Marty finally had to sit and rest achy muscles until they no longer hurt, then Ted helped her get the carrier on so they could cross the augmented stone path together, Ted's hand in hers for balance and reassurance. She gloated about never having to do this strenuous task again, and it did make the trip over much less frightening and dangerous.

She set off downstream toward the meadow, following an obvious trail beside the thickest brush. Along the way she saw plants she wanted to be near, like wild roses with weathered hips that looked like tiny red apples, much like roses that grew near the farm in her childhood. They used to gather wild rose hips, split them open to scrape out the hairy seed mass, then candy the remaining fleshy pulp for healthful winter treats.

Some berry bushes had leafed out enough to recognize and others had begun to bud out or bloom. Waxy pink, cup-shaped flowers hung in sprinkles among unfolding Huckleberry leaves. Holly-leafed Oregon Grapes had deep yellow bud clusters near the center, and many thorny-stemmed briar berries were recognizable. Those would yield so many delicious berries their vines would nearly touch the ground. Her mouth watered at seeing bright white strawberry blossoms.

Moving over here was an excellent idea. More food plants than she'd hoped for grew here.

Cutting across the meadow's center toward its north edge, Marty gathered chickweed, wild carrots, onions, and more fern shoots. She saw more vaguely familiar shrubs not leafed out enough to identify. She followed the meadow's north edge to the east, looking for fresh water to camp near.

When they passed a huge hollow log, Ted ducked down and started to crawl inside. Marty grabbed him just before his head met the gauzy cobwebs across the opening.

"You can't go in there! Some animal might be using that for its home!" She shrilled. "If you go in its home it will be mad. For sure spiders live there, and they bite."

Ted's eyes bulged as he slapped sticky, dusty cobwebs off his head. He backed away.

Everywhere she had a long view of the south cliffs, Marty used the binoculars to scan them. But too many trees crowded the steep side to tell if anywhere could be traversed to get out. All the crest she could see was rocky and covered with dirty patches of snow. That side also looked too steep to climb. The crash site was in those trees. A choking throat lump reminded her of why she had to move camp.

Ted, spotting the dark shape of a Porcupine perched high in a half-grown evergreen, hopped up and down and squealed, "Look! I see a Porkypine!"

Holding the boy in place by the back of his coat, Marty explained about sharp, painful quills that protected the slow, awkward creature that would never tolerate being petted. She hated to disappoint him, but was glad for the distraction.

Ted's head hung as he scuffed after Marty. Sometimes he got tired of playing only with Amy, and wished for other playmates. Someone he didn't have to help take care of.

Marty recognized peeling red bark on woody vines of Kinnikinnick that sprawled in tangled mats in one area. A few dry berries still clung beside new white, hanging-lantern flowers just starting to open. Unsure if it was edible, she cautiously nibbled a dry berry that looked like a tiny shriveled apple. It tasted bland and had no burning or acrid aftertaste—things Gram had warned to watch out for when trying out any new plant. She'd see if it upset her stomach before eating more or letting the youngsters try any. Gram had said her father used the small evergreen leaves to smoke and for a medicinal tea, though Marty couldn't recall what it was supposed to cure.

They sat on a deadfall near the meadow's edge to eat lunch of eggs and cornbread. Tiny, curious chipmunks, daring but nervous, scampered closer and closer as they ate. The bravest snatched a dropped cornbread crumb and dashed a safe distance away. Ted jiggled in excitement. Morsel by tiny morsel, he tossed out the rest of his share so they'd come closer, delighted to at last make more friends.

Marty paid no attention to such tiny harmless creatures, she was studying the lay of the meadow and the distribution of water and food plants, working out where to set up camp so she wouldn't have to move it again. Unless someone happened to find them.

She'd give anything to move into a rescue plane.

Returning to where they'd entered the meadow, Ted discovered a mostly-eaten deer carcass, too mummified from freeze-drying in winter's parching cold to be odorous. Gaping claw marks were still etched deeply into brittle, blackened shoulder hide; Marty assumed this had been prey of the big predator that stayed so well hidden. It had to be what followed them to camp and raided the snare. The hair on Marty's nape prickled and she looked around carefully. No sign of it now, but she hurried back to the ford.

Rekindling smoldering coals, Marty worked on plans for how to accomplish the Herculean task of moving so much weight so far without leaving the children in danger. She brushed a hand over her eyes, trying to remember how she moved it before, but it was only a dim blur.

They stuffed themselves with Dandelion and Chickweed salad, steamed cattail shoots, and pot-roasted grouse that she'd scalded and tediously plucked this time instead of skinning. They washed that down with lightly sweetened, delightfully pungent Spearmint tea.

One woman and two young children couldn't eat so much food. Some of everything was left. Those leftovers would make good soup for tomorrow.

She hadn't made biscuits because she was alarmed at how fast the flour was being used, had no idea how to replace it when the last was gone. But baking yeast bread would stretch it more than biscuits. She boiled the last two potatoes, mashed them in the cooking water and put them in the empty jerky jar to ferment into sourdough starter.

How else could she stretch the flour? Maybe with a little oatmeal, but what would she use when that ran out?

She fretted while arranging clean empty cans and the cheese's peeled-off paraffin in a crate—could that be used to make a candle? It didn't look like enough and she knew of no way to get more.

Distressed, she sat by the fire drinking the last of the tea, thinking about the deer carcass, the raided snare, and the large predator who'd done those things. Its ability to cross the stream with such apparent ease made the hair on her nape prickle. She could swear she felt eyes on her, watching, waiting, though the door was well shut.

Shuddering, Marty busily oiled all the guns, though none had been fired. But she dared not risk them becoming useless from rust. Inside the tent was very damp; nearly always, while they were in camp, food cooked or water was on heating, making steam.

Marty never realized it was Ted's eyes she felt. She thought he was sound asleep. He lay quietly, almost too tired to sleep, watching her from half-closed eyes, curious about what she did after dark. When she started to clean the guns his attention was riveted on her every move. He was puzzled over why. She did many things he didn't understand, but he was learning not to doubt whether she knew what she was doing.

At first, when she was all bloody and scary after the crash, she'd acted strange and he'd been afraid. She didn't act like that now, but the silliest things made her feel bad and he often saw a glint of unshed tears or a special kind of tenseness in her stance or movement. It made his heart hurt that he could not make her feel better.

CHAPTER 9

The snares were empty that morning, but with leftovers to make stew that night, she could stay in camp today. Too footsore to travel far, she decided it was time to wash clothes, since they'd all had to wear dirty ones again.

She shaved Fels Naphtha into the big bucket of heating water to dissolve, then sorted clothes. The pile grew into a big bundle she took down near the spring. She lugged the hot, soapy water down, poured enough into a stewpot of cold water to warm it and started the long, tedious task of scrubbing, wringing and rinsing clothes.

Barely able to grip anything else with such tired hands, she spread clean items over bushes to dry in the sun.

Refilling the rinsed stewpot, she carried it to camp and started the stew of leftovers and the last onions and carrots they'd brought on the plane.

Next morning the snares were still empty so she moved them even farther from camp. Now she had to go fishing or they'd have no meat for dinner. But that wouldn't take long. Then she and the children could rest the remainder of the day.

Looking at the meadow across the rushing water near the pond, Marty considered possible campsites. Daily, the stench drifting downhill form the wreck to camp grew worse. She dreaded the effort of moving, but where they were had become unbearable.

She turned back to hunting bait, smirking at the children. Making silly faces and shrilling giggles and squeals in mock squeamishness, Ted and Amy snatched up worms and grubs hidden under a thin deadfall while Marty held up one end.

A faint trail she hadn't noticed before wound through cattails and willows toward the pond, leading to shore near where the stream spewed out into open water, at what looked like a good place to fish.

Marty let Ted fish while she took Amy to get cattail shoots. When they returned Ted was gleefully trying to get a big flopping trout off the hook by himself. Marty giggled when he grabbed at the fish as it lay gasping between spasms of protest, only to have it jerk out of his hands when he touched it. It thrashed so hard the slimy tail smacked the boy's face but he still grabbed at it.

"Here, Teddy, I'll show you an easier way." Marty stepped on the fish with a waffle-soled boot and showed how to unsnag the hook. She baited it with another wiggly worm and tossed it back out. Before she could hand the pole to Ted it jerked sharply, so she started working the pole tip toward the bank by her feet. Marty cleaned those two fish while Ted caught two more, almost as fast as the bait hit the water. She was relieved to have the fish, but they bit so fast it was almost boring—without the wait for a strike, no anticipation or suspense had time to build.

Four fish was plenty, any more would spoil before they could be eaten. Ted was sad when they quit fishing, though this wasn't as much fun as catching his big big fish.

Not in any hurry, they wandered around the side of the pond, looking for more edible plants. Marty wondered what had made twiggy, conical mounds out in the water. They were unlike the beaver lodge. In school she'd seen a picture of a Muskrat sitting on a mound of greenery out in the water. Could there be Muskrats here? She knew they ate swamp plants, and were eagerly eaten in the southern states.

Seeing movement out in the water, Marty squatted down to point it out to the kids. All three watched as two sets of ripples spread out by the lily pads close to the far side. The V-shaped ripple points headed in leisurely zigzags toward the center, coming closer, followed by something waving lazily and barely breaking the water's surface.

Both children stared in silent fascination as the creatures swam close enough to see the tops of their heads barely sticking out of the water. One dove under and emerged much closer. Its tan-cheeked head was dark brown from nose to crown. It looked like an overgrown mouse with short round ears and beady black eyes that stared at them without alarm. The other paused farther away with its head up just enough so its eyes sparkled at the surface.

First Amy, then Ted jumped up to dance in place and jabber in noisy excitement, pointing at the closer animal. Instantly both creatures dived out of sight and didn't come up anywhere in sight. Marty fumed, the kids' lack of restraint had scared them away before she could identify the animals.

Heading back to camp, Marty thought about the incident. There would be times when the children's failure to stay quiet, to remain unnoticed, could put them in danger of injury or death—an upsetting idea, but true. With the variety of animals here, a time had to come when they'd be in grave danger. How could she prevent that?

To stay unnoticed they'd have to hold still and be silent on command, and only move again when she signaled it was safe. But how? It had to be a signal either child could recognize, but one that wouldn't attract a threatening animal or the signal would defeat its own purpose, would instead draw attention. Animals were especially alert to movement so she had to find a signal with little or no motion—a sound, then. Maybe one so familiar and nonthreatening a predator would ignore it.

She thought of possibilities as they went up the trail toward camp, discarding them as likely to draw the beast's attention, or ones the children might not notice and respond to.

Hearing his friend squirrel chatter somewhere nearby, Ted gleefully answered it by sucking his lips to make a nearly identical sound.

Marty was intrigued. Squirrels sounded off like that at anything that moved and were usually noisy. It was such a common, familiar sound that few animals paid much attention, a sound she and Ted could already make, required no obvious movement, and could be made even with their hands full. It was ideal!

Now, how could she teach them to respond the way she wanted at the signal? Amy was too young to understand an explanation, and Marty wasn't sure about Ted. Maybe she could invent a game that used the signal, a contest to see who could hold still the best . . . Freeze Tag! She'd played it in school, and smiled at picturing the silly positions some players had gotten caught in. Others had toppled, giggling, to the ground because there was no way to stay balanced without moving.

"We're going to play a game." She said with such enthusiasm it startled both children.

Ted frowned sideways up at Marty—she'd never played with them before.

"You two play like always but when I make the squirrel sound you have to stop, no matter how you're standing, and stay just like that without moving at all until I make the sound again. Then you can move. Okay? Ready to try it?"

A long moment after they began to chase each other Marty sucked her lips. Ted staggered a couple of steps, the stood still with his feet apart and offset. Amy bumped into him and giggled on past, not holding still at all.

Marty grabbed Amy and said, "When I go like this," Marty made the signal again, "you have to stop moving and hold as still as you can, like Teddy is. Teddy's doing it right, he plays the game really good."

The second time, Amy took a few steps after the signal, then stood looking from Ted to her mother, but stayed in one spot. Marty sighed deeply. This was going to take time and endless patience.

Near the trail ahead she saw a robin. It sang a lilting cheer-up, cheerily song, hopped with tilted head to listen and then pecked in wet ground to pull out and gobble down a plump, juicy worm. It was already very fat.

Marty made the signal but Amy ran a few steps before stopping, scaring the bird into noisy flight.

"See Amy? You didn't hold still and you scared the poor little birdie away. If you held still when I signaled you could watch it eat worms."

Ted suddenly understood what Marty was doing. "I know!" He yelled, bouncing up and down. "They don't go away if they don't see you move! Right?"

Delighted, Marty nodded and grinned at him.

Onions grew here, so she dug more, tucking them in Ted's pack. The small, potent bulbs made his eyes water. He walked with head ducked forward to escape the smell.

They reached camp in mid-afternoon. Mosquitoes were already thick and hungry. Marty and Amy both scratched bites on their hands and faces, but Ted had none. Unpacking the bulbs, eyes brimming from irritation, Marty wondered if his getting no bites was because such a strong odor bothered mosquitoes. She nearly laughed at picturing the pesky bugs rubbing tears from their eyes, but the reek of death penetrated even the onion odor and quickly sobered her.

Turning from feeding the fire, she saw the sourdough starter had puffed up out of its container and foamed all over the crate where she'd put it to stay warm. Upset at the waste, she was elated that the yeast was actually behaving like it was supposed to, curdling and puffing up, developing a sour, yeasty odor. Despite the mess, she sighed with relief. Enough starter was left to grow more by adding water and flour—in a larger container. Now they could have bread; but she still had to figure out how to stretch the flour.

It would take too long to raise a batch today, so she made cornbread to go with fried fish and fresh greens.

At dusk she approached the snares close enough to see they were empty. While falling asleep that night she mulled over how to set muskrat snares.

In the morning she took time to rebuild the fire and make and drink coffee before going to check the snares. How much had they reduced the nearby rabbit and grouse populations? Would they soon all be gone? She had to go see.

Nearing, she heard a squeaky scream and saw a kicking hare twist and struggle to escape a snare, its efforts making the anchoring branch jerk and whip erratically.

She was appalled, had assumed any snared animal died fast, with little pain.

After a brief, frantic search, she grabbed a stout stick to put the poor thing out of its misery. She was two strides away when a big hawk swooped smoothly down onto the struggling hare. Its outstretched wings narrowly missed hitting Marty. The bird clutched the frenzied, squealing hare with long sharp talons on scaly yellow feet and shrieked in piercing rage at her threatening nearness. It glared at her with bright orange, unblinking eyes, daring her to approach one more step.

Marty froze in mindless astonishment, mouth agape and eyes wide, unable to accept this was actually happening.

The shrieking hawk lurched and flapped slowly, powerfully into the air, trying to fly off with his prize clutched securely in deadly talons, but was abruptly jerked back by the snare line. Squawking indignantly, it struggled to hold onto the anchored game and stay in the air. The limp rabbit suddenly ripped apart from the power of the hawk's flight and its lethally sharp talons. As it flapped rapidly upward, still clutching the rabbit's rear half, the tone of its scream changed from indignation to a clear tone of victory.

The gray-barred hawk was nearly out of sight before Marty recovered enough to realize she'd stood here holding a club and had made no move to use it—hadn't even noticed she held it. She gaped at the tattered front half. The neck had nearly been severed by the noose of fine, strong fish line as the bird strained to fly away.

She was angry at losing food they needed; now, not enough was left for a decent supper. She scrubbed a hand under her nose in irritation; she had to move snares again and figure out what else to get to eat today. She'd wanted so much not to have to travel anywhere today, for a change.

She'd been terrified at the Goshawk's unexpected ferocity and determination, awed by its viciously hooked, yellow beak and nearly four-foot wingspan. Its piercing talons were lethal weapons, its courage remarkable. It was the male of the pair they'd seen in the treetop nest, not an eagle after all. She exhaled hard, astounded any hawk got so huge. But, most amazing, its actions had been purposeful, its eyes acutely intelligent.

Never again would she think of a bird of prey as a stupid creature!

She discarded the scrap of hide. Cleaning that rabbit was simple, the bird had done most of it already.

Before leaving camp, she started a loaf of sourdough bread, covering it and setting it on a crate near the fire to stay warm and be safe from small marauders.

Marty played Freeze Tag with the children on the way to the pond, once even letting Ted make the signal so she could demonstrate how to freeze properly. Amy was slightly better at freezing after that, but the girl didn't really want to hold still; she saw it as a chance to more easily tag the other player.

When Marty realized why Amy refused to freeze, she glared at the girl over folded arms. Her lip scar flared crimson. How could she make the girl understand this WAS important, that this MUST be learned, that her life might someday depend on it? Marty didn't want to give the girl her fist spanking, but knew it might be unavoidable. It was too dangerous for the child not to learn instant obedience to this signal.

By the pond, she discovered a worn trace leading away from the overgrown shore. Many cattail, reed and grass stems were chewed off along that path. She fervently hoped this was muskrat sign.

To set snares here, she cut and sharpened a pair of inch-thick, three-foot-long willow sapling sections for each snare, pounding them into dense, root-laced mud with a rock until the top was a foot above ground. Then she draped the noose top of her heaviest fish line at the top, letting the bottom barely touch the trail, the end tied to one of the props. She didn't know exactly how big or strong these animals were, she'd only seen a picture in a book, and glimpsed them here, mostly submerged, but this should be strong enough.

On the way back she gathered fiddlehead shoots, peeled thistle stems, and a few gnarled cattail roots. No slippery, succulent cattail shoots were left. Some had been chewed off, but most were waist high and now too tough to eat. Tugging another long, twisted segment of cattail root from wet muck and thoroughly rinsing off the mud, she saw a few thin club spikes now poked above the growing leaves. Above each undeveloped club's body a spike of yellowish, powdery pollen was starting to form. Soon she'd have to bring something to hold the fine pollen—it was nearly ready to gather. Could it be used to stretch the flour?

At camp she set the cattail roots near the fire to dry.

The bread was flat and heavy but its aroma and taste were right, reminiscent of home with its familiar routine, security and safety.

Dreaming of home, she cried in her sleep that night.

CHAPTER 10

It took the last grounds from the canister to boil morning coffee. Sprinkling salt in water heating for mush, only a few grains rattled in the metal shaker. Twisting off the pin-holed, domed lid, she pulled out the rock hard salt bag to fill it. Holding the bag against a thigh, she pounded it with her fist to mash the lumps. She opened the bag, saw its blue-bonneted, yellow-haired girl carrying an umbrella through raindrops, and smirked at, "When it rains, it pours." Salt always got lumpy in dampness. The girl looked like Amy.

Smiling as she filled the shaker, she stopped, alarmed that this bag was the last of the salt. Knowing she'd never get more made a chill prickle up her arms. How would food taste without salt?

She shook her head, wiping clammy hands on pant legs. There was no replacement and nowhere out here to get more. Something else she had no solution for, just had to accept as part of life until she found an exit. Well, she'd make it last as long as possible.

Lightly salting the boiling water she thought, so far, getting used to wild foods hadn't been bad. But she dreaded running out of irreplaceable foods—tomorrow she'd open the last of the coffee. At least fishing and snares were keeping them supplied with meat, like grouse, rabbits and trout. But, short of starving, never again would she eat a sucker. Vegetables were there for the picking, and most she knew as edible were tasty. Marty silently thanked Gram for the months of time she'd spent sharing her vast knowledge with a bored and lonely girl.

She needed to get more greens today, which reminded her of the pond snares. Eagerness to go check them made her hand slip as she reached for bowls to dish mush into so it could cool enough to eat, and they fell with a clatter that woke the children early.

Marty's rush to the pond left both children winded. She looked for anything swimming in the pond but only saw more new ducks and noticed a definite increase in quacks, chirps and whistles. Over all that was the unmistakable honk of geese.

Eagerly slipping through fast-growing reeds and cattails to the first snare, she found it untouched. She followed another trace to the next as Ted and Amy wearily followed.

"I got one!" She nearly whooped for joy, but remembered the panic Ted's yells had caused. Stifling elation, she pointed out the brown fur heap to the youngsters. In a soft voice shrill with delight, she said, "That's a muskrat. It got trapped in my snare."

Marty's enthusiasm was contagious. Both children were instantly fascinated, and suddenly not so tired.

Ready to leap away at the slightest motion, she nudged its back with a toe to be sure it was dead. It was limp and unresisting.

This thick-furred animal was over a foot long and a scaly, flat-sided tail nearly doubled that. She tried not to see the resemblance to a huge, round rat, telling herself its long yellowish gnawing teeth were NOT ratty. It looked more like a small beaver, except its slightly flattened tail was thinner in width instead of height like beaver tails. Besides, she shivered, rats lacked the hind foot webbing this creature had.

Removing the snare, she estimated it to weigh around three pounds, meat for two days or more. She'd heard they were good eating—she gulped back queasiness—and were sold down south as Marsh Rabbits.

But she had to eat it, no matter how it looked. They had to have food and what she could get would soon be all there was, so she'd better learn to like it. Or starve. She had to set a good example, had to convince the children it was fine even if she didn't really think so, or they wouldn't eat it either.

She took the muskrat away from the swamp to clean. Cutting down the belly, Marty talked to the watching children.

"This is what you two scared away out in the water when you didn't hold still. It'll be yummy for dinner." She gulped silent doubts away. "We could've had some sooner, But Amy was naughty and didn't hold still when I made the signal, like she was supposed to." She frowned at the girl.

Amy puckered up, her mouth opened wide and tears welled and ran down her cheeks before she uttered a sound. The wail from that wide mouth began softly but grew until Marty wondered how such a small girl could hold enough air to make so much noise. The instant Amy's noise let up so she could inhale, Marty said, "But Teddy was a good boy, he held still until I signaled him it was okay to move again."

Ted puffed up with pride, but felt sorry that Amy was in trouble.

Marty felt guilty for making Amy cry, but she had to make her understand the importance of obeying the freeze signal. She turned aside to clean the game.

When Marty turned away, Ted squatted to hug the bawling child and pat her, whispering *shoosh* like Marty usually did, not understanding why Marty didn't comfort her.

The gutted carcass was still so heavy she removed the head and tail as useless weight, but she carefully saved as much head fur as possible; she didn't want to waste even a thin strip of this thick pelt. She waited to skin it to keep the meat clean.

Even that stripped, it was too heavy for Ted to carry so she took it by a hind foot.

The last trap was also untouched. Marty left the two set, but a muskrat would last much longer than a bird or rabbit.

Remembering they needed vegetables, she found a few cattail shoots to cut.

A courting Redwing Blackbird perched on an old cattail stalk leaning outward, wings spread to display the bright red patch crowning each wing. His black feathers puffed out when he voiced a bubbly *kong-ka-ree* courting song for a drab brown hen perched on a nearby branch stub.

Marty gave the kissing signal to freeze, watching the children from the corner of her eye. They'd been walking behind her, and both froze, Ted at once, Amy after she put both feet down. But Amy held still this time. Barely moving a hand, Marty pointed at the courting birds until Ted and Amy both spotted them. She let them watch a few seconds, then signaled it was okay to move.

Marty picked Amy up and hugged her, cooing, "See, when you hold still you can watch wild creatures without scaring them away. But if they see you move they get scared and go hide." She motioned to where the birds had been.

She put Amy down and hugged Ted. "You both did it really good this time."

When Marty ducked into the tent a mouse bolted out under an edge, squeaking in high-pitched terror. While trembling hands fumbled for wood to rebuild the fire, Marty realized the tiny creature was as frightened of her as she'd been of it. She wondered why any human, so gigantic compared to a mouse, was afraid of such a tiny thing. But it had very good reason to fear humans. She shuddered in relief it was gone, anyway.

When the fire threw enough light, she saw mouse droppings by the food boxes.

"All I need now are mice!" She snarled, put the food away and went out to skin the muskrat, sitting briefly to settle down.

The beautiful rust and chocolate colored fur was one she ardently wanted to save so she was careful not to nick it while skinning it, a task much different than tube-peeling a rabbit. Unsure how to hold it or the hide, she felt awkward. She found a pair of glands not far under its tail, presumed they were testicles, and carefully trimmed them away. She was stumped at finding more glands, one on each side of the abdomen, nearly brushing the 'knees'. These glands smelled awful so she trimmed them away, realizing their distinctly musky odor gave the Musk Rat its name.

She didn't nick the pelt once, but the knife was very dull now. That helped.

This meat was covered with thick fat, which she pared off and tossed into the frying pan to render. She wedged the animal into the Dutch oven and set it on the back of the fire to cook, keeping the frying pan handy at the front. Marty alternated stirring the sizzling fat with scraping fat from the hide with a butter knife, adding every shred to the pan.

Despite all the food they'd used, containers to store gathered food in was a problem. Carefully cleaning the just-emptied coffee canister, she poured oil off shrunken, crisp brown fat cracklins into it.

This new fur was dense and silky, with a layer of fine fur under longer, coarser guard hair. It would be warm in cold weather—if they were still here, and if she could figure out how to tan it.

She examined rabbit skins hung in the tree and decided to experiment first on these less desirable pelts so any mistakes were made on them. She took down the darkest and stiffest one, assuming it was the oldest.

This pelt was like cardboard, surely nothing could be done with it. It felt like, if bent, it would shatter from brittleness. Wondering where and how to start, she knew only that finished furs were soft and pliable. She sprinkled a few drops of water on an edge of the brittle hide until it softened, then twisted and pulled it. Only the crusty inner surface was damp so the hide was still stiff, but its moistened connective tissue coating bubbled loose where it bent. She plucked at a bubble to peel the sheer tissue away. Sticky and slimy, it shredded instead of peeling. The translucent layer she wanted to remove was laced with fine, rigid capillaries full of dried blood. She pulled on a capillary to pry off the tissue but the hair-fine blood vessel broke.

Marty frowned over the pelt a while before shrugging in disgust and tossing it away as useless; that inner layer had to be removed before any pelt was dried.

She hated waste, but especially dreaded wasting this beautiful fur so, after feeding the fire, she started working the connective tissue loose with the butter knife. After starting the edge, she could work out from there under the sheer membrane, scraping and peeling it away. It was not simple to remove, but she was elated at figuring out a way to do it.

When Marty tossed aside the old rabbit skin, Ted picked it up to play with. Pretending it was an animal he had to fight, though it was inside-out, he tossed it up and ran with a bold yell to hit it with a stick when it landed. Each time the pelt leaped from a blow of his stick he beat another enemy. There were many, many enemies.

That looked like fun to Amy. She found a stick so she could beat on it, too. She rarely hit it, but enjoyed trying to beat Ted to it.

Marty soon realized this was not a quick project, especially this first time, and put it aside to finish dinner, smiling over the children's noisy play.

Dipping flour for soda biscuits, she was alarmed to see sprinkles of precious flour on the dirt by the bag. The loss was less than a teaspoon, but even such a tiny waste of food made her heart flutter. She found a thin line of holes in the fine muslin, chewed by the mouse they'd scared away. She jerked the sewing kit from storage and slammed it on top of a crate. Taking a deep breath for composure, she threaded a needle and, unable to find another way, mended the hole with flour still in the bag, just shifted aside.

"Consarned, good-for-nothing mice!" She muttered as she stitched.

Amy wandered off before Ted tired of batting the pelt. He hit it against a tree trunk, watching dust puff out the ends when it hit. That was fun! When Marty called them to dinner he dragged the limp hide in, dropped it by the wash basin to clean up and forgot it.

Marty stayed busy until the kids eagerly started eating, the meat first. Watching their reaction to this dark, greasy meat, she tried a nibble and was amazed at how good it tasted.

After they stuffed themselves, enough meat was left for two more dinners. It was a welcome break from rabbits and grouse, and even trout was getting monotonous. She'd rendered out a cup of fat, and the cracklins that left would make a tasty snack. She put them in a metal mess kit in a cupboard shut so tight not even a mouse could squeeze in.

She scraped the new hide until the kids were asleep then set it aside, nearly finished. Time to sharpen the dull knife; she had to find something else for prying food from hard soil, but could think of nothing. She sharpened the hatchet, dull from daily use, then the rarely-needed double-bitted axe.

Sitting by the fire, she wondered, will we always have to live like this? Is this really going to last forever? Someday the whetstone will wear out, and the cutting tools. How can I replace them?

To ease the sense of isolation, she mumbled aloud. "What'll I do without all the things we brought? I can't get more unless I find a way out and I can't manage without them. Someday everything will wear out. What can I do then?" With a big sigh, she mumbled, "I can't think about that now, I can only keep us alive from one day to the next. That's ALL I can do."

A soft wind gust fluttered the tent's canvas door and carried in a whiff of death stench, reminding Marty how easy it could be to die. She choked back nausea, wiped away a tear, and sat up straight, her face grim in flickering firelight.

It was time she DID something about that stench.

No one else would—or could—do it for her.

Early tomorrow she MUST start moving, and decided on a general area to move to. She glanced around the crowded tent and sagged. She lay awake very late, struggling to figure out how to move so much so far, especially across the stream.

Marty saw vague shadows on the tent roof. Dawn. She was eager to finally do something about the stench that kept reminding her of the catastrophe that stranded them here.

Punching the prong-tipped can opener into the new can of coffee, she leaned close to savor the first gust of fragrance. Instead, because of thin air from high elevation, she heard only a faint hiss, and smelled almost nothing until the can was open. Disappointed, she brewed a fuller, stronger pot than usual, for the boost she'd need to move camp.

Sipping the first cup, she began to sort things into what was used daily, less often, and not at all. Never-used items went in the to-go-today pile: men's clothes, shaving gear, and two of each eating utensils. The sewing kit also went there—no time to sew while moving. Of personal care items, she kept out only the hairbrush, the shrunken Ivory soap bar, a washrag and towel. She packed the shiny metal mirror with its thin, cross-shaped, cut-out area.

She cooked pancakes; more filling than cereal and used syrup, making that can lighter, and finished off the margarine. She ate, then sorted until the children were up and eating. In an empty packing crate she put the last cans of milk, the last two cans of Spam, the can of cocoa, the muslin bag of flour, and packages of rice, beans and split peas. Hefting that, she added the half-used jar of peanut butter, the canister with newly-rendered lard, wedged in a couple of dishtowels for cushioning, then fastened it shut with its metal hasp.

The men's clothes filled two canvas duffel bags, the clothes she and the children did not soon need filled a third. The bag of often-used clothes would wait.

"I'm moving some things to a new camp today and have to cross the stream several times so I can't take you kids every time." She said, while the children ate. "I'll take you when I move the tent, later. Ted, can you watch Amy while I do that? I shouldn't be gone very long each time."

"Yes." He answered, intent on his syrupy pancake.

She grabbed the muskrat fur, felt it drying hard as she stuffed it in a duffel bag. No time to finish it now, this was already later than she planned to start. She tied the men's bags together, leaving the drawstrings long enough to go behind her neck, over her corduroy coat, and balanced them with an arm around each.

"I'm taking these now. I'll be back as soon as I can. You'll be okay while I'm gone?" She asked at the door.

"I can watch the baby!" He said indignantly, his fists on his hips the exact way she often stood.

"Thanks." She piped, ducking out quickly so he couldn't see her amused grin.

She had to go northwest nearly a city block before turning onto the east-bound trail they'd followed before. Slightly over a half-mile on was the stepping stone crossing. She adjusted her bulky load then, steeling her nerves, stepped rapidly over, finding balancing was easier when going fast instead of hesitating each step. Exhilarated by the ease of crossing, she turned west on the faint trail downstream.

She followed that between dense, water-side willows and thick woods for nearly a mile before the trail angled up a gentle slope to an area of scattered saplings. Where these met the meadow's edge she gratefully dropped the bags and went to look around from a nearby knoll while catching her breath.

An ancient Grand Fir towered at the knoll's east edge, its six-foot-thick, deeply furrowed trunk nearly hidden behind long, down-swept bottom branches that curved up just at the ground. West, the meadow's grasses looked about boot-top high, dotted with a few shrub clusters. The meadow reached nearly a mile west, fringed by scattered broadleaf trees lining a wall of evergreens along the precipitous cliffs forming the valley's lower, west end. Left, southwest, she caught glimpses of the pond, maybe four blocks away—in easy reach of its abundant foods.

Southeast, the way she'd come, the trees of the thick woods were so old that a profusion of dead branches lay tangled under them—no problem getting firewood. A stone's throw to the left, a twenty-foot long row of dense roses made a bristly hedge on the knoll's northeast end.

This site had everything they needed. Turning to bring the bags up, a flash of reflection led her to a shallow brook at the foot of the knoll.

Marty slapped her thigh, how could she forget to look for water?

Studying the terrain, she saw its source had to be in the dark coniferous depths footing the north cliffs. Barely visible, grayish snow huddled in those deep shadows. This small brook would hold water most, if not all, summer.

She felt so elated with the site and had taken so long to examine it that she jogged back to the crossing, then had to slow to a fast walk. Though she huffed, she felt strong and supple as her long, smooth stride ate away distance back to the waiting children.

They were playing contentedly in the clearing. She greeted them, hugging each before going in to stoke the fire and drink a quick cup of coffee while it blazed up. Banking fresh coals, she realized she had to get fresh vegetables to go with the muskrat for dinner.

This time she took the crate. It was heavy and awkward. She told the children she'd be back sooner this time and set off, shifting the crate until she found a reasonably comfortable way to carry it. Holding the rope handle on its front with her left hand for balance, she carried it on her right shoulder with that arm curled up around the side so it wouldn't slip off. Long before the crossing, she was glad for the jacket's padding, and had to stop twice to switch shoulders.

Knowing she was too off-balance to cross that way, she wrestled the crate up behind her head, across both shoulders. She held it there by ducking her head forward and clutching each rope handle with an up-stretched hand as she nervously stepped across the rock bridge, returning to the other way to carry it further.

She stayed only long enough to stretch out kinked muscles, and stopped along the trail back to pry up a few carrots and onions, but had to leave the tops on to carry them because she forgot to bring a bag.

Bored by playing while Marty was gone, Ted poked around inside the disarranged tent for something to do. Spotting the binoculars, he remembered her using them, took them out and tried to look through them. Everything was blurry.

Puzzled, he peered into the bigger lenses and saw his reflection. He laughed in delight and showed Amy. She wasn't interested. She was tired and sleepy, yawning. He laid the binoculars down and led her to her bed. She curled up and promptly fell asleep as only a young child can.

The glasses were all dusty when Ted picked them up. Oh, no! Marty would be mad! He tried to wipe the smudges off with his hands, then with his coat sleeve. But dust stuck on the lenses, so he rubbed and discovered that one lens turned. Totally engrossed, he unscrewed it and was amazed to discover that looking in one side made things look big, but the other side made it look small.

Holding the lens out, puzzling over how it could do that, he saw a bright spot of light on the ground. He moved his hand; the light moved. The lens made the bright light! Mystified and delighted, he moved the lens higher; the light circle widened and dimmed. He moved it lower; the circle shrank to a dazzling speck.

This was fun! He ran from one thing to another to shine the spot on.

A jay squawked loudly nearby, startling him. He stood frozen for a second. moving only his head to see what was happening. When he turned back, he gasped in shock—a wisp of smoke curled from the dry leaf on which the bright light was focused! He dropped the lens and stepped back. The wisp of smoke died, but the leaf now had a black hole in it.

His heart raced—he did a bad thing! He'd been forbidden to ever touch fire. What would Marty do when she found out? He hid the parts under his sleeping bag.

He fretted until she returned. As soon as he saw her coming he rushed to bring the lens out and tell the startled woman what he did.

When Ted showed how he'd made the smoke, she knew at once what the lens was from. She felt stupid for not thinking of it, she KNEW lenses did that, had discovered it long ago with a plastic lens from a box of Cracker Jacks. She was profoundly relieved: now she could start a fire without matches—only in sunlight—but better than not at all.

Ted relaxed, Marty was not mad at him, she seemed happy. He brought the other parts and watched her screw the lens back on.

Recharged by a quick cup of coffee, she filled a blanket with loose items, including the tackle box, creel and net, spit bar, baby carrier and the other blanket. Tying diagonal corner so nothing fell out, she hefted its weight and decided to only take that, adding it to the pile at the new site.

She pulled the short camp shovel out and, wishing it had a handle long enough to stand up to use, scraped off the area where she'd set up the tent to prevent dead grass from starting a fire and smoothing most of the lumps.

Walking back that time, each step required conscious effort. She was almost too tired to eat, though she hadn't since morning—she hadn't fed the kids since then either! She struggled to stay awake until the kids settled down, then collapsed into bed, only to drag back out, teeth clenched in anger at forgetting to bank the fire.

At dawn's first glow she stepped stiffly out to get water. Aches from unusual exercise had awakened her earlier than usual. Tight, sore muscles protested each move. But she dared not let camp stay split; survival was tricky enough with everything handy.

While the fire stabilized she filled another crate, to make a trip while the children slept. This one held the food they used daily, except for a pan of sugared cornmeal and dishes to eat it from. Barely half full, she looked for more, saw the sourdough she'd carefully started, then forgot. She packed the jar, the pans and utensils and the saved empty cans.

Gulping a quick cup of coffee while banking the fire, she hefted the crate and had to clench her teeth to stifle a groan at sore muscles. Her muscles loosened as she went, and before she reached the new site all the ache was gone.

Depositing the load, she stretched out new kinks and started back. She reveled at a new, strong suppleness. Remembering how good it felt yesterday to jog, she tried it again. Memories of running hard as a child goaded her to try a hard run. She felt awkward and heavy at first—she hadn't tried to run for years. But she found her stride, her balance, and ran as never before, exhilarated by the newfound ability. Breath came hard and deep, and still she raced, adjusting her breath as easily as she did her stride and balance over uneven ground, until her breathing matched her need for air and the pace of her steps and swinging arms.

She slowed to a walk at the crossing; it was unsafe to run over dewy rocks shrouded by morning mist. She felt a bit tired but astounded at arriving so quickly. Puffing, elated by the ease of the run, she walked quickly on, planning what to get next.

She had to wake the children when the mush was done, no time to wait. They sat on their beds to eat, rubbing tired eyes. She filled Ted's tote bag with personal care items, light enough for him, even that far, then moved everything but the beds out of the tent.

When they finished eating, she took down the tent, using its crease marks to refold it properly. Tying it in a tight roll over the pegs, poles and ropes, she left a loop at each end for carrying handles.

The one-shoulder way to carry the crates also worked best for the bulky tent. The children followed her to the crossing where she left the tent long enough to carry them over, one on each hip, braced in an arm. She knew the route well enough now to step rapidly across. Then she brought the tent.

"Here's our new camp." Marty gloated, dumping the heavy tent on the scraped area.

When the tent was set up, she said, "I have to go for more stuff, Teddy Bear. You'll have to watch Amy again."

"I will." He smiled.

Ted grabbed Amy's hand and started gathering fuel for the new fire. It had become his daily chore to get the small wood they used and he did it now because it was a familiar, therefore reassuring, activity.

She filled the last wooden crate with the empty coffee pot, the Dutch oven holding last night's leftovers, several hot coals in a small pan with a tight lid, and other small items.

Though little food from the plane was left, the total weight she'd moved already was tremendous. And she wasn't done. How much total weight had been on the plane? How had that small plane even gotten off the ground? How had she been able to move it before, with her head splitting and so dizzy she nearly fell every time she turned around? True, it was downhill and maybe only a half-mile. But she barely remembered doing it, let alone how hard it had been.

At the new camp, Marty unpacked the hot coals and dumped them just inside the door on a twist of dry grass. She hurriedly shaved wood chips to add as the grass flared from billowing smoke to greedy flame.

She thanked Ted for getting the wood, then gathered rocks to surround the fire to protect the tent and prop the roaster on while she went for the day's last load. While the fire stabilized, she moved a few items inside, then partly banked the new coals with dirt—no ashes had formed yet.

Struggling to get sleeping bags in their stuff sacks, Marty found sticky pitch on them from the insulating branches underneath. The pitch stuck to everything it touched, even her clothes and skin. It would take lard to loosen that enough to wash it out. Later.

She tied two large bags together and draped the link over a shoulder, using the two small ones to counterbalance the last big one on her other shoulder. Far from the heaviest load, it was the most difficult to keep her balance with. And she was very tired.

Marty's heart skipped a beat when she saw camp—smoke poured out the tent door and both ends of the roof peak!

Fire! They'll die! Heart racing in frenzy, she dumped the sacks and sprinted closer.

Racing by, she saw the children sitting near the knoll's base, playing contentedly. She felt relief they were safe, then terror at having to survive without the tent's shelter.

Panicky when she reached the smoke-belching door, she slowed and pushed inside to frantically peer around, choking, unable to see any flames. The fireplace was still adequately contained, but held the smoking Dutch oven. She jerked the pan off, dropped it and backed out the door, coughing and wiping burning eyes.

If nothing was burning, why so much smoke? She scrubbed at bleary eyes while fighting to catch her breath and calm down. When she quit coughing she went to sit by the kids. Her whole body shook as she hugged them, nearly sobbing at feeling their warm, live bodies. She clung to them for several minutes before she could let go.

A light puff of wind showed why smoke backed up inside instead of funneling out the peak ends like before. There, facing south, wind blew past the door and peak gaps, sucking smoke out on the way by. Here, she'd set it up to face east so early sun could shine inside the tied-open doors. But that put prevailing winds against the tent's back, where it couldn't suck the smoke out, but formed a dead-air pocket, a smoke collector for the indoor hearth.

She tied the flaps back then pulled stakes and loosened guy ropes in an order that collapsed the tent backward, puffing a cloud of smoke as it fell, dragged it a short ways and turned it to set it up facing south again.

The fire was now outside but the weather was warm and this raised site was drier and in sunshine—and easier to see from any plane that might happen by.

Ted held Amy's hand and watched with wide eyes as she moved the tent.

He left Amy and went to help set it back up, then helped pull the sleeping bags free and lay them out, this time on the ground—no padding this time.

Marty took the three big stuff sacks for today's last trip, not daring to leave anything exposed to weather and wild beasts, even for one night.

Rifles went in one bag, the axe and hatchet in another, though she regretted just sharpening them. She nested the washbasin in the big bucket, then wedged them in her pack. Wearing the pack, binoculars around her neck, Marty took a bag in each hand, leaving the last empty bag for later. She traveled carefully to keep from damaging guns or cutting tools.

After they choked down the roaster's few edible morsels, she realized she'd left snares set on the other side for more meat. She was too tired to care just then.

The kids were in bed when she tumbled into hers, groaning, "I'm still not done."

Dragging wearily up the next morning, she whispered past gritted teeth, "One more trip." Limping to peer out at the weather, she was momentarily disoriented with the view in predawn dimness. Oh, yes. The new camp.

She dipped brook water for coffee and breakfast, gulping the welcome brew as soon as it boiled. She ate and got the children eating before leaving.

She went first to the pond's still-empty snares, and salvaged the line. Empty snares didn't solve the problem of what to eat tonight, but saved carrying game so far.

The snares near the old camp were also empty. She tucked those lines in with the rest and put the last stray items in the stuff bag. Careful of the hook, she saved the fish line but left the pole, and unwound the pajama tie from the makeshift broom. She decided to take the dried cattail roots—they weighed little now—adding them to the bag.

Checking around, she picked up the abandoned rabbit fur. It was soft—how was that possible? But it reminded her of those hanging in the tree; surely she could find out how this one got soft. All the pelts went in the bag.

Looking to be sure she'd missed nothing, all that showed they'd lived here for a seeming lifetime was ashes ringed by rock, two short log seats and a pile of boughs in a matted rectangle where the tent had been.

Tying that bag to their clothes bag, she put the link around her neck, grabbed the sooty grill in one hand, the small bucket in the other and set off, feeling almost homesick for this camp. So many delights and traumas of this strange new life had occurred here.

Squaring weary shoulders, she said, "It'll soon be that way at the new one, too. And it won't stink of death over there."

She resisted looking back, blinking back tears that made the path blur and waver.

CHAPTER 11

Startled by sunlight dappling the tent, Marty sat up, groaned at her sore, stiff body, and looked at the jumbled mess in the tent—she'd only dreamt this was cleaned up.

While she fried pancakes the children tried to mix the last oleomargarine. Ted squeezed grease to one end and Amy was supposed to squeeze it back but always managed to squeeze when he did so the bag bulged in the middle. They giggled and giggled over that, making Marty laugh, too.

But that was the last margarine and she'd had to use a can of Spam and the last rice for dinner last night. She'd been too exhausted to gather food or set new snares.

"I MUST do better!" She scolded aloud. "I have to build up supplies not deplete them. What if I can't gather anything for two or three days? These little kids can't do it."

While the kids ate she worked to turn chaos into order, putting away contents of bags dropped randomly inside yesterday. She saw the rabbit skin, now mysteriously pliable.

"Do you know how this got soft?" She held the fur up.

"It got that way when I played with it." Ted shrugged.

"How did you play with it?"

"Oh, it was a animal and I was a Indian, so I chopped it with my Tommy-hawk. Indians's s'posed to kill animals." Ted warily eyed Marty sideways.

"Is that all you did?" She vaguely remembered him hitting something with a stick.

Ted squinted, trying to remember. "I made the dust poof out."

"How?"

"Banged it on a tree a whole bunch a times til the dust didn't poof out anymore." Ted set his empty dish down and edged toward the door.

Marty waved him out and resumed cleaning, amazed that hides were so tough. They had to be handled rigorously, not gently, as she had been.

Unpacking the dried cattail roots, she recalled Gram saying they could be pounded to flour—could it stretch the wheat flour? Only one way to find out.

She found a flat slab of shale, rinsed it at the brook and lugged it to the fireside. Laying a root on it, she hit it with the hatchet back. Bits of dry, brittle root shot off in all directions so she tapped it with one hand cupped close. Fewer chunks were lost, but it didn't break up much. Gram never explained how to do this.

She laid the hatchet's side on the root and pressed to mash the root. It cracked, so she tapped that lightly and the chunks got smaller. She pressed and tapped until powder, small lumps and a few tough, stringy fibers were left. Elated, she put it in the washbasin and jiggled it so the chunks collected to one side, scooped out the lumps to crush finer, and discarded the fibers. That left a whitish powder like fine cornmeal or coarse cornstarch she mixed with enough flour to make sourdough bread, feeding the starter and setting it aside. Kneading the dough in her hands, she winced at sore muscles.

Then realized she also had to get something else for dinner besides bread.

She set snares in bushes just out of sight of camp, gathering unfurled tops of several half-grown ferns shoots on the way. Looking for more, she saw a robin and a blackbird flying by, each carrying a beak full of dead grass and fine twigs for its nest.

Seeing the new grass was high enough to show and the bushes were all leafed out, she was shocked at how much everything had grown. Time was going by too fast! But I've kept us fed, she thought. I have to accumulate a surplus or we'll go hungry. "Make hay while the sun shines, Nelly . . ." echoed through her mind.

Later, dipping dishwater from the brook, she saw paired frogs; they mated in mid-spring. She sighed and gazed up at towering rims. Daily chores of hauling water, finding and cutting wood, tending the fire, food gathering and preparation kept her too busy to look more for a way out—and there'd been the dire need to move camp.

But where else could she look for an exit? She'd been the whole length of the valley, found it surrounded by cliff rocks too high to climb—if she could stand to try. Even the low drop by the middle falls had caused vertigo, something she'd never had before. And even if she could get to the top, how would she get the kids safely up?

Her only choice was to keep them alive with what was here until someday, somehow, a miracle happened that set them free of this primitive place.

She set the kneaded dough in mess-kit lids to raise again. The domed lids shaped it more like loaves, so the bread, at least, was not so strange, like the rest of her world.

She sat by the fire to make sure it didn't over-raise while working on the muskrat fur. It was hard to do now and had to be dampened to remove the last of the membrane. She couldn't stand to beat it on the ground as Ted had, but the skin had dried to the stiffness of heavily starched denim. She squeezed until the pelt crumpled, then twisted and pulled it. That did no harm so she scrubbed it, skin-on-skin, between her hands. That also helped, but her arms were too sore to do more than crush and stretch it now.

Working the pelt, she saw two red squirrels dash around trees, through branches, down a trunk and over the ground, scolding constantly. She envied their energy. They disappeared up a tree as their chatters became loud and irritating, almost angry. Marty looked around and gasped—a fox edged out of the woods nearby.

Frozen by fear, she watched it nervously glide on skinny russet legs, its white-tipped, bushy tail held out behind its grayish body. A loud giggle from Amy startled the fox and instantly, like a puff of smoke, it vanished into forest shadows.

Exhaling, patting her hammering heart, Marty stood on shaky legs to find the children. They were at the meadow's edge on the far side of camp. No wild beast stalked them.

Sitting down, grabbing her coffee cup, she realized what good alarm systems squirrels and jays were. IF she paid attention to them! Her scalp crawled at her failure to watch—that fox could have attacked one of the kids before she knew it was near!

Unpacking, she peeked out often to check the kids, also absently scanning the sky.

Finding the forgotten cracklins, she tried a piece. It was very good. This could be used like crisp bacon for dinner—she had no other meat but the last can of Spam.

She gathered the stew pot full of greens from the meadow nearby and boiled that with the fern shoots and cracklins and a few peeled wild garlic bulbs. The mixed flour bread was delectable, but heavy. She vowed to gather all the cattail roots she could dry and process. The pond held many thousands.

The next morning the snares held two rabbits, all brown now and slightly fat. Over the next four days they caught almost more than they could eat. Instead of taking the snares down she started reheating rabbit for breakfast instead of using irreplaceable oatmeal or flour.

Days were warm enough they didn't need coats to explore. They wore the rucksacks—getting food was the excuse for going—and she always took the binoculars. If they got in a new area she used them to scan all the cliffs; still, no possible way out appeared.

She would find one. She would get them home.

The lower meadow was dry enough to reach the pond without getting muddy, so she gathered duffel bags of cattail roots to dry, carefully washing all the mud off at the water. When back in camp she spread them in the sun to dry.

Yellow Pond Lily buds made her wonder how to reach them, later, to harvest the seeds. Pond shallows held scores of tiny, nearly transparent hatchling fish, fat-bellied black tadpoles waving silky-ribbon tails that stirred up puffs of mud, and rust-brown crayfish with masses of eggs plastering their swimmerettes. How could she catch crawdads?

Some ducks flew by with streamers of vegetation in their wide, flat bills. She eagerly watched where several nests were being built. They'd soon have fresh eggs to eat. Which reminded her of testing a Kinnikinnick berry earlier. She'd had no after-effects. The sprawling bushes were easy to spot by clusters of tiny pink, hanging-bell flowers shining like beacons against its glossy foliage.

"Let's pick some berries." Marty held out a wrinkly fruit like a tiny dried apple.

"Yeah!" Ted jumped up and down.

Amy looked startled for a second, then imitated him. Marty rolled her eyes.

Ted picked several before Amy could see any. Amy, mad that he got more, pouted and frowned to show how mad she was. Marty turned away so Amy couldn't see her smile, or it would encourage the girl to throw a tantrum.

Those few dozen winter-shriveled berries went into varmint-proof storage, filling a spare mess kit, something at last that added to their stored food that would keep a long time; it was handy for them to be dry enough when picked to simply store away.

Meager as it was, Marty felt so elated to add stored food that she romped on the beds with the kids. It became a wild free-for-all of tickling and wrestling. At first Ted held back but Amy's screeches and giggles lured him in. Ted was as ticklish as Amy, and giggling left him helpless.

In the upper valley, she gathered more cow parsnip root and wild carrots, though warm weather was turning them tough, woody and less tasty. She gathered several kinds of square-stemmed mints to dry for tea to mix with dried clover leaves. She dried Yarrow's carroty leaves to use like sage or for aromatic tea; it was in bloom now, easy to find. Miner's Lettuce, Shepherd's-Purse, plantain and Goosefoot for greens grew every sunny place, but stronger sunlight made dandelion greens unpleasantly bitter.

Once, idly kicking a fallen pine cone, she saw four winged seeds fall from between its flared scales. She'd heard of eating pine nuts, so she cautiously tried one. It tasted nutty, not bad in any way. Checking several other cones for seeds, she found them all empty. She'd check the newly fallen ones in autumn—if they were still here then.

Fishing one day, not because they needed meat but were sick of rabbit, she discovered their bait grubs were termite larvae. Rolling a fallen log for fat white grubs, she found a seething swarm of huge, shiny black adults. They used worms for bait that day.

Daily, while dinner cooked, she experimented with different ways to handle new rabbit skins, finding the new pelts softened easier if the inner layer was scraped off while fresh, and that scraping helped soften it. Hide scraping became part of her game cleaning routine. It helped with boredom, but she had no idea why else to bother with them.

Unsure what leather should be like—something she'd never had to pay attention to—she studied every detail of their shoes, boots, her fur-lines gloves, and Amy's furry coat, which was likely rabbit. Then she checked to see how much the new pelts resembled those leathers. She couldn't stand to throw away the older rabbit tubes, but stopped working them, just tucked them out of sight in a corner.

Occasionally she worked on the muskrat fur, disappointed it wasn't softening much. In desperation, she tried Ted's way, beating a newly scraped rabbit tube with a stick, while both kids laughed until their sides ached. Then she whacked it against a tree, shifting her grip slightly between each whack. The kids finally got bored and went off to play tag while Marty gaped in amazement at how much that softened the pelt.

Gathering food plants in the upper valley and, craving something spicier than the usual greens, she went toward where the watercress had been, not far above the middle falls. At the stream she heard sounds like pigs grunting and more splashing than the falls caused.

"Pigs can't be here!" She whispered, neck hair prickling in alarm. She cautiously peered past the cliff edge, toward the steppingstone crossing; the view was partly obscured by trees not too leafed-out to see through so she could see the ford.

A flurry of movement from the pool drew her eye—it was a huge black bear! Struggling to hold a big thrashing fish in toothy jaws, the bear splashed ashore where a smaller, lighter colored bear on the bank raised up in excitement. A mother bear with a half-grown cub!

Marty pulled the children away from the edge and flopped backwards, out of the bear's sight. Amy howled in surprised protest for an instant before Marty clamped a hand over her mouth.

"That's BEARS!" She whispered, her voice squeaky with panic, her lip scar flaring bright red. "If they know we're here they might come and hurt us! Be quiet!" Her fear-widened eyes and quivering body conveyed more warning to the startled youngsters than anything else could.

Marty rushed back to camp via the fault's north end as silently as possible, carrying Amy in case she needed to be quieted again, glancing back often to be sure Ted kept up. She consciously had to resist the urge to blindly run away.

Shocked and frightened to discover bears in their valley, Marty was also fascinated by them. With strict orders for Ted to stay inside with Amy, she nervously took binoculars back to the vantage point. For a long time she watched the animals through the glasses, frustrated at dirt speckling the view in one side, and finally assumed the bears would stay near that falls until the fish run—hopefully salmon—ended. How long would that be?

Nervous and unable to focus, Marty listened for telltale grunts to warn if they came near camp. Despite the guns, she felt more vulnerable than ever. She shuddered to realize the flimsy canvas tent walls were the most substantial thing she could put between them and primitive brutes. Only the pistol, always on her belt, had been loaded; now she loaded the long rifle, keeping the safety on and not chambering a shell, sternly warning both children not to touch it.

Pacing back and forth south of camp with the 30.06 slung over a shoulder, Marty felt relieved at getting moved before the fish run drew bears to the crossing. Now she couldn't go near there until the bears left.

Surely such big fish were salmon. Her mouth watered at the memory of eating smoked salmon; some stayed in a cupboard for months without spoiling. So it could be saved for emergencies—like winter.

It wasn't fair for the bears to hog all that fish! Pacing became stomping. She wanted some salmon!

Stomping over to the woods she cut a new, sturdier fishing pole then, too preoccupied to stomp, returned to rig it with the biggest hook and heaviest line she had. Dad always used salmon eggs for bait, but how could she do that unless she caught one? What else would they eat? And where could she catch them? She dared not go near the bears. Marty growled aloud, stomping back and forth again.

The children crept silently around to the tent's far side to play.

Despite being so frustrated, needing to be sure they stayed safe, she refused to leave the children alone in camp again. Before taking them from camp, she had to reinforce the protection of hiding by holding still she'd begun with Freeze Tag. The rest of that day she practiced with them until even Amy was passably good at it.

While they practiced she fretted about the bears staying there while the fish run lasted. They wouldn't leave the pool until the run ended so she wouldn't have a chance to catch any. She wanted some! But not enough to get injured or killed.

Later, sitting by the fire, she glumly watched a sliver of moon set. Its thin arc meant the phase was a day or two past New—they'd been here a whole month. It seemed like overnight and yet like a whole lifetime. How utterly life had changed in that time. It made the old life seem like a dream. One she couldn't count on ever knowing again.

Feeding a stick to the fire, she realized she had to get serious about storing up food, a lot of it. This warm, easy season would pass, the sun and moon would cycle until autumn came, then winter, when snow covered food plants and hid most animals—hunger would kill anyone not prepared. Echoes of the skeleton nightmare writhed at the edge of her awareness, sent a shiver of foreboding up her back to prickle her nape hair.

Jaw clenched, Marty rasped, "I will NOT let them starve! I WILL NOT!"

At dawn she carried the long rifle to the vantage point to see if the bears still monopolized that pool. After minutes of peering through the glasses, she spotted them laying by the water, playfully pawing at each other.

Should she just shoot them? But what if she only wounded one? They'd all be in mortal danger then. She huffed in frustration, picturing the fish pooling to run at the waterfalls . . . and realized with a jolt this was not the only place they'd do that.

She rushed back to camp, trembling with relief she didn't have to risk shooting dangerous creatures to get any salmon—unless she was wrong about where they'd pool up.

Cautiously approaching the beaver dam, wary of more bears, she stopped often to glass the area ahead and listen. She wore her pistol but had left the rifle, afraid that if she got a fish or two she'd be unable to carry everything, especially without getting the rifle wet.

Satisfied no bears were near, she went just below the dam, where water pooled briefly. She laid the pole and glasses aside to hack willows off at the ground with her knife to make a path to the water, throwing brush aside as she went.

Eyes shaded against reflected glare on rippling water, she searched dim depths, spotted long, silver-flashing shadows in the turbulence and huffed, "Yes! Fish do pool here."

Quivery with anticipation, she fished with worms. No strike. She braved gathering grubs. Still no strike. Not one silvery glint approached the bait.

"Well," she growled in dangerous softness, fingers clawed and shoulders hunched, "they won't get away!"

Glints of silver writhed closer to shore. Breath whistled past teeth clenched in rage and desperation as she grabbed the fishing pole like a spear and jabbed deep at the glint. She gasped in shock as the lunge carried her into icy water past her knees, but the pole met yielding resistance. By sheer reflex she stabbed forward and jerked up hard on the sturdy sapling, sliding another step deeper. As a massive flash of silver fish shot from the water and over her head, she twisted to see where it would land, lost the rest of her balance, and skidded deeper into frigid water. In the long split second she slipped and the fish arced above, she felt a stab of fear: were the children where that huge fish was about to land?

Wailing from dismay and the shock of icy water, she released the pole as the fish slapped down and struggled to turn, to escape slippery mud and icy water. She scrambled up the steep bank and saw both children a few feet from the spasming fish, eyes and mouths wide in astonishment. She noted they were safe the same instant she saw the hard-won fish was about to flop down the bank to freedom. She grabbed a rock as big as both fists as she lurched past it and bashed the fish on the head with all her strength.

Overcharged with adrenaline, she jerked the pole from the quivering salmon and raced down the bank. "Not bite when I go fishing? I'll fix that!" She snarled, squinting into muddy water for signs of more fish.

Another flash, another lunge, and she was waist deep in water, gasping at the cold but struggling triumphantly with the weight on the spear-pole, straining to raise it out of the water before it could work free. She turned and launched fish and pole high onto the bank, then slogged ashore on wobbly legs, gasping, shivering violently, suddenly not angry anymore.

She grabbed the pole as the floundering salmon slid down the bank, barely stopping it before it reached the stream. She shoved the pole on through its belly and held it up off the ground. Icy water pouring off, shivering violently, teeth chattering uncontrollably, she paused to look and catch her breath.

With its head waist high, its tail reached the ground. It was sleek and streamlined, like a giant trout, but solid silver-gray. Its flesh, where it was speared, was light coral. She lugged it on up to where the children stared in awe at the first one.

"That's bigger than my big BIG fish was." Ted uttered in amazement, then grimaced at Marty, "Do I have to fish like that now?"

"No. This is enough." She said, shaking her head. Ted sighed in relief.

But he was right, this was not like catching a couple of trout for dinner—these were huge! She hefted the one impaled on the pole—it had to weigh at least fifteen pounds.

Suddenly weak and shaky, she plopped down by the fish. What could she possibly do with this before it spoiled? She had no way to keep it cold until she could smoke it all. It would take two, maybe three days to smoke, but nothing was set up for that. She huddled with icy hands in dry armpits, trying to warm up. So much to do, so little time to do it, unless she was willing to let some spoil and be wasted. Shivering, eyes squinted and teeth clenched, she growled, "Not one single ounce of this salmon will spoil!"

Both children backed away.

Careful not to cut herself from shivering, Marty gutted the fish then, resheathing the knife, realized the sheath was wet. Heart sinking, she felt the holster; it was soaked too. The irreplaceable pistol had to be cleaned as soon as possible or it would be ruined. But she had to get all this precious fish to camp first.

She pushed the pole, already through the last fish, into the first one's gills and out its mouth to carry it, then asked Ted to bring the binoculars, net and tackle box, and to be sure Amy kept up.

Bracing the pole's thick end between her breasts with crossed arms, Marty shrugged the huge fish over a shoulder, nearly staggering under their limp, floppy weight. She wrinkled her nose in disgust as cold fish slime dribbled down her shirt back and pant leg. She felt her hair getting slimy. Back home she could go clean up in a warm bath, but out here, how would she ever remove the stink from her clothes, hair, and skin?

Glancing back at the kids, she was astonished to see three black crows pecking at the gut piles. One half-spread its wings and squawked a loud warning at something hidden in brush to keep its distance. They sure found that fast, she grimaced.

All the way back she mulled over how to keep any from spoiling before it could dry. She'd have to work fast and, by the speed of the scavengers, would have to stay close to protect it while it dried.

Dropping the fish by the tent, she shivered into dry clothes, but the boots were her only footwear so she could only change socks to dry her feet. The men brought extra boots, but she'd been expected to stay in camp. If she only known . . .

"I never would've come at all." She huffed. "But it is what it is."

"You Indian Braves guard the Buffalo meat while I cut wood." She said, stepping out, and was instantly greeted by loud and enthusiastic, if not very authentic, war whoops. She chuckled and cut short, dull 'spears' and blunt tomahawk clubs. Ted, mimicked as always by Amy, gleefully danced in noisy exuberance, wildly brandishing his spear. Marty cringed, hoping neither poked the other's eye out.

In the woods, she found branches thick enough for a drying rack base, chopped two off six feet out, and trimmed the side branches to a generous foot long, to prop the main part off the ground. Grappling them to camp, she set them parallel six feet apart, then cut a dozen thin saplings long enough to bridge that gap. She wondered if anyone else had ever made a rack this way. She had no way to know if this was right or not, but it was how she could do it out here.

Recalling when she'd watched Dad cut up a deer for jerky, she squatted by the fish and peeled the fine-scaled skin from one side. She spread it scale-side-down to pile the sliced meat on and stripped the flesh with the grain, cutting it into flat, thin slabs like Dad did the venison. When the skin was full, she draped slabs over the crossbars to dry, repeating the routine until one whole fish was laid out.

Marty tried to chase flies away but they flew right back onto the meat. Impatient with interruptions with time so short, she cut willow switches to arm the kids with twiggy flyswatters, asking them to keep the bugs away, then had to warn them not to knock the whole rack down from being overzealous.

Finally, the other salmon was cut. She had to keep out a few slices to eat fresh—her six-by-six-foot rack was still too small. She took the bony scraps to the meadow, hoping the flies would focus on that, washed off at the brook, then sat for a desperately needed cup of coffee. Glancing at the bird and bug-besieged scrap pile, she saw nearly all but the heads were gone—the rack had to be watched every minute to have anything left to store.

By afternoon the pistol was cleaned, oiled and loaded with fresh shells. Unsure if being wet ruined them, she saved the wet ones in case they were still good—no sense wasting anything she couldn't replace.

Checking the fish, she found the tops slightly dry so she turned them over, stretching to reach the center. Some wet undersides had white spots. Curious, she examined one—it was a cluster of fly eggs!

Enraged, she hurled that piece into the brush, then froze; she'd lose all this fish if she did that to every fly-blown piece. She meticulously scraped every egg from each piece, frequently wiping the knife on the grass. Dad said flies only laid eggs on wet meat, so when the meat was crusted with dryness they should stop trying.

She hated having to do this but if she was wrong it could always be thrown away later; couldn't retrieve it if she threw it away without trying. All food, especially meat, was too precious and hard to get out here; she dared not waste any.

They gorged on salmon for dinner, sitting by the drying rack with fly switches handy. By sundown Marty was exhausted from chasing bugs and birds and felt the air get damp as it cooled. Searching frantically for anything to store so much fish in, she finally pulled the liner from a never-slept-in mummy bag.

Putting the partly-filled bag on a crate, she thought it was not much lighter than the two fresh fish had been. Almost too tired to care, she wondered how much longer it would take to dry.

At sunrise she laid it all out again, finishing as the sun's first rays warmed the rack.

Knowing she couldn't leave the meat all day, she'd already done morning chores. The children could guard it if she had to leave a short while, but every time their attention wandered a piece disappeared, usually in the quick claws of an alert jay or crow.

Flies returned soon after sunrise, so when Ted was up to wield his swatter, she hurriedly collected an armload of green hardwood for a smudge fire. She started it under the center, then spread it out once enough coals formed, so cool smoke steadily wafted up under the whole rack.

She stepped away to see if that kept the pests away. After a few minutes she felt it was safe not to watch it every minute, as long as the kids played noisily nearby. She checked often to feed it and make sure the meat didn't get hot—she wanted it dried, not cooked.

Around noon she turned all the pieces again, switching the drier center pieces with the more moist outer ones.

It took two full days of smoking to get the salmon leathery dry. Both nights she took it inside. Noticing how oily it was, she tasted a shred and nearly sobbed in relief—this was how smoked salmon was supposed to taste! It gave off a mouth-watering, hard-to-resist aroma. She did it right!

It shrank drastically. Starting around thirty pounds, it ended up weighing less than ten. She stored it in the same bag, in an emptied crate. The few berries stored in the mess kit seemed ridiculously puny beside the heap of dry salmon.

Every little bit helps, she shrugged.

CHAPTER 12

Marty sighed, disappointed to find another snared rabbit. They'd eaten rabbit stew, roast rabbit, fried rabbit, braised rabbit and rabbit flame-broiled on the spit. It always tasted like rabbit, anyway. If only she could stroll down to the corner grocery . . .

"We only have what I can catch." She grumbled, taking down all but one snare, then paused alertly now in the habit of pausing occasionally to look and listen carefully for bears, or anything unusual.

Too restless to stay in camp, she took the children to look for eggs. In the meadow's drier areas they raided Pintail nests for a dozen pale aqua jumbo size eggs and, near the pond, a half-dozen dusky green Mallard eggs. Marty's mouth watered in anticipation.

She puzzled over how to reach the goose nest, built in plain sight on the overgrown beaver lodge out in the pond. Those eggs were even bigger. She turned away when both geese ruffled feathers and honked at her, even from that distance. "We have enough duck eggs. We don't need those."

They feasted on fluffy golden mounds of scrambled eggs, so tasty Marty nearly wept. Only six of the big duck eggs made that much. They barely touched the reheated rabbit, and the few bites she did choke down made Marty yearn for trout or a plump grouse. The smoked salmon was reserved for emergencies only.

Going to the pond the next day, she saw growing strawberries turning orange in strong sunlight. They'd soon be ripe. Her mouth watered again.

The water was low enough to walk along the pond's edge. Marty saw more edible plants, as well as various blackbirds and a multitude of ducks that squabbled over territory, creating a din that nearly drowned out the sound of the stream rushing into still pond water. The air was permeated by smells of decayed vegetation and faint methane odor, plus each plant variety had its own aroma that, blended together, formed an amalgam of scents unique to old sluggish ponds.

The smells and sounds were so like those from childhood that Marty ached with homesickness while being reassured this was not such a strange place after all. Anything familiar helped ease the displacement shock that weighed so heavily, made this world seem alien, threatening and nearly intolerable.

Following shore toward the beaver dam, she pointed out Alder Flies, fragile Mayflies, and big Crane Flies she called Mosquito Wolves. Below the dam, she peered into the pool to see if any salmon lingered, but the run was over. Trout was a more reasonable size to deal with, and would bite on a hook.

Marty was pleased to see the cattail pollen was now fluffy and ready to gather.

In camp, she moved the muskrat grease to the waxed paper lard carton, then washed out the canister. The children disinterestedly followed her back to the pond to collect pollen by shaking and tapping the spikes over the wide top. Carrying the filled canister back, she was alarmed to see tiny black bugs crawling in the yellow powder.

Refusing to waste any, she jiggled the bugs to the top, spooned them out, and flipped them into the fire. When no more appeared she singed the pollen, cup by cup, in a dry frying pan, to be sure any bugs left were dead and no eggs too tiny to see would hatch. Pollen would only be available briefly and she wanted all she could get. It thickened soup or gravy like cornstarch, except for its distinctive, savory taste.

But what can I store it in? And how much will I need for a whole year? For now, she sewed up one side of a dish towel and stored the singed pollen in that.

At the pond the next day, a duck exploded into panicky flight from near their feet, scaring them with its loud *quaaack-quack-quack-quaa*. When Marty's heart stopped drumming, she found a bulky nest of matted cattail leaves neatly packed with a dozen jumbo eggs. She eagerly took them all, then ducked her head in shame at her greed, and put eight back. She searched until she found another nest but took only part of those, too.

Returning to camp through the upper meadow, Marty picked clover leaves to dry for tea that the children could also drink. She found Elk Thistles big enough to eat but peeled the stickers off there.

They each ate a raw stem. The crunchy white stems were so sweet and juicy she picked all she could find. Searching for more, she saw a clump of ferns whose fast-growing tips were nearly unfurled, too old to eat. Checking underneath for new spears, she jumped in fright at frantic rustles as something larger than a duck fled in alarm to adjacent brush.

Breathless with fright, she wondered why she didn't carry a club for protection from all these creatures who were scaring her to half to death. She might not be so easily startled if she knew she could knock it silly before it hurt them. But she'd mindlessly held a club while the Goshawk took that rabbit—that club had done no good. Having one now likely wouldn't help, either.

Investigating, she found a grouse nest under the ferns, snugly filled with over a dozen brownish eggs. She only took four so the rest could hatch—grouse were good eating.

In camp, after the clover was spread to dry and the pollen taken care of, she broke tangled, dried cattail roots until they were compact and stored them in a denim stuff sack. They dined on raw thistle stems, roast rabbit and scrambled duck eggs. They didn't eat much rabbit.

As they ate chopped leftover rabbit in scrambled duck eggs for breakfast, Marty made another broom like before. Spider webs festooned tent corners and were being spun onto the crates. She lacked the nerve to wipe them out by hand, but a broom was safe enough. After sweeping webs down and squashing a few spiders, she swept the dirt floor until solidly caked grass roots left a cleaner, slightly lumpy surface.

She took children and canister to collect pollen. While Amy napped on a flat, sun-warmed rock, Ted wandered nearby, bored.

He watched tiny black crickets and baby grasshoppers crawl through the grass. He caught one grasshopper after chasing it around and around. He picked it up carefully. It struggled to get away and spit a bead of black goo on his hand; it didn't want to be his friend. He squashed it and wiped his hand off on the grass, nose wrinkled in disgust.

With the canister full of pollen, Marty searched as far as she could reach for any cattail shoots still young enough to be tender, barely finding enough for a meal.

That evening she smelled roses. Puzzled, she walked around camp until she saw a sliver of bright pink in the nearby rose hedge. The aroma reminded her of the wild rose arbor by the farmhouse, long ago. She picked a big handful of leaves to dry for tea. Spreading them by the nearly-dry clover, she wondered where the bears were now that the salmon were gone.

With the long rifle slung over a shoulder, they went up through brush and thin woods to the vantage point, stopping often to listen for telltale grunts. She knew they could be heard a lot farther away than they could be seen in such brushy woods. She did not want to get close, only to locate them.

They passed several tall Serviceberry bushes, each covered with clusters of small white starflowers, but hordes of bees prevented getting close enough to smell them. Nearby, dozens of waist-high Chokecherry bushes bore creamy flowers in large hanging clusters, so aromatic they didn't need to get close to smell them. A short ways farther she saw many Blueberries and Huckleberries nearly in bloom.

So many different berries grew here! She'd have to be ready to pick and dry them when they ripened. Drying them like raisins was the only way she knew to keep them out here. That would not be soon, though.

Peering over the vantage point, Marty was relieved not to see any sign of the bears. But where did they go? And where did they come from? She looked around nervously, did they grunt like that all the time? She fervently hoped so. Just in case, she'd stay away from the mid-falls a while longer; and this was enough exploring for one day.

Returning to camp, a buzzing shadow sped past Marty's head, making her cringe. She heard it and felt the breeze of its passage, but didn't see what went by. She turned to go on and froze in astonishment. Hovering a yard in front of her was a tiny copper-colored Hummingbird. Its fast-beating wings were mere shadows beside its delicate body. She heard the faint buzz from its wings. Pinpoint, shiny black eyes traveled up and down her body and with each head movement the tiny orange throat flashed gold in the sunlight. Then it flitted in a blink to hover a few short seconds in front of each child, looking them up and down, too. Marty's jaw sagged—it was studying them!

In a thrumming flash of iridescent olive green the tiny bird disappeared. Dumbstruck, she looked all around for it, remembering the intelligence in the huge hawk's eyes.

"Dumb animals are not dumb at all!" She exclaimed.

Ted trailed Marty and Amy to camp. He knew Marty was thinking hard and wondered if that tiny, pretty bird that looked at them was the reason. Other birds had looked at him, too, though never right in front of his face like this one. Why should that surprise Marty?

Back at camp, Ted wandered off with Amy to look for more tiny birds. He'd heard no sound but its wing-buzz so he didn't know how to call it. But he could call squirrels! He puckered up and made the kissing sound they always answered.

Amy froze for a second, looking at him. Was it time to freeze?

Ted called over and over until he got an answer. Catching Ted's excitement as answers sounded all around, Amy totally forgot about holding still at the freeze signal.

One big squirrel popped its head out of evergreen needles and two others about half its size appeared in different places. Little kid squirrels had come to play with them, too!

Marty was nearly frantic when they returned to camp.

"You stay out where I can see you from the tent. Those bears are somewhere in this valley and I don't want you where they can hurt you." She scolded.

"Okay." He said, excited. "We saw some little kid squirrels!" He bounced.

"That's nice." She said, absently, while dishing up dinner. "Get washed up."

Ted frowned, digging a toe in the dirt, stung that she didn't care about his new friends.

That night the Full Moon reminded Marty it had been a month since she'd realized no one was coming to rescue them. Had anyone even looked for them?

She still felt aching loneliness and deep sorrow but not such intense, heart-rending anguish now. She accepted they were stranded, at least temporarily, but could not, would not accept it as permanent. Either there was a way out—which she would find eventually—or someone would find them, if only by accident. They would get home!

She looked at camp in the flickering glow of hazy firelight, smelled wood smoke, felt a light breeze across her cheek, and sighed deeply. This was her world.

"Always be prepared for the worst." Mother had drilled into her. Well, she was, if only half-heartedly.

"There must be a thousand rabbits here!" Marty fussed, checking the snare the next morning. She was tempted to leave it, but thoughts of what it would take to get other meat made her decide not to. She took down that last snare. Later today she'd set some out in the meadow. A grouse would be a very, very welcome change.

Fleshing the new pelt, she occasionally checked the heating bath water and added wood to the fire, thinking she had well over a dozen rabbit tubes now. She was still unsure what to use them for, but couldn't stand to let them be wasted. The pelt was scraped when the water was steamy hot.

She was dismayed to discover how much the children had grown since their last bath; Amy barely fit down into the big stew pot. Had it really been a whole month since they'd bathed? She gulped in shame.

This time she saved enough for her bath, taking it when the children went out to play—too many hungry mosquitoes were out in the evenings to wait until then.

Flies had become as thick and irritating during the day as mosquitoes at night. They buzzed endlessly, crawled over everything, and swarmed on any moist food. Today they were sluggish, landing back where they'd been when she waved at them.

Lines of ants raided, following invisible trails to food storage and eating areas, gleaning every tiny crumb and grease speck they could reach. She stomped them to obliterate them and their trail, only to have one make its way under her pant leg to bite bare skin above her boot.

By afternoon she was shocked to realize the air was cold and a brisk wind hissed through the valley. Stepping out, she saw dark roiling thunderclouds up far enough over the west rim to partly obscure the sun. Calling the youngsters in, she grumbled at herself for not watching the weather.

Earthshaking thunder cracked, rumbled and echoed from a long series of glaring lightning flashes but little rain fell, only a few huge, scattered drops. Ted and Amy were terrified of the sudden dazzling flashes and tooth-jarring peals of thunder. The first clap made Amy scream and clutch Marty in terror, and sob wildly at the second one. Ted's eyes widened until the whites showed and tears brimmed, but he stayed silent, refusing to cry like the baby. He huddled against Marty, too.

"That noise is thunder. It's the sound of God laughing so hard He cries and that causes the rain. The lightning is Him winking at His own joke." She said, repeating what she'd been told as a child.

"What joke?" Ted grimaced.

Marty had never wondered about it, and stammered, "I . . . . I don't know."

The storm was brief and blew over so fast she saw it move and felt the air warm.

Finally all the newer rabbit skins were worked soft enough to bend, but nothing near Amy's fur jacket in pliancy. The pelts were thin, their strength limited, but no hair fell out, as she'd feared it would. She tried working the muskrat fur the same way but, turning frying rabbit, accidently splattered grease on its skin side. Nearly weeping, afraid she'd ruined the beautiful fur, she scrubbed that part between her hands, then noticed the oil had made that area much softer. She smugly added that to her growing knowledge of processing hides.

She smeared stale lard on an older scraped hide. Little lard was left so she only used a dab to see if it worked like the hot fat. Hot fat worked better, she decided, but even cold fat helped soften the hides considerably.

The next morning Marty found a snared grouse and nearly sobbed in relief. "This is silly." She mumbled, resetting the snare. Her step had a new bounce as she returned to camp. No more monotonous rabbit for a couple of days.

Later she went to dig onions, grumbling at having to use the knife to pry them out of hard, dry ground. A faint echo of thunder interrupted. She looked, upset at not watching the sky closer. Again!

Towering masses of thick black clouds loomed over the west cliffs. She grabbed Amy, called Ted, and ran for the tent. This storm left a coat of white hoar frost and a penetrating chill that had them huddling together for warmth in the flimsy tent. It seemed closer and louder, and even frightened Marty. The cold drove bugs inside. Silverfish, pill bugs, millipedes, black wood ants, and different beetles crossed the floor, looking for safety. Marty squirmed, wondering how many bugs were trying to crawl up her back. She clutched the kids close, trying not to think about it.

Finally, she draped a blanket over the children and, shivering under the other blanket, vigorously worked grease into another pelt. What would she do with all these pelts? She turned one right-side-out to study and realized it would be simple to sew the narrow parts shut to use for food storage. Most would hold two or three pints, others more.

This storm worsened rather than fading away. Wind blew and rain poured, making its own thunder on the taut canvas roof. Wind gusts thumped the shuddering tent like a giant hand slapping its flimsy fabric. Wind-driven rain drummed onto dry hard ground, but not loud enough to drown out the wind whistling and howling. She worried about how much pounding the poles and stakes could stand before one broke or pulled loose and dropped the whole tent on top of them.

Cuddling the children, now as scared as they were, her heart thumped so hard she feared they'd feel it and know how afraid she was.

Not far away something huge crashed resoundingly against something else and thudded to the ground so hard it jarred the tent worse than the fierce wind. Cringing, Marty fought to keep from screaming in terror as she stared up at the flapping tent roof, trying to will it not to collapse on them. Ghostly shadows of branch scraps appeared briefly, quickly swept away by the same swirling, wrenching gusts that tore them from the trees. Would a bigger branch come crashing through the tent? She shuddered, remembering the branch that nearly hit her head.

Rain and wind eased but temperatures dropped and a thick, roiling fog descended, darkening day to twilight gray. They shivered under wool blankets with teeth chattering.

They needed fire inside—how familiar that was! Marty rushed into the cold rain for wood and returned dripping wet with an armload. She rushed out with frying pan and spatula for hot coals, but was too late, even the coals were drowned. She could do nothing but sit huddled and shivering with the children until the storm ended, so terrified tears slipped unnoticed down her rain-soaked cheeks.

After what seemed like hours, the sky began to brighten. Marty searched for dry wood, had to break squaw wood from the enormous fir near the tent, the only place with branches even partly dry.

It was so late she was terrified the sun would set before it could peek past the last storm clouds. Using the binocular lens on stored cattail fluff and a pile of squaw wood shavings, she nervously waited for a shaft of sunlight, finally got a brief one that enabled her to restart the outside fire.

While hot coals glowed under roasting grouse she gathered wood to keep inside to dry. It was very late before the bird was done enough to eat.

This time they'd been extremely lucky that the sun peeked out enough to start the new fire before it set. They might not be so lucky again, she thought, arranging a place inside for a fire; one rain couldn't quench. She had to watch the sky closely for storms, even on hot days.

The incident reminded her that food wasn't all she had to gather. Dad and her brothers had cut, split and stacked huge ricks of firewood every fall.

The next morning she asked Ted to help her start a woodpile near the tent, showing him how to tell which pieces were pitchy by the smell and weight, and tossed amber beads of highly flammable pitch on the fire to demonstrate its value. Pitchy wood and bark was set aside for kindling, piled under the Grand Fir's droopy branches to stay dry.

Starting a ways from the tent, they began to heap wood nearly to the big tree, about a fifteen foot space. Dry wood was kept inside—enough of being caught unprepared.

The storm had broken off so many branches it seemed they had to move a year's supply to reach seasoned wood that burned with less smoke than green pieces. Many new pieces were pitchy and Marty gladly added them to that stack.

Going past the rose hedge for more wood, she noticed something was different. She went on a ways, then saw a mature evergreen had been blown against another and the two had crashed down together to form a huge X, only a long stone's throw from where they'd huddled in the flimsy canvas tent.

Foul weather hadn't damaged the strawberries. Marty found many ripe ones in the meadow and spent most of a day tediously gathering half the canister full, to try drying. But a swarm of fruit flies immediately appeared and green mold spread rapidly right after she spread the juicy berries on the flat rock by the fire to dry—no wonder she'd never heard of dried strawberries. Disgusted at the waste, she chipped a shallow trench a short ways into the meadow and planted the moldy pulp, hoping to grow more.

After that they gladly ate every ripe berry they found.

Masses of big black carpenter ants appeared with wings to fly awkwardly or swarm clumsily over everything, terrifying Amy. The girl's too-frequent shrieks of panic grated on Marty's nerves so she sent Amy into the tent, the only place without airborne ants.

Ted enjoyed swatting them out of the air with a switch as they floundered by. Marty jumped in fright at his version of war whoops as he pranced around flailing madly at flying ants with his twiggy flyswatter. Marty wiped both hands across her face. Too many things startled her out here. She simply had to get hold of herself, to regain a measure of control over her world.

After two nerve-wracking days of Amy's screeches and Ted's war whoops they began to see a few shed wings laying around, and the ants seemed less dense. Two more days and the only sign was an occasional stray, detached wing on the ground. At last, Amy could be allowed out without hearing constant screeches of terror.

Stream water had dropped inside its banks, and snow had disappeared under all but the densest trees that edged the valley. The trio wandered all over the meadow and, at the west edge while searching for more eggs, a swirling gust of wind scattered dried leaves and debris past them, dropping a whitish snarl of rubble nearby. Intrigued, Marty examined the tangle. It was hair! Long and matted into a big, dirty wad the texture of wool. But, she frowned, no wool grows that long. What animal grew this?

Feeling the long, thick hair and thinking how empty evenings were and how she used to knit to pass the time, she looked for more, grabbing every wisp and wad to stuff into her pack, hunting through the brush in all directions. She didn't find more or the animal it came from, so she went back to egg hunting.

Knitting in the evenings would be nice, but how could she turn this into yarn? She'd heard it had to be washed, combed, carded and spun—but how was each supposed to be done? Washing she could do, but comb it? That would be to align hairs for twisting into a continuous strand. Her brush should work for that. But what was carding? And how could she go about rolling and twisting it?

In camp, she put the fresh foods away, stirred up hot coals and fed the fire, washed the wool in cool brook water then laid it to dry on the tent's leeward side, where no breeze would blow it away again.

That evening she brushed out the worst tangles, a task that sounded easier than it was.

It took a whole evening to get the long, strong, white fibers untangled and aligned. It was far too little to knit anything useful. Carefully tying the bundle with thread, she tucked it in with the men's clothes. She'd watch for more, but she also had to figure out what to do about knitting needles. She slapped a thigh in frustration—why was everything so difficult out here?

Considering what food to get today while the children finished breakfast, Marty tucked the hatchet under her belt, just behind the knife sheath. They went to the north meadow so she could check grouse snares.

All were untouched so she took them down and went to where she'd found the wool. She searched a wider and wider area there, while the kids sat to rest. She didn't find any so they went on down to the pond's drying bank to look for duck nests. She still had eggs at camp, but wanted to locate more to get in a day or two.

Near where marsh plants were gnawed off at the ground she set three muskrat snares like before, across the pond. This time she used the hatchet to cut stakes, its blunt back handier than rocks to pound them into root-laced shore muck.

She decided to explore along the stream now that the water was low. They could walk along its sand-scoured edge below the banks. Where bordering brush and trees reached far over the bank in a canopy, they had to crouch down and edge along the embankment to keep their feet dry.

The piercing *kill-dee, kill-dee* call of a Killdeer echoed along the streambed. Marty glanced at the bird with the double chest band, absently watched it scurry over gravel to peck one spot then rush on long skinny legs to peck further on. Ted giggled softly and dashed ahead. It would make a good friend. When he neared though, instead of flying away like most birds, the bantam Killdeer shrilled alarm as it fluttered and struggled along the rough gravel dragging one limp wing, staying just out of his reach.

"Oh, no. The poor birdie's hurt." He whispered, his heart welling with sympathy. It he could catch it he could take it to Marty to fix. Marty could fix anything. But he couldn't quite catch the floundering bird and was soon out of breath from trying. The second he gave up chasing it, the Killdeer sounded a strident warning and flew quickly and easily back to where he first saw it.

Sad and winded, he plunked down on a rock. He swallowed at a lump that hurt his throat and tried to figure out how the injured bird flew away so well.

At last they could go no farther without wading. Marty led the kids back to where the bank was sloped enough to climb and brush was sparse enough to squeeze between. Not far through the brush they came to the trail between the stepping-stone crossing and camp. She saw an Elderberry bush crowned with huge flat umbels of creamy flowers. Remembering what Gram said about them, she pulled a tall, pith-filled stalk down far enough to pick three broad flower clusters.

Later, to go with duck eggs, she dunked the sprigs of Elderberry blossoms in pancake batter to coat them, then set the flat clusters, batter side down and branching stems up, in a pan of hot grease to fry to a crisp golden brown. They dipped the fried flowers in syrup and ate them off the stems, not even noticing sticky syrup dripping onto their chests.

Marty woke feeling smug at keeping them fed and warm despite lacking most of the conveniences she'd been raised with.

Remembering the new pond snares, she eagerly and cheerfully rushed through her morning routine. Her mood was contagious. The kids bounced with energy and playfulness as they followed her directly toward the new snares. She glanced at the meadow and stopped. A doe grazed near the far edge. Should she return to camp for a rifle to shoot it?

The doe lifted her head often to look carefully in all directions, her long mulish ears constantly flicking and turning, then glanced with nervous intensity at a grass clump for a few seconds before taking another bite of forage.

Intrigued by what seemed odd behavior for a deer, Marty made the freeze signal and studied the doe, wondering why it tensed up when it looked at that one spot. She finally realized the doe had a fawn hidden in the grass clump—she wouldn't shoot that doe, it had a young one to protect, a fawn that would die without the doe's protection.

She made the kissing sound to tell the children they could move again as she went on to the pond, not noticing that Amy never did hold still.

When the trace they were wearing into a trail neared the brush edging the pond, Marty heard a sharp puppy yip. She paused to peer intently at the brush, thinking, there can't be any dogs out here. But the bears had sounded like pigs, so what, in this valley, could sound like a puppy?

Ted heard it, too, and alternated between craning to see the animal and watching Marty search for it. He was excited but, except for his eyes and a slight head wobble, held still because Marty only stood that way if she saw something unusual.

Another yip, then a whining growl helped her locate the animals. Two small furry bundles erupted from thick bushes and tumbled over one another in the mock ferocity of play. Their almost catlike faces were dominated by pointed noses and dwarfed by huge, perky ears, showing her what they were.

Squatting to Ted's level to point them out, she lifted Amy so she could see. Pointing, she shushed softly, and whispered, "Those are baby foxes. If you stay real quiet we can watch them play."

Both kits tumbled and growled, the dark gray one more often the aggressor than the silvery one. A third kit, with dark gray fur highlighted deep orange, cavorted to a spot near the others and sat to watch them with aloof interest.

Marty felt a rush of maternal tenderness at their fat-bellied fuzziness, guessing they were only a few weeks old.

Ted, wanting to pet one, could wait no longer. He jumped up and took a step . . . and his butt hit the ground next to Marty, her hand still gripping his shirt.

"Those aren't puppies!" She hissed, eyes flashing and lip scar blazing red. "Those are wild baby foxes! Mama Fox will bite you if you get near her babies!"

Ted looked around but saw no other fox. "But the Mama isn't here." He whispered.

"She's somewhere close, even if we can't see her. No wild mother leaves such young babies alone in the open." She searched, too. "Mamas protecting their babies are the most dangerous creatures in the world. They don't understand you only want to pet the babies, they think anything that comes near them wants to eat them."

"Oohh!" Ted whispered, shifting onto his knees so he could watch them play.

In a moment the kits stopped playing to stare into the brush then bounce out of sight.

All three pond snares held a muskrat. Marty jiggled in glee. This was enough meat she wouldn't have to go anywhere for four days! But, more important, here was plenty of fat to render into lard. Rabbits contained only a trace of fat, if any, and grouse not much more if skinned. The remaining lard tasted so rancid she was unsure it was fit to eat—even here, where nothing edible could be wasted.

Carrying the game aside to gut, she noticed one was half the size of the others. She was sad it was so young, such a waste to kill.

"But if the others are its parents it would probably die anyway." She mumbled. Though she felt bad, it was dead and she couldn't unkill it, so there was no sense letting it go to waste.

Both bigger muskrats had much thicker fat than that first one. Some chunks of fat clung to the entails, and a thin sheet of hard fat lined the gut cavities of both, all of which she trimmed away and kept. It was enough fat to last several weeks if she was frugal, so now the rancid lard could be used to soften all the hides.

Removing the lines but leaving the posts for use later, she gathered greens on the way home. As soon as the small one was on roasting in the Dutch oven and the fat set to render at the front of the fire, she started scraping the fresh pelts. She'd learned a lot about how to scrape a muskrat skin before, but figured out how to do it more easily with these, finishing all three that evening.

Chapter 13

For four days they went to the pond every morning and again after Amy's nap. On morning trips she half-filled the stewpot with cattail pollen. The pot held much more than the canister, saving time and trips. If the last muskrat snare was empty she gathered duck eggs for Ted to carry in his pack. He was so proud his face glowed and his strut was comical.

While Amy napped Marty debugged pollen and poured it into rabbit tube pouches. The narrow front leg and neck openings were bound shut with fish line, another line laced through holes poked around the back opening with the meat fork then pulled shut and tied. Each filled tube hung from the ceiling pole, safe from bugs and mice.

Oiled, the tubes were flexible enough to turn right-side-out and pull shut. Crammed with food, the pouches stretched and pollen compacted, so each pouch held nearly half a stew pan. The oldest skins shed so badly she hid the motley pelts behind the men's clothes.

After Amy's nap they went to the meadow for edible plants then around to the pond. Marty gathered another half pot of pollen, and sometimes a few green clubs or tangled roots. She boiled the narrow green cattail clubs to serve like corn-on-the-cob. The taste and texture were unlike corn, but reminded her of familiar foods, and helped her feel more at home here.

They ate duck eggs as fast as she got them since they might spoil if kept very long. One evening she cracked an egg open and was horrified when a half-developed duckling slid out—never before had she thought of eggs as containing live baby birds!

"Every farm girl should know that!" She snarled, appalled at her thoughtlessness.

All day she struggled with guilt for killing a helpless chick. They had to eat. Without meat, they needed eggs. If they had meat it meant an animal was dead. Either way, some creature had to die for them to stay alive.

She decided they'd had enough eggs, they could fish if the snare was empty. They hadn't fished lately and fish never seemed alive quite the same way as birds or mammals.

From the meadow, she now harvested various Lily species in bloom to identify which was safe to eat. Also, plants with long edible taproots like dandelion and Salisfy. She hated using the knife to dig in rocky soil for roots and bulbs but, still unable to think of a substitute, used it as gently and carefully as possible.

A sliver of New Moon showed, their third here. Time passed so quickly! Without moon cycles she'd have no idea how long they'd been stranded here. Would she soon lose track of months? She lost track of time before, since being here. What if, later, someone found them and asked how long they'd been here, and she couldn't remember?

Aghast, she peeled a finger-thick, two-foot-long stick to record their time here. She cut two marks and almost laid the stick on a crate but pictured the kids losing it, so she used fish line to hang it far back on the roof support pole. When rescued she could say, "See, I kept us alive this long." She wondered if anyone else could ever know what it took to survive in such primitive conditions.

Earlier than usual, billowing thunderclouds darkened a bright day to gloom. Thunder ushered dark curtains of drenching rain. This looked nastier than the usual, almost daily, midday storm.

Marty called the kids and moved hot coals in onto shavings kept ready. She'd learned the hard way that if the western sky was cloudy by midmorning it would storm that day. She hoped the weather would not be that way all summer, but adjusted her routine so she had an inside project to do while it lasted. The storms were so frequent they were no longer frightening. Amy slept through them and Ted seldom slept but rested on his bed while it rained.

This crackling storm brought torrential rain that saturated the meadow's lowest corner.

When only trailing, gray-marbled clouds were left, they went to look for food on the north, higher meadow edge where the ground was less soggy. Swishing through rain-drenched grass, they avoided dripping trees and temporary puddles. At the west end, mucky dips forced them farther back into cliff-flanking trees than they'd been before. Marty worked along the faint game trace taking them past a rock slide that had, months ago, broken from the steep cliff face.

A hint of unfamiliar odor made her examine the jumbled rocks, where she found scant remains of some large creature. Sharp horns grew from a thick-boned, battered skull with a nose jaggedly broken off near the eye sockets. The spike-horned skull, a few shattered, sun-bleached bone fragments, and wads of matted, dirty white hair identified it as a Mountain Goat.

She'd been told Mountain Goats could survive on any cliff. She looked almost straight up at the dripping, broken rock of the precipice towering so near above. "Even Mountain Goats can't always survive here." She mumbled, throat tight with emotion. Her hair prickled to realize how dangerous and unforgiving this primitive place was.

And, again, of how thoroughly trapped they were.

She gathered all the hair, crammed soggy handfuls in her pack, filled it to bulging before she found no more. Now she had enough raw material to make something useful—if she could figure out how to roll it into yarn, and how to make knitting needles.

"What's that?" Ted squinted, curious.

"This is Mountain Goat hair."

"A Billy Goat Gruff?" Ted jerked back, brown eyes bulging. "Did a Troll get it?" He edged closer to Marty and glanced around nervously.

"I don't think any Trolls live out here." She struggled not to smile, tried to reassure him. "I think it just fell off the cliff."

"Billy Goat Gruffs live up there?" He saw no reason for any animal to want to live up there. He squinted murky brown eyes sideways up at Marty. It seemed more likely a Troll got it. He stayed closer than usual, peering around, his neck tight, until they moved well away.

From partway across the meadow he squinted back at the unevenly broken cliff, wondering what a Troll looked like, exactly. He didn't see anything strange, and Trolls hid under bridges. He didn't see any bridges but ran to catch up with Amy and Marty.

Despite the frequent thunderstorms, the weather warmed enough that the children wore only underpants all day, saving Marty the effort of washing so many clothes by hand.

Ted lost reluctance to be undressed in front of Marty, and now it was she who failed to strip down to comfort, sweating miserably in a flannel shirt and corduroy pants. She had no actual warm weather clothes, but couldn't stand to wear only bra and panties.

When first going barefoot the children's tender feet got so sore they gimped along. But their feet toughened quickly and soon they ran as hard and fast as they had with shoes.

One day, when no clouds showed by late morning, disgusted with her body odor and the children's ground-in dirt, Marty decided it was time to bathe in the pond. Shuddering to think of swimming in undergarments in front of the children, she dug through men's clothes until she found one of Eddie's rib-knit, strap-shoulder undershirts, tucking it into a pair of his boxer shorts to keep them from falling down. Feeling totally ridiculous but delightfully cool in the baggy clothes, she wore them to the pond. She didn't wear her bra and panties and felt too exposed, so she wore the shirt over the swimwear. She took several barefoot steps on the dirt floor before deciding to wear boots to the pond. Her feet were terribly tender.

Ted was shocked to see her wear the flannel shirt with boxer shorts that hung nearly to her knees. Trailing her, he giggled softly at her pale-skinned legs, bare only from mid-calf boot tops to baggy, red-and-white pinstriped shorts. She looked so silly! He walked to the pond with both hands over his mouth to muffle laughter he couldn't quite hold in.

Marty shed boots and shirt at the pond. Amy grabbed her hand and pulled her to the water. Ted took her other hand and side-by-side they slowly waded into placid water so cold that stepping ankle deep took their breath away. After a few hesitant steps, each punctuated by a chorus of shivery *oooh* and *aaah,* the water started to feel less cold.

Despite chilly water, the inch-deep mud felt warm. Marty wriggled her toes and grinned in delight as thick mud squished between them. It had been years since she took time to go wading, had forgotten what a delight plain old mud could be.

Amy loved water, warm or cold. When she stopped gasping, she kicked a big splash and giggled as cold drops splattered all over them. Marty dropped their hands to duck away, gasping in shock. Ted kicked water back at Amy, spraying Marty, too, then scooped water in cupped hands to splash them, giggling mischievously. Amy gasped, teetered, screeched a giggle, and tried to scoop water back but lost her balance and plopped down waist deep. Her gray eyes widened for an instant but she never lost her grin or the giggle.

Smiling, Marty stepped warily to the water's edge to let them splash each other, close enough to reach them if one went under. It made her realize she had to teach them to swim. They could easily drown if she wasn't near every second they were by any water. Their safety depended as much on learning to swim as on freezing to avoid attracting dangerous animals.

It was several years since she'd taken time to swim, years she'd been too busy being an adult. "I'm not too busy now." She smiled. Knowing she'd get splashed again, she braced herself and waded to the kids.

"I'm going to show you how to blow bubbles." She said, grinning.

Amy cheered so enthusiastically she fell down again, but no longer gasped at the cold of rib-deep water. Marty chuckled and led them out by the hand until Amy stood waist deep. She showed them how to hold their breath then lean down and blow bubbles with faces barely submerged. When both understood they had to lift their face out of the water to inhale, she encouraged them to dip their heads deeper to blow bubbles. Then, as one clung to her leg for balance, she held the other so they felt secure enough to sink all the way underwater to blow bubbles, prompting them to open their eyes and look around.

She was amazed at how fast they learned and how little fear they had of water. They were so eager to do more that she taught them to float, facedown first, then on their back. When her back ached fiercely from bending over so long, she called time out for a rest. Neither wanted to get out so she grabbed their wrists and pulled them out—she needed to rest. Once free of water's buoyancy, they no longer resisted taking a break.

All too soon though, they wanted to go practice. Marty stood at the edge to watch. She saw that most of the dirt ground into their feet, knees and elbows was gone and decided every warm day they'd swim to get clean. It wasn't even out of their way, since they were by here so often.

When they started to shiver, she rubbed them briskly with her palms to roll off dead skin. Then she had them dunk and blow bubbles while she briefly scrubbed their heads. This time neither child resisted getting out to rest on the warm, sunny shore.

"You both stay right there. It's my turn to get clean." Marty waved a warning finger, then waded out waist deep to dive under. Now the water felt invigorating. Diving felt so delightful she went under several times and swam parallel to shore so she didn't get far from the kids. Each time she surfaced she looked to see if they were staying put. Reassured, she dived and swam slowly, luxuriating in having water all over her at once.

The spellbound children watched her dive with a small splash at one spot and appear a short time later several feet away. Ted craned his head, puzzled at how she did that.

Marty finally, reluctantly waded ashore, slightly winded, shaking off water before briefly sitting by the kids.

As supper cooked she noticed both children were turning red from sunburn. Sitting them by the fire, she smeared old lard on the red areas. At dusk, she felt her back and shoulders burning and awkwardly smeared lard everywhere she could reach.

The next day a rainsquall without much thunder did little to cool the air. When it passed she decided to start their food-gathering trip with a short swim.

Nearing the pond she noticed the usual noise was different. Ducks quacked, geese honked, and blackbirds squabbled as usual, but none sounded quite normal. Near the willows across the pond she saw a huge, hump-shouldered bull moose, partly submerged!

She gaped and froze in utter astonishment. Following closely, both youngsters stopped abruptly, though she hadn't thought to make the freeze signal.

Where did that monster come from? Marty's mind reeled. It hadn't been around when she explored the valley end to end and she'd found no possible way for it to enter. That would have been a way for her to escape this place!

She never had figured out where the bears came from, or where they went. Glancing at continuous cliffs bordering the valley, she frowned. Most of the valley was filled with trees and heavy brush. The moose could have moved into them when they neared. She hadn't noticed many things that she'd learned to watch for since, why not this, too?

Even from that distance the animal's size was awesome. It stood belly deep in water. A bulbous nose bluntly overhung a long jaw underlined by a long pendulous dewlap. It was so ugly! Yet so magnificent! Its short, heavily muscled neck swelled to a massive chest below, a high hump above, and to bulging shoulders. The bull's hindquarters looked ridiculously small for its body. Only a tail stub showed in the light rump patch. A drab gray coat, shed in ragged patches, made it look mangy and bedraggled.

The bull stood sideways, looking toward them. His long ears constantly moved under barely-grown, velvety antlers, searching for any further sound from them as they stood transfixed in amazement.

Marty's heart thudded as she tried to judge whether he might charge. Nervously feeling the flap holding the pistol in her holster, she doubted that small weapon would help if he did charge. How fast could such a long-legged animal cover that distance?

As far as she could tell it couldn't see them well, but had heard them approach.

After staring myopically a short while, small eyes focused off to one side of them, the bull dunked his head underwater for a long minute before raising it again with his mouth trailing streamers of pond vegetation. Water ran off the growing antler nubs and dribbled from the beard-like dewlap.

The instant it dipped again, Marty spoke softly, her voice quivering. "That's a moose. He's very, very dangerous, even if he is only a bull. A cow moose with a calf is even worse. They're so big they can squish you to death just by stepping on you." As the bull raised his head to chew another mouthful, she paused, unwilling to risk talking while his head was above water.

"Mamas with babies are the most dangerous animals of all, especially a cow moose or a sow bear." She whispered as he dipped again.

When he dunked again, she squeaked, "We have to get away from here." She pulled the children a few steps farther each time it submerged until they were out of sight and could safely hurry away on trembling legs.

They certainly couldn't swim in the pond while that was there! She glowered, the bears took the best fishing spot and now the moose has the best swimming spot!

The next day grew overcast and so windy the treetops whipped with such force she nearly fell over from looking up at the towering fir's thrashing tip. She made sure dry wood was inside and the indoor hearth ready to light, though few sprinkles of rain fell. Her knapsack still held tangled wool she could stay busy with. It wasn't washed, but she tried to untangle it anyway. That didn't work, it had to be washed first.

The children sat on the dirt floor playing with sticks, bark scraps and a handful of colored rocks.

As the moaning wind grew more turbulent, she faintly heard cracks and thumps over its howling as fierce, buffeting gusts wrenched branches from trees in the dense woods east of camp. The tent fluttered and shook, the roof and sides first sucking in, then ballooning out, as if it was alive and breathing. She huddled with a child under each arm, terrified of what might fall and crush them.

The storm blew past by mid-afternoon. She welcomed the chance to walk around and look at damage from such ferocious winds. Where the brook emerged from woods at the meadow's northeast edge, a quarter mile away, a huge old maple had blown over. Long massive branches on its underside were broken from the impact and now those thick stubs held most of the trunk more than eight feet off the ground, leaving a labyrinth of tangled branches between trunk and soil.

Awed by the gusting wind's power, Marty saw other trees with newly broken tops and branches—now she understood why so much scrap wood was available. She'd assumed the valley's depth gave protection from strong winds. Obviously, it didn't always.

Profoundly glad the tent was not near other trees, she thought the huge fir survived undamaged so long only by having exceptionally strong roots, branches, and trunk.

Looking at the maple, she saw bright shells under a nearly hidden, sculpted grass-and-mud nest. The eye-catching color was Robin's-Egg Blue. Marty picked up a shell scrap, wondering if the chicks had learned to fly yet, or if the storm had killed them.

Ted looked hopefully at the shell. "Is this an Easter Egg? Was the Easter Bunny here?"

"No." Marty shook her head sadly, thinking how chancy survival could be for any creature in such harsh conditions. "No Easter Bunny lives in this valley."

Ted sagged in disappointment.

Crossing the meadow toward the old dam, they passed scores of buzzing bees industriously gathering nectar from late spring flowers. Frightened by a bee buzzing too near, Ted ducked and swatted, striking it a glancing blow. The angry bee clung to his hand and stung. Ted screeched at searing pain and raced to Marty, screaming and frantically shaking his hand. Marty slapped the bee off, used fingernails to remove the raggedly torn-off stinger, then blew cool air to ease the hurt. As she dabbed mud on the sting, tapping it with a fingertip to work the venom out, she recalled Dad apologizing for being so poor they had to use home remedies like this, or grease on sunburns. She was thankful for knowing them now, though she'd been ashamed of being so poor then.

To distract Ted long enough for the mud to drain some venom, she showed him how to blow on dandelion heads so the miniature seed-bearing parachutes would drift away. Amy blew and blew on top after top until she was so dizzy she could barely stand.

With warm weather spiders invaded the tent, built webs overnight, and bit all three as they slept, the bites easy to identify by two tiny punctures in an irregular red blotch.

Shortly after laying down to sleep that night, Marty heard a shrill mouse squeak and felt something tiny skitter by in the dark near her head. She cringed and growled, "You better not get into any food, you little pest." Mentally reviewing where food was stored, she was sure it was beyond reach. "You can clean up any crumbs you find." She whispered. "Then I won't have to sweep this blasted dirt floor with that pitiful broom."

She was half asleep when a mouse skittered into her hair and instantly became tangled in it. Marty screamed and frantically scrabbled to get rid of the struggling, squeaking creature. In blind panic, she screamed until suddenly the creature was gone, her screams scaring all of them half to death.

It took a while for everyone to calm down and for the youngsters to get back to sleep, much longer for her to feel relatively steady. She needed to find some way to get the beds up out of reach of foraging mice and biting spiders and lay awake trying to think of a solution, then remembered one of Edward's luxuries was folding camp cots. But she hadn't seen them—where could they be? Where had she not searched the plane? The only place she could think of was the partly crushed nose. How could she get them out? And how could she carry them so far?

Could she stand to face that horrible place again? She thought about the mouse in her hair and of spider bites and knew she had to, that she couldn't stand NOT to go.

Very early in the morning she went to see if the bears were still gone from the middle falls, taking the long rifle the short way along the stream. She found only weathered tracks and old scat full of shiny fish scales.

The next morning, at dawn's first hint, Marty set out at a slow jog, carrying the big double-bitted axe over a shoulder. She risked ruining one side, but could think of no other way to get into that space. She slowed at the crossing, then walked quickly to the old camp to reach the worn trail up the steep hill to the wreck.

Puffing and thirsty, climbing the grade made her slow to a plodding pace. She drank at the small brook above the old camp and sat long enough to catch her breath. It had been over a month since she was here but everything looked so different, then she realized that was because her surroundings no longer seemed strange and threatening. Instead they were part of her world that daily grew more familiar.

When she went on, each step up through towering, shadowy evergreens brought more emotion until she had to choke back fresh sorrow and revulsion. Suddenly she felt rage at the whole world for her isolation—no one had even looked for them!

At the first glimpse of the wreck she stopped to stare, aghast at the devastation. A two-foot-long section of broken propeller projected from a huge trunk. A wing was broken off along the outer edge of its wing-mounted engine; that mangled wing leaned against a trunk long paces from the fuselage, and a torpedo-shaped pontoon, once firmly braced under it, dangled by one strut next to the tree. The other wing, with its motor and bent, cracked blades, drooped down on the plane's far side, still connected by thin shreds of metal at the back, by the passenger door. Gaping in awe, she wondered how any of them had lived. She recalled searing head pain, dizziness and terrible confusion. No wonder!

Remembering to hurry, she edged closer, and finally lowered the half-forgotten axe to the ground. The plane looked smaller now, but its top was still above her reach. A puff of wind brought a foul odor that made a lump form in her throat.

"Don't you dare cry!" She growled aloud. "Do what you came here to do." Mice and spiders suddenly seemed minor problems compared to this, but she didn't want either child to experience the terror she felt from that mouse, and she had no medicine but first aid cream. She had to protect them, had to do what she came for!

Or they might die, too.

Focused on the aircraft's nose, she tried to open the hood, but it was too jammed by the tree trunk that still lay along its length . . . and beyond. She chopped into the side, astonished at how easily it cut through thin, soft metal. Then she used the axe to pry loose and peel back the razor-sharp edge until she had a big area of safe access to the storage area. She pulled out cots, one at a time. Seeing other shadowy objects, she dared to reach in further and retrieve the tent's ground tarp. Then, quivering nervously, a rubber raft she hadn't known was brought, and a full size handsaw. Each seemed ridiculously extravagant, more that overloaded the small craft and contributed to the crash. But both were sorely needed.

She peered into the nose one more time and saw packed parachutes, but left them because they were useless on the ground. Nearby, she saw things she'd missed: a hand compass, an olive-drab tubular tin of paraffin-dipped wooden matches—tears of relief fell at seeing those!

She found several pieces of rope: tie-downs, a long line for raft mooring, and cotton ropes attached to wooden chocks—which she cut off as useless. She salvaged broken fishing poles, hoping to use them to dig roots, as skewers, or something else useful. They had full reels, giving lots of snare material.

Using tie-down ropes, she bound together all four folded, lightweight but bulky cots and used the ropes to brace them across the back of her shoulders. She set off downhill, upset that it would take at least one more trip for everything.

Both kids were up but still rubbing sleepy eyes when she reached camp. Ted's eyes bulged when he saw the cots.

"Where'd ya get those?" He asked.

"From the plane. I don't want any mice to get caught in your hair. That was too scary. These will get our beds up high enough the mice can't reach us. Should keep spiders from biting us, too." She said. "I have to go back tomorrow for more things I found."

Wide-eyed, Ted saw her as magic. She could do anything!

Marty gathered extra food and cooked a stew big enough to reheat leftovers tomorrow. Moving things never left enough time to forage and cook.

Early the next day she tried to get everything in one load, her attention focused only on the task. The rolled and tied raft and paddles made one bulky, rather heavy bundle and everything else fit in the ground tarp, bound with mooring rope. But the weight and bulk of both was too much. She left the tarp for yet another load, though the round trip was about four miles, some very steep, and meant time away from the unguarded children.

Late that day she returned with the last load, plodding with exhaustion and glad for leftovers that only needed to be heated.

Waking late, she did the morning's wood, fire and water chores before untying the cots, upset to find part of every cot surface and a corner of the ground cloth had been chewed to shreds by rodents. The cots had to be repaired before they could be used or the holes would rip wider, might even allow a child to fall through. The only cloth she had that was sturdy enough to use was from a duffel bag.

Opening the cots outside she cut patches with her freshly sharpened knife to fit each hole. The meager sewing kit held a few tiny thread spools but no thread heavy enough to use on canvas. Searching men's clothes, she unraveled cotton stitching from the newest denim leg seams, then struggled to work such thick thread into the largest needle's eye.

She sewed the entire day, first repairing the cots. Without a thimble, her fingertips soon became very sore, so she used a small, rough rock to help push the needle through one layer at a time. She finished the cots, but would wait for sore fingers to heal before doing the ground tarp.

She rearranged the tent, putting one cot along the back wall for storage and another parallel it for the kids to sleep on foot-to-foot, leaving just enough room to walk between. Her cot went closer to the front, up against theirs to leave floor space. The last cot didn't fit end-to-end across the back, so it went along the side not far from the foot of the others. She left it far enough from the rear wall to store guns, hatchet and axe, both saws, the shovel and the fishing tackle out of the way. She put the rolled-up raft and ground tarp on that cot. It filled over half of that wall, but left enough room for some dry wood inside the door.

She left the crates near the fireside, lined along the wall at the head of the beds. The nested cooking gear fit on the crates. Their clothes went on the back cot in neatly folded stacks instead of stuffed in bags; she was thankful for the empty storage bags. The men's clothes bags went under the rear cot. Anything else went under the side cot.

Elated to finish an emotional, tiresome task, Marty cheerfully took the kids to gather food. Now only meadow snares were set for grouse. Muskrats had been avoiding the pond snare and she couldn't yet stand to eat rabbit again.

Wandering diagonally across the meadow toward the dam to check that last snare, they followed the path where Ted got stung. Partway across, she stopped to dig several Salisfy roots growing in a clump. Amy paused, then wandered on. Ted followed her, hunting for a ripe strawberry. They knew Marty would catch up.

A sharp snort halted Amy. Ted glanced up from picking a berry. A large mule deer doe stood between the children and small, speckled twin fawns. Head high and long ears out to the side, the doe glared defiantly at the surprised children.

Marty glanced up at the snort, sucking her lips to signal freeze without thinking.

Amy totally ignored the freeze signal and started to run toward the fawns, giggling in anticipation. The snorting doe charged with head straight out, eyes glaring. Amy saw the doe coming and shrieked in ear-shattering terror. The doe froze, head up, eyes rolling, startled by this unknown noise.

Marty raced over rough ground, waving her arms, screaming, "No! Leave her alone!" to distract the doe, though her heart pounded in terror she refused to slow.

The doe trotted away, zigzagging to warily glance back from one side then the other while herding her fawns to shadowy safety across the meadow.

Relieved, Marty slowed, but the instant she reached Amy she yelled, "When I signal you to freeze, you freeze!" She punctuated each angry word with a loud smack on her behind. Amy's screams of terror became screeches of outrage.

Marty was now thoroughly determined to enforce instant freeze in obedience to the signal—their life DID depend on it!

Ted had frozen at the signal and watched without a thought of moving anything but his eyes. At first he was terrified for Amy, then for Marty, sensing the doe could be deadly. He knew from her movements and voice that Marty was terrified of it, but she'd still protected Amy. He was stunned when Amy screeched in outrage at being spanked, reminded of what Marty said about dangerous mothers—Marty was a mother, too!

Even people mothers were dangerous!

The next day, approaching the meadow's brushy northwest corner, they first smelled, then saw a herd of ten grazing Bighorn Sheep. Sounding the freeze signal, Marty saw they were ewes because none had big horns and most had lambs nearby, barely showing above the grass. She watched the ewes intently for several minutes.

"Duck down and hide between these shrubs." She whispered. "Do NOT move until I say to! Is that understood?" She shook a finger to emphasize each word. Both nodded mutely, Amy cowering against Ted with shoulders hunched.

Circling behind bordering trees for cover, she raced to camp for the light rifle, loading it with shaky, sweaty hands. She chambered a shell there, where the noise wouldn't alert the sheep. In case her thumb slipped and the rifle fired too soon, she stepped outside to ease the hammer down while pressing the trigger. She sighed in relief when the hammer stopped. She'd have to cock the hammer to fire, but that was a much quieter than chambering a shell with the lever. This was the only safety she knew of for this gun.

Back by the children, she whispered, "Stay where you are until I come back, or you might get hurt or scare the game away." She glared briefly at each child for emphasis.

Ted raised up just enough to watch her over swaying grass tops. Pouting, Amy stayed crouched exactly where her mother said, not trying to watch.

Like when she hunted deer after the crash, Marty felt an adrenalin surge, making every sense acute, her thinking crystal clear. She crept closer, using every bush or grass clump for cover.

As unmoving as possible, she looked the herd over to be sure she wouldn't leave an orphaned lamb, finally spotting a fat, barren ewe. Palming back the hammer and aiming with trembling hands, she pulled the trigger, winced at the solid recoil and painful sound blast then let the rifle sag down as she craned to see if the shot had hit.

The ewe jerked violently, stumbled down on its front knees, its nose drooping to the ground. The others disappeared into the trees faster than she could blink, the sound of pounding hooves faded away nearly as fast. The ewe struggled, stood, and stumbled after the herd as Marty watched, open-mouthed, holding the forgotten rifle.

Trudging back to the kids, she scolded herself aloud for being such a poor hunter. A real hunter killed clean, without just wounding game. And she was ashamed of missing so much meat, again.

Seeing her blazing scar on pursed lips and her scowl, Ted asked, "What you mad about? We stayed like you said."

"I only wounded it, I didn't kill it!" Marty growled. "The poor thing will hurt now, maybe go off and die and all that meat will be wasted."

Ted was deeply impressed that not killing what you shoot at was a VERY bad thing.

CHAPTER 14

Because the days became quite warm, they sweltered when in camp, especially while the sun glared on the tent's pale gray canvas. After cool, impossibly short nights, the inside became so hot Marty tied the doors open early every morning. Thunderstorms were rare now, but the inside fire was always set up, but unlit, in case it was needed.

Marty's boots felt so hot and heavy she started going barefoot in camp where stickers and sharp rocks were rare and heavy use had made the dirt hard and smooth.

She shifted the two extra sleeping bags from their beds to the back cot, under their clothes stacks instead of in their stuff sacks; she needed those too much for storage. She had to duck bulging rabbit tubes hung from the rear of the ceiling pole to reach that cot. Even if only cattail pollen, she was proud to have food stored in them, food she could only get in spring.

Done with morning chores, she put boots on to go see if the moose was still hogging the pond, letting the kids stay barefoot; their soles were as tough as shoe leather.

Peering at the pond through shrubs, she saw he was gone. "Now where did HE go?" She asked, her voice shrill with frustration.

Marsh birds sounded normal again, so she snuck closer, listening and looking.

A row of huge, split-toe moose tracks and a line of flat, drying cow pies were the only signs the massive bull had been there, that she hadn't imagined him. She could now reset muskrat snares and gather pond foods, and they could swim again.

Cattail clubs were browning, too old to eat, and the top spikes were bare of pollen. The new leaves were taller than last year's dry ones, so the only usable part now was the starchy roots, but she had enough of those and nothing to store many more in. Storage containers were such a problem!

On impulse, she cut a bundle of long cattail leaves and sat by the water to experiment with them while the kids splashed nearby. She'd woven a paper-strip Easter basket in school, now she wanted to try it with leaves.

It took a while to find a way to split the long, rather flat leaves thin enough to flex easily. She finally braced the knife tip on a rock and pulled each leaf past the blade to split them to half thickness. Then she split them lengthwise so their width and thickness was similar to strips of construction paper.

When she went under and over the spokes radiating from the center, the narrower leaf she wove with went over the same spokes each round and it fell apart when she released the middle. She growled frustration, finally realizing the spokes had to be odd-numbered so the weave alternated over a spoke one round and under it the next. Then it worked right.

When the bottom seemed wide enough, she bent the spokes and wove up the basket side. But it became lopsided and round-bottomed. By the time she tucked the loose spoke ends back to bind off the top, it wouldn't sit up without holding weight to keep it from rolling on its side.

She took the pitiful basket home as proof she remembered weaving basics.

The fresh leaves shriveled and shrank overnight. The next morning, glaring at the pathetic thing, its uniform gaps gave her the glimmer of an idea how to make a sifter or crawdad net—items requiring even holes. These gaps were too wide for those, but . . .

Picturing cutting a large bunch of cattail leaves to dry for weaving, she thought, why not go out farther? We can now, with the raft. She'd never been in one, had only seen others in them a few times. It was time to learn to use it.

The next morning she blew and puffed for what seemed like hours to inflate the two-man rubber raft. It's outside was three feet wide by five feet long. A rubber seat strap stretched across the narrower inner gap near each end, barely above the soft rubber floor. It held an appalling amount of air.

When she'd blown it up as much as possible she plugged the blowhole and carried it up-side-down over her head. Ted carried both wooden paddles over a shoulder and Amy sulked between them because she had nothing to carry.

By the water, Marty saw it had to be blown up more or the rumpled floor would be too loose to walk on. But it would still float now.

Sliding over the bulging black rubber side, she crawled unsteadily to sit on the far seat strap. She helped the children in, seating Ted on the other strap, his feet between her outstretched legs and her feet nearly alongside his torso. Backed against Marty, Amy filled most of the floor space. Her feet reached Ted's knees.

Focused on how to use the paddles, she picked one up. Then discovered the loaded raft sat solidly on mud, too near shore to float. Grumbling, she untangled herself from crowded arms and legs and stepped into squishy mud to push them far enough out to float with her weight added. She slid back in and they scrambled over and around each other until they fit again, like jigsaw pieces, only now they were all smeared with smelly mud from her boots. Marty grimaced, this was not starting out well.

At first, nervous about how to paddle effectively, she stayed near shore where they nearly dragged the bottom. Finally confident the raft couldn't tip over, she learned to steer where she wanted and went farther out.

Ted and Amy giggled at this new fun. They stared quietly when Marty paddled near muskrat feeding piles, which looked like floating haystacks, then far around the old beaver lodge. She glowered at seeing that the moose had eaten nearly all the water lily leaves and flowers—that was HER food! She paddled hard, fuming, but soon forgot the irritation, distracted by fuzzy chicks and ducklings out swimming, peeping shrilly, shadowing alert mothers. Five goslings had hatched, rather cute babies of dangerous parents. Marty gave them plenty of space.

When Marty's shoulders started to ache from using new muscles she showed Ted how to paddle, directing his zigzag path toward the swimming beach. She pulled the raft out and inverted it over a pile of rocks for next time.

She shed muddy boots and dared the youngsters to beat her to the water, letting them get a head start. She taught them more diving and swimming skills. Then it was time to set two muskrat traps and gather food for dinner.

The weather stayed clear and warmed more and they spent much time wandering the valley. Marty still couldn't find a way out, though she looked from every angle.

Fruits suddenly approached ripeness in high elevation's sort season, startling Marty.

They ate any strawberry they found and saw Holly-leafed Oregon Grapes' darkening berry clusters. Serviceberry and chokecherry fruits darkened toward ripeness. Along seeps and springs she found tart, golden Salmonberries they all eagerly ate. She pulled the long, prickly canes down for the children to pick the purple-tinged, raspberry-like fruits.

Onions bloomed, each pair of round, hollow leaves separated by a stalk topped by a clump of blue or white flowers. The bulbs, fat and tender in the spring were now thin and tough, their stored energy spent on blooming and setting seed. Domestic onions kept best if dug and cured during a late dry spell, so now she only noted where they grew. Later, she'd come and harvest them. But fall was a long ways off, and this ripening was only of the earliest varieties. There was no hurry.

With the heat and few storms, the last snow melted, so the small brooks dried up and the stream fell enough to bare gravel and sand spits its whole length. The pond water was also low, and now and then another stick gave way in the worn dam, but so much debris had accumulated against it that it held water to a minimum level.

The pond snares caught more muskrats, fatter than ever. Marty experimented more bravely with these hides, scraping vigorously and thoroughly while they were fresh. She beat them against a tree trunk to break and soften skin fibers, gripping the pelt's edge in several places in turn to pound and stretch it equally from all sides. Rather smugly, she thought she was much better at curing pelts. These felt more like store-bought leather, but still not the same, especially in color. And some of the luxuriant fur fell out. She hoped it was because this was normal shedding season and not from any mistake she made handling the fur.

She had no idea what to use the furs for, but felt challenged to make them as good as possible. She couldn't bear for anything to go to waste, even inedible items. If she had to kill an animal to eat, at least she could use every possible part of it. Killing to eat felt less shameful that way and she had, finally, found a use for the rabbit tubes, so she would for these, too.

One day, a dark gold blur streaked through brush and grass close behind a smaller creature moving as fast. Freezing, Marty tried to think what each could be. The tawny, long-legged cat pounced, snagged and fumbled its prey, almost let its frantic victim escape, caught it again and bit hard on its neck with an audible crunch.

Appalled, she recognized the hunter as a Bobcat, similar to but much bigger than a house cat. Its prey was a tiny chipmunk. The tuft-eared cat carried its limp victim away to eat, rumbling a menacing growl at the astonished trio. Wide cheek tufts of thick gold-and-brown mottled fur framed greenish-yellow eyes that glared defiance at them. Marty shuddered, wondering how dangerous a wildcat might be to the children.

Ted froze when she did, though she'd been too startled to give the freeze signal. He stared at the tiny white-striped chipmunk with his breath held, trying to will it to escape. But the cat thing killed it. He struggled not to cry. Chipmunks were his friends and now a friend was dead—and getting ate! A fat tear scalded down a cheek.

Seeing his shocked dismay, sadly understanding it, Marty thought of all the animals they had to kill to eat.

"That cat is a hunter just trying to stay alive. It has to kill to eat, the same as we do." She said, rubbing his back for comfort.

"Do deer kill to eat?" He asked after a moment.

"No. They don't hunt. They eat grass, not meat. They're the ones who get hunted. We eat animals that eat grass. Or we WOULD if I could ever HIT one!" She stomped.

Very sad, Ted knew that when they walked all day his stomach growled and ached with hunger. Marty no longer brought a lunch, hoping to find a few bites of something fresh along the way. He knew animals wouldn't like hunger pangs, could see why they tried to make it better. He wiped the last tear away and gulped at the ache in his throat.

Another day they saw the fox family. From the color mix she knew it was the same one and it was the mother who'd snuck into camp. Where's the male? She wondered, peering around. Did vixens raise kits alone? Or did something happen to the male?

Both days and nights grew warmer, so they started sleeping in the sleeping bag liners, on top of the bags. But mosquitoes feasted on them all night and left them miserable, so Marty draped the wool blankets over the liners and that was comfortable, though a bit warm. Hot middays they spent by the water, mostly in or on the pond. Cool mornings were spent getting that day's food.

Marty added a notch to her calendar stick at the new moon. They'd been here three months. She shook her head: time slipped by so fast, so unnoticed.

She wore fewer clothes in the growing heat and finally hemmed the boxers shorter and put a tuck in the waist so they'd stay up. She tucked in the t-shirt and strapped the hot leather belt on top to carry the holstered pistol and sheathed knife. She even got brave enough to wear the altered clothes without bra or panties. It was cooler, but she was glad only two small children could see her dressed like that—she blushed hotly.

Her feet were so tough she only wore boots to go far from camp, not just the short way to the pond. She enjoyed feeling damp tickly grass, scratchy, shifty dirt or sand, and sun-warmed rocks on her feet. She could grip things with her toes and bend her feet to fit uneven places, which improved balance.

The kids wore only underpants until voracious mosquitoes appeared at dusk to bite bare skin. Then Marty put shirts on them for protection.

They all became so tan they no longer sunburned. After the first burn peeled they burned again, less severely, peeled, and burned again, until their skin became a mosaic of mottled browns, tans, and pinks.

Their hair, the top layers sun-bleached, had grown long enough to blow in their eyes with any breeze. To control it, Marty braided long, dried cattail leaves into wide loops to wear like crownless, brimless hats. Besides holding hair, the headbands gave some relief from sun glare and kept sweat from running into their eyes. In a few days the bands made a definite less-tanned line across their foreheads.

Amy, whose burn-and-tan mottled face was now lightly freckled, had lost her chubbiness. She was leaner, tougher, and more coordinated from frequent long walks and energetic swimming, and daily running and wrestling in play.

Ted's thick brown hair, bleached pale on top, began to curl at the ends. Already lean, eating all he wanted of the great variety of foods they lived on added weight only in bone and muscle as he grew taller with astonishing speed, reminding Marty of a leggy colt. He'll get as tall as Eddie, she thought with a twinge of heartache, and it looked like he'd stay as thin. But the trigger to her deepest ache of missing Eddie was Ted's dazzling, whole-face grin, just like his father's.

They spent much time in the pond, either Ted or Marty at Amy's side while the other was free to explore, usually underwater. Amy dog-paddled well but had no idea of where it was safe to stop paddling and often tried to stand up in water over her head so, always, someone had to be near enough to pull her back up before she drowned. Ted swam like he'd been born in the water and quickly became proficient at maneuvering underwater. He spent most of his turn away from Amy exploring the pond's muddy bottom. He even managed a few short dives nearby while watching her.

After his turn ended, he dived, curious about how underwater plants grew. Pulling a sturdy aquatic plant loose from the muddy bottom, he saw a long thread going from its base into the mud. He surfaced for quick gulps of air then followed the thread to a lump at its end, a tuber. He examined it while catching his breath and letting the mud settle.

"What's that you found?" Marty asked.

He gave her the fat-radish-sized tuber, shrugging that he didn't know what it was.

"Where was it?"

"In the mud. It was on this." He pointed to the thread and attached plant floating nearby.

Marty rinsed mud off to examine the leaves. She recognized it as Arrowhead and grinned in delight. Gram had said native women harvested Arrowhead tubers by holding onto a canoe while loosening the water plants with their toes, then tossed the floating tubers into the canoe. She tasted a tiny nibble then let the kids try it. The flavor reminded them so much of potatoes that both kids whooped in delight. She warmly thanked Ted for finding it. He grinned back.

To his delight she had him find more. She gathered the tubers that floated up, rinsed off clinging mud and carried them to pile on shore.

When Ted stumbled ashore to catch his breath, Marty told him to stop for the day. They were delighted with the harvest, though the smallest rabbit tube would easily hold it.

Since cattail pollen, spikes and sprouts, and eggs, were no longer harvestable, they'd stopped wearing packs to the pond, so she made a special trip to camp for a bag to carry the tubers in. The children rested on shore while she went. The plants and dirt felt good on her tough bare feet. Even stepping on an occasional rock didn't hurt much anymore.

She spread the tubers to dry overnight then stored them in the small stuff sack from Ted's sleeping bag, eagerly planning to add many more. But each was so tiny even the several dozen they had didn't fill one corner. It would take a long time to fill this bag.

One big flannel liner now held dried salmon and a large stuff sack held dry cattail root chunks she powdered as needed. She knew she should powder them all to make room to store something else in that big bag, but nothing else was ripe yet. No hurry. Besides, what could she put the root flour in? Nearly all the rabbit tubes were used for pollen and she had no other small bags. The only use she'd found for the root powder was to mix it with the flour for bread . . . why not add it with the flour as she powdered it? The flour sack was not very full. Yes, she'd do that, real soon.

For storage containers, she still had both empty duffel bags their clothes had been in, and three empty denim stuff sacks. All but one of the bags were big and would hold a lot, but figuring out what to store smaller amounts in was a problem. She rolled her eyes, thinking she might have to weave more baskets, hopefully better than that first one.

Each day seemed busy, never boring. Marty thought about now, only occasionally about steadily approaching fall and winter. She was still amazed at the number of useful plants and glad they had so many to choose from. Maybe it wasn't so bad here, after all. Except she got awfully tired of only having two youngsters to talk to. She'd always been quiet, but liked to talk with adults now and then.

She was amazed one day to find ripe blackberries. She'd started wearing her pack again since having to go back to camp when they got the Arrowhead tubers. She was tempted to pick the berries, but was afraid the juice would ruin the pack. Strawberries had only molded, not dried and these were at least as juicy so, afraid they'd go to waste otherwise, they ate all the ripe ones they found.

Looking around, she saw that many sagging, yellowed grass heads also appeared ripe. Examining a few grains while munching sweet, juicy berries, she realized she also had to figure out how to harvest and process wild grass seeds for cereal and flour. She could only guess at the procedure, but knew the result. How were oats flattened? How was grain ground to flour as fine as dust?

She shrugged, something else to find out the hard way. Grain should dry easily and how to harvest it was obvious, though it would take time to strip off so many seeds.

Walking near the north cliffs, mulling over how to process grain, her eye was drawn by matted clumps and wisps of Mountain Goat hair. As the nimble goats shed old tangled wool to grow sleek new winter coats the wind blew the shed hair down into the valley from their high territory. She eagerly gathered all she found, ashamed she'd done nothing to the rest but wash, dry and brush it, then stash it away.

Scant steps into the meadow, alerted by their distinctive smell, she saw the herd of Bighorns grazing near where they'd been before. Marty's spine tingled with excitement as she slowly edged back out of sight. Determined to aim better this time, she hid the children like before and quietly ran through the tree fringe beyond the herd's view to get the rifle and leave the pack of fresh roots and wool. She was so excited she nearly forgot to load the gun, lever a shell in and lower the hammer, then quietly rushed back.

Using any bush she could hide behind, she inched closer and closer to the herd until she had a view of her intended target. Moving very slowly, she palmed the hammed back and eased the rifle to her shoulder as she rose slightly. This time she was calm when she aimed at the fattest ewe's side, just behind the shoulder, taking care to make this shot count.

The rifle butt slammer her shoulder as the sharp crack stabbed her ears, but the ewe fell so abruptly all four feet jerked off the ground before the animal dropped from sight in the grass. It didn't struggle to rise as the herd thundered away in panic.

"I got it!" Marty shrieked, jumping and waving the rifle over her head in exhilaration. Racing to the downed ewe, she circled warily to be sure it was dead.

Vividly recalling one of Dad's bucks having its throat deeply cut to drain its blood, she slit its throat, slicing deeper and deeper until blood trickled from the deep gash. She sighed in relief—this must be right.

She tugged a leg to judge its weight and realized it had to weigh over a hundred and fifty pounds. About three feet high at the shoulder and nearly five feet long, nose to rump, the old ewe had a thick, stocky body covered with gray-brown hair. It had short, straight, sharp horns. She saw the wound exactly where she'd aimed; from now on she'd aim for that spot, this animal hadn't twitched after it fell.

A small circular wound, nearly healed, was at the bottom of its chest—this was the same one she shot before! Feeling the old wound, she realized the first bullet had slid under the skin and shaved the ribs without going through them, then came out a slightly bigger hole low on the other side, far too low to kill.

"I didn't waste the meat after all." She gloated. Somehow she had to get all this meat to camp before some did go to waste. But no big trees were close by where she could hang it to gut it. Jerking at a limp hind leg, she realized she couldn't even drag it until it was gutted.

She pursed her lips, wondering: how do I gut something this big? The men always did it at home. But no men were here, only her and the kids—the kids! She whirled, then saw with relief they'd stayed put. Both were craning their necks to see what she was doing, so she motioned for them to come. Ted led Amy by the hand because the girl was too tired to watch where she was going; it was far past her nap time.

The dead ewe fascinated Ted. It looked enormous. Amy glanced with little interest, sat down, and fell asleep as she rolled down into a loose curl.

Marty'd only watched Dad and her brothers butcher a steer, but they'd used a block and tackle to hoist it. Her brothers got in the way so she didn't see much, only helped Mother with the liver, heart, kidneys, tongue and tripe as the men handed them over. Without block and tackle or even a handy tree, how could she manage this?

Finally she had Ted watch Amy while she trotted directly to camp to get the strongest rope and leave the rifle.

Panting from the jog back, she squatted in front of the ewe to slit through the belly hide from ribs nearly to the tail, surprised at the skin's thickness. She cautiously cut back up, going through nearly an inch of fat and barely through the abdominal muscles, careful not to puncture the gut sack—the thin, filmy membrane holding the coiled intestines tightly together—since a tiny nick could ruin a lot of meat.

She turned aside to gulp fresh air and consider what to do next. Though this was much larger than other game she'd cleaned, the procedure should be like on small game, just bigger in scale. The object was still to remove all unwanted matter.

Reassured, she slit the hide up between the front legs, but couldn't figure out how to cut while holding the leg out of the way.

She was only trying to get rid of enough weight to move the animal, so she left the hide on. Shifting, she pulled the gut sack aside with fingertips while cutting carefully beside them, working inward to detach the connective tissue between muscle and gut sack until she was nearly elbow deep. When she felt sharp spine projections she stopped, could go no farther on this side. Standing to gulp clean air, she flexed her aching back and wiped her nose on her shoulder. Wild sheep smelled worse than tame ones; no wonder she smelled them before seeing any.

She wrenched up on the bottom legs to roll it over on the other side, worked the rest of the sack free as far as she could reach then backed off to rest. This was much, much harder than dressing a rabbit!

Finally, she moved to the back end, cutting around the openings to cautiously work them down into the gut and out without touching anything. Blindly working along the spine, she worked the last few attachments loose so the gut pile rolled out and flattened against her boots and shins. She grimaced but dared not back away or she'd never be able to finish all the way up.

"Oohh, that one has lotsa guts!" Ted exclaimed, pop-eyed with amazement.

She finally had to step away and let it ooze on out, gasping for fresh air. Never again would she wrinkle her nose at cleaning small game!

"Guts and guts and lotsa guts!" Ted jiggled in delight.

Marty chuckled.

Awake, Amy rubbed her eyes and stared at the strange scene by Mama. Ted knelt with an arm around Amy; Marty's frown showed she needed to focus to do this and keeping Amy quiet was the only way he could help.

Finally, she tugged until the windpipe and esophagus, leading up through the neck, were all that was still attached. Too tired now to care if she ruined a little meat, she hacked the tubes off as far up as possible.

Keenly grateful she'd never been squeamish, she stepped back and studied the pile, trying to find the heart and liver, the only organs she wanted to keep. She estimated roughly a quarter of the weight was removed, leaving a bit over a hundred pounds. Moving the meat would not be easy, but now she could manage, somehow.

She carved the heart and liver free and tucked them far into the chest cavity to avoid carrying them separately. She puzzled over hard chunks of beige tissue coating some of the intestines. It seemed to be fat, but it was not familiar, and she would have too much trouble getting this to camp without adding more weight, so she left it.

She rolled the carcass away from the innards and tied the rope to a hind foot to drag it, quickly realizing the hair slanted the wrong way to drag it from that end. She put the rope around the neck, relieved she hadn't cut the head off to get rid of more weight.

Thinking how suddenly everything was getting ripe, Marty felt a twinge of fear. No time was left to set and check snares every day, so she had to save as much of this precious meat as possible. And the scant remnant of lard was so rancid she feared it was unsafe to eat now, so this fat was just as urgent. She had to hurry to finish this so she could begin harvesting the grains and berries that were ripe, and the fall-fattened bulbs and roots. If she missed them now she'd have to do without them until next year—they could never survive the winter without those foods, or this meat.

She had to move this meat, now! She pulled with energy born of desperation, the rope gripped tightly in both hands, draped over a shoulder so the carcass slid up over tall grass. Leaning forward, she jerked hard, felt her boots slip though the short summer hair now eased the drag as it bumped along. Every few yards she had to switch shoulders and catch her breath.

Leading Amy behind, Ted wondered how bad it hurt the animal to be pulled by the neck like that. He remembered Marty saying dead things don't feel pain. Wondering how that could be so, he rubbed his own neck. It would hurt him!

After a third stop, Marty shed her boots to dig her toes in for traction. Tying the laces together, she asked Ted to carry them. He flashed his dazzling grin—it felt good to help her, even only that much.

Marty's traction was much better, but her feet quickly became sore from the harsh dry grass. Panting, she plopped down for a break. Her whole body ached with fatigue and both shoulders were raw from the rope, but camp was still a quarter mile away and slightly uphill. Then she had to drag the meat past camp to reach a tree big enough to hang it in. Unless it was hung she'd never be able to skin, slice and dry it before scavengers got to it, even with a big gut pile to distract them. This meat would be much safer in a tree.

Marty put her boots back on for the rough part and, jaw clenched, hauled with renewed determination. She left the meat at the meadow's edge to clear a path to a big maple, calling the kids to help. Ted was confused: the tent was that way. He saw she was clearing a path and remembered she said she had a reason for what she did, even if she forgot to tell him what it was. He shrugged and helped toss debris from the new path.

When the ewe was under the maple, Marty boosted Ted up on a thick branch so he could climb higher and drape the rope over an even higher one. She hovered below, afraid he'd fall, ready to catch him if he did.

Scared at first, he felt braver as his tough bare feet curled to grip the rough bark. He grinned down at Marty. He was doing something she could never do. He had to wait for her to tie on a longer rope to put over the high branch. After being up there a while he was enjoying the tree climb, but didn't know how to get back down. Marty explained how to face the trunk, work down to the low limb, slip down to hang by his hands, then let himself drop to his feet. He did that, but when he let go he fell, then rolled up onto his feet, laughing hesitantly. It was scary-fun. He felt very, very daring.

Marty hoisted the ewe up by the neck, inch by inch, high enough so no fox could reach its hind legs, then struggled to anchor the taut rope to a branch stub. She jerked back in terror as the forgotten liver and heart suddenly plopped on the ground at her feet.

"Well. I guess we eat fried liver today," she huffed, "and heart tomorrow."

Dragging with weariness, when the pan of sliced liver was set over the growing fire Marty plodded to the brook to wash off dry blood that seemed to coat most of her.

They all gobbled generous portions of fresh liver. None had eaten since morning and were ravenous but Marty was almost too tired to eat.

Though still tired, when it was light enough to see she started a fire under the drying rack and began to skin the ewe from the bottom up, lowering the carcass only enough to work on. She peeled the skin back to thinly slice thick rump muscles, draping slices on the smoke-shrouded rack until it was full.

The old ewe was extremely fatty and Marty gratefully saved every shred of precious fat. Tempted to use the rock by the fire to chop the fat on, she realized having the big saw allowed her to make a cutting board. She sawed diagonally through the thickest wood the saw could span, making a second cut a couple inches farther back to free it. Shaking out aching arms, she rinsed the big oval board off at the brook and gloated in triumph. Now the knife was less likely to be ruined, solving another problem of living in this primitive environment.

As meat smoke-dried, she discovered how well tree knots worked to hold fire all night. That dense wood smoldered slowly for hours, perfect for drying meat. But knots were so rare that she had to use regular wood during the day, which required frequent attention so she had to stay nearby all but a few minutes at a time.

With the racks full and the fire tended, there was little to do. Time hung heavy. She brooded: each hour spent here was an hour less to gather foods they needed to survive winter. But meat wouldn't wait, had to be cared for quickly or it would rot. Being busy help pass the time, so she carved off and rendered all the fat she could reach and skinned the rest of the hide to scrape while it rendered.

Meat was the most important survival food. Unable to travel to get fresh vegetables, any time they were hungry she sliced off a slab of mutton to fry. She let the kids eat strips of steak by hand. They ate juicy, stringy, fatty meat and more meat until their tummies bulged. It tasted delectable after only fish and lean small game.

As more meat was carved away, she wondered what to do with the bones. Mother had stewed them; always simmering on the back of the cook stove in the biggest pot, stew became a staple at every butchering.

These bones were covered with shreds and chunks too small to drape on the rack to dry, and the racks were full of meat that would take another two days to dry. So, one by one, she sawed up the leg bones to fit in the stew pot then smashed them smaller with the hatchet back. Day after day the pot bubbled, stewing off scraps and thick, rich marrow.

Each morning, as soon as the meat was rotated and the fires tended to, she scraped the cold fat off the broth to put with the rendered lard, and picked out bone fragments. Then she added more bones to the broth. If it got too thick she added more water and few grains of precious salt. Now they ate bowls of rich stewed meat whenever they were hungry.

The long ribs looked tempting, but much of it was pocked with bullet-shattered splinters and lead fragments. She dumped those and all bullet-damaged meat far from camp.

Fat, rendered to lard and cracklins, was of secondary importance to survival. She poured new lard into the original coffee canister, then the empty peanut butter jar, then the jerky jar. Crunchy cracklins, hard and brown, tightly filled mess kits. As fat rendered, she scraped more from the hide to add.

The hide was a bonus, but she wasn't sure what to do with it once all the fat was off, so she worked at scraping it to help pass the time. This hide required different handling than small ones, needed more vigorous scraping before it dried, but drying took much longer.

She couldn't imagine beating it against a tree to soften it—not twenty-plus pound of limp weight that was hard to hold onto. The unappealing coat was thin and bald in places from the long slide getting here. She had no idea how to remove the rest of the hair.

While scraping, she realized this hide was much thicker in proportion to its size, especially along the spine. This skin was four-and-a-half feet long without the head and four feet wide without the leg extensions, while the scraped, softened big muskrat hides ended up eighteen inches long by nearly as wide. She couldn't think of what to use it for but couldn't stand to waste it.

When the last meat was drying and the last bones stewing, the hide was well scraped and still she felt restless. So she decided to try making lye soap. Plenty of wood ash was handy. Filling the big bucket half full of ash, she added water and let it soak overnight. Then carefully drained only the water into the wash basin. In the Dutch oven, she added some new fat to the old lard until it was about equal to the lye water and set it to heat. When it melted, she cautiously dribbled the lye solution in, stirring it with a stick as it sputtered and foamed. She stirred and stirred until it boiled down to honey-thickness, then poured that back into the wash basin, nearly filling it to the brim. To keep it safely out of reach until it cured and was no longer caustic, she slid it far under the side cot.

By that evening all the meat was dried, stored in the other never-used big sleeping bag liner, and stored in the meat cupboard, next to the smoked salmon.

She was crushed that so much struggle and work had only yielded around thirty pounds of dried meat.

CHAPTER 15

Marty awoke satisfied at a big job well done and eager to roam after being confined to camp so long to protect drying meat. Discouraged yesterday at the meager amount of jerky such effort produced, today that supply reassured her she could get enough food to last the whole winter. Like everything out here it required unexpected time and work.

Now she could get other food, starting with berries. Hopefully all the briar fruits like blackberries were ripe; they ripened before others, like blueberries.

Picturing sharp thorns, despite the heat, she wore pants and boots and found protective clothes for the kids. Jerky chunks went into a pocket for a lightweight lunch.

"I can't button these." Ted complained, unable to fasten his pants.

Marty was shocked; the pants were only snug two months ago. She found his biggest pair and turned back to Amy. He got those on but they were short. Despite the girl being slimmer, her pants were also too small. By double-rolling cuffs and sewing a tuck in back, Ted's smallest pants fit Amy.

Neither could get their shoes on, and Ted's were far too big for Amy. They'd have to stay barefoot. Marty stared at the worn shoes. Before, this would be a minor problem but here, with no store to buy more, outgrown shoes presented a serious difficulty. She couldn't make new shoes—if she knew how, which she didn't—materials and equipment were unavailable, but would have to make something for their feet. Gram wore leather moccasins. Marty wished she'd paid more attention to how they were made.

She felt proud to be able to feed them enough to grow so much, but now she had to make bigger clothes for both children. She led them to the pond, the clothes problem in the back of her mind. Winter was still a ways away.

She enjoyed the trilling songbirds, the sun's vital warmth, the kids' boisterous play, the mature lushness of trees and bushes by the path now so well-known each was a friend. This world had become known, no longer fearfully alien. She glanced at familiar towering cliffs, reassured by their stony sameness as she strode along, the smaller bucket swinging at her side, pacing each step.

She searched the streamside trail for blackberries, dusky dewberries, red raspberries, and skimpy, ruby red Thimbleberries. Few purple-tinged, golden Salmonberries remained. Before the middle falls she found a copse of blackberries with the three end berries ripe. The others were still green, not in full fruit yet. Time was not as short as she'd feared. But they were here so she let the kids eat all they wanted while she stepped deep into the clump and picked.

Despite the strawberry drying failure, she wanted to dry some of these; no other way to save any out here, and the air was hotter and dryer now.

By mid-afternoon the ripe berries were picked. She took the half-full bucket home, disappointed at the labor, time and backache required—and the vines had exacted a fee for the fruit by ripping tiny, stinging shreds of skin from her arms and hands.

She spread a thick layer on the breadboard out in the sun, sure that if turned often they would dry without mold. The rest she stewed into a puckery dessert without sugar.

Leaving much earlier the next day, she headed up the thick woods' north side. It was light enough to see but the sun was not entirely up yet. Neither child was fully awake, and unenthused, so Marty walked slower than normal, surprised to see dew on tall yellowing grass after a cloudless night and the activity of birds and animals as they sped about eating almost frantically.

In a Hazelnut grove halfway to the fault squirrels bound from branch to branch, scolding unusually loud as they neared. Marty saw nothing to explain the loud warnings until she peered into the tall shrubs and saw a few twin nut pods in leaf-like husks.

A squirrel cut a pod loose with sharp teeth tossed it with a flick of its head. The nut-filled husk shot by to land by her feet and she wondered if it was meant to hit her, almost giggling at the idea. The squirrel jerked around to face her with fluffy reddish tail waving brazenly, its legs braced firmly, chattering loud defiance.

"This must mean the nuts are ripe!" She chortled, reaching for the pod as the squirrel vaulted into safe sheltering leaves to proclaim its outrage.

"Those must be terrible curse words in squirrel language! Did you see him THROW this at me?" She asked the delighted children, grinning broadly.

Ted giggled; Marty liked his friend squirrel!

She peeled off the husk, trying to avoid its layer of tiny, sharp bristles, cracked both nuts between rocks and tasted one. It tasted green, but good. Dividing the rest between the kids, she decided to get these now. Despite squirrel protests, they filled the bucket, the kids scurrying through tangled gaps to retrieve a few that were cut but not collected.

Marty got the most by pulling down a whole bush section—which set off an assortment of protests—holding it with one hand and picking with the other, dropping them in the pail at her feet, soon understanding why squirrels jerked so hard as they bit tough stems.

She hated taking their winter food, but reasoned that squirrels could find more of them easier than she could, and such tiny animals needed much less food than three humans. Long before the bucket was full their fingers stung from the almost invisibly tiny bristles. The kids scrubbed irritated hands on their rough pants. In childhood, her family wore gloves to pick domestic Filberts when the husks browned; these were green. If she waited until they turned brown the bristles might not be so bad.

Their hands were too sore to pick anything else that day. By the brook, they scrubbed their fingers through sand, trying to wear away the bristles. She dumped the unhusked nuts into the other small stuff bag to stash in a crate. She'd figure out how to husk them when they were dried; enough sore fingers for now.

She spent a frustrating day doing little because of sore fingers. But the next day she was back out with the bucket, this time searching the meadow for berries, finding a type of blackberry that grew on a long, low vine easily found by dragging her feet through grass until one caught her ankle. These berries were small and seedy, with few on each vine, but fully ripe, so she picked all she found.

Hot, dry weather forced her to dig their bucket-filling spot in the brook deeper as it diminished to a slow trickle that took hours to fill. Soon she'd have to go the quarter mile to the stream—returning uphill with full buckets. At eight pounds a gallon, seven gallons would get very heavy, even after she'd carried it every day for weeks.

The weather was hot every day and warm at night, so only the outside fire was used. Drinking fireside tea in the evening quiet, she saw the moon was a new crescent and carved another mark on the stick. Four months now—they left home April eleventh so it must be August eleventh. She peered into the little mirror in flickering light. The scars from the wreck had faded, except the hot pink lip scar. Her deep tan made her eyes look darker and . . . less like a frightened animal. Her gaze was steady and alert, plus something she couldn't name; something she'd never seen before. Abruptly she put the mirror away. Didn't want to look anymore.

Hunting berries in the upper valley the next day, she realized the extra elevation made foods here ripen a bit later than below. The blackberries she found were just starting to ripen at the end of each cluster. Knowing other foods had to be ready, she looked around, saw the dense, slender Lodgepole Pines across the stream. Gram said her people made special trips into the high mountains to cut and peel those for long, thin, lightweight but strong poles for their teepees.

'High Mountains' echoed, caused vague discomfort, so she focused on finding food.

She cringed at a jerky rustling nearby. Shrill giggles from the quivery ripples changed her fear to a nervous grin. Amy was totally hidden in such tall grass and only Ted's crown bobbed above sagging, grain-laden tips. He pushed through thick grass in anticipation of 'capturing' Amy.

She called them and went to dig a huge cow parsnip root for dinner. That towering plant was easy to spot over the grass.

Once clear of the grass Marty noticed sharp-awned grass seeds stuck in their clothes and hair. One awn was buried like a sliver in tender skin between Amy's toes. Amy wailed loudly, without tears, from seeing it until Marty removed it with sharp fingernails.

Working down-slope, she discovered ripe Sorrel seeds. Standing above long-stemmed, wavy-edged leaves that made such good greens, the seeds looked like dense spikes of coffee grounds. She still savored one or two cups of coffee every morning, but as her supply of grounds dwindled each brew was a few grains weaker, steeped longer to extract all possible flavor. She nibbled a raw Sorrel seed. It tasted like rye or buckwheat but looked so much like coffee grounds she picked a seed stalk to try brewing, and possibly stretch her coffee supply.

Nearby she saw blue Chicory flowers, much like Bachelor Buttons. She'd heard of Chicory root being used like coffee so she dug up a few of those dandelion-like roots to try.

After dinner she put Chicory roots on to roast and tried brewing the Sorrel seeds. The seeds tasted grainier than like coffee, disappointing. She toasted a few in a dry pan then brewed that. It worked better, but tasted more like buckwheat; she loved buckwheat pancakes, so she'd get all these seeds she could find.

She crushed the browned Chicory root on the flat stone by the fire. Purple stains on the breadboard reminded her the blackberries had dried to a seedy pulp that would keep well—another small success.

The brewed Chicory root tasted better than Sorrel seeds, though both lacked the lift of real coffee. Mixed together, they were good enough to extend her coffee.

The next day, nearing the pond, Marty smelled its stagnant reek and immediately gave up wanting to swim there.

Feeling lost, she looked around. May as well gather what's ripe while we're here, she thought. Young birds, loudly voicing panic at their approach, caught her attention. Standing quietly to let them settle down, she noticed all were growing flight feathers. Most were learning to fly and all had grown considerably since they were here last. Startled, she realized they hadn't been here for many days.

The goslings, no longer cute fuzzy babies, were now awkward and gangly, almost larger than the adults. The ever-protective parents, scraggly from molting all their feathers at once, swam unusually near to threaten loudly and boldly.

"If I looked that pathetic I wouldn't want anybody to see me either." She smirked over a shoulder at the children. They laughed so hard the goslings fled in splashy panic, tailed by the scruffy adults.

She wedged the kids into the raft and paddled out to check the ripeness of the remaining Pond Lily seedpods. Though fat, they didn't seem ready. Not sure how to tell when they were ripe, she decided to wait. She paddled over to pry Arrowheads from the bottom with a stick then pulled the whole plants up to pick the tubers off hair-thin runners. Cattail spikes looked brown and full; she wondered if their seeds would make good tea as well as spice. Maybe the seeds weren't fully ripe; better wait a little longer to be sure.

Leaving the small pile of Arrowhead tubers in the beached raft to retrieve on the way back, she led the way to the mid-pool to swim. Stepping down the gradual bank into the pool, she saw many of the rocks she'd used to expand the crossing had washed on downstream. The water was so low the bridge now marked the pool's lower edge. She and Ted replaced the loose rocks plus many more to make the footbridge into a dam to deepen the pool.

With both kids preoccupied with finding pretty rocks at the shallow edge, Marty dived and swam into the luxuriantly cool, clear water. Clunks, gurgles and deep murmurs from water movement made the dive noisy, unlike the quieter pond water.

When it was Ted's turn to swim he dived and tried to catch a whole school of almost transparent pinhead hatchling fish. His efforts were futile but it was fun to herd them with a hand to one side or the other, giving him a new sense of power. He herded tiny fish around until he simply had to come out to catch his breath.

Today Amy was happy to sit waist deep by shore and feel around the rocky bottom for pretty pebbles. She stacked her treasures in a pile at the water's edge.

After they all soaked enough, Marty scrubbed them gently with the fine sand until all grime was gone. Clean, cool and refreshed, they wandered back down in the streambed. Some places were a mere trickle, muddy from moving rocks upstream. The water barely gurgled now. Not so long ago it had been noisy, at times nearly roaring. Most bank tops were about even with Marty's shoulder, some places deeper, others shallower as both streambed and banks raised or fell along its course.

Just down from where Ted saw the Killdeer, Marty spotted a Raccoon. Automatically signaling the kids to freeze, she inched closer to clearly see the ring-tailed animal, not far from the pond. The masked creature frantically washed something, nibbling it between dunks, continually making a chittery-grumbling sound, as if scolding its food.

Ted peered around Marty's leg. Wide-eyed with amazement, he saw it wash its hands like people did. 'Hands' was the only way he could think of its front paws since it used them to scrub and hold its food, like he did, only quicker.

Amy peered timidly from Marty's other leg, very careful to be quiet.

When Marty edged a few steps closer, a child at each leg, the Coon abruptly fell silent and turned its sharp-nosed face to stare intently at them with bandit-masked, glittering eyes. It vented a short, gurgling snarl and bared needle-sharp teeth for an instant before shuffling away in a peculiar humpbacked gait, hurrying up the south bank, its black-and-yellow ringed tail disappearing last.

Marty sidestepped up the sloped north bank and knelt to lift the children, looking across the stream and wondering how dangerous Raccoons were to humans—especially young ones. But she'd heard of Coon hunters and assumed they were good to eat. This one weighed at least ten pounds, bigger than a grouse or rabbit. Its grizzled, brownish fur was long and thick, unusually so for warm weather. But how could she catch one?

The next day, hunting ripe berries near the stream bank, she cut willows away so she could reach more vines. Hacking the brush, she bumped the back of a hand against a berry sticker, jerked at the sharp stab and dropped the knife. She saw it plunge into shady depths, then was stunned to see sparks fly from where it landed.

Carefully sliding down the steep bank, she grabbed the irreplaceable knife, checking the blade for damage. She found a fresh chip in a rock where the knife hit, and picked up the sepia-toned rock to study. It was glossy, like greasy glass. Its many irregular faces dipped in slightly, each faintly ridged with concave lines like in-curving rainbow arcs. Unable to believe she'd only been seeing things, she struck the unusual rock with the back of the knife and saw sparks fly in all directions!

Too stunned to move, she recalled Dad saying he was glad he didn't have to start fires with flint and steel as he struck a match to light fire in the heater stove. The knife was steel, so this had to be flint.

Her mind reeled—now she could start a fire without matches or sunlight! To be sure, she struck again, lips pursed in concentration. Obviously it would take practice to get sparks to land where they were intended, and such fine sparks would require very flammable tinder. But, she jiggled in excitement, what a lifesaver this flint rock was!

She scrabbled up the bank and dropped the rock into the bucket; it was too big to fit in a pocket. Berries needed to be picked.

The early berries, the briar types, suddenly seemed to be all picked. She had dried a lot, but it was so seedy it was nearly tasteless. Smooth-skinned later-ripening berries were still too green, sour, or not full-grown. She eagerly anticipated drying many of them to raisin-like nuggets of sweetness.

The break in berry picking left time to collect other foods. Where the squirrels harvested Hazelnuts, she scoured every bush for nuts but only found a few. In one entire day she only managed to get half a bucket full. Determined not to leave these for later, too, she spent that day painfully shucking off the bristly hulls. Then, with her mouth watering in anticipation, she cracked them. But shell after shell was empty or the dark nutmeat shriveled. Only a handful was fit to eat. Upset at wasting a whole day's effort, she realized these were squirrel rejects. She huffed: how could those little beasts tell which nuts were bad without even picking them?

Drinking evening tea, she remembered everything in the upper valley ripened later. The next morning she found several clusters of Hazelnut trees up there. She wore the hot, fur-lined leather gloves to pick, warning the children to only point them out for her, not touch them. With them pointing she picked as fast as she could grab and soon had a knapsack full. That evening she singed off the brownish husks by laying them near hot coals, scooping them away with the pancake turner before the shells scorched. Tucking them away, she gloated at finding an easier way to do another tedious chore.

It was too soon to dig roots so she did neglected camp chores. The tent was cluttered with dust, ash, wood scraps, bugs and cobwebs. Using the makeshift broom to whisk litter off the packed dirt floor, she scowled at big mousy droppings and relentlessly swept out small, brightly colored stones Amy must have brought in.

Dishwater heated while she shook clothes and bedding outside and swept away cobwebs. Washing the few dishes, she realized she'd cooked very little in the heat. It was so easy just to chew on a piece of jerky and nibble a few berries.

Drying the last dish, she realized some silverware was missing. She searched every inch inside then, feeling closer and closer to panic at not finding a single irreplaceable fork or spoon, searched outside. Totally annoyed and unable to imagine what else could have happened, she scolded the kids for playing with and losing the utensils.

"And find someplace besides the middle of the floor to leave your precious rocks!"

Two sets of wide eyes focused on her, expressing only bewilderment.

She plunked down by the smoldering fire and sipped the dregs of adulterated coffee to calm down. How could she replace those utensils? She used to have wooden spoons, but what kind of wood were they made from? It was strong, didn't splinter and had no resin taste. Carving anything with a stout skinning knife would be difficult, at best. Finding the missing ones would be much easier.

Searching outside again, she saw more rodent droppings, too big for mice, too small for rabbits—rat size. Stunned, she remembered hearing Packrats stole shiny things to take to their nest and left something in its place—she might be able to recover them. But what did a Packrat nest look like, and how could she find it?

Determined not to lose more, she poked a hole in a tall empty can and hung it on the ceiling pole with fish line, to hold the remaining utensils.

That night, in bright light from a nearly full moon, she silently watched from her cot for any motion on the shadowy dirt floor. Her eyelids had grown unbearably heavy when a faint scurry jolted her wide awake, heart hammering. Stifling terror, not moving, eyes straining against the dimness, she finally spotted a fluffy-tailed creature slightly bigger than a city rat.

Trembling, she watched it nose around the indoor hearth, sure that cramping muscles would force her to move before it found the shiny teaspoon left for bait. A white agate glowed in place of the spoon as the small beast shuffled importantly out the door with the spoon flashing moonlight. And she thought the children were storing those treasures! She felt mean for scolding them as she tiptoed out to follow the fluffy white tail in bright moonlight, nearly stumbling until her legs stopped cramping. She tracked it through shadowy places by faint rustles. Far into the east woods she lost track of it.

But she'd come this far, she wouldn't quit now. Standing still, she strained to hear any sound, scanning bright areas first then, slowly, the darker depths. She listened until her ears hummed and looked until her eyes watered, but . . . nothing. Did they dig a burrow? Or did they construct a nest?

Defeated, she heaved a big sigh—and nearly choked. Barely breathing while searching, she nearly gagged now on an overpoweringly foul stench. Gasping, she fled, but paid sharp attention to where she was, scuffing a foot now and again to mark the way so she could return in daylight—she refused to argue with a bunch of rats, Packrats or not, over anything in the middle of the night!

Early, armed with a stout stick and all the courage she could muster, she returned via her scuffed trail. In daylight, the Bushytailed Wood rat's elaborate stick nest, built over and around a long-fallen trunk among low bushes, was obvious.

"Give me back my silverware!" She snarled, stabbing the stick's sharp end into the tangled nest, prying and twisting to break it apart as savagely as she'd speared the salmon that refused her bait.

She jumped and shrieked when rats darted away, each in its own direction. The largest turned back and briefly stared at her from the edge of thick brush. With unusual clarity and fear's heightened awareness, she was shocked to see its face was not ratty, more like a muskrat or squirrel. It was rather pretty, covered in gold-brown fur with dainty white feet and chest, and a white bushy tail more like a shorter-haired squirrel's than any rat's. Its perky ears were also more like squirrel's, but slightly bigger. Only its bulgy eyes looked rat-like.

"How can anything look so pretty but smell so bad?" She grumbled. Cringing, she pried and tore sticks away until she found the hoard of missing items in the fetid, long-inhabited nest. Ammonia fumes made her eyes burn and her nose run. She hurried away, gasping fresh air.

In camp, she scrubbed them with syrupy lye soap and sand. Her first attempt at making soap had thickened poorly, but cleaned effectively. Despite the heat, she stoked the fire to boil the silverware to be sure using it was safe. Drying them, she saw worn areas in the silver-plate; it still had to be replaced, just not so soon.

The next most urgent thing to do, during a short lull in food gathering, was to make bigger, warmer clothes for both children. In dimming twilight she tucked them into bed and stoked the fire up enough to see by. Pulling out duffel bag scraps left from repairing the cots, she basted together an outline of her foot, using fish line. If she could fit herself, she could scale that down for the youngsters. If the fit was wrong she had only to snip the end knot to try it differently, saving line and canvas.

Darkness and fatigue forced her to wait until daylight to refine her own fit. She slept poorly that short summer night, dreaming fragments of making her own moccasins. The dream rehearsal clarified details so, before noon, she found a good fit for herself. Only then did she cut the heavy canvas down to narrow seam allowances.

She undid her pattern and reduced it to fit Ted's foot, then reduced his for Amy. She used the canvas patterns to cut moccasin pieces from the thick, sturdy ewe hide. Because her only scissors were from the tiny sewing kit, she laid the hide over the breadboard to carve with the freshly sharpened knifepoint. No remaining needles reached through the leather so she used the sharp meat fork tines to poke holes around the edges, then worked stiff fish line through those holes.

While sewing the children's moccasins, she thought about how often she'd needed dry footwear, and had only her boots to wear. Only the men had brought a change of footwear. Thinking of her boots wearing out, she tried on the men's. Edward's were far too big but, by wearing extra socks, Eddie's would fit her in an emergency.

Digging through that bag, she decided to try on some of the men's clothes. Eddie's olive-drab combat jacket was too big, but might work if her coat was ever soaked, and it would fit over her own for extreme cold.

Edward's coat was too big for her to get her arms out the sleeves but was made of many layers. She needed material to sew kids' clothes, and it had plenty.

In that bag she found the forgotten wool. The smallest part of it was clean and combed, the rest unwashed. She'd gathered the dirty wads the day she shot the ewe and had tucked it away and forgotten it.

"I have to do this, too." She groaned, tucking it back away for now.

Though sad at how the men's clothes had become spares, she was glad to have that material. Some of Eddie's clothes fit her with little alteration, like her summer outfit. She stacked the largest denim pants, flannel and wool shirts and Army surplus fatigues in a pile with Edward's coat to take apart.

Most of the sewing kit thread had been used for repairs so, while taking garments apart she saved all useful thread, refilling the small spools, sorted by thread strength, not color.

On her cot, she piled scraps of cloth by type: flannel, denim, wool, fatigue twill, and pocket or waistband linings. When one pair of Edward's pants and two of his shirts were apart, enough thread was recovered to start sewing. She studied the shape change of the two sizes and mentally scaled them down to fit the children, with lots of room to grow. Using Ted's outgrown pants to find the minimum length and width, she cut reclaimed material, doing Ted's first so if she was wrong, she could reduce it for Amy. The knife left poor, ragged edges. Hide was easier to cut evenly.

With only adult sized zippers, she puzzled over how to fasten the new pants. She finally put waist darts in that could be let out later, for growth, and overlapped the front with wide flaps and ties. Now no zipper was needed. She made the legs straight but loose and hemmed deeply, to let down later; much easier than making new ones!

Reclaiming cloth, cutting, and sewing took a whole day to make one pair of pants. The next day she made a second pair for Ted and two for Amy from his outgrown ones. Stitch by tedious stitch went so slowly she wished for her good scissors and treadle sewing machine. But they were hundreds of miles away, at what used to be home.

Using their pull-over pajama tops for patterns, she made shirts with straight, loose sleeves ending in snug, narrow cuffs. Unable to figure out how to make adequate buttonholes with these needles, she also put ties at the top and midway down the center of overlapping neck openings that reached halfway down the front.

Stitching the last of two shirts each, Marty fretted about nearly being out of thread again, and supposed there must be a lot of it in the unused chutes in the plane. They'd never be needed for anything but salvage. And, opened out, a canopy would be big enough to dry a lot of berries at once. She sat bolt upright: one could even be tied up off the ground by its shroud lines, so food dried faster. Each chute had several long shroud lines—just those lines would be very useful—and a canopy was useful for many things besides drying berries or taking apart for thread.

She was so excited it was hard to fall asleep that night. She slept lightly and woke early, leaving for the plane as soon as growing light allowed her to see the path.

By the time she started climbing the steep slope, painful memories rushed at her with each step. But she had to salvage the parachutes. She clenched her jaw and forced herself on. She'd done this before and could do it again for such a worthy cause.

She pulled four chute packs, each with a tangle of OD, thickly woven cotton straps and zinc-plated buckles, from the open gash in the plane's nose. Why were there four, not more, not less?

Each bulky chute weighed nearly twenty pounds, but she refused to make two trips again. With two buckled together and slung over her shoulders, one in front, the other in back, she dragged the other two clear back to camp. She'd had to stop three times to unburden and rest, but only had to make the one trip.

Panting and trembling with fatigue, she dropped them by the tent door to brew coffee mix and cook breakfast for the hungry children. After eating, she examined a pack. It was duck fabric, very tough and durable. Tugging and pulling various places, she finally discovered the ripcord ring. It took a definite yank to make it come loose, but when it did, the whole pack fell open.

Four sets of three shroud lines connected the harness to the neatly tucked and folded canopy. Each slender, braided cotton shroud line was fifteen feet long—she'd find lots of uses for those!

Grabbing an edge of the canopy she backed off, further and further. It was astonishingly huge. Spreading the silk all the way out, she stepped off paces—it was twenty-four feet across! And all the many seams were machine lock-stitched, the easiest of any to remove without breaking. One canopy had enough thread to sew dozens of garments!

Feeling she'd found a treasure trove, Marty nearly sobbed with relief. These four chutes would yield plenty of material and thread, even with rapidly growing children. She was disappointed to see the eighteen-inch wide central canopy opening, reinforced by a rubber ring. That hole had to be closed before using it to dry berries or they'd fall through.

By noon, a foot-long stick was wound to the thickness of her wrist with sturdy thread in long, long pieces. She was ecstatic. Once started, the lock stitch unraveled without breaking and, for each foot undone, yielded about three feet of thread. When one canopy was undone, she sewed storage bags from several of the wedge-shaped gores of thin, fine-woven silk.

For now the other chutes were left unopened. She coiled shroud lines to store in the emptier clothes bag with the wool; she'd need them eventually. Surely each pack's tangle of cotton webbing, buckles, and frame would also prove worth saving—each and every item here from the old world had assumed new importance.

Marty was finally forced to haul stream water, dipped from above the pond's staleness. Adding that toilsome chore to her morning routine, she moped about having so many strenuous, time-consuming chores to do every day, like getting wood, and water, and food for the day . . . and worst of all, the sheep jerky was nearly gone. They'd snacked it all away in less than a month when it should have lasted more than two. Now she had to hunt another big animal. Smoked salmon was strictly for winter, when they couldn't fish. She'd shamefully wasted the hard-won meat when she should have been snaring more rabbits, birds or muskrats.

The next morning, while her world was still a hazy, grayish blur, she set bird snares in the meadow, sturdier ones for muskrats by the pond, and more for rabbits near the pond trail. She dreaded eating more rabbit but shrugged, that meat would dry, too.

Now she had widely spaced snares to check twice a day, plus a half-mile loop to haul water. Life had already been busy. Time, and a growing sense of urgency pressured her until she began to feel guilty and edgy if she wasn't busy every minute, almost couldn't bear to do only one thing at once.

Since she was out checking snares in dawn's and dusk's soft light, when game moved the most, she took the short rifle to hunt along the way. On the morning snare-checking loop, she left the buckets at the stream on the way out, swinging near enough to see the pond snares. Then she rounded the meadow's center to check bird snares, alert for larger game. She cut back across to check rabbit snares and ended up back at the stream to fill the pails to lug to camp with the light rifle slung over a shoulder. The late loop was the same, without the pails, but in reverse order.

Not forced to wait for the children, the loop took about an hour. Faint trails were now familiar, her body hardened by months of continual activity, her stride long and confident but off-the-heel soft, even in boots, so she'd scare no game away. Though sign was plentiful, she never saw any, and wondered why.

Gazing over the lush meadow as early breezes rippled heavy-headed grass, she noticed the wind direction. Dad had discussed wind directions with her brothers before a hunt, and how to stay downwind so they didn't spook the game. With that in mind, she studied the wind's pattern and direction. It blew mostly from west to east. Occasional short gusts swirled back toward the west cliffs from near the meadow's center. Rather than her usual route, she'd be less detectable by approaching from north or south. Routes can be changed, she smirked.

Three muskrats were in pond snares that day, and two the next, with the bigger one barely half grown. Each adult weighed around four pounds, but the last two were barely a pound each. The muskrats needed time to grow—she wasn't hungry enough to eat baby animals. She took down the pond snares. Rabbit and bird snares would do until she could get bigger game.

Now she had several various-sized muskrat pelts, the biggest eighteen inches long by nearly as wide. She was still unsure what to do with them but even the summer fur was thick and soft, more so now than the earlier ones. Thankful for her habit of wasting nothing, she knew she'd find use for them.

All the muskrats had thick body fat, which she needed to replenish lard going rancid in summer heat.

Returning from evening rounds, she paused to pull off and chew a plump grass seed. It was tough and tasted . . . grainy. Not knowing what unripe grain would taste like, she thought they looked big enough and dry enough to harvest. The outer husk wouldn't chew up so she spit it out; that would have to be removed, somehow.

After her morning loop, followed by rambunctious youngsters, Marty took both knapsacks to strip grain into. How much did she need to harvest?

In four months they'd used less than the twenty-five pound bag of flour she'd brought, but she'd been very frugal with it. The kids ate more now and their appetites would continue to grow. They all ate more meat, nearly the same amount of vegetables, and much less flour and cereal than at first. So, two or three pillowslip-size silk bags should be plenty for a year. But that would still only about double the combined flour, rice, oatmeal and cornmeal they'd brought.

Determined to get plenty, day after day she picked any grain she could find, all kinds in together, spending hours tediously filling one knapsack. That rather small amount was unexpectedly heavy. She stripped grain until her fingers were raw and one big duffel bag was over half full—and almost too heavy to move. This would have to be enough, she could find no more anywhere in the valley.

To get rid of the sharp awns and hulls, she rubbed a few grains at a time across the breadboard with a gloved palm. But she still had to figure out how to separate them from the grain, and how to make chunks for cereal and fine powder for flour. After struggling overnight to recall everything she knew, the next morning she spread the ground cloth and tried to winnow grain in a slight breeze so the tarp caught it. Most of the chaff floated off to the side. The mostly-hulled grain went into a small silk bag. She'd work on it as she could, this would be a longer process than she could do now. Other things urgently needed doing.

The shrinking days cooled gradually, the nights more quickly. One morning was so chilly Marty needed a full set of clothes and even an extra shirt. The kids could barely squeeze into their coats. Coats took so many layers to make . . . she looked at rubbed-smooth fingertips that were tender and pink from stripping grain. She didn't want to sew that much, not yet. The children slept the coldest part of the day, while she checked snares and hunted. If she lit the inside fire at night, they'd stay warm until night's chill dissipated soon after sunup. Then they wouldn't need a coat. She could let her fingers heal before making the coats.

On the loop before filling water buckets the next morning, she looked to see if other berries were ripe. Dark blueberries, translucent Red Huckleberries, pale-powdered Blue Huckleberries, blue-powdered purple Oregon Grapes, and apple-red Kinnikinnick berries made her mouth water.

Marty and both children spent a whole day picking ripe berries, tossing all types in the small pail. It was nearly full when they quit in late afternoon. While they picked the next day, birds, squirrels and mice pilfered berries drying on the tarp, breadboard and flat rock back at camp. Only their return scattered the raiders.

Half of what had been spread to dry was gone or ruined by droppings. She had the kids stay to chase away thieves while she hurried out to pick more. The hungry children ate many of the berries before they were full.

While grabbing more berries, she saw fresh bear prints by a stripped and bent Huckleberry bush. Heart pounding in panic, she rushed back to the kids. But they were safe, their faces and fingers smeared with incriminating berry stains. She was too relieved at their safety to be very mad about all the fruit they'd eaten.

Rifle in hand, she checked the area around camp for bears, then opened a new chute canopy, hung it folded in half, and poured berries to dry in between layers, safe even from birds.

She kept the kids near her, except to haul water and a quick jog to check snares twice a day. Picking berries, she paused often to listen for telltale grunts, but never heard any.

They also picked half a knapsack of hazelnuts from the upper valley, but most were culls. What they'd first picked would have to be enough.

Smelling onion after stepping on one reminded her of harvesting those while they would dry well. She dug one to check its readiness, and was pleased to see it was fat and juicy. She knew where lots and lots of onions were but didn't want to dig them all with the precious knife. She rubbed oniony hands across her face; what else could she use?

Later, searching the tent for a digging tool, she found the spit bar—that would work.

She spent the next day in the meadow prying up potent bulbs, getting many pounds while the kids romped noisily nearby. The day after, she filled the knapsack from the upper valley, and a second one from farther out in the meadow. But, being a farm girl, she always left enough to reseed next year, and scattered any seeds she found.

Squinting against the robust fumes, she spread the small bulbs to dry in the sun near the tent, and minced the hollow leaves to dry for seasonings.

CHAPTER 16

Nights were now so cool Marty kept a fire inside, stoked it to cook supper and sit beside for a while, banked it for night, rebuilt it for breakfast and brew her drink mix, then banked it for the day. Days also cooled abruptly, enough she had to wear a jacket all day. The children were so active they stayed warm without coats, with a double shirt layer.

They missed going barefoot. The youngsters liked the moccasins she made but halved laces from Edward's boots had to be added to tighten the tops or they fell off. The rawhide soles easily became soggy so she made a second pair to wear while wet ones dried, then rubbed in lard for water resistance.

At sunrise, dipping water from the shrunken stream above the pond, Marty saw a moon sliver in the rosy eastern sky. A New Moon, already. Frowning, counting on her fingers; it must now be September eleventh. Time was going by much too fast!

No leaves had changed color but winter was near. Most leaves looked old, a tired, faded green, others were drab yellow-brown and withered. Marty shivered with dread. Soon snow would hide everything, including food plants. She wondered: how much is enough?

Scattered, steel gray clouds thickened soon after sunrise, brought drizzly rain. Distraught at this interruption in drying masses of onions and shriveling berries, she raced to take them in, glad the chopped onion tops were safely dry and stored.

They stayed in the tent, unhappy but not chilled by getting wet. Marty was too tired to be very upset at a day's harvesting delay, but hated being idle. For days in a row she'd walked the valley to dig onions and pick scattered berries, and twice a day had jogged the full snare line, which had produced only an occasional muskrat. She fretted at wasting precious harvest time, haunted by picturing aged, snowy leaves.

Restless and impatient, though weary, the need to care for all she'd gathered registered. Unsure where to start, she edged around the cluttered tent, shifting silk bags and stomping on scurrying bugs. She dipped into the partly filled bag of hulled grain, letting seeds trickle between fingers, puzzled at how to make flour from such hard chunks. It had been done, so there was a way—but how?

Gram said her grandmother ground roots, seeds and grains by rubbing and pounding them between two rocks. A smaller rock was pushed and pulled against a larger bottom rock—preferably one with a dip worn into its top—to grate and crush the bits fine. Marty braved the cold drizzle to gather two fairly flat rocks, smaller than the heavy one she had, and rinsed them off outside.

Grinding stones worked better on cattail roots than crushing with the hatchet; none shot off in all directions, wasted, and tough fibers worked out the sides. But hard grain took far more pressure to break up and much longer to grind fine.

She held the small rock by its ends to avoid scraping her fingers and leaned forward to press as she pushed and pulled it over the grain, now and then twisting the top rock and leaning hard. It was an effort but she could see that using those rocks was quite effective.

When a double handful of grain was finely powdered she scooped it up and put it in the flour sack. For a whole year they'd need at least double that bag full of grain.

She hoped what she'd picked—all she could find—would last the year. Arms and shoulders throbbing, she looked for what to do next. Other foods had to be harvested now, but what would she store them in?

The partly full silk bags all looked alike and she always had to look in each one to find what she wanted. None stacked well and shifted unpredictably, often spilling. Even her lousy basket wouldn't do that. She should weave baskets, however poor, while it rained. She dared a quick dash to the pond to gather cattail leaves and long willow shoots. Pond Lily seeds must be ready now, and she had to get lots more Arrowhead tubers. Rain would freshen the pond enough to dive for tubers—much faster than loosening them from the raft with a stick.

Puffing, she toweled her hair and glared at her first pathetic basket, tucked in a corner. The fishing creel was woven wicker, similar to willow shoots; she studied every detail of its material and weave before trying to make another.

Cold drizzle continued for two more days. It was too wet to go out except for a quick dash to get water and check nearby rabbit snares, the only ones still set. She focused on learning to weave better, quickly finding there was more to it than she would have guessed without trying it. Some failures had round bottoms and sat crooked, others grew lopsided if she pulled the weave tighter on one side, making that whole side lower.

She found problems with sturdiness and how to bend corners without breaking a thick stay, causing a weak spot or hole. Some withes were too thick to bend enough to weave except so loosely the basket would only hold items Hazelnut-size or larger. Or the material, like one woven from thin willow bark, was so flimsy it was limp, more a floppy sack than a basket. It was important to choose materials for each container's sturdiness to hold a specific food—how could she foresee that?

Making baskets for farm food would be no problem, but out here? Not the same. The whole process was frustrating. Weaving should be simple! Like knitting.

Her best basket was barely acceptable but had to be good enough, she had no more time now. Even poor ones would hold roots and tubers she didn't want mixed together.

The rain stopped but the air stayed chilly from an overcast gray sky that made the valley—her entire world—seem bleak. She eagerly returned to harvesting, despite the bleakness and, still afraid the bears might find the youngsters alone, took them along. After three days of confinement they were ecstatic at a chance to run off pent-up energy.

Ted proudly carried newly gathered food in his knapsack. Marty was glad to let him.

They stopped to watch squirrels cut newly ripened pine, spruce and fir cones, then toss them down to collect and cache when each tree was stripped.

They were astounded when a slim-bodied Pine Martin appeared, and gaped as the lightning-fast hunter ran down a darting squirrel in a brief, frenzied treetop chase. The Martin paused to glare at them, dark eyes glistening triumph, the hapless squirrel dangling from its jaws, then hopped feather-light into shielding branches.

For a dozen hammering heartbeats Ted froze in horror—another friend was dead—then wilted into wracking sobs. Shocked at his intense grief over a silly squirrel, Marty silently held him and patted his back. Amy sniffed in pouty-lipped sympathy and hugged him.

Even after resuming harvesting many hours each day, every evening Marty worked at weaving baskets, briefly. Nights were longer now but not enough to stay up late and still rise at dawn's first glow so every minute of daylight was spent on work impossible to do after dark.

Nights grew colder under cloudless skies, so she relined their cots with sleeping bags so they stayed warm underneath. Each day, shortly before sunset, dank, wispy fog formed near the stream, pond and lower meadow, persisting until midmorning on overcast days. On clear days the fog burned into high, thin clouds soon after sunrise.

Even cloudless, the sky stayed a depressing steely-gray that made the air seem smoky. She soon realized the gray haze was fine dust blown up by increasingly blustery winds in autumn's dryness, despite the recent drizzle. A baby powder-fine layer coated everything, even in the tent, out of the wind. Trees and bushes, now dusty, looked even older, more faded and dry than a few days earlier. Some leaves drooped, others curled under at the edge; Marty thought they must also mourn the end of warm weather.

Noting all that on the way to the pond, she frantically dived to loosen Arrowheads from thick mud. The pond smelled fresher, but was already uncomfortably cold to swim in and each loosened plant added silt to cloud nearly motionless water. She pulled all she could find then, shivering, gathered an armload of the floating plants to pile on shore. While the children splashed nearby she searched the tangle for tubers, piling them on the barren shore strip.

Calling the children to warm in the sun, she wrung the last water from her hair and replaced the braided cattail-leaf headband to keep wet hair off her face. She changed into dry clothes, then scooped the tubers into a silk bag while the children dressed.

In the meadow, using the spit bar to pry them from hard, dry soil, she gathered roots and bulbs while Ted and Amy played tag, screeching delight when one tagged the other.

Wild carrots, now at their largest, were as thick as her thumb at the top, tapering to a sharp tip, skimpy despite being as long as cultivated carrots. But they were a familiar link to her past and no matter how skimpy, she cherished the taste.

Dandelion, Chicory and Yampa formed taproots bigger than wild carrots. Though she gathered Chicory to roast for her morning drink, the Yampa was her favorite. Raw, they tasted carroty but cooked, they were more like parsnips.

Tomorrow she'd pick blue and Kinnikinnick berries, then get the Pond Lily seedpods from the raft. She'd look for Sorrel and Mustard seeds along the way, but could only gather so much at once. Part of each day had to be used to sort and dry foods then, when dry, store somewhere in the increasingly crowded tent.

At bedtime she stepped out to get morning wood. Twilight was chilly and damp, with swirling mists glowing white from the nearly Full Moon's pallid light. She gasped and ran for the date marker—had she marked the last New Moon? Only four lines; scowling, she etched a new one. Her heart thumped. She couldn't lose track of the month, when at home she always knew the date and day! Too many comfortingly familiar things had suddenly and irrevocably been stripped from her life; allowing more was intolerable.

That short night was filled with vague dreams of people and things she'd lost by being stranded here. Her unconscious response to those dreams was to feel more compulsive about collecting food. She even gathered a large duffel bag full of fresh-cut, sticky green cones, though she felt guilty for taking more squirrel food.

She didn't taste any cone seeds but recalled the bland nuttiness of the weathered cone's only remaining seed last spring. The sticky pitch liberally coating the cones attracted dirt like a magnet to her skin and clothes, and was hard to remove. Lye soap worked, but lard dissolved pitch best. Only, she still had to use soap to dissolve the lard. She was happy to dump the cones in the two biggest baskets, so poorly made she gladly designated them as throw-aways. She'd think about how to get to the seeds later, no time or energy for that now.

Storage problems worsened. Assorted silk bags of all sizes filled the space under or on both back and side cots—she needed more stackable baskets. The year's last fruits, seeds and roots were ready now.

Daily she grew wearier from relentless physical drudgery as she forced herself to tramp through the long, steep valley to pick or pry out various foods, or dive in the pond for others, and then lug heavy, unwieldy, hard-won loads back over rough, circuitous and often overhung trails. Still, she stayed up late each night to make more baskets. Each took many evenings to finish and was slightly better made but, even now, none were very good.

Toiling to gather every edible plant she could find, Marty worried about their winter meat supply. Dad always butchered during cool weather. The snares had been yielding nothing for all the effort it took to set, move and check them. So, in spite of feeling as tired as the leaves looked, in addition to her many other chores, she was again up and out to hunt at dawn's first hint. She'd welcome more rabbit skin tubes for storage, and gladly eat their meat again.

The third morning of also hunting, so exhausted it was hard to get up and moving, she groggily dressed before disturbing the banked fire. She checked that the lever-action rifle was loaded and left, hoping the predawn chill would help her wake up.

She groped through misty gloom, past gray and tarnished silver plant shapes, edging along the path to the mist-shrouded stream burbling into the pond. Guided more by sound than sight, she stepped upstream toward the sluggish pool where she filled the buckets, and saw faint glints on the gravelly shore. Jerky, wavering, disconnected spots of silvery glint.

Suddenly wide awake, she held steamy breath and peered through fog to watch moisture seep into narrow, split-toed tracks sunk into wet sand and fine gravel.

Deer tracks!

Tense and alert, she watched water fill the tracks in jumps and jerks. The deer had been here only seconds ago! Barely daring to breathe she slowly peered into thick mist. Faint stirs in brush across the stream filtered through sound-muting fog. She stared that direction, heart thumping madly and hands sweaty despite the fog's penetrating chill. It was still nearby!

Another crackle, the exact location hard to pinpoint. A breeze swirled mist into vortexes of thicker fog, leaving thin wisps of clear air to twist to silvery oblivion. She glimpsed furtive motion in dense willows on the far bank before thick mist returned.

Exhaling softly, she waited for another thinning to aim and shoot, body strung tight with tension, fearing any sound might warn of her presence. And intent.

Her scalp prickled—she'd forgotten to bring the buckets! But the metallic rattle would have scared the deer away before she saw it—first time she'd forgotten them.

She slipped the sling off her shoulder, trembled as she aimed toward the deer's sound, and saw she hadn't cocked it! No shell in the chamber, either, and so she had to work the lever—so much noise would scare it away!

With a thumping heart, she heard the marsh erupt in a strident din of squawks and honks, quickly worked the lever and palmed back the hammer, straining to hear any sound from the far bank—nothing.

Fog swirled again, clearing briefly to her right. She heard a rustle straight ahead. Taking a deep, silent breath, she waited for the break in thinning mists, teeth gritted to steady shaky hands, thinking she'd done this before, she could do it again.

A puff of breeze split the fog across the stream, following the south bank's brushy hedge. She took aim at where the deer should be, caught a quick glimpse of it staring toward the pond, spike-antlered head high and big ears cocked, adjusted her aim and fired. The shot's flat crack seemed deadened by fog as the deer convulsed in the instant before fog intervened.

Her heart pounded wildly—did she only wound it? She levered in a new shell and cocked quickly. She jerked the gun up to aim a second shot as a following swirl briefly thinned the mist but the erect flag-tail disappeared behind thick brush. Unable to see, she strained to listen, heard the wounded spike crash down, its fog-shrouded position marked by desperate thrashing.

Edging closer, knowing it would flee if it could, she huffed in exhilaration. This made all those fruitless trips carrying the rifle worthwhile. She wiped a sweaty hand down her jacket, over the forgotten pistol on her belt, and felt stupid for going clear to camp for the rifle to shoot the ewe and lugging a rifle all this time when she always wore the pistol—she could've snuck closer and shot the ewe with that! Planning to hunt she'd brought the rifle today but had become so used to wearing the pistol she'd forgotten it. Would she soon forget she carried the rifle, too?

Letting things get so familiar she forgot them was dangerous! She'd held a forgotten club while the hawk tore the snared rabbit in half in front of her. Visions of being attacked by some beast and not remembering she wore a gun made her shudder.

Listening for the wounded deer—it was dangerous to go near too soon—she tipped her head forward to ease an aching neck, and saw she was halfway across the stream. Her feet were dry. It was very shallow here! Salvaging parachutes, she'd gone clear to the mid-pool to cross, following that path from habit when she could have cut off over a mile each way by crossing here. Anything getting so familiar it became a mindless habit caused waste and serious danger out here!

The wounded animal's thrashing finally stopped so she dared to push through thick, fog-soaked brush to find it, then nervously slit its throat. She cleaned it where it lay in the thrashed-out space—no nearby large trees here, either. She paused to stretch kinked back muscles and evaluate her routine for what else needed to be done a better way. Reason and forethought eased so many tasks.

Get rid of all the dead weight first, this time, she thought. Too much of the sheep was bone and waste. Considering what parts to leave, she eyed the young deer with its first set of spike antlers. Slightly taller than the ewe, it was much leaner, not much over half the ewe's weight. Almost light enough to carry; getting it to camp would be so much easier if she could. But more had to be trimmed away first.

The lower legs were so thin they were mostly tendons and bone, but she need all the hide she could get. Already the kids' moccasin soles were wearing thin. She didn't need all the bones and could leave the rifle while getting the short saw to cut bones. Hurrying to camp, she remembered she had to get water, too. But meat came first.

She stripped leg skin back until she found enough meat to bother with and sawed vigorously, cut the head off, then the tail. Already the saw was noticeably dull. She tucked the heart and liver back inside with a few chunks of fat off the intestines, and bent to lift the carcass to her shoulder. She growled aloud—nothing was left to get a grip on! So much for finding a better way to do things!

After several strenuous tries, she finally got the unwieldy carcass up over a shoulder and clutched all four empty leg skins to hold it there. Panting, she pushed through brush, skidded down into the streambed, slipped and stumbled up the other bank and struggled along the worn path to camp.

So exhausted she nearly collapsed when releasing twisted leg skin, she was convinced carrying it had been easier than dragging. But this spike, stripped of all possible waste, was the absolute limit of what she could carry.

She sat to rest. Considering how fast they ate the mutton and how much it shrank in drying—it would take many times more than this to get them through a whole winter.

Stoking the fire and putting coffee mix to brew, she used the last stale water to clean up, changed into a clean shirt, wiped blood off her jacket and hung it on a cupboard near the fire to dry, then plodded down to fill buckets, shivering without the jacket. She got the saw and checked snares on the way by. Still empty. Surely they hadn't eaten all the rabbits in the valley! She removed the snares to reset elsewhere.

Deciding not to hang the deer to cut it up—nothing was left to hang it with—she laid it out by the drying rack where fire was forming smoky coals and skinned back the hide on top to slice meat off the whole side. Crowded on, those thin slices filled half the rack. She rolled the carcass over with the stripped bones on the ground and did the other side. The meat boiled off the sheep bones hadn't been worth the time and work.

The convoluted spine sections had enough meat to boil off, along with any bits too small for the rack.

She vigorously scraped the worst of the unwanted tissue off the hide but had no time or energy to do more now so she spread it over bushes to dry.

By mid-afternoon the diced heart was simmering with the scraps and spine. Dandelion roots and Arrowhead tubers roasted at the fire's edge. She quick-fried thick liver slices when the roots were tender.

By the time they finished eating day was fading, plenty of fuel was stacked nearby, and the rack fires replenished with wood too green to flame up and overheat the meat. It had taken most of the day to get the smoky fire right. If she took the meat in for the night it would take most of tomorrow to get the coals right again but if she kept guard all night it should be dry in about one more day. It had taken over three days before, days she'd been stuck in camp to guard it, unable to harvest anything. She was worn out from the hectic pace, but she could do this, had to.

She hugged and kissed each child and sent them to bed. Drained, she sat down and leaned against a young alder near the rack to guard it. Too weary to weave baskets, she thought if she sat still a while she'd be rested enough to guard the meat all night.

Later, when rising moonlight brightened the roof, Ted awoke and rubbed bleariness from his eyes. Marty's cot next to him was flat and empty. He heard nothing. Frightened, he went out to find her, shivering in night's chill. He saw her sitting near the drying rack and trotted over to sit by her, holding his hands out to catch warmth from smoldering coals. Turning to say he was glad he found her, he saw her eyes closed and her mouth hanging open. Her head sagged against the trunk and her breathing was deep and steady. She was asleep! Sitting up!

Ted covered his mouth to muffle soft giggles. Sometimes Marty was funny!

He huddled quietly, comforted by her presence even as she slept. He shivered. He didn't want Marty to get cold so he went in and got a blanket to drape around her—as she'd done for him a hundred times—gently, so she wouldn't wake. He tucked it snug and ran back to his warm bed. But he was afraid to stay in the dark tent without Marty. He led Amy, more asleep than awake, out next to the slumbering woman, wrapped the girl in the other wool blanket then snuggled against her warmth under the cover. He fell asleep immediately.

Marty woke and sat bolt upright, blinking the world into focus. She was surprised at her cover, positive she'd just sat down a short while ago without it. She leaned forward to stretch oddly kinked muscles then saw the kids snuggled under the other blanket beside her. She saw growing, misty daylight—it was dawn!

Touched by figuring out what Ted had done, she rubbed her face and groaned.

"I did fall asleep." She whispered, looking around. Several chunks of meat were gone from the rack's far side. "Might as well have slept inside." She growled softly.

Later, sitting near the newly replenished fire's thick smoke, Ted gnawed a half-dry chunk of venison. He tipped his head thoughtfully. "Are dead animals meat?"

"Yes." Marty answered absently.

"Meat is food." He said.

"Yes. Probably the best food." Still absently.

"Are people animals?" Ted took another smoky nibble.

"Yes . . . sort of. Humans are a kind of animal." Marty listened closer.

"Are people meat?"

"Yes. Our bodies are made of meat." She felt vaguely alarmed.

"Are people food?"

Her whole body tingled with horror. "Anyone who eats another human is a cannibal! Cannibals are savages!" She shouted, "WE ARE NOT SAVAGES!"

"Oh." Ted nodded and ducked his head. He glanced covertly at her lip scar. It was bright red. He would not ask about that again.

Amy listened, chewing and sucking her meat as she looked from one to the other, gray eyes flashing with intense interest.

Marty thought, picturing her method of spearing the salmon, "I have resorted to being savage here, more than once, but at least not a cannibal-type savage.

Marty picked the big clusters of Elderberries and hung them over a branch to dry. So many small berries crowded the clusters it didn't matter if birds pilfered a few. She still wondered how much food was enough. The tent was already very crowded, all spaces under the cots stuffed with bags from nearly empty to nearly full and stacks of more-or-less filled, poorly formed baskets.

She was haunted by a dream of the tent bulging but still too small to hold all they needed to get through winter and until food was available in spring. The skeleton nightmare haunted her, kept reminding her of her vow not to be helpless, not to let the kids starve. The worry of being wrong about how much food they needed for half a year obsessed her, drove her to find and gather even foods that were past ripe, edible but no longer tender or tasty.

Though food was primary, it was not her sole concern. She cut and dried bundles of cattail leaves and thin, pliant willows for winter weaving. She laboriously dug or pulled up and rinsed more cattail roots. The sidewall tent became frustratingly crowded with newly gathered, unsorted food piled high in every space except next to the hearth, kept burning against the advancing cold. Some overflowed the canvas-flap doors and lay stacked outside, waiting to be cared for. No room was left inside to keep kindling or wood dry or handy; each day's supply had to be piled beside the door.

The woodpile they'd started was so depleted she had to cut more. Most wood was too far into the woods for Ted to drag in and they'd used all the nearby dry wood, even chunks too big for him to move. She sagged at being reminded of the need for winter fuel, but drove her aching body to search nearby woods for anything movable, seasoned or green, taking no time to cut up more than each day's supply, or to chop up big pieces. She was too exhausted for that.

Dragging load after load of long, wrist-thick or bigger limbs to camp, she tried to picture how much fuel they'd used in the warm half of the year. It would take much more to get through the cold half. How big would the pile be if she'd gathered it all at once? A whole winter was going to take a staggering amount of wood!

Wearily piling wood, some green, some dry, between the tent and the towering Fir, she put all pitchy pieces under those down-swept branches to stay dry. It was ten long strides from tent to tree. Surely that space would hold enough!

She vowed to gather more every day until snow prevented her from finding more.

But she was so very, very exhausted.

And so very, very afraid.

CHAPTER 17

Marty shivered awake despite wearing flannel pajamas inside a flannel sleeping bag liner, tightly wrapped in a wool blanket; it had been enough a few nights ago. Seeing breath cloud the air, heaviness filled her. She shivered through dressing in dank clothes to step out.

Overnight the year's first frost had turned birch, maple and aspen leaves to a riot of amber, gold, orange, bronze and red. A few bushes were nearly purple. Autumn tang freshened the air. She knew, heart pounding and knees shaking, she'd run out of harvesting time.

Frost shouldn't come yet! Pumpkin vines died at first frost, near Halloween. Seeing the sliver of New Moon rising in the east, she counted on her fingers; it should only be October eleventh, now. Too early!

The elevation! Winter came earlier up here; mountains always had snow before the farm got frost. Not too early, then. Snowy weather could set in any day.

She studied the frosted camp. Winter snow reminded her of the spring storm, being so cold, and of the tent roof sagging. So much more would fall in winter—how could the tent withstand that hard season and keep them warm? A shiver reminded her of needing firewood. She had to get so much before snow buried it. Dry shelter and warmth were as vital as food, and though she'd spent weeks getting food, she feared that was not enough.

She notched her date stick at the right time this month. Six marks—they'd been here half a year, the easy half to live through. The hard half was starting. Now.

Sitting on the log seat, shivering from icy drafts across the cluttered dirt floor, she glanced at the sleeping youngsters, thankful for the cots keeping them above the draft.

She sat extra-long to sip coffee mix and warm boot toes near comforting flames, trying to think of how to block drafts and keep the tent from collapsing from snow load.

A childhood blizzard had gone on and on until drifts covered halfway up the downstairs windows. Dad went out every couple hours all night to dig drifts away from the doors so they weren't trapped inside; her brothers took turns during the day. That had been near sea level, snow would be deeper here. Marty shuddered, recalling the bark-scarring teeth marks she'd seen high overhead last spring.

Too agitated to sit, she grabbed buckets and went to check rabbit snares. Still empty. She took them down, daily use of that path must have chased the game away. She'd reset them farther off. Again.

Filling buckets at the stream, she was startled to see how far south the sun now rose. How far south would the sun be by Winter Solstice? In deep winter would it even shine over the south cliffs or would the valley stay shady all day when the sun's warmth was most desperately needed to counter harsh cold?

She set bird snares up toward the scarp's north end, hoping the birds had moved to the sheltering woods. Along the meadow's northeast corner, near the half-downed maple a long quarter mile from camp, she also set several rabbit snares.

Being tilted hadn't killed the maple, half its roots remained buried. The rest, raggedly broken or ripped whole from mucky soil, now poked futilely into the air. The beautiful tree would die, though not this year. It reminded her of one she'd climbed as a child. Its impending death was another break with familiar ties.

Back inside, she worked the stalest grease into moccasins to keep the kids' feet dry, the only thing she had that might help, gloating at the job she'd done making them, even to getting and treating the hide and making the pattern.

Cutting the day's wood small enough to fit the fire pit, the steady *thwack, thwack* of the ax woke the kids from late sleep. A drowsy voice summoned "Mama?"

Marty set the wood inside and dressed her. Amy's jacket was hard to get on, but without it her other clothes were not warm enough. Besides hunting meat and cutting stacks of wood, warmer clothes had to be sewn for both youngsters—never enough time to do all that absolutely had to be done!

Ted was astounded at the new colors. They were like Halloween. His birthday and Trick or Treat came when leaves looked like this.

"Is it Trick or Treat time now? Daddy promised me a birthday party at Trick or Treat time." His lip trembled.

Marty gave him a hug. "I can fix a party for your fifth birthday. It's too important not to have one." She turned away bleakly, wondering how to keep that promise with what she had. So much for cutting wood all day.

Using the last irreplaceable sugar in cake batter, she knew that without eggs the cake would be crumbly but beat it longer to bind better. She cringed at forgetting Amy's birthday on October first—a few days ago. I forgot my own daughter's third birthday!

So this party would have to be for both, nothing was left to mix more cake batter.

The batter filled two greased mess kit lids that baked in the fold-up camp oven. She stirred a handful of dried berries into the last dribble of pancake syrup for topping.

The cake was flat and tough, but tasted great when drowned in the fruity syrup. Both children were ecstatic over the sweet cake and the Birthdays Party, Marty was sad that the sticky mess was the only present she could give. She felt terrible at forgetting, did that too often—had even forgot her own birthday in July.

She rubbed calloused palms across her face. Too much was too different out here! There were no familiar routines to remind her of things she'd never forgotten before. All her attention was required to keep them surviving.

Since all nearby small wood was gone she was forced to chop up big pieces, going into the nearby woods to find that. Using the freshly sharpened double-bitted ax, she relentlessly hacked whole fallen trees into logs small enough to laboriously drag in and tip up into a pile near the tent. Despite bone-aching weariness and broken blisters, she also chopped down young trees with four-to-six-inch-thick trunks for green wood to hold fire through lengthening nights. Green wood was much heavier than dry chunks and had to be chopped shorter to be moveable. She piled it separately between the Noble fir and the drying rack; it would also be needed to smoke meat when she got large game.

Her only effort to get food now was to check the snares twice a day, rifle in hand in case she saw something bigger. All day every day she spent cutting and hauling wood, one heavy awkward chunk at a time. Evenings, she sewed children's clothes by dim, flickering firelight, not weaving more baskets.

Following the shirt design, she pieced together oversized jackets, so they'd fit all winter. They had a layer of denim from men's pants, interlined with wool from the heaviest shirts, and faced with warm flannel or cotton from lighter shirts. Ties down the overlapping front held them closed. Using reclaimed material required so many seams that it took sewing every evening for nearly a week to make one coat.

During those grueling days of chopping and hauling wood, at every pause Marty watched colored leaves start to fall, Maple and Aspen first. Incessant wind varied from gentle sighs that swayed clinging leaves to hard gusty blasts that wrenched them loose and swept up those fallen to swirl with whispery rustles into deep piles under branches that daily grew more barren.

Any breeze rattled leaves. Loose ones fluttered with soft popping sounds as they struck branches on their erratic way down. Fir and pine needles, shaken loose by blustery wind, sounded like pattering rain. Stately cedars with frothy pea-green foliage underlined by lacy, ginger-colored dead sprigs shed until a coat of tarnished gold underlay each tree.

Seeing dead trees and branches became easier and thinning leaves allowed light into the dense forest, revealing a few asters and dandelions still in bloom as frantic, pollen-laden bees sped from one to another in a constant drone.

Like all children, these two reveled in noisily diving into or tunneling through crackling piles of dead leaves, playing with such constant shrieks and giggles they were easy to keep track of while Marty wielded the heavy ax.

As the last Aspen leaves flashed gold in fading autumn sunlight, accompanied by the boisterous youngsters' laughter, she could finally see the kaleidoscope of colors as beautiful. The distinct fall aroma made her wonder if Dad had won the County Fair's Blue Ribbon for his huge Hubbard squashes this year, as usual.

Several nights after the first frost a hard freeze iced their world with puffy white hoar. More leaves fell. Trees and bushes so familiar Marty considered them friends were suddenly strangers. Everything looked so different she felt disoriented, even in the most familiar places.

She undid the bird snares; they'd caught nothing in the woods, either. She had no idea where to trap birds. They weren't where they'd been. Most waterfowl had migrated out, but surely not all birds would. She realized she was no longer being awakened by birds greeting the day. When had that stopped?

She listened. The pond was spooky quiet. Straining, she heard faint, persistent, two-toned honks in unfamiliar stillness, sounds she'd heard many times. At last she looked up at a high flying flock of Canada Geese winging south in their unique V-form, their continual cries echoing in the hush. Heart aching, she wished she could fly away with her young trailing like the geese.

To her relief a rabbit snare caught one every few days. She didn't even mind eating them now, especially since they had a light fat layer. They were changing from brown to white, their bodies speckled with both as the dark hair fell out at a touch. Their oversize feet were covered with long thick hair, especially around the edges.

She hunted every morning. Though snares caught some meat, they needed much, much more. She carried the rifle with a shell chambered so she had only to palm the hammer back to fire. She handled the gun very carefully, it could fire with any hard bump, this way.

Out hunting in early morning fog, in sight of the fault's north end, Marty looked above the haze toward the towering promontory until she saw its sentinel trees at the cliff's brink. Slightly below that she was stunned to see dark shapes, barely recognizable as Bighorns, moving over rocky outcrops of the cliff face. They'd gone from the meadow to near the cliff top!

There was a way out! Her heart raced with excitement, feeling a desperate need to find that exit. Over and over she thought: the leaves are down so I can see better and we're all stronger. We walk long distances, even Amy. Now we could at least carry blankets and some food. It would be hard to leave all the food and wood she'd toiled so relentlessly to gather, but getting out mattered more.

All the next day she led cold, irritable youngsters around the edge of the deep upper valley, stopping often to study every inch of soaring, broken cliffs from every angle. Depressed but refusing defeat, with no idea where else to look, she went to bed that night determined to search again tomorrow. There had to be a place she missed!

The dream began as a memory of a childhood zoo visit. Her nose wrinkled at powerful odors, some worse than on the farm. She was fascinated by a shaggy, thin-legged gray wolf who trotted endlessly around and around the wire mesh boundaries of his concrete-floored cage, toenails clicking, clicking, his dripping tongue lolling as he panted, his slate-gray eyes desperate as he searched mechanically, mindlessly, for a way out. Then she was inside the cage, her toenails clicking, clicking, her dripping tongue lolling as she panted from endless circuits of her cage, desperate to find a way out, unable to accept the loss of the world she'd known.

Marty woke drenched in cold sweat and panting for real, feeling the caged wolf's lingering desperation. Frantic, she jumped up with hands so shaky she could barely hold the green hardwood poker to stoke the fire. Blanket-wrapped, she sat by the growing fire, rocking back and forth in agitation, horrified at the trapped wolf's plight—and her own. The wolf's pacing search did it no good, as her search had revealed no way to freedom. With a jolt she saw she'd done that same futile thing almost continually since the crash. She sobbed softly into deep, thick folds of warm blanket.

Finally she brewed soothing tea and sipped it with the thick blanket clutched tightly for defense against more than night chill. Startled, she understood the wolf had been alone in its cage, but she was not. She had two youngsters who needed her. Their lives depended solely on her, on how well she fed and sheltered them. She was ashamed at forcing them on her endless searches for the exit. She'd been unfair to drag them around the valley time after time, after time, when she'd long ago seen there was no way out.

But how did so many animals—bears, moose, and sheep—get in and out? Farm animals couldn't climb places she could. But these are wild animals, not tame ones who live with our help, she chided. They'd always lived in these conditions.

Marty envied animals their four legs, their claws, their bestial strength, fish for their ability to swim, birds for their freedom of flight. Human were inadequate by comparison. But, she reminded herself, on two weeks' food and temporary shelter she'd kept the three of them alive for over six months. She felt a little better about her survival ability, then.

At last able to crawl into bed she drowsed, vaguely aware of a soft steady wind and the tent flapping gently, soothingly. She woke suddenly, very cold. Clenching her jaw, she stepped out. A brisk, cold wind stung her face. A nearly Full Moon peeked between scattered black clouds, lighting a ghostly view of black naked branches poking from stark whiteness of new snow. Knowing winter was here and not, almost safely, just around the corner hurt, made breath come hard.

With sinking, thudding heart she knew this remote wilderness valley she could not escape would forever stay her entire world.

An inch of snow had fallen. At first delighted, the children were soon distressed by its shallowness. It wouldn't even form snowballs but was surprisingly slippery, even with Marty's waffle-soled boots. By mid-morning it was melted to slush.

Tipping another hard-won log onto the pile, Marty shook ache from weary arms. A sudden crack echoed distantly through the forest, startling her. The distant sound came at odd intervals as she cut more wood. Eventually she grew worried enough to take the children and loaded rifle to look for the source. Since the slip-fault gave the best view of the valley she went to its north end, pausing at the top to listen.

Another crack resounded but she couldn't pinpoint its source. She edged along the worn path, alert to everything. The children, warned by her anxious scrutiny and stiffness, followed silently.

A flat *clack* sounded ahead, then huffing and snorting. Heart pounding madly at this unknown thing, Marty signaled wide-eyed kids to be quiet. She edged closer, unconsciously crouching to peer over a large boulder, and saw three does huddled together.

So excited she could barely breathe, Marty huddled near a leafless, twiggy bush, kneeling in slush to peer through. Ted and Amy crept up alongside and found gaps to peer through.

Two heavily antlered bucks struggled with heads down, antler to antler, twisting and bending, straining muscles rolling beneath sleek skin. One buck slipped in yielding slush and nearly fell, scrambled back. Both bucks huffed and snorted, their gasps creating vapor a chilly breeze blew toward the immobile does.

One buck went down on his side, writhed back to his feet and fled in exhausted, heavy-footed humiliation. The victor stood with antlered head hung, gasping.

The children stirred. Marty leaned close and whispered, "Don't move. I want to shoot."

The regal buck ambled slowly to a doe. The others shuffled aside. She shifted to face away from the buck, stretching her head forward. The buck sniffed her hock and tail, then reared up and stepped forward to ease his weight down, front legs dangling. He stood puffing, hips barely moving for a few seconds before moving off to stand beside her.

Tightly clutching the forgotten rifle in hands covered with unnoticed blisters, Marty stared, breathless and tense, aware of a nearly forgotten hunger low in her belly. She gulped and glanced at the children, embarrassed they'd seen the mating. Seeing farm animals breed when she was young had not aroused her, so she hoped these two wouldn't think much of it.

"What are they doin'?" Ted whispered into her ear, frowning.

"Mating." Was all she could think of to reply, relieved at his unemotional curiosity.

"Why?"

He would have to ask that, she thought, glancing away. "They're making babies." She whispered.

The deer began to browse. Marty shifted to bring the rifle up and palm the hammer.

"But the stork brings babies." He whispered, dark eyes going wide. "Does he get 'em from DEER?" His voice was loud enough to startle the deer into abrupt flight, each its own way, the buck springing off with regal antlers arched high.

"Look what you did! You know animals run away if we make noise!"

She leapt to her feet in anger. It had been a perfect chance to shoot.

"I wanted to shoot one for meat. Now I can't." The crushed look on his face caused a pang of regret for being so harsh.

"Are we gonna get another baby?" He asked very softly.

"No." Marty brushed cold slush off her knees, "Deer make deer babies, fawns. Every kind of creature makes its own babies."

"But . . ."

Marty blushed, thinking: I went this far, I may as well go all the way.

"It takes a daddy and a mama of each kind of animal to make their baby. We won't get another one because there is no daddy."

"But . . ."

"I don't want to talk about it!" Her lip scar flared red as she stomped away so fast Ted had to jog to keep up, and Amy had to run.

Amy slipped and fell in the slush and started to cry. After seeing the red scar, Ted went back and helped her. He was afraid of what Marty might do when she was so angry, maybe go away and never come back as his mother had.

He would never again ask about storks and the babies they brought.

Despite deep fatigue from cutting wood all day and sewing each evening, Marty had trouble sleeping that night. Why did people lie to children about things like the stork? It was easy to tell them part of the truth, they just didn't need all the details until later. And, just before sunset, dark, thick clouds promised more snow overnight. How much would it be this time? Enough to cave the tent in on them?

Marty leaped out of bed with a stab of fear as soon as she saw the tent roof sagging, and pounded upwards to knock off the snow. Peeking out to see how much had fallen, she was relieved to see only a couple inches. But it was obvious the roof had to be shielded from snow weight—today.

All through stoking the fire, a quick jaunt to the slightly replenished stream for water, and another to check snares while coffee mix brewed, she sought a solution. Would the unused canvas ground cloth work for a hood to deflect snow to the side? When she dug it out she found holes mice chewed months ago still had to be patched.

Struggling to sew on patches cut weeks ago, she realized this camp was too open and unprotected, but she knew of no better place. At least here no trees would blow down on them, but she had to make this place more suitable.

The patched tarp was too small to help. How had Gram's people solved the problem? Picturing a sharply pointed conical tepee, she brightened. Three parachutes were left whole and the open canopy shape was like a very blunt tepee. A chute canopy would be light enough to easily put up and would reach well past the tent's corners.

She circled the tent to study what it would take to add a hood without adding weight to the tent, steep enough for snow to slide off to the sides. Finally she cut eight thin maple saplings, each about twenty feet long, limbed them and tied their tops together. She opened a new parachute and struggled with yards of slippery silk to get the poles' tops through the rubber-ringed center hole and tied the ring in place at the top.

She struggled inside the canopy to tip the poles upright, then divided the poles in half, alternating sides of the tent they went on, until it stood on its own. Patiently, she worked one pole at a time out until the tent was centered and the end poles cleared the corners. She made sure the peak was low enough that the whole tent was sheltered, but steep enough so any snow would slide off.

Stretching kinked neck muscles, she realized the new legs might slip outward at any added weight, or wind. So, using the sturdy spit bar, she chipped a hole in frozen soil to set each pole into, stomping clods and rocks in to hold it stable.

With gentle tugs on attached shroud lines, she distributed the canopy as far to the front and back as possible to take up the slack so wind couldn't get under a loose edge to blow the whole hood off. Then she secured the shroud lines to stakes pounded deep between support poles.

The front slack, hanging loose, blocked the wind suction at the tent peak, and already smoke was building up inside. Frustrated, she squatted on one heel to study the problem. A breeze fluttered the loose door flaps, giving a glimpse of crowded interior. Something had to break the chilling wind's force at the door without blocking it from drawing smoke out the peak. She also needed more space to pile dry kindling and wood by the door.

Suddenly inspired, she took the ax to cut long, thin saplings to build a frame to fit the ground tarp, and additional lengths for bracing to keep it in place. She lashed the tarp to the frame with shroud lines then braced it at a slight slant on the windward side of the door so it deflected wind under the hood while shunting it away from the door. Then she tied the loose part of the canopy front to the outer edge of the tarp frame. Now the hood also shielded out past the door, forming a small porch wall and roof.

She was pleased with her solution to weather proofing camp, but it looked awfully strange.

The outside fire pit was useless until spring, its rocks now in the way so Marty used those rocks to deepen and enlarge the inside pit. Inside the tent already felt warmer, so the time hadn't been wasted.

She thought one day of wood gathering made little difference since downed wood was already harder to find, hidden under thin snow she'd have to brush off to cut the logs. Plus, temperatures had steadily dropped until she needed gloves so her fingers wouldn't freeze. How might wearing gloves to chop wood affect her many blisters and calluses? She hoped they didn't create new ones. Her palms and fingers looked mangled as it was.

Snow fell nearly every day, but usually only an inch or two at once. The well-used path to the toilet area quickly packed down from use and the trampled snow turned to rumpled ice; it became treacherous to go to the latrine. So, taking time out from cutting wood, Marty laboriously cracked the ice apart with a stout, jagged stick, and used the sharply pointed but woefully small camp shovel to scoop the loose chunks aside. She cleared ice off down to rough, frozen soil they could safely walk on, then repeated the wearying process in the trampled area directly in front of the tent.

The soft, fur-lined gloves did not protect her hands from new blisters.

To fill long dim evenings, now that the children's jackets were done, Marty worked to soften the deer hide she'd tossed over a bush to dry and forgotten. It was a bit shrunken and very stiff. After being left untouched so long, and because of its size, it would take a great deal of work to soften, though it was now less than half its wet, fresh weight. Still, the big pelt would be needed for a wrap-around to sit by the fire, to cut off icy floor drafts against their backs while their feet and legs toasted by the flames.

Before taking it inside, she examined the hide for parasites. All were gone, but the edge that had hung lowest from the bush was hairless. Mystified, she saw a faint tracery of tiny tooth marks and remembered the squirrel gathering moss and shredded bark to insulate its nest. Some tiny creature, also wanting to keep warm, must have stripped the hair off to line its winter nest.

Still feeling silly for doing it, Marty beat the stiff hide against a tree trunk. Every few whacks she shifted handholds to a new place on along the edge until she'd gone all the way around at least twice. Though much softer, the hide still looked shrunken, its coarse fur unattractively bunched. She had to find some way to keep big hides from shrinking as they dried. She'd stretched rabbit skin tubes while they were wet and they hadn't shriveled up like that. But she couldn't tube-peel a deer, so how could she stretch a hide this size?

Examining muskrat pelts for shrinkage, she saw their fur looked bunched and messy, too. She sighed in discouragement. All pelts must need to be stretched to dry while fresh. Muskrats could be tube peeled and stretched on a willow hoop like rabbits, but pelts much bigger than that would be physically impossible. She rubbed rough, sore palms over her face—another solution to find. That wouldn't help the already-damaged hides.

When the deer hide had been wadded, pulled, twisted, and worked between the heels of her hands until it was more-or-less pliable, Marty gave up trying to further soften it. It was good enough for a cape.

Dumping icy clumps out of Amy's moccasins that evening showed Marty the need to find a way to keep snow from getting into them. She cut and sewed ewe-hide legs on the children's moccasins. Again using the meat fork tine as an awl to poke holes, she used a very narrow strip of hide for heavy thread to lace the pieces together. She cut other, slightly wider hide strips for wrap-around ties to hold the legs up to the youngsters' knees.

The children's new pants were not warm enough to wear outside, so she sewed them three-layer snow pants and lined their other pants with wool, then cotton. She sewed a deep dart in back to alter a pair of Eddie's olive-drab fatigue pants to wear over her own; that took less sewing and materials than lining all her pants.

She wondered if game animals saw color. If so, the OD-green of her over-pants was good camouflage. Her corduroy coat was already a sun-faded, dirt-mottled brown.

Except by the fire, it was chilly and forever damp in the tent. As Marty dropped a just-dried butter knife into the tin utensil can, the knife broke through the can's rusty bottom and nearly fell in the fire. Other pieces slid down and jammed the new hole, or it would have fallen. That can was useless. Unable to find anything else to keep tableware safe from packrats, she wove a deep, narrow basket to replace the can. Weaving a container that narrow and tall made it obvious she needed to find weaving materials between the size of cattail leaves and willow shoots, and some much finer than either for tighter weaves.

Something ELSE to find a solution for.

The cold weather also meant they couldn't bathe again, except to wipe off a small area at a time with the washcloth. With no quick way to dry it, she dared not get their hair wet to wash. The tent was too cold even with a fire blazing as high as she dared build it. They would stink unbearably by spring. As she washed it, Marty looked at her face in the small mirror, relieved to notice her forehead and cheek scars were faded. Her not-very-narrow lip scar had become a pink, slightly crooked line.

Nights were now cold enough that by early mornings a thin crust of intricately patterned ice lined the stream edges with only the fast moving center staying completely ice-free. So Marty shifted hauling water to mid-afternoon, when the weakening sun's rays melted most of the ice. The weather was usually cloudy. Wind ranged from a gentle, sighing breeze to tree-whipping, whistling gusts that never totally stopped. Newly fallen snow packed down and partly melted. Then it snowed again, and packed again, over and over. Snow was now about six inches deep, dense and hard-packed except on top.

The children were delighted that the snow was finally deep enough to play in. Marty bundled them up in thick new jackets, snow pants and knee-high moccasins, and their old knitted wool caps and tight mittens. They whooped outside, bursting with youthful energy to slide and tumble, giggling all the way, down the slight slope toward the dry brook on their bellies with arms and legs sticking up every which way.

Ted seemed less bothered by the cold and snow than Amy. Wondering how the tender youngsters could ignore the ache of cold toes and fingers, Marty felt most affected by it.

Snow worked down the neck of the romping youngster's clothes and caked under mitten cuffs. Their fingers stung with cold and their feet grew so numb they stumbled at every step. Marty called them in to clean snow out of their clothes before they became soaked from it melting against their bodies. Their fingers were beet red and they sniffled but were so bursting with delight and exuberance she decided not to keep them in. Instead, she used the axe to slice through bark around a large birch trunk and peeled off the section for a thin sled to keep snow out of their clothes.

Trying to slide down the bumpy slope on the slightly curved, oblong sled, the kids instead slid off the bark's smooth inner surface. When they held the bark edges to stay on, the snow's thin, sharp crust scraped their fingers. Marty tied a short loop of rope through holes poked near one end for them to hang onto. She was rewarded by heart-warming, piercing shrieks of delight and bubbling laughter as the sled careened down the slope with its precious cargo. She had to smile.

She realized the bark sled would also work to haul wood if she used a longer rope to drag it by. It would be much easier than dragging a rough heavy log over tangled, snowless ground had been, or trying to drag each one through the slippery snow.

Watching the noisy play, she worried the children's mittens were not warm enough. Those were also nearly outgrown. How could she make Ted mittens so Amy could wear his hand-me-downs?

Despite the braided cattail leaf headband she always wore, the wind blew Marty's hair across her cheek, blocking some of the wind's chill. The light veil of hair strands held in heat from her exhaled breath and warmed her face slightly. No wonder so many men grew winter beards to protect their face, she thought, turning to go inside, reminded she had to make more cold weather clothes.

That evening she made wide fur strips into headbands from the smallest muskrat pelts. The thick fur loops were easy to slip down over their ears to go outside. Then she stitched narrow, double-layered strips of thick wool into the split seams of Amy's mittens so they fit Ted. Ted's old mittens went to Amy. Now they both had mittens big enough to go out and play. Marty had only the one pair of fur-lined leather gloves, but aside from being rumpled and dirty they were in fairly good condition.

The children's old knitted wool stocking caps were rather snug but still fit. Marty had not brought a hat so she fashioned herself a hood out of two muskrat furs by trimming the legs off and stitching them together along the curved side edges and down one end. Worn fur side out, the hood broke the wind's chill, except when facing into it.

She knew the youngsters would soon outgrow their old stocking caps so she studied yarn strands in their topknots and how they were made. She'd heard of spinning wheels for twisting wool into yarn, but couldn't figure out how they worked. The large wads of unprocessed wool she had was enough to knit several cap and mitten sets, but first she had to find some way to twist it into useful yarn.

The next morning she got out all the goat's wool she'd found and washed what was dirty and matted in warm water, indoors. Draping the clean wool over the nearly snowed-under drying rack, she was careful to cover it with thin branches to keep the wind from blowing it away. When it was dry, she combed out all the tangles and remaining debris. Now she had to figure out how to roll yarn from the fluffy heap of long, combed, ivory colored fibers.

Acceptable knitting needles could be made from long, slim suckers from the Red Osier Dogwood tree, so easy to find now by its distinctive bright red twigs. The switches only had to be peeled and trimmed to the desired length, and the narrow end smoothly tapered. The diameter was right for most knitting projects. She knew that even thin dogwood twigs were extremely tough and durable.

Marty used the last of the rolled oats and cornmeal while occupied with cutting wood. Now she was upset at having only seared and husked half a silk bag of the gathered grain. And she'd only ground a small portion of that. Should have done all of it before storing it away, she frowned. It took hours to cook the whole grain soft enough to eat, so she tried soaking it overnight. That shortened cooking time considerably, but still took much longer than the processed grains she'd brought on the plane. She tried cracking whole grain into smaller pieces with the grinding stones. That shortened cooking time for soaked pieces to under an hour. Thankfully, it swelled so much in soaking and cooking that only a cupped-hand scoop of cracked grain made all they could eat for breakfast. The last sugar had been used for the birthday cake, so she added a few dried berries to add a hint of sweetness.

It quickly became part of Marty's routine to crack a handful of grain each evening and set it by the fire in heated water to soak overnight. The soaked grain went on to cook when she started her morning brew. It was usually ready when the children woke, as ravenous as only healthy, active youngsters can be.

Every time she cracked grain for cereal, she ground up extra, putting the finest in the flour sack. Any chunks not needed for morning went in the empty oat bag. While the rocks were out she often ground a few more dried cattail roots, putting that fine meal in the flour, too. She hoped, eventually, this bit of extra grinding every day would give enough surplus that, if pressed for time, she could skip this tedious chore.

She still had to figure out how to get the seeds out of the pitch-covered cones but put off tackling that chore in dread of getting pitch on everything in the crowded tent. She gladly tucked the heaping, pathetically-made baskets of strongly aromatic cones far back under the rear cot to attend to later.

Most Hazelnuts were still in their bristly husks, in a small stuff bag. Remembering sore, raw fingers, Marty also tucked that far back alongside the cones. Those could also wait.

CHAPTER 18

Wind slapping the silk hood against its support poles woke Marty before dawn. She yawned, stretched, nestled down into her thick sleeping bag's warmth, and wondered how near dawn it was. She shifted to exhale with mouth wide open, saw traces of white vapor, sighed deeply and stretched again. To see her breath meant it was growing light. She may as well get up.

But she delayed a few minutes—for once she had no need to hurry—to luxuriate in the warmth of her soft, thick bed. She listened to the wind vary from whispers and sighs to moans and whistles, once briefly building up enough force to growl eerily through the trees and loudly flap the silk again.

She groped in the sleeping bag for her clothes, kept there at night to be warmer and drier when it was time to dress, sat up to shrug out of the pajama top and shiver quickly into a flannel shirt. Then she slid off pajama bottoms and struggled into pants. Fumbling blindly in the bag's depths, she finally located a sock and slipped it on. She had to stand to find the other one and gasped at the dirt floor's shocking cold on the bare foot. She slipped into cold boots and shivered into her dank jacket before tying bootlaces.

Going more by memory than sight, she found the hardwood stick and stirred deep ashes until several red coals glowed dimly in the darkness, scooted them all together then blew on them until they glowed almost white. Pattering softly past the door flaps, she fumbled in the dark to find a handful of thin dry twigs that would ignite easily from glowing coals in one hand and some brittle-dry, finger-thick lengths in the other. She laid twigs then slim branches against the coals and blew on them. Yellow tongues of flame licked up through slim twigs to curl around the larger chunks, emitting faint, glimmery light through swirling, pungent smoke plumes, breaking the intense darkness and throwing huge, flickery shadows on smooth canvas tent walls and soot-darkened ceiling. She ducked to rub smoke from stinging eyes.

She set larger chunks on the growing fire until flames licked the underside of the metal grate over the fire pit and felt its welcome warmth. Sighing in satisfaction, she ladled water into the soot-caked coffeepot, dumped in a measure of adulterated coffee, and set it over the fire's hottest part to brew amidst curling smoke. The soaked cereal went beside it.

Tiny ice particles, torn loose from slightly crusted snow by the wind, lashed Marty's bare face and stung it fiercely as she stepped out shortly before sunrise. Snow had fallen nearly every day, though usually only a light dusting of hard specks little bigger than dust motes, then the sun partly melted the surface so it packed down more. But snow accumulated until it reached Marty's mid-calf boot tops. Thin crust crunched at each step, making her steps seem unreasonably noisy in the intense snow-muffled silence.

Going to the latrine, treading carefully on the packed, shoveled, and repacked path, Marty noticed the clouds were broken into thin rows with narrow gaps. The gaps gave a glimpse of the faint crescent moon, nearly overpowered by the rising sun's cold white glare. Since it was always crisply cold out, the sky usually cloudy and gloomy, she seldom went out now except to check snares, bring in water, or gather wood, so she'd nearly missed seeing the new moon. Swallowing a surge of fear, she scolded herself aloud to be more careful not to miss her only measurable reference to time's passage.

When she returned to the tent's growing warmth she marked the seventh line on the date stick, thinking it must be November eleventh. So far, the weather hadn't been as bad as she'd feared, and the tent was crowded with bags and baskets of many food varieties. Perhaps winter wouldn't be so bad after all. The pesky flies and mosquitoes were gone—an immense relief—as well as dangerous bears.

She was pleased that all snow falling on the strange-looking hood over the tent was being diverted into scalloped piles around the tent sides, and as the piles deepened they blocked off more and more of the cold draft that used to blow under the tent's bottom edge.

About mid-afternoon, when it was warmest out, she went to get water. The rippling stream sprouted tiny wisps of swirling vapor, but bubbled and gurgled along undaunted by cold, by the snow-wreathed banks, or by intricately patterned ice that fringed the slower-moving water near its banks with a translucent gloss.

Then it was time to find wood. The grueling, unending chore of finding and gathering each day's wood was eased by hauling it on the bark sled. She refused to use any of the stored wood until she had no choice—winter was just beginning and she might be unable to gather more when the snow piled deeper. Already, downed logs were impossible to find. Wind-blown snow grew more level at each fall until its surface was now too smooth to see many revealing lumps hidden under the white mantle. She was forced to look for reachable dead branches to burn, though she could now gather many that had been just out of reach before the packed snow gave her a slight boost up.

Trudging daily through the pristine whiteness of the snow-shrouded forest's growing familiarity, sinking nearly to her knee at each crunching step as she searched for wood, Marty began to feel a deep spiritual kinship with her small, remote corner of the world.

She preferred going out when it was overcast, though it was colder then. Each new inch of snow added intensity to glaring whiteness that was lessened only by the gloom of clouds or nightfall. If she was out very long in such dazzling brightness she developed a raging headache and burning, watery eyes.

When she did go out she heard an odd, intermittent "crack" that echoed so far. It was frightening. She couldn't figure out what was making it, and carried the rifle slung over a shoulder when she left camp, worried the pistol was not enough to protect her from whatever made the noise. It might be some dangerous creature she'd never heard of. At times she also heard a high wavering whistle echo off the cliffs, but guessed it was some trick of wind playing off rock walls. Flowing through thick vegetation or across the rugged, soaring cliffs, the wind made an amazing variety of sounds.

It was startling to see or hear a hawk, raven, gray jay, or the huge soaring eagle in the muted silence. She often saw or heard the twittering flock of tiny Black-capped Chickadees and welcomed their cheery perkiness in the solemn quiet. She even began hearing spooky hoots of more than one variety of owls at night. The eerie, haunting hoots always made her neck hair prickle and goose bumps run down her arms.

From waking until sunset, the children wanted to go out and play in the snow. Marty worried they'd get sick from the cold, so she usually kept them in. Only on fairly warm afternoons did she allow them out to play in the trampled area by the tent door; beyond that, the snow was too deep for them to navigate without her help. It nearly reached Amy's waist and Ted's thighs.

Chopping the day's haul of wood near the woodpile, listening to pleasantly noisy play, she realized they'd gradually stopped playing 'Town' or 'House Building', and now only played wild animal games, like 'Otter' while sliding downhill on the sled, 'Hunter' like her shooting the ewe, or 'Indians' like when guarding the drying rack—when had that changed? Now they were playing 'Fox', pretending to sneak up on drying meat chunks that were wood chips laid on twigs stacked like the drying rack. Amy threw poorly made snowballs at Ted—the fox—to chase him off; good thing all the rocks were buried and her aim was so bad.

The last grain of salt was gone, though she'd tapered off its use and hoarded it as long as possible. Marty savored the last few grains, carefully scraped out of the two-layered paper bag, too torn and tattered to be worth saving for anything but fire starting. She knew they'd miss it for a while but their tasters would adjust as they had with the end of the sugar. She'd learned that flavor and taste preferences depended on what one was accustomed to.

They now had to dress in several layers to go out longer than it took to grab a quick armload of wood, and also wore more than one layer inside. Drafts lessened as the roughly oval snow-wall built up around the canopy sides, but inside the tent was never really warm, just not as cold as outside.

The nearby brook was frozen solid under the snow and the stream was ice-fringed nearly to its still-flowing center, even in the warmest part of the day. Marty could no longer reach a bucket out to the running part without danger of falling through intervening thin ice, and was afraid such cold would paralyze and quickly kill her if she fell in even partway. She didn't dare take the chance so, to avoid that risk, she began melting buckets of snow for water. It shrank drastically as it melted; a tightly packed bucket melted to much less than half, and that always held soot and other fine debris. Melting took so long the big bucket was always on heating, melting more, while they used what water they needed from the smaller one.

Ted's daily chore now was to scoop the big bucket full of snow from slightly beyond their play yard's trampled edge and drag it in. Amy delighted in helping him fill it, throwing in crumbly snowballs and nearly standing on her head in the bucket to pack it down at the bottom, her shrill giggles echoing up from there.

Marty piled each day's supply of cut wood, some green, some seasoned, in the slanted and braced tarp's shelter, bringing the chips and finest pieces in for kindling. Since Ted couldn't get any wood from the snowy forest, Marty gathered the wood and, not trusting the boy with the sharp axe, the chopping.

Her hands had become coarsely calloused but no longer blistered from using the ax, regardless of whether or not she wore gloves.

Amy brought an occasional small chunk inside—which she got from the pile just outside the flap-door. That always amused Marty, but she would enjoy it more when both children grew up enough to be of real help. It was nearly impossible for one person to do all that had to be done to survive in such primitive conditions.

Ted was also assigned the never-ending job of using the small shovel to scoop up any tracked-in snow chunks, mostly from Marty's waffled boot soles, before it melted and made the dirt floor muddy. Little snow clung to the children's moccasins.

They all ate when they were hungry, but supper was the meal they always shared. Out of boredom, they often ate four or five times a day though meat, being the hardest to get, was rationed to that one meal a day. When Marty was not asleep or getting wood, something was on to cook, roasting, baking, bubbling or sizzling over the grill next to the snow-melting bucket. Cold had ruined the yeast starter, so she baked flat pancakes of mixed flours and grains, grinding more grain as needed, often altering the flavor with cattail pollen or a few berries. It was too cold to winnow more and grain was too precious to risk losing in the snow, so they learned to tolerate tough hulls, spitting out into the fire any hulls that escaped being ground. She still regularly cracked some to cook for cereal, and faithfully put a small pan of it to soak every night.

Marty tried to recall what Gram said about how her family processed grain. Like a hundred other times since the crash she regretted paying so little attention to all the old woman told her. But now and then, for no apparent reason, all or part of a conversation came to mind to ease the intense silence. Marty eagerly latched onto those memories, thankful to get even piece-meal bits of memory refreshed.

In a monotonous struggle through yielding snow, step by high-lifting step crunching through to sink deeply, pulling the slightly curled bark sled piled with tangles of foraged limbs and branches around snags and obstacles toward home, one of Gram's stories of an ancient buffalo hunt ran through her mind.

"The old ones," Gram had started, "those of our ancestors who lived before the days of the white man, used to gather at the edge of the far prairie," she waved eastward, "every fall for the year's biggest buffalo hunt. It was a time of joy, when relatives visited for the first time in a year. They gathered in such numbers because it took many braves to hunt buffalo with success when they had to do it on foot. This was before they had horses.

"The fall hunt was the year's most important one. Braves had to kill enough meat in that hunt to last their family through a whole winter, half a year, and the women had to preserve it all before it could spoil. Everyone spent much time preparing. Men made arrows or new bows and bowstrings, while women sharpened their stone or bone skinning and butchering tools, cleaned and readied the stiff rawhide pouches that would hold dried meat, and tied up bundles of long sticks to build drying racks.

"Everyone also prepared spiritually. A brave had to be full of courage and energy for the rigors and danger of hunting down and killing three or four huge buffalo—much, much bigger than any beef cattle ever grew—for his family. Plus, each brave tried to kill an extra animal for any family without a hunter. The slightest hesitation in shooting accurately at the exact right time would mean the brave missed many hundreds of pounds of meat, or was faced with an enraged, wounded animal. They fasted and danced to lighten and invigorate the body, sharpen the senses, and build hunger—a hungry hunter is always more successful than one full of food!

"While dancing, they prayed to the Spirits to make the game willing to die for them. That was VERY important!" Eyes going wide for emphasis, Gram had nodded sagely. "No animal can be killed for food unless it is willing to share its essence, its being we know as Soul, with the hunter. Just as important, each beast that allowed itself to fall to the hunters had to be thanked properly afterward. If not thanked with proper reverence all the game would disappear and the people would starve.

"The hunt was always very dangerous. Every year one or two hunters were wounded or killed. All braves stripped down to moccasins and loincloths to hunt, so if they were gored the wound would be clean, not full of leather shreds that would make the wound fester. A clean wound healed easily and well, with little attention from the Healer.

"The whole camp moved near the chosen herd, staying very quiet to avoid a stampede. Then, before light, the women, children and old people hid in a sheltering grove of trees or a jumble of big rocks where they couldn't be trampled. The hunters readied their weapons, applied their hunting paint and offered up a last silent prayer. They crept silently into a line around three sides of the peacefully grazing herd, leaving open only the side they wanted the herd to run toward. That way led the herd to the cliff-top they would run off of—if things went as planned—where most would fall to their death on the rocks below. Then, before any could escape, the hunters had to quickly reach the cliff base and kill with a well-placed arrow or stabbing spear all those only wounded. Buffalo are very dangerous and unpredictable at best, but a wounded one is a demon!

"One brave at the center of the line lit a torch and passed fire out in both directions, then they all ran at the herd waving the torches. Fire was the only thing buffalo had any real fear of and it terrified them into running. Getting the herd to run in the right direction was the hunt's most dangerous part.

"As soon as enough buffalo had run off the cliff and the wounded were killed, the women hurried up with their tools and started butchering by cutting them open and pulling out the livers. They sprinkled it with bitter gall and everyone ate raw, hot liver with great relish, but always the hunters ate first. Then women cleaned the kills and cut meat small enough to haul to the drying racks on dog-pulled travois, where they sliced it thin to dry fast. As it desiccated in the dry air and hot sun of late summer, they feasted on all the best cuts like the tongue and hump ribs until they couldn't eat another bite, and danced in thankfulness to the buffalo spirits for their sacrifice.

"They wasted no part of any animal. They even ate roasted small intestines, delighting in the contents, what we'd consider a vinegar-dressed salad."

Marty thought about the story while she chopped wood and piled it by the tarp. Unspoken details showed that Indians, even before white men brought metal tools and weapons, had ways to make everything they needed to live, all clothes, tools, shelters, and storage containers. Even sharp knives; Marty knew by experience that nothing dull could slice fresh meat thin enough to dry quickly.

But how could a knife be a knife unless it was metal?

Each day felt distinctly colder than the last, so Marty turned the fur of her hood to the inside. When that was no longer warm enough, she added a second layer of muskrat fur, skin sides together so fur faced out on both inside and outside. Then, to protect her neck and throat from the increasing cold, she attached a short cape to it that draped her shoulders and overlapped snugly at the front. Her caped hood required seven muskrat skins; the hood itself had two skins facing inward, two outward, plus three more to make the cape. Ties of narrow hide strips held it securely under her chin.

She also made one-layer fur over-mitts, pieced together from all the legs trimmed off the muskrat hides used for her hood. All were sewn with short snare line scraps, to save the alarmingly depleted fish line not already cut up; the salvaged silk thread didn't seem nearly strong enough to use for connecting pelts, and it would be too difficult to get through the punched holes with the few needles she had left.

Slipping the children's moccasins off to put warmer ones on them, Marty noticed that after only an hour or so of being outside, their poor little feet were blue with cold. One hand slipped down into a moccasin showed her why; the leather was not very thick, and though the fur helped a great deal to hold in heat, the holes punched to lace the soles to the tops let in too much icy air. What was left of their socks was too thin to hold more than token warmth. Since the hide and fur were both dry the moisture-sucking cold solved much of the waterproofing problem.

Glad for something to keep busy with, Marty sewed on a second sole of tough ewe hide, the bristly hair side facing in. She packed the space between sole layers tightly with dry moss and cattail fluff just before taking the last few stitches. She made sure the outer sole covered all the stitch-holes of the inner layer. Then, stitching only into the outer sole, she sewed a second layer over the tops, stuffing that, too. No cold air could work its way through that maze of layers, even with the most vigorous movement! She was quite pleased. But insulating all four pairs of small moccasin took every last scrap of thick, sturdy ewe hide.

If she spent much time outside during the day, Marty's eyes got sore and felt grainy and irritated from the unrelieved white glare. When the sun peeked out, even briefly, her head ached fiercely from blinding brilliance. No longer able to get water from the stream, even in the warmest part of the day, she also adjusted her wood-gathering routine so she was most often out very early or very late, when the sun couldn't shine unexpectedly. But it was noticeably colder then. If she stayed out long in early mornings, when it was coldest, her breath vapor quickly froze to her hood, building up layers of glossy ice on the fur near her face.

Restless and bored from being confined indoors so much, she also made two-layer, caped, muskrat fur hoods for the children to wear over their jackets and old stocking caps. Now only their chins, cheeks and noses could get cold, all else was covered. But, with so many warm clothes on, they had trouble moving when they were out.

Marty was glad she'd made their clothes so big. She hadn't thought of needing room to wear them in layers. But she'd never been in a place this cold before. At last she hadn't had to learn something the hard way!

By the time a full moon brightened night so much it was hard to sleep, Marty was so bored she began to recomb the long white goat wool. After careful thought, she laid a tuft of several long wool strands on her thigh, slightly overlapped it with another tuft, and slid her flat palm over the top so the strands twisted and rolled together between palm and leg. Each time the overlapped tufts were twisted past halfway, she added another tuft and rolled that, continuing until the thinly rolled strand was long enough to wind around the other hand. It took long, patient work, but eventually she had a fair-sized skein wrapped loosely around one hand.

Testing its strength, she found the single strand broke too easily to be useful. But the yarn used in the knitted caps was three or four strands thick, so she rolled several skeins of single-strand yarn. Then she twirled three of the fine strands to form a large skein of thick yarn. The resulting yarn was lumpy, but was now strong enough to be useful. Learning to roll it evenly was obviously going to take a lot of practice.

For her first project, when enough yarn was rolled, Marty used the carved dogwood needles to knit a scarf to wrap around her face and mouth, leaving only her eyes showing, as further protection from growing cold. It took a surprising amount of wool to roll the yarn and knit it into the one muffler. She was glad she'd found so much wool.

She rolled more yarn and made the kids bigger caps and mittens, though seamed thumbs had to be sewn in, and then a scarf each. It didn't take much new yarn to make the caps because part of the yarn used for those was from unraveling the ones they brought.

Thoroughly enjoying being able to knit again, especially badly needed items, she made a pair of thick socks for each of them. But they had a shameful seam down one side—she'd tried, but was unable to do seamless socks or gloves without a matched set of double-ended needles sturdier and smaller than she could figure out how to make. And she could not remember how to turn the heel of a sock. So they had to make do with seamed tube socks.

For days and days she spent most of her indoor time rolling yarn and knitting. Her most consuming worry now was frostbite or freezing to death.

While her hands worked mechanically at the repetitious moves of knitting, she realized the dogwood's hardness made it ideal for carving big spoons from, someday. Carving them would be difficult because of that hardness, but each would last a long time. They might never wear out.

From chopping them, she'd soon learned that poplar, aspen, cottonwood and willows cut fairly easily; their soft wood was light-colored with excellent, lovely grain patterns. While they lacked the resinous smell or taste that saturated coniferous wood, anything made of those woods might wear out too fast to be practical for some carved utensils. Still, it would carve much easier than dogwood.

The snow was now slightly above Marty's knee. It still packed a bit after each fall, but less and less as the sun retreated further and further south and the air stayed colder. Being much shorter than Marty, the snow looked deeper to Ted, and more so to Amy—if she could stand on dirt, snow would now reach her shoulder.

Looking out and seeing such deep snow, Ted asked, "Are we at the North Pole?" Pausing sadly, he picked at his fingers. "Where's Santa Clause? He comes in snow time." A fat tear ran down one cheek. "Can't he find us here?"

Marty was startled. It was not December yet—was it? Well, she gulped silently, I may as well do something for Christmas now as later. Teddy expects it.

"Oh," she mumbled lamely, "Santa's not supposed to come for a while yet." She crossed her fingers behind her back for the fib. In truth, with only an estimate of the date at each new moon, she didn't know the exact date.

While the children slept, for many nights in a row, she secretly worked with pitifully meager supplies to make a rag doll from various cloth scraps. And painstakingly carved a rough toy rifle out of a branch off the birch tree from which she'd peeled the sled's bark. The wood was soft and carved with relative ease, but her skill was crude.

She was careful to keep both projects well hidden.

The morning after the toys were as good as she knew how to make them, she snuck out and used the small saw to cut the top off a young, nearly buried fir tree. Making doubly sure the children were sound asleep before sharpening the lower end with the hatchet, she brought it in and poked the point down into the packed dirt floor where wood was usually stacked, pushing and twisting it until it would stand alone.

She decorated the tiny tree with scrap strips of bright cloth and thread bits, and laid the unwrapped gifts under it. The decorated tree was pathetic in its make-do meagerness. But, try as she might, she could think of nothing else to add.

At the first sign of the children stirring to wake up, she called out in her cheeriest voice, "Wake up and look! Surprise! Santa came last night!"

Two heads popped up, one from each end of their shared cot, and two bleary-eyed faces poked out of thick rolls of rumpled sleeping bags. Amy didn't understand; she couldn't remember her other two Christmases. But she loved her dolly. She giggled and squeezed it so hard Marty was glad it wasn't real. Amy did remember she used to have a whole bunch of dollies. Ted tried hard to act happy, and he really was delighted at his toy gun, but he knew Marty made their presents. He felt bad for having no gift to give her.

But worse, Santa couldn't find them.

Over a steamy breakfast of boiled grain and berries, Marty told the story of Rudolph, the Elves, and the other Reindeer helping Santa deliver presents all over the world.

"What do Reindeer look like?" Ted finally asked, after a thoughtful silence.

Marty tried to describe them, finally saying, "They look a lot like the deer we saw fighting, except their antlers are different."

That triggered memories for Ted. "Oh yeah!" He yelled, remembering pictures of the sleigh and the Reindeer, and Santa and Mrs. Santa at the North Pole.

While the children played with their new toys, Marty sadly realized she'd somehow forgotten all about Thanksgiving. Too. But, shivering and adding wood to the smoky fire, she could think of nothing except the three of them still being alive to be thankful for.

All that day and in dreams that night, she relived memories of past Thanksgivings and Christmases and happy family reunions and dinners at tables laden with food that took days to cook. Everyone thinks we're dead, she moped. What would they do if they knew how we live now?

What COULD they do?

Dawn, the next morning, was obscured by a raging snowstorm, by far the worst since they'd been there. Howling wind flapped the silk hood until Marty was afraid the whole canopy—and the tent—would collapse around them. Huge fluffy snowflakes came down so thickly that going out to the latrine was impossible, especially for the children. Any more than four or five steps away and the canopied tent nearly disappeared in a light-choking, disorienting swirl of wind-whipped snow, when it should be full daylight.

From dire need, Marty layered dry moss thickly in the bottom of a poor basket for an emergency toilet. She set it in the corner where guns and fishing gear had been, then stacked enough bags on the end of the side cot to give as much privacy as possible. She was relieved to discover the corner was so cold that the basket's contents quickly froze solid.

For the first time since setting them, she failed to check the few set snares that morning. And now was the time to start using the precious hoard of piled wood. The raging storm went on and on until it seemed like she had never known a time without a storm. By how many times they ate and slept, Marty guessed it lasted three days and nights, but that was purely a guess. She saw no change between day and night because, with thick storm clouds closer than the cliff tops, the dimness was constant from one time to the next when she dared to dash out and grab more wood.

The storm dumped huge mounds of new snow, and icy moaning winds erratically drifted it. Outside was very, very cold, and inside much colder than usual, so cold they were forced to wear snow pants and coats at all times, even to sit near the blazing fire.

Marty dressed in every warm thing she had to go out, but even then she dared stay out no longer than it took to scoop a bucket of snow or grope and scrape through the woodpile's snow drift to fill her arms with wood chunks chipped apart with the hatchet—the wood had frozen solidly together.

Late in the storm, when the wind finally slowed to less than a howl, a sudden shuddering rumble vibrated their entire world. Marty sat bolt upright in bed, hands clutched over mouth to keep from screaming, looking around wildly, feeling totally helpless, near panic. She'd been in earthquakes in LA, but none worse than a quiver. Was this a bad quake? The rumbling sound and ground shaking grew louder briefly then faded; in a few short seconds it died.

It was hours before she could slip back into the peaceful oblivion of sleep.

It took a long time to locate and gather the long-neglected snares. A stiffly frozen white hare led her to one. How was she going to tube-skin that? The creature was so rigidly frozen she thought bending a leg would snap it off. The meat should be good, she shrugged, nothing that frozen could possibly rot.

Returning to camp, winded from struggling to wade through such deep, yielding snow, Marty paused to catch her breath in thin, cold air. The cloudless sky was a gloomy gray-blue. She glanced east to see how long it was until sunrise, when the world would become unbearably dazzling from cold sunlight reflecting off this sparkling new snow. She saw the sharply-pointed, snow-burdened twin peaks with narrow sinuous indigo ridges slanting down their asymmetrical flanks, saw streaming veils of windblown snow trailing the high wind from those majestic peaks into far distances. She could not imagine the ferocious wind power required to uplift such massive volumes of snow and keep it suspended in a fading streamer as far as she could see. Perhaps, though they held her captive, the cliffs were much greater protection than she knew.

Hearing another suddenly growing rumble, like the terrifying one last night, wide-eyed and heart thumping madly, Marty whirled toward the sound to stare at the west cliffs. Through thick layers of packed snow under her feet the earth trembled as a wide swath of jumbled snow and rock gyrated inexorably down the nearly vertical cliff, spreading, gaining mass and momentum as it roared downward, leaving a wide sweep of treeless devastation at the base . . . Near where she'd found the Mountain Goat skeleton and wool! Now she knew how such a nimble creature had died—it hadn't simply fallen off—an avalanche had swept it to its destruction!

Shaken that such sudden devastation could crush even a Mountain Goat's thick skull, Marty turned to look at the much closer north cliffs, terrified a slide might occur there that could reach camp and bury them.

When her pounding heart and gasping breath slowed to normal, she studied those nearest cliffs. Thick stands of well-grown evergreens stood between camp and the cliffs. In front of that was a narrow strip of barren deciduous trees, then the meadow. She felt reassured no avalanche could reach this far, but now understood why so many shattered trees were tangled amongst the rocks at all the cliff bases.

So many grave perils haunted this wilderness valley! Each peril lay in restrained suspension for some luckless or unwary victim to set it into deadly motion. And, unless some unforeseeable miracle occurred, this valley was her home for the rest of her life. Shuddering violently, Marty wondered how long the rest of hers and the totally dependent children's lives, could possibly be.

Later that morning, relieved to be able to empty the 'potty basket', she toiled to clear the path to the latrine with the tiny camp shovel. At every step she sank past her knee in powdery snow, even then her feet did not actually touch the ground, only the more densely packed snow under the softest, most recent layer. Before half the path was cleared, she had to stop to carry each child out and back, in turns. Ted had tried to get there by himself, but sank in up past his waist at each step.

It was so hard to keep that path clear! With some snow falling nearly every day, and nothing better to use than the puny shovel, it was simply too much. But what place closer to the tent would work? She frowned and decided stink from a new site was no problem until spring thaw released the odor, and spring was awfully far away—she refused to consider they might not survive that long. They needed to use a place they could get to NOW.

At the Grand Fir, just past the woodpile's bumpy ridge, she diligently plied the big saw to trim off the lowest branches on the wind-sheltered east side so they could use part of the area under overhanging boughs for a winter toilet. For a screen, she jabbed the butts of trimmed-off limbs down into the snow to anchor them, and sort of wove them into the attached limbs. She felt silly—no one else could see them use it—but felt too insecure to use that space without the shield. Besides, she rationalized, it helped divert icy wind from otherwise exposed skin.

The lumpy, snowy woodpile protected the new path from wind on one side and the long mound was easy to follow in the dark. Marty still had to clear the path each time it snowed, often every day, but it was much closer than the old one, and not already so packed as to be treacherously icy. Now Ted could reach there without her having to carry him. But she still had to take Amy—the three-year-old couldn't undo and redo so many clothes by herself.

Late one cloudy afternoon, struggling back past ragged fronds of white-coated evergreens with a sled of wood, Marty realized her feet breaking through the sharp crust and sinking far past her knee in the soft snow at every step was exhausting. It took as much effort as climbing up a steep bank because her feet sank back down level at each step but she had to raise each foot up out of the snow to move it forward. The sharp crust was tattering her pant legs and causing long thin bruises across her thighs, even through layers of heavy jeans and lined snow pants.

The abrupt flight of a panicky snowshoe hare made her jump violently. Its pale face, with black-tipped nose and ears, and shiny black eyes, was obvious against the snow as it zigzagged away, glancing back at her first over one shoulder then the other, to a hidden place of safety. Fascinated, she saw it easily dart over drift-tops without ever breaking through the crust. Wishing she could skim the crust as easily, she paused to study its footprints, so disproportionately huge for its body size.

To copy a rabbit's ease of movement over snow, her feet had to be bigger! That was why people invented snowshoes, and why these creatures were called Snowshoe Hares. How she could make snowshoes for herself? She'd never seen any, only a picture of a distant man using them.

Stepping into the tent to warm cold-stiff hands before chopping wood, Marty saw the latest rabbit skins, stretched over willow hoops and hung near the back wall to dry. The flattened shape was similar to her foot's outline but much bigger. She blew a huge sigh of relief—perhaps making snowshoes was not as much a puzzle to solve as it seemed!

She didn't know how anyone else made them but that hadn't been an insurmountable problem when she built the drying racks or set up the spit. Even if unique in detail, her methods were still based on the same general idea others used to solve identical problems. Just knowing someone else had found a solution gave her confidence to find her own method. If they did it, so could she.

From handling so many rabbit skin tubes, Marty knew the hides stretched far less nose-to-tail than sideways. A big Snowshoe hare, the largest wild rabbit variety, can weigh up to five pounds. As an unstretched tube their flattened pelt measures fourteen to seventeen inches from ear base to tail base, and six to ten inches wide. After being scraped and stretched until quite dry they were about eighteen inches long by about a foot wide. The size was ideal to make into snowshoes, and the tube shape simplified keeping the pelt stiff enough to provide flotation over the snow.

The wide rear opening from one hind heel up past the tail to the other heel made it easy to turn the hides and insert the willow hoop, but it left an excessively wide opening for this new purpose. She had to find a way to keep the willow drying hoop from working out that wide rear opening when walking on the flattened tube. The neck opening was much too narrow for the hoop to come out the front.

She examined the two pelts most equal in size and tried one against the sole of her boot. How could she fasten them to her feet? She frowned in concentration for a while before removing the sturdy leather laces from Eddie's spare boots and cut them in half because they were so long. Adjusting the hoops inside the rabbit tubes so the narrow front legs pointed upward, she threaded a half-lace in one front leg, around the hoop, and out the other. With the front legs poking up near the front of her boot heel, she tied that lace in front of her ankle so it tightly held the back of the snowshoes.

Satisfied with that end, she crudely bound the center of the wide rear opening shut with a short length of snare line, so the longer hind legs stuck up near her toe. Threading the other half-lace through the willow hoop and hind legs, she crossed the ends over her arch and tied them behind her ankle. Lifting and wiggling the foot, she was pleased at how securely that held the toe end. Maybe this wouldn't be as hard to figure out as she thought.

She secured the other snowshoe and took a few tentative steps in the tent. Each step was clumsy and awkward. They'd take more than a little getting used to. Are real snowshoes, ones made by people who know what they're doing, as clumsy to use as these? She wondered, then shrugged. If they kept her from sinking deep into snow, they were a huge improvement—even if they weren't perfect.

Without removing the makeshift snowshoes and with legs further apart than was comfortable to avoid stepping on one broad snowshoe with the other, she slogged to the edge of the cleared play area to try them out on the crusty snowdrift. The steeply slanted snow bank formed by repeatedly shoveling the area clear presented an unexpected problem. At first she tried to scale it as she normally did, by poking her toes into the dense snow bank in four steps, but at each step the slick-bottomed, wide-toed snowshoes slid back down as soon as she eased weight onto it. In exasperation she finally turned each foot sideways and stomped each 'shoe into the packed drift's side to create a diagonal series of more or less level spaces that enabled her to step sideways up the bank.

Jubilant at gaining the drift's rumpled top, Marty waved and grinned at both curious faces peering intently from between door flaps. Eager to demonstrate this new skill to her attentive audience, she took two quick steps without watching her feet and promptly tripped and fell in a tangled heap, partially sunk into the more yielding snow past the shoveled-onto area. Mortified at taking a clumsy tumble in front of the children, who were now laughing hysterically, she softly chided herself, "Pride goeth before a fall!" Her cheeks blazed with embarrassed heat.

Struggling to regain her feet in yielding snow, she floundered helplessly. She had nothing more solid than the thin, crumbly crust to push on, and under that, softer, more powdery snow slid erratically out from under her hands and knees.

Ted and Amy screeched with laughter.

Exasperated and feeling more ridiculous than ever, she resorted to rolling over and over until she reached the more solid edge, then slid over it until she could stand in the packed doorway clearing. Thoroughly disgusted, she jerked the ties loose, kicked off the 'shoes, and stomped in to get warm. At each step, clods of packed snow fell from inside her pant legs and flaked off the entire surface of her clothes onto the dirt floor.

Both youngsters bent over with laughter, holding their belly with one arm and pointing at the clumps of snow with the other, unable to speak from laughing so hard.

Marty growled wordlessly and squirmed to dig snow from the neck of her clothes. Snow caked against her throat and breasts was COLD!

Big brown eyes glittering in poorly suppressed mirth, Ted snickered softly as he scooped snow back out. Watching Marty be so silly was worth cleaning up so many snow clumps.

Blushing again, this time at the bother she'd caused the boy—and he giggled about it!—Marty stepped out and shook out each pant leg, beating the icy stuff off her whole body. She glowered at big clods that fell out of her pants. From now on she'd have to tie the cuffs down over her boot-tops to keep snow from working up past them. "Can't tie the neck of my shirt closed, though," she growled. "Just have to be careful not to fall down again," she scoffed.

Warm, rested and with pant leg bottoms securely tied, she dug a long thin pole from the woodpile to help with balance and getting back up after a spill when she tried to walk on deep snow again. The pole idea sounded great, but its narrow end sank so deep in the snow it made keeping her balance even harder. After thinking briefly with teeth clenched in frustration, she widened the pole end by lashing on fine branches much the same way she'd made the broom, only splayed out to cover a wider area.

Afraid to get into a dangerous situation, she cautiously stayed near camp to learn how to manipulate the new snowshoes. When she understood how to keep her footing reasonably well, Marty realized the hide tubes, whose willow hoops framed only the outer edges, were stretching in the middle. The thin pelts had pulled far out of shape, forcing her to step awkwardly high because the under layer's center sagged below her foot each time it was lifted. Under weight, that slack allowed her foot to sink into the snow until even the wide edges were below the surface—the snowshoe now acted more like a blunt wedge, not the flat plane needed for good flotation.

Huffing indignation, Marty sat inside to study the problem, wondering if the whole frustrating project was going to be worth all the bother. And humiliation.

Finally she wove a grid of willow shoots, gathered weeks ago to make baskets, and secured that to the hoop to reinforce it, expanding the hoops enough to hold the stretched skins rigidly flat. She put the reinforced frames back in the same tubes and retied the open end, relieved she hadn't yet sewn them shut.

She had to walk with legs slightly apart but no longer sank more than an inch into the lightly crusted surface. Elated at that hard-won success, she cautiously stepped out further from camp, watching her feet at first to avoid stepping on one 'shoe with the other and using the altered pole for balance. After a few minutes of practice at that, she dared to start walking on level areas of deep, unshoveled snow. Delighted that walking was so much simpler and less exhausting now, she quickly adapted her balance to accommodate the wide-legged walking posture, her body swaying from side to side at each step.

Early the next morning she eagerly wore the 'shoes to check snares, surprised by sore ankles and a stiff ache in the tendons running from hip points to thigh muscles. Still, it had been well worth the trouble to make them. It took much less time or energy to check snares and return. But she had concentrated so hard on the snowshoes that, for the first time in weeks, she forgot to take the rifle.

After feeding the children, with the pole in one hand and the rifle in the other, Marty triumphantly shuffled back out of camp toward the slip-fault, hoping to find game. She was elated that walking was so much quieter now than before, the furry 'shoes helping to muffle every crunchy step. Still, each step was heralded by a *hiss* from a slightly dragging 'shoe heel as she stepped forward, a soft *plop* from setting the foot down, and a faint *crunch* as she shifted her weight forward and the 'shoe settled into the snow crust, leaving a trail of shallow oval dents. The result was a soft, repetitious *hiss-plop-crunch* at each step that was so amusing she giggled aloud. That sound reminded her she was hunting, a poor time to make unavoidable noise.

Learning to turn was more difficult because she had to place each foot far enough out to be clear of the next. Going up or down even the slightest slope was also tricky; the least foot slip and her balance had to be adjusted—thank goodness for the pole! The kick-step she'd used to make steps out of the play area, was necessary to keep from sliding while walking across a slope. Scaling obstacles like rocks or downed logs high enough to protrude above the snow were the hardest movements to figure out.

Learning to use snowshoes was exhausting, but each small success encouraged her not to give up until she was good at getting around. Each time she went out to learn to use snowshoes better she gained confidence, muscle tone, and balance in using them without having to pay conscious thought to each movement. The first few trips, when she was supposed to be hunting, required so much attention to travel that she forgot to look for game.

One overcast afternoon, when muted snow glare made it possible to be out in the warmest part of the day, Marty tucked the hatchet under her belt and went searching for wood. One hand held the empty sled's rope. It trailed behind with a softly buzzing vibration in counterpoint to the *hiss-plop-crunch* of her steps. The rifle was slung over a shoulder so her other hand was free to use the balance pole. Wondering if the west end's bordering fringe of trees were worth searching for wood, Marty squinted into the distance across the drifted meadow, and was astounded to see several elk pawing at the snow.

Stumped at how such huge animals could possibly get into the valley, she stopped to watch, squinting in open-mouthed fascination as a massive elk pawed or nosed through shallower areas of snow to reach dried grass while others casually nibbled bush tops sticking through more deeply drifted spots near trees bordering the meadow's far edge.

The two largest elk regally bore astoundingly huge, thickly tined antlers that extended back over nearly half their body length and spread double the width of their horse-sized shoulders. A third bull, lacking the darker neck color of the other bulls, had only small, short antlers, though he was near the older males in size. Marty assumed any without antlers were cows and the smallest ones were last spring's calves.

Suddenly excited, she tried to sneak near enough for a shot but the herd paced gracefully into the trees, necks held forward so their extended heads nearly paralleled the ground. None seemed to hurry, but they disappeared with amazing speed. Snow did not slow them. She envied their long legs.

Disappointed at not getting close enough to shoot, Marty moped about how easily she could have pulled a yearling elk in the sled over the meadow's gently mounded smoothness. With adults as big as a horse, even a young one would provide meat for all winter. She wouldn't even need to set any more snares.

But they'd seen her, and were gone into the trees. It was futile to try stalking them, today, at least. They already knew where she was. She slogged toward the pond, trying to figure out how to approach within shooting distance of the elk.

Movement of widely palmate antlers protruding from tall brush down past the side of the pond revealed a huge bull moose quietly browsing twigs in dense willows. He was back!

She was stunned to hear coughing grunts from other moose near the bull. Instantly excited, Marty edged cautiously along the willow fringe between meadow and pond, trying to get in position for a shot, heart racing and gloved hands trembling in anticipation. Despite being muffled by the fur snowshoes, snow crunched with alarming loudness at her steps, in contrast to the normal, deep wilderness silence. So, to her absolute dismay, she got no closer than she had to the elk before all three moose shifted warily away.

The enormous bull, looking as large as a Percheron draft horse she once saw at a County Fair, a cow, and a half-grown calf effortlessly stepped away through the snow. Now she understood why they needed such long legs. They trotted through the snow with awesome speed, hopped with astounding agility across the ice-shrouded stream below the beaver dam, paused casually to look back, and finally disappeared silently into thick brush like smoke blending into fog.

How could creatures of such vast size move silently through brush so thick she could barely squeeze through it? Marty shook her head, mystified. Wild animals could easily accomplish feats she couldn't begin to imagine how to do. Maybe they really did know how to get up and down the valley cliffs. It wouldn't surprise her. Well, not too much. She had no answer for how they did it but accepted, finally, they could move in and out of the valley in some mysterious fashion she, not being born and reared in the wild, could not ever hope to match.

She felt woefully inadequate—again.

Day after day she stubbornly tried to get near enough to the huge animals for a shot. She saw them often, but they never quite allowed her within range. How could they know she was armed, and how far a bullet could reach? She had no answer for that.

At the new moon Marty etched the eighth mark on her date stick, thinking it must be December eleventh. Oh no! I did Christmas too early! She thought, grimacing, but was relieved they were through almost a third of winter. It hadn't been as bad as expected; at least, not so far.

She was grimly determined to keep trying for a shot at either an elk or a moose but, unable to figure out how she could possibly move one any bigger, hoped for a shot at a yearling.

She fervently wished she had a man's strength, or—infinitely better—a man around to help.

CHAPTER 19

Restless from the monotony of interminable nights and daily confinement in the cramped tent during brief, blinding-white daylight, Marty tried to clean up scattered soot and ash and rearrange food storage bags and baskets to leave more play space for the children. For too long their play area had been restricted to the beds or the cramped hearthside. She hated having to bundle them up to go out in stinging cold to play in the shrinking trampled area outside the door. And, from eating often while unable to exercise, the children were so plump their heavy clothes, loose when made, were so snug it was hard for Marty to dress them warm enough for outside.

Despite her earlier fears, she'd been able to feed them more than adequately. She smiled smugly, feeling a flush of pride.

Searching through each food bag she came to, she was devastated to discover how many hard-won foods had spoiled from relatively warm, unending dampness, or invasion by furtive mice and annoyingly robust and persistent insects. Pitifully thin to start with, some carrots had shriveled to pencil-lead size for more than half their length and much of that was coated with sage green mold. She'd laboriously gathered many dozens of them, but almost a third was spoiled.

Scowling at irreplaceable loss, she tossed the moldy ones out onto the snow bank just past the windscreen tarp. She pointed them out to Ted, "When you scoop the snow-melting bucket full, be sure not to get close to that. I threw it away because it's rotten, and we don't want it in our water. It would make us sick."

Ted squinted against the outside glare to look at the tangle of wrinkly, fuzzy greenish roots. He nodded soberly, his eyes pumpkin-pie orange. He'd avoid those yucky things!

Sorting more, Marty found many of both Yampa tubers and onion bulbs slimy with foul smelling black rot. She sighed despondently. These foods, long-familiar carrots, onions and sweet potato-flavored Yampa, had been reassuringly familiar; now many were ruined. At least they'd eaten the Arrowhead tubers before they spoiled.

The few remaining Dandelion and Chicory roots were shrunken and shriveled, yielding to her touch, but not rotting. She set them over the fire to roast in the Dutch oven. She'd grind them later, when the stones were out to pulverize tomorrow's cereal grain.

Many other foods were soiled by telltale mouse droppings, nibbled on or pilfered by the rodents gaining entry through holes raggedly chewed in nearly all the silk bags. Marty was momentarily tempted to save unrotted roots from those bags to use. Racked by a shudder of dread, she swallowed rising bile at the filth that touched that food. She had no medicine if she was wrong and using feces-contaminated food made them sick. Reluctantly, she tossed those foods out on the mat of spoiled roots.

Starting to refill the narrow corner where the guns and fishing pole had been kept, she decided it was better to leave that space empty for when another storm came. There surely would be several before winter ended, a horribly discouraging thought on an already depressing day.

Forcing herself to keep cleaning and sorting, jaw clenched in determination, Marty uncovered the wicker fishing creel, sitting empty except for the rust-mottled stringer. She felt foolish at overlooking that storage space when, in the crush of harvest season, she'd frantically woven crude baskets far into the night so many weary nights in a row.

Trying to cook and eat them at dinner, she realized many dried greens had been unchewably mature when gathered and others were too bitter, useless as food. She also tossed those, both cooked and uncooked, out on the growing pile.

Numb with despair, she heated a precious little snowmelt to wash dishes, and sagged to see the syrupy homemade soap was nearly gone. Plenty of ash was handy to make more, but she dared not use any dwindling lard; that was needed much worse for food. She decided to use crusty snow to scour the dishes clean—no danger of running out of that!

At daylight's first pale glow, Marty was astounded to see a tangled maze of tracks at a rumpled bare spot where garbage had been so glumly tossed. Only scattered droppings and jumbled footprints remained. Judging by the number of tracks, many creatures had eaten the spoiled food—mold, rot and all!

"I could've used that for snare bait." She grumbled, vowing to save rotten food and scraps for that, feeling inexcusably wasteful for not thinking of it sooner.

With all compulsively gathered, inedible, and spoiled foods eliminated, Marty calculated how much food remained and how much longer it was until spring brought enough new growth to identify edible plants. She couldn't depend on getting more meat than an occasional snared rabbit and, until spring, all plant food was locked as securely away as the outside world.

With a pang of fear she realized the food was going much too fast to last that long. She could only allow two small meals a day for the rest of winter! Unless, by some unforeseen stroke of luck or genius she figured out how to get near enough to big game to bag plenty of meat. She couldn't count on that!

They could eat less, they'd all grown fat—even her clothes were snug. "We do have to eat enough to maintain body heat or we'll freeze!" She whispered hoarsely, bitterly regretting not rationing food to start with. It had seemed like so much!

She gazed in despair at the flimsy, ever-chilly tent, now smoked gray-brown. Soot caked the slanted ceiling above the fire. Marty gulped down fear. Now she understood how dangerous this primeval valley was because inexperience had so poorly prepared her for the endless, unique rigors of the mountain winter's deep snow and cruel iciness.

Survival required so much thought to solve each unfamiliar detail! Even in warm weather each day had brought its own challenge of finding solutions to problems that mattered little or not at all when living among other people!

Except for a few snared rabbits, she'd bagged no meat since shooting the spike deer because deep snow had kept her near camp. Since learning to use snowshoes she'd been able to range much further out to hunt, but had yet to figure out a way to get near enough to shoot big game. A few chunks each of jerked mutton and venison were the only meat left. Soon they'd have to use the smoked salmon, but that was a food of last resort, not to be used yet.

She grimly persisted in hunting any day the weather allowed, slowed by the unaccustomed weight and awkward bulk of snowshoes that softly made a familiar *hiss-plop-crunch* at each step. The slightly straddle-legged walk required to use them was now second nature. It was easier to watch for game when she no longer had to watch her feet to keep from tripping. Aside from a few birds too small to shoot, she saw no game but the persistently distant moose and elk. She sighed, perplexed at how to get closer. At least the moose ran away from her, so she needn't worry about being trampled. Still, whenever she neared a streamside fringe of willows she half hoped, half feared one might charge.

When hunting that area, she carried the gun in one hand rather than slung over a shoulder, wielding the balance pole with the other hand. She now made separate trips for wood and to hunt because the moving sled was so noisy, but she always carried the slung rifle when getting wood—just in case.

Finally forced to serve dried salmon, she examined every piece minutely for maggot damage or spoilage, sagging in relief that it looked and smelled fine.

When one small, oily chunk apiece was served at dinner Ted was delighted. "YEAH! We get to eat Buffalo fish!" He beamed his whole-face grin.

"This is salmon. I don't think there's such a thing as Buffalo fish." Marty said, wondering where he got that name as she savored a rich flake of oily, smoky fish.

Ted's flashing grin faded to a puzzled frown. "But you said, 'you braves guard the buffalo meat', when you did that stuff to those fish bigger than my BIG one."

With a jolt, Marty realized he was right. "I did say that." She admitted, amused that he remembered so well. How do you explain an analogy to a five-year-old? "That was sort of . . . pretend. Honest, it really is salmon." She grinned tolerantly. "We'll call them Buffalo Salmon anyway. How's that?"

Both children whooped and laughed, parroting "Buffalo Salmon, Buffalo Salmon," over and over. Amy's tongue got tangled and her words became garbled. The kids broke into gales of laughter, intentionally mispronouncing and getting sillier and giggling harder until they rolled on the cold dirt floor in laughter.

Marty was tempted to go . . . do something, until they stopped. Such hilarity was annoying when having to use the last kind of meat, the one reserved for emergency. It was no joking matter to be reminded they could still starve to death—soon!

But, reminded of catching salmon she wondered, why not try fishing again? Surely the hatchet can chop through the pond's ice. She'd seen many pictures of heavily clad people fishing through holes cut in ice. Some built fires on the ice to sit by as they fished. She wondered how to build a fire on ice without it melting through.

Intent on ice fishing, Marty shuffled along on snowshoes, pulling bundled youngsters on the bark sled so they could burn off energy nearby. She'd made them promise to stay on shore; ice was too slippery to be safe for them.

Studying the pond's irregular contours, trying to decide where the best fishing might be, Marty saw the old beaver lodge and a half-dozen muskrat mounds projecting from the ice. She wondered if ice was thinner and weaker near those, but shrugged, it was not worth the risk to find out; best to avoid them. Besides, they were built in shallows, unlikely places for fish to hole up in such cold. The pictures she'd seen were of people fishing far out on frozen lakes, not near shore.

Leaving the children to romp noisily by the sled, Marty carefully inched out on the icy pond to where she thought it was deepest. A frigid breeze stung her face as she squatted to chop a hole with the hatchet to fish through. Icy wind made her eyes sting and water, and bit the inside of her nose with each breath, the moisture-sucking cold making her nose painfully dry. So the kids wouldn't think she was weak, and determined to do this, Marty clenched her teeth and ignored the stinging cold.

Soon worn out from fighting soft snow, Amy stood near the sled, sunk down too deep to climb on it, whimpering and shivering from biting cold despite layers of warm clothes. Her teeth chattered loudly between blue lips. Also shivering uncontrollably, Ted swallowed a whimper of his own. The cold hurt, biting and burning him now that he wasn't romping and having fun. He squinted at Marty, kneeling on the ice, stubbornly trying to chop through it with the small hatchet. Cold seemed not to bother her, so he refused to show his growing distress. He didn't want Marty to think he was a baby—like Amy. Babies had to have someone else take care of them.

He understood why Amy whimpered, and felt sympathy for her. Marty was busy. He would take care of the baby again, as he did most of the time. Awkwardly boosting Amy onto the sled, he noticed how warm her body felt, even through all her clothes. The brief warmth felt good, so he struggled up beside her to hug the whimpering, shivering girl and share body heat. Close contact soon helped warm him, too, slightly.

Watching Marty chop deeper into the ice, spraying sparkling ice chips far out onto the slick surface with each whack, he wondered who could warm her. Maybe she was magic with the cold, too, like she had been in soothing his hurt from the bee sting. He remembered the times her warm, cuddly hugs were mysteriously comforting in his grief. Such soothing comforts had magically eased his distress.

Marty finally had to admit the motionless pond water was frozen too deeply to chop through with a hatchet. Unwilling to give up fishing, and recalling that moving water had to be colder to freeze, she moved to where the stream entered the pond.

Without melt-water, either from the glacier or thawing snow pack, water barely moved under the ice. Pausing to decide exactly where to try, Marty very faintly heard water trickle in the snowy silence. Hacking with new determination, she soon discovered the stream was also frozen too deep to chop through. She shuddered. How low did the temperature have to be to freeze water that deep?

Drooping with cold and defeat, she turned back toward the sled. Aghast at seeing the children's blue lips and hearing their chattering teeth and Amy's faint whimpers, Marty hurried to get the youngsters back inside the tent, feeling unforgivably cruel for bringing them out in such punishing cold.

Stripping off overmitts and leather gloves to stir up the fire, she started a pan of rose hip and cloverleaf tea. While it brewed she pulled off their cold-stiffened moccasins and mittens to chafe bloodlessly pallid, thoroughly chilled feet and hands between hers until some warmth returned. She helped them put on freshly warmed moccasins, though Amy continued to whimper and fuss from the pain of warmth returning to such chilled flesh.

They sat huddled tightly together on a log bench, cold feet stretched toward a blazing fire, the rather stiff deer hide thrown around them and tucked under at the edges. Savoring the steamy tea's fragrant aroma, they clasped metal mess kit cups in warming hands to sip the rosy liquid. At last they began to feel warm, though frost-nipped fingers, toes, and noses still stung and burned with returning warmth. Marty was sure, from the deathly white pallor of their skin, that frostbite damage had been imminent. Not again would she make the mistake of taking tender youngsters out into such harsh cold!

Marty developed an unexpected, insatiable craving for greens, or anything fresh. The hatchet hadn't cut very deep into thick pond ice, but she assumed it would chop through the stream's shallow edge where ice had to be thinner. The hatchet was easy to carry when tucked under a rope tied over her many clothing layers.

Unwilling to take the children out in the cold again, she left them in the tent's safe warmth, the fire carefully stoked with large chunks of hardwood so it would smolder for several hours without attention. Intending to be out longer than usual and determined to protect herself from the ever-growing danger of frostbite, she bundled up in the usual layers of double socks, one pair the wool tube socks she knitted, lined snow pants tied down over regular pants that were tucked into boot-tops, and three layers of shirts under the corduroy jacket. She also wrapped the knitted goat's wool scarf around the neck of the double-layered fur hood and tucked its long ends far down into her jacket front to secure it. She tied on the belt-rope and slipped the hatchet under it, donned snowshoes, fur-lined gloves and muskrat overmitts and, out of habit, slung the rifle over a shoulder. A small silk bag was tucked in a coat pocket to carry whatever she found.

Deftly wielding the balance pole, she worked her way above the slip-fault, heading for the stream's watercress patch. She hoped to chop loose some of those peppery greens imbedded in thin edge ice and then thaw them out of that to eat, and silently hoped she'd see game near enough to shoot along the way.

Slogging over various types of terrain to get there, she soon discovered that not all snow was the same. Texture differed sharply between shaded snow and exposed patches, and she found rough, unyielding icy patches around trees where slushy sun-melted snow had slid off the boughs, then refroze where it fell. Her gait had to be altered for each type: grainy and relatively solid snow, exposed to sunlight some part of the day, was easy to walk on though it crunched loudly at each step; soft, fluffy, sun-shielded snow was quieter but easy to sink deep into, requiring each foot be raised high enough that the snowshoe's toe couldn't scoop up an awkward load of heavy snow and thus trip her; icy patches were best avoided. Where that was impossible or impractical, she learned to edge across the icy section by easing each foot a scant inch or two ahead at a time, knees flexed for better balance on the glass-slippery, slightly creaking surface.

Once above the fault's north end, Marty glanced at the sun to see how late it was, saw with a jolt of alarm that the mist-shrouded sun was partly obscured by the southern cliff tops, though it was late morning. Most of the valley's width was now in perpetual shade. She frowned with worry over how much further south the sun would sink before starting to cycle back up higher overhead. Would it soon fail to rise enough above that steep soaring ridge to shine directly into any part of the deep, narrow valley?

Gaping at the expanse of shadow filling the valley's center and south side, struggling to remember when the shortest day of the year was, she thought it was near Christmas, and that on the shortest day the sun was as far south as its orbit would go. But, she rubbed the back of one overmitt vigorously across her nose in frustration, she had no way to be sure when Christmas was. Frowning in concentration she recalled the last new moon, some days ago, should have been December eleventh. So it was now . . . very nearly Christmas. But the moon should be nearly full by then and it wasn't yet, so the shortest day of the year was still to come. Soon though, very soon.

It was terrifying to realize it was not yet the shortest day of the year, nor was it the coldest part of winter. It already seemed like winter had lasted many months.

This was by far her longest excursion since snow had become deep enough to make travel difficult. With grim determination, she forced tiring muscles on up the steepening, increasingly slippery grade toward where she'd once seen watercress. But the mantles of snow made everything look so different that, search as she might, she couldn't locate the spicy plants. Carefully scrutinizing every inch of thin edge ice, Marty worked down-stream, cautiously inching along on the slippery ice because it was so much smoother than the snow-shrouded, brush-tangled bank.

Her heart lurched at a sudden groaning crunch of ice cracking under her feet; by reflex, she lunged onto the snowy, overgrown bank. Lying frozen with terror while she caught her breath, she reached a mittened hand out to brush a thin skiff of snow off the ice. Shallow, convoluted, various-sized air pockets and tunnels, easy to see so close under a bare, clear surface, created otherwise unmarked thin spots in the seemingly solid ice.

Realizing how much danger she was in while on that ice made her head swim. It would only take one foot plunging into an air pocket enough to throw off already precarious balance and she'd fall on the slippery surface—and probably break a leg! Then all three of them would surely starve to death!

No, she grimaced, exposed as she'd be to night's ruthless frigidity, she'd freeze to death first. The children, even in the tent with all the blankets and sleeping bags, would freeze to death before they could starve—Ted didn't know how to keep the fire going. She'd forbidden him ever to touch it! Maybe that was a mistake, maybe he needed to know such a life-saving skill; but only while under her direct supervision.

Marty felt abrupt relief at realizing she'd been warned, without injury, of the danger of traversing the smooth, inviting expanse of ice-immobilized stream, shuddered at knowing she could have discovered the danger of air pockets by falling into one.

Getting shakily to her feet, brushing off clinging snow and retrieving rifle and balance pole, she wondered why the pond lacked evidence of air pockets when the stream had so many. Had she simply stepped on the right spots?

Hunting watercress was useless; no summer landmarks were discernable under this thick, obscuring snow carpet. Though it was so far away, she decided to go to the pond. Maybe a few cattails were in ice shallow enough to chop through. She doubted any dead parts were edible, but even fresh, undried roots would provide a welcome change of diet now. Her mouth watered at the thought.

Automatically, she set off to go the long way, following near the fault's edge across the valley to the easy descent at its north end. Halfway there, wishing she didn't have to go so far to descend the drop-off and then come back to just below here, Marty was momentarily tempted to step off over the scarp into the solid-looking snow drift not far below. Then she recalled how far down bare ground really was. It was not possible to tell if the deceptively deep drift was too soft to support her, or if she'd be buried by it. A flimsy balance pole would certainly not be any help getting out of that!

Stepping nervously away from the edge, she went *hiss-plop-crunch* to the gentle slope at the very end. Then she slipped and slid precariously down the bumpy incline until, stomping down through the thin snow crust to keep from falling, she accidentally discovered the usefulness of punching each heel down into the snow for traction when descending. That meant she no longer had to turn sideways to go down.

Because of the build-up of drifted snow against the abrupt scarp's face she had to walk a ways out from the base going back across. Reaching the forest's wind shelter, halfway to the twin Cedars, she found that the thick stand of trees had trapped enough blowing snow so only shallow drifts lay below the drop-off. From there to the stream she used the smoother trail she'd used before it snowed, but still had to travel to the stream to get past the huge grove's dense trees.

From the middle falls to the pond, it was easy to follow the unbroken area over the deeply buried path, marked by trailside willows now buried nearly to their tips that had once been more than shoulder high. Aghast at how deep snow already was, though winter was only halfway over, she groaned aloud. How deep would it get before it started to melt? How could so much possibly ever melt?

Picturing the tooth-marked bark she'd seen last spring on a branch high overhead, she now knew how an animal had been able to reach so high!

Marty punched her heels in to descend the slope where stream widened into pond, poking each step down through the crust. Her hips, legs and ankles screamed with throbbing aches by the time she reached water level. Even after so much strenuous activity since being in the valley, her leg muscles were poorly conditioned for so much of the wide-stepping, side-swinging, knee-bent, gliding gait required for snowshoe use.

Afraid to cross the shorter pond center, which might contain hidden air pockets, she wearily inched along over shallow ice near shore, edging the bulky snowshoes between withered marsh plants to a spot near a cattail clump where she could easily squat to scoop back the snow.

The yellowed cattail stems proved too tough and fibrous to break off, and the plant-tangled ice impossible to chop through, so she bent the leaf-sheathed stalks over at the surface to hack them off. So great was her craving for anything fresh, she was determined to eat the bases up to where they were dead and unchewable.

After chopping through several stalks, some with a ring of jagged ice around their base, she tried to peel off the dead leaves. Her mouth watered at seeing several short root-runners caked in the ice-rings. Her grip was too clumsy from wearing both gloves and overmitts to pull any leaves off, and her cold-stiffened hands would freeze without them, however briefly. She'd simply have to carry the whole bundle home to strip, where it was warm and safe to remove hand gear. And where she could sit and rest.

Struggling to summon energy to get home, she slung the rifle over one shoulder and carried the bulky, leafy stalks, almost too many to fit, curled under that arm, the balance pole in the other hand helping her trudge wearily along. Her legs quivered uncontrollably with fatigue. Today's tortuous travel was several times longer than any since the first snow, two months ago.

The sun's last rays glinted over the southwest cliffs as she slid down the abrupt snowbank by the tent door. She'd traveled the entire short day!

She was relieved to see the children had curled up together on her bed, wrapped in a wool blanket, and were sound asleep, safe and warm.

She waited until after supper was cleared away and she felt slightly rested to tackle the stalks she'd brought. Aching fatigue made them seem unimportant, but gnawing cravings gave her no peace. She struggled to peel layers of sheathing leaves from the stems. She was too weary and they were too tough to pull loose, so she carved away the leaves, one by one, where each attached around the stalk.

Only after tediously peeling back and trimming off layer after layer of leaves, now dry and yellow-brown, did she find a few small, pale green, sharply conical sprouts near the stem bases. Out of a whole bulky armload of stalks, she could find only a small handful of very short edible sprouts and runners. The rest was dead and terribly fibrous.

She left the tangled mess of leaves strewn on the dirt floor long enough to share the disappointingly few raw bits with the youngsters, seated beside her near the fire. She wouldn't bother to get more until spring thaw, no matter how much she craved fresh food.

Cleaning up the mess, Marty noticed that the dry leaves easily split lengthwise into thin flat fibers. The fibers were surprisingly strong, even strips only a quarter inch wide.

Intrigued, she studied the tough strands. Eventually, she'd run out of fishing line, it was down to the last unused spool now, and the salvaged thread wouldn't last forever. Perhaps she held a replacement for both.

Weary but too achy to try to sleep yet, time hung heavy. Nothing urgent was left to do. So she split several leaves into narrow strips and experimented with twisting the long fibers together. She tried handling them like the wool to make yarn, but thin, flat fibers didn't roll over her leg like wool, they had to be rolled between her fingertips.

A single twist of overlapping layers made a very sturdy thread thickness. But, in running her fingers along the fine length, she realized she'd have to sew with it from the starting point to prevent the ends of each individual strand from snagging and sliding back to form a knot. When two twisted strands were coiled together, it made a twine she estimated to be strong enough for snare lines. Coiled in four strands, the fibers yielded a light rope, pencil thin but extremely tough.

She wearily crawled into bed feeling triumphant at having figured out such an all-encompassing solution to the problem of replacing not only thread, but of rope, twine and string. Though she had rope and fish line to last for a while, it was an immense relief to know she could make more whenever it was needed.

Drifting towards sleep, she smiled grimly; for once, she'd found a solution to something before she needed it—a most welcome change.

Late the next night, Marty grumbled under her breath at having to get bundled up just to go out to the toilet. It would be so much easier to use the indoor basket. But without a storm she couldn't justify using the moss-lined basket indoors.

Stepping out from the huge fir's protection into a steady wind, she paused to survey the familiar scene, bright from the nearly Full moon, partly shrouded by high, broken clouds. Something was different.

She was startled to realize the oddness was caused by eerie, blue-white shafts of flickering light that wavered in fluted, shifting bands across the velvet black of the star-dappled sky. The Northern Lights! The unique sight made her neck hair prickle under the warm protective hood.

Brisk wind soughed through the trees, made them sway almost hypnotically as their starkly naked branches raked futilely at the vast panorama of sparkling stars and dazzling light bands. Scintillating, erratically shifting Aurora Borealis ribbons bathed the snowy camp in a spooky, shimmering glow while wind swished naked branches back and forth. Marty swayed almost drunkenly to one side as the flickering, wavering movements made her stomach churn. She had to lean on the depleted woodpile and look away from the Lights to keep from falling. Studiously directing her gaze down to keep from getting dizzy again, she hurried back inside.

She knew what the Northern Lights were, had heard of it more than once, but had never in her life expected to see it. How could they be far enough north to see this? She worried, unaware the Lights sometimes appear far south of her location in these mountains; even rarely extending to the southernmost states.

The last venison was eaten days ago. Now only a few chips of mutton and half the salmon remained. Marty had to get meat—they couldn't eat just grain and cattail roots, the only foods she had much of. All other food was gone except remnants of flour mix, dry berries, coffee mix and tea makings, a very few spices, and cattail pollen.

Day after day she slowly wandered around on sore legs, going through the motions of hunting while trying to figure out how to get meat. Big game avoided her with infuriating ease. There must be a way to get close enough for a shot! She fumed.

She finally abandoned hunting elk or moose, and morosely headed up the valley. Maybe deer wintered there, and would be less wary because she'd only gone up there once in over two months.

Below the promontory—disgustingly no longer occupied by any Bighorns—and above the slip-fault, Marty veered up-slope from her usual route, following the base of the northern cliffs. After going a few dozen yards, she discovered a wide path worn deep in the snow. It originated from a jumble of snow-mounded rocks at the cliff base and angled toward the valley center. The path reeked of strong urine and had obviously been well used since the last snow.

As quietly as possible, tingling with excitement, she followed the packed furrow to the base of a thirty-some foot tall evergreen whose bark was mottled with irregular cream-colored patches of bare wood. High up in the young tree, she easily spotted the bristly silhouette of a porcupine, feeding leisurely and paying her no attention.

She felt a warm surge of elation—fresh meat near enough to shoot! It looked like it had to weigh a good twenty-five pounds—days of meat! Raising the rifle to aim sharply upward, she realized the creature was too close to shoot with that gun, but she wasn't sure of hitting such a small target if she backed away. After a moment of turmoil she drew the pistol, always carried under her coat, and shot with that, dismayed that it took three shots to make the creature fall.

An abrupt ground-jarring rumble echoed the loud, sharp pops of pistol fire. Marty fought brief panic at the shot-triggered avalanche, somewhere up higher in the valley. As the echoing roar faded she heaved a huge sigh of relief that she was not in danger from the safely distant avalanche. She had to be very aware of her proximity to any cliff when shooting, or an avalanche that caused would bury her!

Worried she'd only wounded the animal, she slowly approached the dark bristly heap lying quietly in the snow by the tree, stepping carefully to avoid the many scattered chunks of greenish feces that smelled strongly of rotting wood. A maze of hare tracks were interspersed with the feces and scattered, green-needled sprigs the porcupine dropped as it ate the tree bark. She wondered how good green sprigs might be for snare bait, and if porcupine trees were where all the rabbits had gone.

Near the quilly beast she was engulfed by a feces-and-turpentine stench. Gagging, she regretted her poor shooting. This porcupine was gut-shot.

Gingerly trying to find a safe way to pick it up without getting the stink on her mitts, Marty finally tipped it onto its back with the balance pole. Avoiding the mass of dangerously sharp quills, she pulled off her mitts and sliced down the quill-free belly with the hunting knife.

Greatly relieved at the unexpected ease of skinning it, she worked the meat free of its poorly attached skin, but was astounded at how much smaller the body was than it looked under all those jutting quills interspersed with thick fur. It only weighted about half her estimate. She drooped with disappointment.

Gutting was a horribly fetid but fairly simple chore, much quicker than the spike deer or ewe. She carved away all bullet-damaged meat as fast as she could hack it loose, holding each choking breath as long as possible. Gasping fresh air desperately, she stepped back to don her mitts, wipe all traces of blood and stink from the knife in gritty snow, and replace it in the belt sheath.

Carrying the carcass by a naked leg, she shuffled hurriedly toward camp on hissing snowshoes, disappointment mixing with triumph, hopeful anticipation, and revulsion. Her elation at finally getting meat was ruined by the horrible odor. She paused often to roll the meat over and over in clean snow to rub away the blood, hoping the terrible reek came off with it. The snow scrubbings helped, but not much.

She cut the meat into small chunks and set it to boil in the Dutch oven, leaving the heavy lid off in hopes that more stink would dissipated as the water boiled. The youngsters, who seldom noticed any bad odor, complained loudly about the awful stink.

Though the meat was barely edible, they managed to choke it down; only increasingly distressful hunger pangs made that possible. The children normally ate everything she cooked with gusto, but complained now about the strong resinous taste.

Offensive as the flavor was, the porcupine gave them three days of all the meat they could choke down.

That third morning Marty set rabbit snares among the nearer trees, and baited each with a fresh sprig of evergreen needles, hoping that would work faster than waiting for a large hare to happen into the noose.

The next morning she was delighted to find she'd inadvertently caught a grouse. They were still around! She fairly purred with elation while cleaning and vigorously plucking the bird. Her mouth watered in anticipation of a roasted bird's savory juiciness.

The bird had no fat, its taste was bitterly resinous, and the meat tough and stringy. It was almost as bad as gut-shot porcupine. But, she shrugged, fresh stringy meat was better than hunger pangs, at least it slowed the weight loss from a rigidly rationed diet.

Now she knew why winter ended the farm's butchering season; winter meat was lean and almost too tough to eat.

Frowning with worry, Marty watched the hungry children wolf down the last bites of braised mutton. Swallowing the last shreds of her own small piece, she tried to ignore the ever-present ache of emptiness in her belly. For the dozenth time, she resisted the temptation to increase tomorrow's ration of dwindling grain and cattail roots. She still had a small amount of smoked salmon, but it would do for no more than three meals.

Hoping to find something she'd missed, she diligently searched through every inch of makeshift cupboards, shuffling empty containers into some semblance of order. One of the closed mess kits rattle as it was moved. Startled, she opened it carefully to avoid spilling whatever it contained. It held a few dozen dry Kinnikinnick berries she'd been so proud of storing many long months ago. They'd been the first thing stored away for winter. With new hope of finding forgotten food, she nervously grabbed the other two stored mess kits. Both were unexpectedly heavy!

She nearly sobbed with relief to find both tightly crammed with muskrat and bighorn fat cracklins. Brushing unexpectedly bleary eyes with a cold hand, she gloated at finding what now seemed like priceless treasure, despite seeming so unimportant when she stowed it here that she'd forgotten it.

Though rationed to one small chunk per person each day, and much stronger tasting from age, the minced cracklins were a welcome addition to a daily stew of crushed grain flavored by cattail roots and pollen. The steady diet of stew was monotonous, but filling for the amount, and the token amount of fat the cracklins provided was badly needed for more energy to heat quickly thinning bodies in the bitter cold.

The moment daylight began to brighten the highest clouds, Marty stepped outside to line up the Grand Fir's soaring top with a thin cloud streamer to see how fast the clouds were moving to tell if the weather was good enough to safely hunt far from camp. Wind speed up high was one thing she'd learned to use—the hard way, of course—to see if the weather was about to be nasty. The faster the high winds blew, the more likely it was to turn inclement.

The cloud streamers moved to the south, not east, like normal. She'd never seen them do that, and wondered what it meant. But the clouds moved so slowly she thought the weather would stay good long enough to hunt.

Still unable to believe she could get near a moose or an elk in the lower valley, she planned to hunt the upper half again, near the north edge, which should be less taxing than when she looked for watercress. She'd found the porcupine along there. Next time she shot at one, she grimaced, she'd back off and aim for the head with the rifle—if she ever got up enough nerve to try again!

Going up near the valley's top was much further to travel than around the lower section, and the days were now so short she'd have to keep going even if the sun came out and the glare hurt her eyes. But, for several days, the sun had cleared only a few low places along the south crest; usually it was down behind those peaks so most of the valley lay in all-day shadow, which was not as bright and painful to her eyes as it had been earlier. It was a trade-off: less glare, but much colder. Soon the sun would again rise higher—surely the shortest day had come by now!

Alert for game, the loaded but uncocked rifle in hand, huffing from trudging steadily up the steepening grade, she learned to punch the snowshoe toes in for uphill traction to prevent sliding back nearly as far at each pace as she stepped forward.

Marty stopped short, gasping in open-mouthed in awe and disbelief. Without realizing, she'd traveled so far up the valley that she faced a thick, braided column of twisted, glistening ice where water from the upper falls had frozen solid as it fell!

How cold did air have to be for that to happen? She stiffened and turned—how had she come so far without noticing cold or distance?

Engrossed in hunting and in not sliding back, she'd come further than intended without seeing a hint of any creature. She became aware that everything was eerily still, with no sign of the ever-present Bush Tits, Crows, or Gray Jays. Numbly, neck stiff with tension, she scrutinized her surroundings, wondering why not a single bird was active. She couldn't remember one daylight hour in this silent valley without seeing or hearing ANY noisy birds.

In a spasm of choking alarm, she KNEW something was terribly, dangerously wrong.

A few fat snowflakes drifted down past the front of her hood. Panic wrenched her gut as she looked up. Her heart skipped a beat at black, roiling clouds scudding low over the north crest, rapidly moving south. The clouds dribbled snow that brushed down the face of cliffs much too steep to stick to.

Another snowstorm! And she was more than four miles from home!

With a suffocating sense of impending doom, Marty now understood what wind from the north meant. Trembling with fear, she shuffled as fast as possible on the awkward snowshoes, slipped and slid down the undulating slope, nearly ran toward home in rapidly increasing gloom as a solidifying black cloud mass rushed on overhead. Snow fell thicker as wind began whipping down off the cliffs to swirl and growl menacingly across the narrow valley.

The falling snow's confusing, swirling motion obscured more and more scenery as it thickened, until only dimly seen cliffs nearby could guide her toward the remote safety of home.

Long before she reached the slip-fault, turbulent black clouds obliterated the cliff tops and the wind grew viciously strong and icy. Her heavily clad body perspired from fear and exertion despite the frigid air. Her face and nose stung like she breathed fire, so she shifted the knitted scarf up over her nose and mouth for protection. Her face immediately felt warmer. Air that filtered through the scarf was less biting to inhale, but it was alarmingly difficult to get enough air unless she slowed down so she didn't have to breathe so fast; it was that or risk uncovering her face and having her mouth or nose frostbitten in plummeting temperatures.

Breath vapor soon froze to the scarf and clogged its breathing gaps. Every few minutes she had to shift the scarf to breathe through an ice-free area. After the third shift she paused to pull the scarf off and pound out the caked ice, while the frigid wind sought to suck away each breath. Freezing air brutalized her bare face, brought tears that froze on her stinging cheeks before they could trickle to her jaw.

Marty shook with panic as she rewrapped the scarf, felt fear-sweat further dampen her body and saturate her clothes, cooling with alarming speed and draining precious body heat. She shivered uncontrollably.

It was nearly impossible to see ahead through the obscuring snowfall so she barely avoided tumbling down the scarp path. She kept reminding herself to travel slower to keep from getting short of breath. The shielding scarf again became clogged by frozen vapor and again she had to bare her face to the intense cold to clear it.

Below the drop-off she could no longer follow the cliff's shadowy landmark, had to angle away from it to reach camp by the shortest route, and had to peer more intently through cloaking snowflakes to see the way. Boiling, snow-laden clouds were so thick the day was now as dim as late dusk, making it harder yet to see where she was going so she blundered into the edge of the dense forest below the fault. Even in the best of conditions that was too hard to get through but its fringe led toward camp, though she repeatedly had to veer back to the right to stay near that edge. The density of those trees did help break the frigid wind's biting force.

The constantly erratic swirls of snow were dizzying and disorienting. At each wind shift the angle of falling flakes altered and so did her direction of travel, without her being aware she'd veered from a straight line. Dense swirling flakes made it impossible to be sure of direction as she focused solely on getting home.

Near collapse, sapped by cold, terror, and the long forced pace through difficult terrain, Marty finally had to stop for rest. Wriggling past thick, snow-laden evergreen boughs to be near a shielding trunk, she sat hunched on a branch sturdy enough to support her weight. Shuddering violently, eyes shut against the cold, she concentrated on regaining her breath and energy.

"Don't you dare lose your head in this, you'll die if you do." She admonished herself aloud to stay calm and rational, her scarf-muffled voice further muted by howling, whipping wind.

When her breathing slowed she unwrapped the rime-stiffened scarf to again pound out most of the brittle ice, struggling not to inhale the bitter air until the scarf was safely back in place. Then she pulled off one snow-caked overmitt to brush fine ice crystals from her eyelashes and around the muskrat hood's rim. The ice stuck fast to the hood's thick fur.

Vision was limited to a few feet. She squinted at the dim, shifting curtain of white and shuddered at knowing how easily she could get lost in the confusing swirl of snow and freeze to death, though surely she was less than half a mile from home and safety. At the image of freezing to death a mere stone's throw from camp, she laughed bitterly. The harsh sound shocked her out of the growing lethargy of frigid weariness.

She no longer shivered, but felt overwhelmingly sleepy despite agonizing cold. She laughed aloud again—freezing to death was supposed to be painless. This cold HURT!

Sobered by the image of dying where she sat, she forced herself to move again. But every step was so hard! Her strained muscles were stiff, her energy spent. She managed to get moving again, very slowly, only through sheer willpower and knowing that two precious children utterly depended on her and that no one else in the whole world could keep them from dying. She absolutely could not stop! As long as an ounce of strength was left, she could not let them die!

She worked back out to the very edge of the woods to keep from getting lost in its tangled, snow-shrouded depths, though the wind at the edge howled viciously past, pushed at her, nearly knocked her over with its relentless, gusting force. The intense cold was more penetrating in the open fringe of woods, its maliciously biting chill was excruciating. She was startled to hear whimpering moans, astounded to hazily realize the sounds issued from her own throat.

The world was unreal, like a horrible, vivid dream, snow swirling erratically this way then abruptly that way, causing her to feel so dizzy and disoriented she staggered with each shift in direction. She fought to move snow-shoed feet, edging further and further in the fluffy morass of new snow, step by slow endless step along the slight down-slope at the forest's fringe, toward where home and the children should surely be.

She wanted so much to sit down and rest!

Her frosted lashes drooped lower and lower until she stumbled and fell. Something thumped her head just behind an ear, cushioned by the thick hood. Exhausted, swaying on hands and knees in the soft fluff, Marty dimly became aware it was the barrel of the slung rifle that had bumped her head, that somewhere she'd lost the pole, and that she'd forgotten to put the overmitt back on. Both mitt and pole were irretrievably lost, and her right hand was so stiff from cold, even through the fur-lined glove still covering it, she could not move those fingers.

It was so tempting to lay her hurting, weary body down on the inviting softness of clean new snow—only to rest for a short time. It would be like lying on the spotless white sheets that covered Gram's cushiony-soft feather bed.

She was so sleepy . . . so very, very tired.

Marty abruptly jerked her head up, knew death was close, too close, and had nearly lured her into a fatal mistake. To rest now was certain death.

Without enough energy to grit her teeth in determination, she began to mumble aloud to keep her attention focused. Words were obscured to vague rumbles by the ice-crusted scarf, but she knew what they meant. She reprimanded her body harshly when a leg refused to move at her command, or an arm failed to shift with the need to change balance and nearly toppled her again.

At a faint whiff of smoke she froze. She could see no more than ten feet in the swirling, shifting gloom of the storm. No smoke was visible. A fresh surge of hope and energy, though sluggish, roused her. Through a haze of exhaustion she knew that as long as she'd been gone—had that truly been less than forever?—even the best laid fire would be low by now so she had to be very near camp to smell smoke.

Two more tottering steps and sharp thorns unexpectedly pierced through the layers of her pants, stinging the cold, clammy flesh of her thighs with startling new pain, dimly noted by her foggy mind as something important. She paused, swaying with exhaustion, to study the dim row of bushes she'd staggered against. Even snow-coated and leafless, something about it was familiar. She struggled to think what it was.

The icy wind briefly shifted again; another, stronger wisp of smoke suffused her awareness—now she knew exactly where she was! She'd blundered into the bristly rose hedge at the edge of camp.

Turning slowly, swaying, she painstakingly peered into obliterating flakes, searching for some glimpse of the uniquely pointed hood over the tent. Or the rumpled mound of the woodpile. Anything to show what part of the curved hedge she'd come up against. Near the end of a full circle, through a brief thinning of the dense, obscuring snow, she spotted darker shadow—part of the towering fir by the tent!

A few more steps and she'd be home!

Home, where the children were, where her reason for living was!

Home, where warmth and safety and rest waited!

She staggered with grim determination in that direction, reeling perilously from side to side, stumbled and fell over the woodpile, tumbling in a tangle of fur and snowshoes and sprawling unresponsive limbs into the once-shoveled path to the new latrine.

Too spent to stand, her right hand too numb to feel her weight on it, Marty awkwardly crawled the last feet to the tent, every shred of energy focused pointedly on the singular goal of reaching that door, of getting home.

Huddled together on Marty's cot, shivering, trying to keep warm in the deepening cold under both wool blankets, Ted and Amy waited quietly for Marty. With her return, the life-giving fire would be replenished, the tent would again be warm enough for comfort, and she'd cook something good to fill their grumbling, hours-empty stomachs.

Ted jerked up to stare past the edge of the blankets at a loud thunk and a muted, peculiar moaning sound near the door. His hair prickled, his wide eyes went black-brown with dread at the eerie, unfamiliar noise. His heart pounded hard in his chest as he stared helplessly at the shadowy doorway. Sometimes the wind moaned—it did now—but not like that! He was frozen with terror of that unknown, moaning THING that slowly came closer and closer to the door. The door moved—the Thing touched it! It was coming in! It was going to GET them!

Gasping and cringing in abject terror, Ted horrified himself by shrieking: "Mama!" His terrified cry shocked Amy into shrill, anguished howls of panic.

Their piercing screams instantly penetrated Marty's haze of frozen exhaustion. Her children were in danger! She had to reach them, had to save them from this new, mysterious threat!

Through tangled webs of lethargy she fought the hardest battle of her life, the battle to overcome her own exhaustion and confusion, to get to the aid of her precious babies.

"I'm here! I'm coming!" She croaked through a cold-dried throat.

Ted finally, barely, recognized her voice, and realized the snow-caked form crawling so arduously through the door was Marty. He nearly sobbed with relief.

But why was she crawling? Was she hurt?

He slipped out of the covers and, trembling fearfully, edged toward her, his heart pounding at this unexpected emergency. He tentatively reached out a hand to touch her face; it brushed the rigidly frozen edge of the scarf covering the lower half of her face. He jerked the hand back in alarm then reached forward again, careful to avoid the scarf. Where he touched her temple, just below her headband, the skin was nearly as cold as the icy scarf. He stared in awe, at a complete loss for what to do.

His tentative touch partly revived Marty. Through the murk of utter exhaustion she heard his soft boy's voice, "You scared me, I thought sumpin' was gonna GIT us."

And she knew the children were safe though Amy still sniffled, that she'd been what frightened them and made them scream. Relief washed through her—she didn't have to get up and fight some unknown thing to save them—but left her totally used up.

Too cold and spent to do it herself, not even able to get up onto a log seat to sit by the fire, Marty slumped on the cold, packed-dirt floor. She mumbled through half-frozen blue lips, instructing Ted how to rake up live coals from the dying fire, then how to lay on kindling, blow it to flame, and when to add bigger wood. He was very careful how he followed her instructions, too many times he'd been strictly forbidden ever to touch the fire—or else! If he did it wrong now, she might never let him do it again.

"Water." Marty croaked hoarsely, motioning feebly toward her mouth with a mittened hand. Ted dipped out a cup of cool, sooty water from the bucket always over the fire to melt more snow. She drank with quivering hands, so dehydrated from moisture-sucking cold that it hurt to swallow.

The fire slowly grew and warmed inside the tent to a more bearable temperature, and heated water in the bucket. Marty pointed mutely to the small silk bag of tea makings. Finally understanding, Ted nervously made hot tea. He tried so hard to do it right he spilled some. When it looked dark enough he dipped the metal cup full and helped Marty hold it steady while she drank hot, reviving liquid.

Still following Marty's hoarse, cryptic instructions, Ted heated several cracklins in a frying pan, divided the rest of the tea then distributed a generous handful of dried berries to each for their meager supper.

Drinking hot tea and eating even that meager amount revitalized Marty, slightly. It would take at least a good night's rest to regain energy. Her right hand was too stiff and numb to grip with, and she was still so spent she couldn't even remove her icy, snow-caked outer clothes without Ted's help. She sat for a while longer on the snow-spattered dirt, shivering in sweat-soaked clothes, until at last she could summon enough dregs of energy to crawl to her bed and drag her spent, trembling body up onto it. It was impossible to force her body the short distance to the fire to bank it for the night. Again, she had to talk Ted through doing it.

Her heart welled with tenderness and tears slipped unnoticed down her tingling cheeks as she thought what a good boy he was. He'd done an excellent job of fixing the fire and feeding them, especially for a first try. She knew he'd watched her fix the fire and cook countless times, but it was far, far different to actually do it himself.

Her last mumbled, raspy words before dropping off into exhausted oblivion were, "You did real good, son. You two go to bed and sleep now."

Ted puffed up with pride, feeling very pleased that she had trusted him to do things he'd been forbidden to try before. He smiled and nodded to himself as he led Amy to her bed and helped her snuggle down deep into it. Marty had said he did real good and had even called him son. He felt very grown up and capable as he nestled deep into his own bag.

At that latitude the year's shortest day was less than nine hours, so night lasted more than fifteen. The ferocious blizzard that started that day howled and raged for three or four days—light stayed so dim Marty could only guess its duration. Slowly regaining strength and the use of her right hand, she constantly agonized over how long this storm might last, and how much snow it would add.

With weather far too severe to venture out into, except the unavoidable, still-wobbly dash for wood from the drifted pile, she again used moss to line the poorly made basket in the corner for a toilet. The increasingly offensive odor, despite severe cold, was a constant reminder to empty it the first time she could possibly reach as far as the tree.

While the blizzard raged endlessly on, she used the last of her precious coffee mix. With no Dandelion or Chicory roots to roast for more, it was a trauma to use the last few stale granules. Desperate to keep this long-familiar daily routine, she fry-toasted cracked grain chunks to brew, and was amazed to discover that it was the reassuringly familiar ritual of brewing and savoring a hot drink that mattered, not which ingredients went into it.

Hunger gnawed at them constantly. Even after eating a strictly rationed, scant bowl of monotonous stew, their stomachs rumbled with hurtful emptiness. Licking an irreplaceable, softly cooked grain morsel from a fingertip to keep it from being wasted, Marty remembered pushing baskets of hazelnuts and pitchy cones into the far corner under the rear cot. She rushed eagerly around the beds to pull them out.

Dried by time and cold, the prickly husks readily fell off the hazelnuts but the stickers were more irritating now than when they were green. Too hungry to ignore this food, she meticulously picked all the nut-filled shells out of the bristly mass of husks anyway, then took a deep breath and quickly stepped out to rub rough snow granules on her stinging bare hands to scrub away the minute stickers.

It was tedious to pick shell fragments from the nutmeats after crushing them open between grinding rocks. Tired of doing that, Marty dumped several cracked nuts in a small pan of precious water, hoping to separate them more easily. But some shells sank, and so did some nutmeats, the rest, some shells and some kernels, floated. She went back to the tedious hunt-and-peck method, painstakingly salvaging every tiny morsel of nutmeats to share with the children.

Because the entire supply was about a rucksack full, each day she shelled only until a small handful of the highly nutritious nutmeats could be shared. It took an amazing number of nuts—and time—to yield that much.

The daily, token amount of nuts made only a slight difference in appeasing their grumbling bellies. Marty was hungry enough to try getting the seeds from the pine and fir cones in the other poorly made baskets. Hesitant at first, for fear of getting pitch smeared all over again, she was happy to discover the cones were no longer sticky. The coating pitch had dried to hard, translucent grit.

Pleased to find some cone scales loose and partly open, she tried to shake seeds out from between their protective scales. The scales had not opened enough, so she used a table knife's blunt tip to help pry the scales loose. It seemed to take forever to accumulate a small handful of the split-pea-sized seeds. There must be an easier way. Discouraged but remembering how easily pitch burns, she tentatively set a cone in the edge of the fire, where it soon blazed hotly. The scales opened wider as they burned. Marty hastily grabbed the pancake turner and nervously flipped the burning cone out of the rock-lined pit, aghast at helplessly watching most of the precious seeds drop into the fire and burn up or disappear into deep, hot ashes.

Determined not to lose more seeds that way, she put a cone in the soot-caked frying pan and used a blazing twig to ignite it. She was afraid of ruining the irreplaceable pan, but they absolutely had to have those seeds to eat. As seeds slipped free of the burning core, she shook them to one side of the pan, saving them from also burning up. After each cone burned out she set its dark-toasted seeds aside to dump the ashes in the fire pit. She did half a dozen cones before deciding that was enough for now—it was a long time until spring.

When she turned to hand equal portions of precious seeds to the eagerly waiting children, she groaned at dense, black, sooty smoke filling the tent.

Though scant, the crisp, oily seeds were so delectable she judged them well worth any harsh black smoke produced in separating them from their cones. But next fall, when squirrels cut and tossed the ripe ones down where she could gather them, she vowed to do the smoky chore of seed separating outside! Then she would only have the small seeds to store, not the bulky cones.

As soon as the storm ended Marty rigged a new balance pole. While binding sturdy branch tips to the bottom to prevent it from easily sinking into the snow, she realized the woodpile she'd dug it out of was depressingly shrunken, especially since they were only halfway through the long mountain winter. Remembering how much wood she'd amassed to begin with, she knew she must concentrate, during every break in the harsh weather, on getting more wood. Food was scant and monotonous so hunting was also urgent, but without wood they'd only survive a few hours before freezing to death. Especially during a frigid storm, when temperatures plummeted to devastating levels and wood was impossible to gather.

It was already near twilight so Marty dared not start out for wood today. Instead, she considered the problem of getting both wood and food from every angle, while keeping her hands occupied by sewing the last muskrat pelt into a new overmitt to replace the one lost in her brush with death. This time, to prevent another loss that she now had no fur to replace, she used a length of twisted cattail-leaf twine to tie the mitts together, running the line up through one coat sleeve and out the other.

At the first faint light the next morning she set out resolutely toward the meadow's northern edge where the sun would, near late morning, briefly warm the lower valley. She was relieved to notice the sun now rose slightly higher over the crest. Its welcome warmth was still terribly debilitated, but its slow return proved they'd passed the year's shortest day; from now to mid-summer the days would grow longer and life should at least seem less bleak.

Stopping a ways past the tilted maple, she left the sled to prowl through leafless, scattered trees. Searching the distance for any sign of game every few minutes, she studied each clear space for fresh tracks before entering it to look for wood. She sought game first; it could move quickly away, wood could not.

The blizzard's effect on this particular area of the valley was astounding—layers of snow left by gentler falls had been torn loose and whipped away to land against anything that broke the force of the storm's relentless wind. The thin skiff of remaining snow now exposed once-buried wood, big, dry chunks she had to strain to pry loose from the frozen ground.

With no choice but to do a man's work without his strength, Marty was forced to use her weight for leverage, securely grabbing protruding limbs and jerking her whole body backward or to the side to wrench the wood free of its icy anchor. Then she pulled the bark sled close and wrestled each chunk onto the sled the best way she could, rolling, tipping end-for-end, or sliding, any method that would move them.

But short rations in such cold had weakened her so she tired fast and had to rest often. During one such rest, sitting on a chunk of wood just broken loose from the soil, she glanced at the bare dirt of the log's imprint. Several small white spots embedded in the rigid ice-bubbles of the frost-heaved ground puzzled her.

Leaning closer to see what the whitish dots were, she was astonished to realize they were hibernating grubs. Automatically shrinking back in revulsion, she sighed and shrugged—it was impossible to fish until the ice melted. Then she recalled telling the kids that grubs were edible, and laughing with them that they'd rather use the horrible looking things for bait and eat the fish. Squinting, she recalled that crawdads had also seemed gruesome, until she tasted them.

Thoughts of food made Marty's empty stomach rumble in the snowy quiet. Eating these was better than starving to death, a too-real possibility. She hadn't seen a single fresh game track since the blizzard so it was now imperative to gather anything possibly edible. Reluctantly, steeling her nerves, she used a broken stick to chip away frozen soil to flip free of their haven every grub she could find. She carefully piled them on a corner of the sled. She broke loose and looked under several successive chunks of old wood, moving them only enough to search underneath.

Faced with moving the bouncy sled back to camp, she puzzled over how to save what grubs she had, maybe a scant half-cup. It was too far to go home for a special container for so little, so she dropped them in one overmitt to carry home.

In the tent, Marty used her body to block what she was doing from the youngsters while using the back of a large spoon to mash the soft white grubs into a formless lump with flour and cattail pollen. The mashing and mixing disguised the telltale shapes so they seemed less repulsive, even to her. Patiently blending the caked remnants of stale powdered eggs with that and water, she scrambled the mixture in a dab of lard.

Nearly gagging on the first bite, she had to pause with her mouth full to regain self-control. When she could finally force herself to chew, she was surprised to learn the taste wasn't bad, except for the unpleasant flavor of dried eggs, which overwhelmed all others. Bland, faintly sweetish and richly fatty, she decided grubs were not so bad after all—as long as she didn't think about what she was eating!—and intended to gather any she found. But she was relieved they'd finally run out of powdered eggs.

Solemnly watching the youngsters hungrily gobble their marginally larger-than-usual portions, Marty envied their innocence and lack of prejudice, then wondered how they'd act if they knew they just ate grubs. Relieved this worked out better than trying to eat bony suckers, she grimaced. She'd even welcome those now.

Seeing the bright sliver of the New moon sink westward just behind the sun, Marty realized she'd missed noting the Full moon, again. Faithfully etching a line in the date stick, she assumed it was the eleventh of January, and they'd spent nine full months here. Though proud to have kept them alive so long, she knew starvation was an increasingly serious threat, and the deepening cold still potentially lethal.

Due to weight loss from a strictly rationed, nearly fatless diet, all their clothes, so recently almost too tight, now hung on them. With any luck she felt they could still survive until spring, but it was getting scary just to make it through each day. She was constantly reminded of the skeleton nightmare's prophesy, was haunted by it, but each time she visualized it she stubbornly renewed her vow not to give up.

A third of the original amount of grain and a quarter of the cattail roots remained, but the pollen was nearly gone and dry berries were rationed to a scant handful per day, cooked into morning cereal. They'd all grown so weary of monotonous stew that dinner now consisted of grain and cattail roots, boiled soft then mixed with one or two finely minced cracklins and fried into flat cakes in a dab of stale lard—sort of makeshift fried biscuits. It was the same ingredients she used in stews, but the texture was different, so it seemed less repetitious. Nuts and cone seeds were alternated from one day to the next, half a palmful split three ways, only a nibble.

Sleepless in the stifling silence of long evenings, broken only by faint hisses and crackles from the fire and the resting children's soft, even breathing, Marty pledged a solemn oath to be more prepared next year, or find way out, no matter what that took to accomplish. Unable to think of any new way to find an exit, she soberly assessed all the remaining tools and equipment, concentrating on how long each might last, and pondered what to do when they wore out. She focused on Gram's story of the old time buffalo hunt, considering for the first time all the ramifications of the tools those people had to have personally made and wielded, and their uses for parts of game that wasted none of any animal they killed.

Her own discovery of twisting cord from cattail leaves was vastly reassuring. One way or another, she knew she could find solutions to replacing tools as they wore out. But it was obvious she had an infinite amount of learning to do.

Her head sagged low. Most of that learning would continue to be the hard way.

CHAPTER 20

Before the new moon grew enough to notice, Marty used the last cracklins, pollen, and dried berries. She searched the crowded tent for any forgotten food more thoroughly now than a month ago. While looking, she shook dust and debris out of several empty bags, folded the cloth ones and stored all but two in empty cupboards to protect them from mice and dirt, both still a problem despite thick snow and harsh cold. How could mice live through winters like this when there was nothing for them to eat . . . "Except our food!" She growled, tapping on empty rabbit tubes once stuffed with pollen, hoping to salvage a tiny bit more. Then she folded the pelts enough to also fit in the cabinets.

She frowned in concern while inventorying the food. They still had nearly half the nuts and cones, several pounds of unprocessed grain, and a silk bag the size of a bed pillow of dried, partly crushed, gnarled cattail roots. The skimpy amount of flour had actually grown from being mixed with what was left of each day's finely ground grain and cattail root powder after she scooped up the rationed amount of coarser grain to soak. But she was saving that few cups to make gravy—if she ever got more meat to use it with—which would extend it much further than making biscuits. She dumped the half-cup of pollen shaken from the tubes into the flour bag.

She also found a tangle of various lengths and thicknesses of weaving materials, and a medium size silk bag each of dry moss and cattail heads.

Dumping the cattail heads out onto another bag, she stripped them for their minute seeds, pushing loose fluff back into the first bag. Adding a pinch of tiny seeds to each pot of monotonous stew would change the taste a bit, though it would add no bulk.

The gradual shrinkage of food left enough room to store each day's fuel inside to thaw, but she cut it outside. She cautiously chopped today's wood near the door, in the shrinking clearing whose snowy sides had grown to just below her shoulder.

Chunks often flew up and hit the tent, but it was the only place she could get a firm base to lay the wood on, everywhere else was too deep in snow for her swings to bite deep into the wood. She was careful to stay between the wood being chopped and the kids inside, so no flying piece could hurt them. An occasional chunk, hit slightly wrong, hurtled up end over end and fell back to bounce and hit her, causing big dark bruises, even in places padded by layers of clothes and only nicked lightly. Her many painful bruises were very slow to heal because of mild scurvy from no fresh foods to eat.

Forced to go out every day the weather allowed to get any wood she could find, Marty noticed the towering Noble Fir's long, long shadow shortened a tiny bit each day. The sun's light was still weak and gave no real warmth, but it did shine almost imperceptibly deeper into the valley bottom each day it broke through multiple layers of lumpy gray clouds.

The brightness and glare of the sun shining however weakly on the solid white coat of snow became an increasing problem. It gave her a fierce headache if she stayed out long but it was too frigid out in the dimmer parts of the day, at dawn and dusk, to be out very long without her hands and feet getting dangerously numb, despite wearing thick, warm, knitted goat's wool sox over the thin cotton ones she'd brought, and thickly furred overmitts over fur-lined leather gloves. The overhanging fur hood adequately protected her face with the knit wool scarf shielding her lower face and holding the hood's attached cape tightly around her neck. Under that, the wide headband of muskrat fur stretched across her forehead, down over her ears, and under the nape hair. All those layers made it protectively warm, but made it difficult to turn her head and even harder to hear small rustling sounds. She learned to turn her body to see in another direction.

Marty chuckled aloud, thinking how expensive and fashionable all her fur garments would be Out There, as she now thought of the rest of the world. She smirked at the irony that now, where no one could see them, she had no choice but to wear furs to stay warm enough to survive.

They all slept long hours at night and napped often during the day out of boredom and to stay warmer, but also because they were weak from cold and hunger. Marty woke often to make sure the fire still burned hot enough. She constantly feared frostbite, even in the hooded tent. The nights were now extremely cold, the days not much warmer.

The daily ration of evergreen cone seeds or hazelnuts had to be decreased as those supplies dwindled. But even a small nibble of either was a treat that helped break the tedium of grain and cattail roots—except that the seeds and nuts were also getting monotonous.

Marty handed first Amy, then Ted their daily ration of four shelled hazelnuts each, feeling terrible about the amount being so paltry. Amy's attention was focused on hungrily stuffing her mouth with all four at once and trying to chew them. It made her sunken cheeks bulge out like a chipmunk.

Ted eagerly bit into one nutmeat, more willing to savor his share. With a startled yip of pain, he touched his lip with a fingertip, looked at it and saw a smear of blood.

"Oh! Let Mama see." Marty automatically reached for him in sympathy, afraid he'd cut his mouth on a shell fragment she missed.

Ted stared blankly at Marty. His only response to her gesture of concern was to pull back slightly.

She hesitated at his reaction.

Continuing to stare blankly at Marty, he dug in his mouth with a fingertip, exploring a strange gap in his bottom front teeth and a sharp thing lying loose under his tongue. Marty called herself "Mama" again, he thought, still staring at her without expression. The word "Mama" brought a shadowy memory of a woman walking away, a woman he never saw again. Remembering her made his throat feel full and hurt worse than his torn gum. He didn't want to think of that, but "Mama" echoed in his mind as he continued to stare at Marty. Daddy said Marty's my real mom now, he thought. His throat hurt again to remember Daddy went away, too. And Grandpa. He didn't want to think of things that made his throat hurt.

Ted focused his attention on spitting the hard loose thing into his hand. He studied the tiny tooth in his palm, fingering the gap with his other hand, until he understood what it was.

At seeing the tooth, Marty leaned back and sighed with relief that it hadn't been her carelessness that hurt him, but only the normal event of losing a baby tooth.

"Is the Tooth Fairy gonna come now?" The boy's voice was soft and husky. His wide brown eyes looked bigger than ever in his hunger-pinched face.

Marty looked down and sighed sadly. "The Tooth Fairy can't find us out here. And there's no place to spend the money if she could." Marty answered, gently wiping pale blood from his chin, concerned at how much his gum was bleeding, another scurvy symptom.

Ted nodded in mute resignation. Santa and the Easter Bunny couldn't find them either, and Santa was more magical than anybody, except maybe Marty.

At Ted's question, Amy looked up from eating her nuts. She'd had to spit them into a hand and chew a small amount at once. She stared in fascination at the tiny tooth. After a long moment the girl stood up and crowded in front of Ted to peer into his mouth, prying his lips apart until he opened his mouth wide for her to see. When she sat down, frowning in concentration, her fingertip probed her own mouth and teeth.

Nibbling slowly on her own meager share of nuts, savoring each one, Marty realized her own gums were almost too sore to chew. Perhaps she was only feeling sympathy for Ted's sore mouth. But, now that she thought about it, she noticed all her teeth hurt to bite down on, and the gums felt sore, slightly puffy, and unnaturally soft.

That night a nearly windless storm deposited several more inches of fluff on the old snow's thick crust. The conical hood over the tent deflected some of the new snow to the sides, but the pointed top allowed snow to build up to a narrower and narrower gap overhead as it deepened. The tent walls bulged relentlessly inward, discouragingly unlike her dream of having so much food the walls bulged outward. Marty sulked at having so little food left, feeling helpless to solve the dilemma, brooding that it wasn't possible to make the walls bulge out with too much food now, not even if she got a whole elk. She sneered bitterly. No chance of that!

Feeling claustrophobic with the walls bowed in, Marty moved aside one cot at a time and used the breadboard as a flat surface to push hard against the walls to press loose snow back until it became packed too solidly to move further. Though the walls were not moved back out much, the tent sides hung straighter and made it seem less crowded in there. But she realized that those walls could not be moved out again, not until spring thaw, and continued to sense the force created by the sheer weight of snow building ever higher over their flimsy shelter. She shuddered, feeling more helpless than ever.

Snow was now so deep that the dug and redug path to the tree-side latrine was no longer down to dirt, but had become caked ice more than a foot deep, and still the snow bank alongside the path was up near Marty's shoulder. She was forced to carve out new steps up that bank, wide enough to wear snowshoes on, to get onto the snow surface so she could leave camp to hunt or get wood. And so the children could get up to the latrine path.

Near the top she paused to catch her breath and glance up at the snowy peaks with their shadowed blue depths, amazed again at their beauty, then turned back to digging steps, clearing off the near side of the woodpile, and unburying the icy path to the tree, all the while thinking how treacherous those beautiful peaks were, how infinitely dangerous.

Though dismayed by the deepening snow pack, Marty understood it further insulated them from the increasing cold. However, so much snow made it impossible to find bared wood or grubs. All were deeply buried again.

With the passing of that storm the sky cleared entirely and the days became achingly bright and cold. Nights were crystal clear and extremely cold. Untold stars sparkled like glittering ice crystals in the black night sky. The second time that night Marty woke to feed the fire, she was startled by a loud, sharp pop. Puzzled, she wrapped in the deer hide to sit by the fire, holding the loaded pistol. This dawn, night's coldest part, was so cold that even beside the fire her breath formed a dense cloud in front of her. She soon heard another pop and another, and more, getting closer and closer together until they were almost continuous, though some sounded much further away than others. Her eyes rolled in fear in the near darkness of a partly banked fire. She could not imagine what caused the sound and recalled she never did figure out what had made those echoing cracks last fall, when it first turned cold.

Laying three more thick pieces of wood on the coals, she huffed in exasperation and was lost momentarily in a thick cloud of white vapor. This primitive valley had many strange things that made unknown noises. Their very mysteriousness was spooky.

She finally had to go back to bed to sleep more, her sore eyes refused to stay open any longer.

Outside in the sub-zero cold wave, more standing trees cracked with a sound like gunshots from their sap freezing solid. Many branches fell, broken by traces of sap expanding into wedges of ice. That ice pressure caused some whole tree tops to split into long thin strands of wood fiber that arced out and down from the gaping trunk splits. The tips of some strips bowed so far down they touched the snow, lending an eerie other-worldliness to the winter forest.

In the painful brightness of a clear mid-morning, Marty was horrified to realize that all the exposed chunks in the depleted woodpile were frozen solidly together. Most pieces buried under the deep drift were not as securely stuck together, but she found it impossible to get such long sections untangled from the frozen top pieces.

Desperate for wood to keep from freezing to death, she tried to chop down a fairly small standing tree. She swung hard with the sharp double-bitted ax, but it ricocheted off without gouging deeper than a shallow chink in the bark. Marty blinked in astonishment and bent close to examine the small nick, then stared around at other trees, seeing the few within sight that had split and arched into grotesque shapes. Her scalp prickled as she realized with a sinking heart that all standing wood was too frozen to chop into, let alone through. She could see a few freshly broken branches within reach in the nearby woods. They would have to do; they were all she could get.

She soon realized many of the fresh branches were green and that reachable dry wood was very scarce. All nearby squaw wood had been gathered, too. She clicked her tongue, chiding herself for not leaving the nearest of those for times like this.

Pulling the noisy bark sled, she set out to gather older broken branches still caught on other branches, which she could only now reach because the snow was just enough deeper. She grimaced, thinking how naive she was in being so careful to get enough green wood when now dry wood was what was so desperately needed. Other things learned by experience.

Ted wiggled and picked at his other bottom front tooth, which was also loose, until it fell out a few days after the first. Marty had even more trouble getting the new hole to stop bleeding. She blotted thin, pale blood away with a cold wet cloth, wondering if this was normal. His gums looked oddly bruised, but she could already see the tops of both new teeth near the surface. As they very slowly grew in, the new teeth began to look enormous in his hunger-pinched face.

While grinding a day's ration of fast disappearing grain, she realized that, for sure, there was not near enough food to last until new foods could grow in the spring. So, despite their already half-starved condition, not knowing what else to do, she rationed their scant portions even more severely. But she cooked that set amount and fed the kids first, then ate what was left.

Day by day though, she became shakier, weaker, and thinner until her clothes hung so loose they were hard to keep on. Her joints swelled and ached, her leg muscles grew so hard and stiff every move became harder to make, and always, always she was tormented by the burning, gurgling, hurting emptiness inside. In a very few days the least amount of exertion drenched her with sweat, which could be deadly if she was outside very long. After only walking to the latrine and back she felt so shaky she was afraid she'd fall. She was horrified to realize she was now so weak it was impossible to go hunt food or gather wood!

She understood then she had to make a choice, possibly the hardest one of her life: eat more of the scant daily ration and feed the children less so she'd have the strength to keep them warm and fed enough to stay alive, or continue to feed them part of her share and doom them all to certain death. Even if her babies cried from hunger, she had to maintain enough energy to keep searching for food, and to keep gathering wood or they'd freeze. She was plagued by guilt at failing to provide for them. They were already slowly starving to death and now she had to feed them even less.

That night she ground a bit more grain and roots to soak for breakfast, intent on eating enough to go get something edible tomorrow. Going out for an arm of wood just before retiring, she saw a glittery bright full moon rising, lighting the snow until it was nearly as bright out as a cloudy day. She sighed frigid air, another full moon. Will we be alive to see the next one?

She did feel better after eating the larger breakfast, enough stronger to go as far as the overhang where they'd sheltered from rain so long ago. Gram had said rock lichens could be eaten if you got hungry enough to get past their bitterness, and some grew there that the snow hadn't buried. She hoped.

Though shaky with fatigue when she got there, Marty did find the cavelet enough protected from snow by the dense forest fronting it that she had no trouble going inside. While carefully scraping lichens off all the rocks she could reach, she saw that the stone making up the overhang was solid enough that snow could never cave it in on top of them, and realized those walls cut out all draftiness except from the open front. But there was no way she could move the tent and the rest of their belongings, not even just the absolute essentials, in her current state of weakness. She shook her head at not thinking of moving here before she grew so weak. It would be so much warmer than the hooded tent. But she could not think of a way to block the front or to move enough to keep them alive. The tent would have to do.

When she had all within reach, she took the lichens home and ground the brittle plant-like growths like the grain, added them to cattail root flour, and mixed in enough water to make a thick paste that she boiled like dumplings in water with a trace of nearly rancid fat. They were gooey, soggy, somewhat bitter dumplings, filled with sand from scraping the rock, but it was something different and slightly more to put in empty bellies, and had some nutrition.

Near dusk, returning from the latrine, Ted said, rather indignantly, "I saw a deer. I didn't see no babies! You said . . ."

Marty jumped up and frantically layered on her outer clothes, then loaded the rifle with shaking hands while answering, "Some babies take a long time. Animals have babies when it's warm out so the babies are big and strong when it gets cold again, or else they'll die. Animals can't store food like we do." She started to rush out, turned back. "Where was the deer you saw?"

Ted stepped back out the door and pointed to the deepest part of the woods to the southeast. Marty's heart sank. Could she find it before it was too dark to see it in there?

Though she looked and looked, she could not find even a fresh set of tracks, the snow was too rumpled from clumps of snow falling off branches and her many wood gathering trips. She'd never had to learn to track game, and was no good at it now. She slouched back home, weak-kneed and dizzy, shaking from hunger and adrenaline letdown.

Marty sat resting, feeling suffocated by guilt at letting them all down, by failure to find the deer. Her empty stomach grumbled and knotted with hunger pangs. She simply had to find a way to get some kind of food! What would Gram do, if she were here and got this hungry?

But Gram had been this hungry! Marty reviewed Gram's tale of starvation that one severe childhood winter. There were no leg bones here to make gruel from, but Gram had described the maple tree whose inner bark kept them alive for many more days. Gram had ever after felt sorry that stripping its bark had killed that tree.

Marty sat bolt upright and growled: "I know a maple that will die soon, anyway!"

At daybreak the next morning, grimly determined, Marty took a knapsack and the hatchet to the edge of the drift marking the mostly buried, half-downed maple. She stripped thin bark from all the exposed branch tips, stuffing the chunks into the pack until no more would fit without falling out and being lost. Marty grumbled at herself for not bringing a bigger bag, then remembered this was only an experiment, in any case. If it was good, she could come back for lots more; she had lots of empty bags. Even such a small bag forced her to struggle home regretting she forgot to bring the sled.

Safely inside, stoking the fire, she wondered which part was edible. Gram said inner bark. When she examined a chunk by firelight she could see the outside was rigid and fibrous and the inside coated by a thin, slippery layer that scraped off fairly easy with a butter knife. Recalling festery bark slivers, she wondered what it would do to their stomachs if she were wrong. Hesitantly, she nibbled a tiny shred. Raw, the texture was rather slimy, the taste bland but vaguely sweet. After stripping all she'd brought and stewing it until the mixture was thick, she tasted a little before deciding it was safe to feed the children.

She could see it would take a huge amount of bark to strip enough of the edible layer to matter, and moving it would require the sled and lots of empty bags. Likely the tree would not yield enough to last very long since most of it was buried in a hulking snowdrift she'd have to somehow dig it out of. She shook her head at that image.

Once there, Marty used the woefully small camp shovel to laboriously bare more branches to strip, working in closer to the steeply sloping trunk to reach more, digging deeper and deeper as she went. Suddenly a foot slipped and she plunged down into a hollow formed by the raised trunk and dense branches. Snow caved in behind her and entirely buried her, shutting out both light and fresh air.

Feeling suffocated, certain she was going to die, in panic she thrashed and struggled in loose puffy snow then stopped, gasping, thinking, 'I didn't make it through winter after all.'

But my babies! I can't give up!

Still trying to catch her breath, Marty realized breathing was not so hard if she held still. Finally she calmed enough in her tiny pocket of thrashed-out space to see the faint glow of daylight overhead. Though she still had to strain to keep from giving in to panic, she began to systematically push snow, a mittened hand scoop at a time, from overhead to down under her feet, where she could stomp it tight enough to work her way up through narrow gaps between tangled limbs. When the last layer above caved in and fell past her face and she saw open daylight, she gasped huge deep breaths of fresh icy air, nearly sobbing with relief.

She was going to live after all!

Now she was infinitely thankful she'd refused to give up, and was able to calm herself enough to work the rest of the way out.

Too spent and shaken to strip more bark, Marty searched in vain for the camp shovel, and then tightened snowshoe laces loosened by her struggle. The rest of her meager energy was used up just getting home. After eating some of the newly gathered inner bark, she decided she was too exhausted to clean the dishes, and left them for morning, when she'd be rested. She used the handy scraped chunks of outer bark to bank the fire by overlapping several of the pieces over the top of large wood chunks before going to bed. But that was so effective it became painfully cold inside.

Marty's night was filled with bad dreams. She kept seeing the tent sides and ceiling bulge inward more and more until she felt as smothered as when she'd been buried in the snow. In the dreams she suffocated in the collapsing tent, squeezed to helplessness by snow weight as they all smothered to death.

The next morning, she chided herself aloud for being too enervated by the scare to do the dishes. Now they were dry and hard to clean. She should have felt invigorated by the success of staying alive, not sapped. Her tongue clicked as she mechanically scoured the bowls and soupspoons with gritty snow to clean them, which reminded her of scouring the same silverware with sand after retrieving it from the pack rats.

She set the cleaned dishes aside and brushed ice granules off her gloves, wondering how good pack rats were to eat. They were a rather pretty kind of rat, and their tails were fluffy, not ratty. But the very idea of eating rats made her skin crawl until she remembered how delicious muskrats tasted. She wondered where the muskrats went in such cold. Surely they weren't frozen under ice all winter. They'd drown immediately!

She warmed her hands with a quick cup of weak tea, then bundled up to go look for the pack rat nest from which she'd salvaged silverware. She had trouble finding it in the deep woods, had to wander around in the general area for a while before faint steam coming from small holes in a low mound pinpointed it.

Using the balance pole's sturdy top end, Marty scraped soft snow aside to bare the crown of the nest then used it to wrench and pry the tangled nest apart. She staggered back and yelped in fear when rat after rat frantically jumped out through the open top of their twiggy nest. They tried hard to run away, but floundered helplessly in the deep soft snow, only moving away very slowly. Desperately, Marty bashed each of them in the head with repeated blows from her pole, growling and shaking violently from the effort by the time they all lay still.

There were four. Each was a bit over a foot long, less than half of that tail, and weighed about a pound. Timidly gathering them up by their beautiful fluffy white tails, she tried not to look at the flattened bloody heads. She felt unbearably savage and cruel for killing the small, pretty, white-footed creatures, but she also felt victorious that she'd finally gotten meat, enough to last several days if she rationed it. Sometimes being savage was life-saving.

She tube-peeled them to save the pelts, knowing she would never waste another scrap of fur after experiencing this cold. She laid the entrails out to freeze, so they could be used later for some sort of bait. In the back of her mind though, she knew that if death became too likely from starvation, she would even resort to trying to eat those. An overwhelming urge to gag made her shift attention back to now.

She looked up above the snow piled so high by the entry it was hard to see over. It made her realize how far she'd been climbing down to get into the tent, and how much the pointed canopy let the deepening snow pack closer and closer in over top of them. She found it scary to go in and see the sides and top bulging inward from all that pressure. Marty shuddered in dread, thinking that maybe the dream was really a warning that it would collapse on them, and not just aftershock from being buried under the snow-shrouded maple.

She kept the pretty Wood rat tails but wasn't sure what to do with them, so she laid them out to freeze dry, and left three of the cleaned and skinned packrats outside, hung up under the windbreak to stay frozen and keep longer. The largest went in to be cooked. Thankfully, all four had a layer of fat over their muscles.

Her mouth watered and her stomach rumbled the whole time it took to cook the meat from its bones. She added flour mix to thicken and flavor the large pot, and kept cooking the bones until even the tough bits of gristle at each joint slipped off easily and were soft enough to chew. Halfway through, the sleeping children woke from the aroma and sniffled and whined with impatience until she finally dished up broth for them. They loved it!

Marty finally tried a bit of broth and found the taste similar to muskrat or rabbit, and decided it was acceptable as long as she didn't think about where the meat came from. Then she wondered if the savoriness was due to extreme hunger or because they were normally tasty; no matter which, it tasted good now.

Because their stomachs were so shrunken, none of them could eat much at once, which amazed Marty. She'd always assumed a starved person could eat enough to regain their weight in a short time, but now realized that was not so. In any case, these small creatures wouldn't last long and had to be rationed to not much more than they'd been eating. The fat that coated the game was thin but did help stop their weight loss, for now.

When the stew had thickened further from a meager handful of added grain, they ate again. Marty decided pack rat really was as good as muskrat and rabbit. But she had no idea where to find more.

By the next day they all felt slightly stronger from having meat again, and from eating three small meals instead of only two. It was obvious to Marty that they didn't have to have a lot more food each day to survive winter, but more than they'd been eating.

When Marty was not reliving the horrifying skeleton nightmare in her sleep, she kept having the same dream about the tent caving in and all of them smashed and suffocating while she was powerless to save her screaming children. One or both dreams disrupted her sleep, over and over, until she was nearly incoherent with nervous exhaustion.

Exhaustion did not stop the gut-wrenching dreams.

On the third morning after getting the pack rats she discovered that more snow had fallen overnight and saw with hammering heart that the wind had drifted it even higher over the canopy. Soon they actually would be buried alive! She had to do something, now, today!

In desperation, she loaded the bark sled with their clothes bags, the guns, ammo, tackle box with spare knife and whetstone, the axe, some kindling, several large coals in some ashes in the Dutch oven, and, at the last moment, added the two unopened chutes and the precious date marker stick. After tying everything in securely, she struggled to pull the sled up the slight grade near the forest edge the mile to the fault-side trail, then another quarter mile to the overhang.

Catching her breath, sitting on the raised ledge in back, Marty studied the recessed area. When she gathered lichen here recently she hadn't paid attention to it as a place to live in. Most of the snow ended just in from the mound of nearly buried rock that had formed the cutback space. The entry needed to be off to the side of that rock because it would be dangerously slippery now. Again she judged the area to be nearly triple her height from side to side, and well over her height in depth at the deepest point near the center. Plenty of space for everything they had left plus room for dry wood.

She rose and went out to snap off an elbow-to-fingertip size branch of cedar to sweep skiffs of snow out of the way, then used the coals and kindling she brought with blown-in duff already there to start a fire in the end with the highest ceiling. It was the end that curved sharply outward, forming a good corner to help contain the blaze and reflect heat. She was far too weak to bring fireside rocks or the heavy grill up from the tent, and any nearby moveable rocks were hopelessly buried under all that snow, but with what she had left to cook, she could simply scoot the pan sides against the coals.

When the fire was stable she piled on big pieces freshly cut from the fringe of nearby woods and left to move more from the tent. She hoped the rock walls beside the fire would soon warm up enough to amplify the fire's heat, to make up for this shelter's open front.

Next she brought the kids wrapped in all the furs and bedding, plus what was left of the food and cooking gear. She'd decided not to bother with the wooden cupboards, the raft, or the empty storage bags and baskets. This load was almost more than she could pull, and she wasn't sure she had strength left to make another trip, even if she waited until tomorrow.

Building a big fire, she felt relieved to have lots of wood nearby. Though the shallow cave was fairly wind sheltered by the nearby thick forest, even with a big fire it was still too cold to remove even their outermost clothes.

Shivering despite all her layers of clothes, Marty cut long, thin poles from the edge of the woods and tied a pole top to each shroud line along most of one side of a new chute canopy. Then she struggled to tip them all up to lean against the outer edge of the overhang so that the poles held the chute up to cover the entire opening with the poles underneath to give a sloped shield from the winter cold.

When smoke quickly started to build up inside, she cut another long pole, leaving a side branch near the end long enough to catch the edge of chute's center ring to hold it up in place. She shifted that pole until the canopy center was directly above the fire corner to vent smoke. That left a space near the fire for a doorway, opened simply by moving that end of the canopy.

Adjusting the pole bases out as far as possible without the bottom of the canopy raising from the ground, she secured the chute bottom to the poles at the ground, hoping that would break the worst of the wind and cold. The support pole tops held the canopy's upper edge slightly above the fault top, but left a few narrow wrinkle-gaps above the rock lip that let some heat escape. Picturing how far she would have to travel to get above the shelter to change that, she knew she lacked the strength to fix that slight loss.

The poles that held the canopy side up also held it out from the overhang so living space was less constricted. The children could now move around a little bit more than before, though they had little energy to play. This new shelter was still not very warm with only a sheer layer of moldy-smelling silk between them and the punishing cold, but soon became nearly as warm as the canopied tent had been.

Unable to even consider moving the cots, she cut evergreen boughs from the woods to sleep on, to cushion and insulate against the hard rock floor's biting cold. The aroma of fresh evergreen boughs was pleasant and helped mask the chute's awful mustiness.

The next day, using more new poles and the last parachute, she rigged up a lean-to between the two cedar trunks, away from the heat, for a food cache and freezer. She put the last solidly frozen wood rat and all the saved entrails in there. The other frozen carcass she took in to cook, hoping to make it also last two days though it was smaller.

She was exhausted and debilitated again from such strenuous efforts. This winter now seemed so long it was hard to recall any time it wasn't winter. The dark and cold were as depressing as the hunger and discouragement at not being able to kill more food than she had. So, to keep from worrying or getting more depressed, and to reaffirm her determination to stay alive, Marty decided to spend much of her indoor time weaving, using materials gathered last fall. But she had to make another trip for those the next day, though it was difficult to force herself to go inside the nearly buried tent. Then, since she was there with the sled, she also decided to bring the men's clothes bags to lay in front of the low beds to block the cold floor draft.

In the new shelter she laid aside all the weaving materials so carefully gathered and saved when she'd been so busy harvesting food. She unpacked and sorted the men's clothes, looking for more wool scraps, finding many large socks, mostly thick warm ones. What a welcome find! Now she could also wear those in multiple layers. Eddies' coat even fit over her corduroy jacket. That was much warmer but awfully heavy when she was so weak.

She discovered the gloves both men brought. Edward's were big enough to fit over her leather gloves and she could still squeeze her overmitts on over those. Trying that out while cutting the day's wood, she found she could use that double layer of gloves better than her own gloves with overmitts, but adding the muskrat fur mitts while traveling kept her fingers warm enough to be flexible when she did choose to shed the third layer to use her fingers.

The last useful thing she found in the men's clothes were two knitted hats, like larger versions of the children's. That brought a smile to her face. She could just picture Edward planning on teasing the children about the men having stocking caps like theirs. It also made her sad.

She hadn't missed any wool, earlier; all but a few feet of yarn had been used weeks ago, so she put that away with the needles for next year. As she did, startled, she realized she was automatically acting on the belief that they'd now survive through this harsh, endless winter! When had that changed?

Plus, she realized she now had time to think of solutions to problems that had come up when she was too busy or too new to the situation to consider solving. So, busy weaving to fill time, she figured out how to make loose weaves in a bowl shape for two sifters, one coarse and one finer, by weaving two strands side-by-side then pulling out one of the two strands to leave even gaps. The finer sifter was simply woven of finer material. It seemed ironic that she could find this solution only now, when there was nothing left to be sifted.

While working on weaving those she taught the bored, listless youngsters, especially Ted, to count. He's almost old enough to go to school, she reasoned, a good age for learning.

Ted easily learned to count to ten, had some trouble learning the teens, and less trouble with higher numbers until they went over a hundred. At that point the numbers ceased to have any meaning to him. Amy learned to count the fingers of one hand, but couldn't always count in sequence. She did understand she was three years old, all but her thumb and little finger of one hand, and Ted was five, one whole hand of fingers.

Gathering wood near the forest edge in gusty weather, Marty noticed that when the wind blew the trees swayed enough to pack more and more snow around the trunk into a hard circular gap. Thinking about the power of the wind in accomplishing that, she stretched to break off a piece of squaw wood. A stab of fear pierced through her as a snow-shoed foot unexpectedly slipped into one of those slick, treacherous dips and sent her sprawling with that foot wedged deep in the trunk pit, the other leg bent under her.

Staring up at the towering tree above her, gasping in panic and struggling to free herself, she groaned, "No! I can't get hurt! We'll all die!"

A gust of wind pushed the swaying tree trunk hard against her foot and ankle, crushing it mercilessly into the solid collar of packed snow. Marty cried out in pain and terror that such pressure could break bones and cripple her. The gust died and the towering tree straightened, loosening its hold. She struggled to pull her foot free before another gust came, but the snowshoe was snagged. Forcefully swallowing her panic, she wiggled around until she could reach down and untie the snowshoe and lever the foot out with her hands. She retrieved the snowshoe and gingerly felt her foot and leg, not sure how to tell if anything was actually broken. Wiggling the foot was a bit painful, but nothing seemed badly damaged. Sending up a silent thanks, she retied the snowshoe.

Careful to avoid the dip, she cautiously stood, pulling herself up with the help of the balance pole, and gingerly tested her weight on that foot. The muscles and tendons ached from her weight, but not severely. She heaved a deep sigh of relief at being able to take firm, though somewhat painful, steps. Apparently no bones were broken—she was so lucky! That one single second of inattention, when she stepped too near the packed, icy rim could so easily have been a fatal accident!

Again, like when she'd nearly broken through into the frozen creek's ice pocket, she'd been shown she must be careful with every move and take absolutely nothing for granted as being safe! She must always be aware of what she was doing and what might be dangerous.

Thereafter she kept a cautious distance from all trunks, reasoning she could always use her walking stick to knock dead branches loose or snag them a tiny bit closer to reach them safely.

That night she was awakened by a throbbing ache in that foot, ankle, and calf. She sat up and reached down into her sleeping bag to rub the ache away, appalled to feel some swelling in the arch and around the ankle. Swinging out of bed, one hand braced against the steep back wall to ease weight off the hurt foot, she limped over to stir up the fire so she could look at it. Her hands shook and her heart pounded—maybe she was more hurt that it had seemed at first!

But the arch and ankle were the only swellings and didn't look as bad as it felt in the dark. It would certainly be sore for a while, but she doubted it would stop her from doing absolutely necessary chores nearby, though it might slow her down.

The next day she limped around to gather the rest of the easy-to-reach squaw wood nearby. Her foot and ankle ached but not more than she could almost ignore. The day after that she had to go further out for wood.

Limping and squinting sore, gritty eyes against the aching glare, she hunted wood on the windblown gradual slope from the old camp, where thick-crusted, hard-packed snow was fairly shallow. With each piece of wood she pried free of the frozen ground, she searched fruitlessly for more grubs. The wood rats had all been eaten and the bones boiled so long they crumbled into tasteless mineral.

Looking up for more squaw wood, she stumbled into an exposed low-growing mat of aromatic evergreen shrubs nearly ten feet wide. The deep turquoise, sharp-needled Junipers had dry, wine-purple, waxy looking berries with a gray powder coating sparsely scattered on its ground-hugging limbs. They'd just recently been bared by wind shifting the snow or some other hungry creature would have eaten them.

Marty was proud of herself for recognizing them, and remembered Gram had said they were edible if not many were eaten at once. She tasted one. It had a thin, oily, gin flavor that reminded her of the one drink—a Gin Gimlet—she'd had with her honeymoon dinner with Eddie. It still caused her heart a stab of pain to be reminded of him.

She gritted sore teeth and blinked back tears at both the memory and the increased ache in the ankle at stumbling, and picked those few Juniper berries, stepping cautiously between slim, waist-high branches coated in loose-scaled, paper-thin, reddish-chocolate bark. At last she'd found a fresh winter food to vary the bland flavor of grains and cattail roots. Aware their taste could get overpowering, she decided to use only one or two in the daily stew.

Limping to gather more wood, she caught slightly resinous whiffs of the pungent berries from her jacket pocket as she moved. The smell had an alpine tang that reminded her of Gram brewing spruce needle tea. She knew spruce trees grew in a straight dense spire with no other plants close under them, and bore each needle from a woody peg base in spirals on rough, warty twigs. Those details made it easy to locate and identify the trees. She gathered several sprigs from branch tips of the next spruce she saw. They could safely have much more of this than Juniper berries.

At first she tried to boil a sprig of needles into tea, but ended up with an oily, offensive mess totally unlike what Gram prepared. But gently steeping another sprig in a closed pan yielded the remembered highly pungent, lime green, delicious tea that helped quell the incessant craving for something fresh. Marty was nearly weak with relief, so elated she felt giddy. It was easy to get plenty of this!

Despite being out of meat again, their scurvy symptoms improved as they all greedily gulped the vitamin-rich spruce tea several times a day. Their teeth quickly became less hypersensitive to the pressure of chewing and the gums stopped bleeding at every bump. Marty's persistent leg bruises finally started turning a sickly greenish as they faded. The tea was low calorie but vitamin rich, and did help fill the aching emptiness in their rumbling bellies for a while. Plus, it was a new flavor, not a jaded one like the rest of their meager fare, though the Juniper berries also helped with that for a few days.

Out early hunting and getting wood in dim light and cold, Marty saw another new moon sliver in the east. Limping back home, she marked their tenth new moon since being here, thinking with mild relief it must be February eleventh, and that winter was almost over. She only had to get them through another four or five weeks, then the first new greens would start up. But how could those grow with so much snow still on the ground? She pushed the thought away; it would surely start melting any day now.

She noticed that, even with their layers of clothes, all three of them were very thin, except for the children's oddly bulging tummies that rumbled so often from hurting emptiness. Both of their pixy faces were thin and pinched, with sad, dark-circled eyes that looked much too big for their faces. They were constantly listless and cranky with hunger and seldom played, hadn't for a long time. They slept most of the time, often whimpering with hunger in their sleep. Marty nearly cried every time she looked at them, and their whimpers always brought tears to her eyes.

She was afraid to look in the shiny metal mirror at herself.

Dreaming again of the gruesome skeletons' accusing glares, she awoke sobbing softly. In desperation, she increased the amount of morning cereal from two cups cooked to three. She was terrified of running out, but it would do no good to hoard some for later if they died of starvation before they could eat it.

All that was left would be wasted, then. So would their lives.

While grinding grain that evening, Marty recalled she never did reap any seeds from the abundant reeds, or water lily seeds or roots. Next summer she would have to get brave enough to shoot that moose before it ate the Water lily leaves and blossoms.

If they lived that long.

While out getting wood she realized her snowshoes no longer made the *hiss-plop-crunch* they had at first. She couldn't remember when that stopped, but now they only made a slight *hiss-pat*. Stopping and bracing herself steady with the balance pole, Marty lifted one foot to look under the snowshoe. All the fur had long ago worn off, and now even the woven wood brace inside showed through the tattered fur in many places. She sighed. This meant she had to go into the nearly buried tent to get rabbit skin tubes to replace these worn ones. She dreaded that with all her being. But she hadn't brought those skins to the new camp, hadn't been near the knoll camp for what seemed like weeks.

Trying to stay positive, she thought some game might have moved back into that area that she could hunt on the way. She swung closer to the north cliffs than usual, limping along, forging a new trail around the clumps of evergreens, watching keenly and pausing now and then to listen for game, trying to ignore foot and ankle pain. She needed all her attention on hunting.

After maybe half a mile down the valley along that area she was astonished to see another porcupine waddling importantly along a well-worn path between the snowy, jumbled rocks at the cliff base and a clump of evergreens. She grimaced. Could she stand to eat one of those again? Her stomach grumbled as she thought of pinched faces and hunger-swollen bellies of the youngsters dependent on her for their lives. She had to get any food she could.

But, this time, she would be more careful where she shot it!

Cautiously approaching the creature her mouth began to water. She admitted she was hungry enough to choke its meat down again.

The bristly creature was not the least bit afraid of her. It stopped and stared at her in curiosity while she very carefully aimed the pistol at its head a yard away from the menacing quills; no way was she getting nearer while it was alive. It looked quite large with all those quills. This close, one shot was enough.

As before, she skinned and gutted it on the spot. She wouldn't save these odorous entrails for bait. She rubbed snow all over the meat to rid it of residual odors, though this porcupine didn't seem as offensive as the other.

Feeling invigorated by the successful hunt, even if it was only a porcupine, she hurried back to camp with her prize, gritting her teeth at the painful ankle. This one felt heavier than the first, but she assumed that was because she was weaker and had since been taking only packrat-size game.

When she got it to camp and tried to stuff it into the Dutch oven, she realized it was only about the size of the biggest rabbit she'd cooked, barely five pounds, skinned and cleaned. She knew they could not eat much at a time, so she cut off the front legs and neck to cook, and put the rest out to freeze in the lean-to.

When they ate thin grain and meat stew that night, she was pleased to discover this porcupine tasted better. It was not gut-shot. It still didn't taste very good, even in their starved condition, so it took them several days to force the whole creature down into rumbling bellies, a few bites at a time.

Totally forgotten was the need to retrieve other rabbit skins to repair her snowshoes.

CHAPTER 21

Because of starvation weakness, they all now slept far more than they were awake, especially the children, who were also bored. Though Marty hunted every day it was not too stormy to be outside, she'd become so discouraged at such poor results that she often had to remind herself to watch for game. The hazelnuts and cone seeds were long gone, and even the grain and cattail roots were down to meager remnants. She did brew fresh spruce tea every day, making sure to pluck fresh sprigs on every trip. Though the bruised ankle and foot continued to ache when she walked, she was now forced to find another spruce further away. Both closer ones had been stripped of all the reachable sprigs.

Now, more than earlier, after every winter storm she felt jarring avalanches and heard their nerve-racking freight-train-at-her-back roar. During the day these were unnerving enough but at night the rock floor of the overhang vibrated with each one and spooked her from even the soundest sleep. To Marty's immense, if shaky, relief, they were now in a safe location, in no danger of being crushed by snow.

Wood was much easier to get here; in her weakened condition she wouldn't have been able to get enough to keep them from freezing to death if she had to go as far as at the tent. In that way, also, the move here had saved their lives. But the change to the overhang had not solved the food problem; they were now more likely to starve to death than ever.

She no longer had the nightmare of having the tent collapse on them, but night after night the skeleton dream haunted her. The fresh, grisly skeletons of Edward and Eddie, horribly smashed but still intact, loomed over her beside the small frail skeletons of her starved-to-death children, all grinning in ghastly mockery at her immobile helplessness. It still made her come awake gasping in panic and anguish that she'd failed those two little trusting helpless souls, her precious children. No matter how many times she had that horrible dream, it continued to affect her as deeply as the first time. That dream goaded Marty to force herself to hunt much more than she had real strength for, though still with little success. She seldom saw sign of any game and when she did they disappeared before she could get near enough to shoot.

One overcast day, weak, half-frozen and in pain from hunger and the aching ankle, out hunting for anything to eat in the stark white stillness, she came nearly face to face with what she assumed was the male fox; one she hadn't seen before. For a split second she and the startled fox stared in frozen astonishment at each other, she into those bright yellow-gold eyes. Marty was so amazed at the eyes that she hesitated a split second before moving the rifle to shoot at it. The fox darted into the nearby thick forest before she could even swing the rifle up. Her hands shook and her heart pounded, disappointment burning tears down her icy cheeks. She had failed again.

She blinked back tears and thought she might have to resort to stripping more maple bark for food of any kind. But that tree was such a long ways away now, and still as dangerous as ever. No. Surely something closer would be safer.

She glanced around and recognized an alder. She wasn't sure about those. She peeled a twig and chewed on its trace of raw inner bark scraped free with the knife. The taste was unpleasantly astringent, nearly bitter, but she choked it down. Sudden stomach pain bent her over and her mouth watered until she vomited the tiny scrap of inner bark and bitter froth. She would certainly avoid eating alder bark from now on! But surely if maple was edible, there must be other trees she could safely strip.

Gulping, catching her breath, she saw several birches nearby with branches reachable from such deep snow. Some time or other she'd heard of Birch Beer. Did that mean the trees, or parts of them, were edible? Very cautious now, she broke off a twig to sniff, and was astounded that it smelled like Wintergreen! Eagerly, she nibbled the tiniest tip of the twig. It faintly tasted like that kind of candy, but not sweet. Was this where Wintergreen came from? No matter, she happily broke off a big handful of slightly sticky twigs to take home to brew. The children would be delighted. If nothing else this would vary the now monotonous spruce tea.

After a few moments, still feeling no ill effects from nibbling the pleasant birch twig, she reached in further to cut through the branch bark and strip it away, staying very aware of how close she was to the tree trunk's dangerous ice collar. Heartened by the twig's taste, she scraped free a small shred of inner bark to nibble. It also tasted of very dilute, faintly sweet Wintergreen. Marty sighed deeply in relief, she could get plenty of this; many birch trees grew all over the valley. It tasted altogether different than the maple inner bark's hint of maple syrup flavor, but was apparently as edible. Maybe alder was the only exception.

Looking back at the branch for more bark to strip, she noticed long hanging male catkins were just starting to open out to shed pollen. Mouth watering, she remembered the cattail pollen's broad usefulness. Shaking equally from weakness and excitement, she plucked all she could safely reach. Aromatic twigs crammed one pocket and equally aromatic catkins filled the other. She peeled bark from all the branches within reach and laid them on the ever-present sled. But she peeled none from the trunk to avoid killing the handy tree. She only wanted to take enough from it to keep them alive.

Both youngsters were overjoyed at this fresh taste.

"Did you find Santa Clause?" Ted asked hopefully. "I had candy like this at Christmas, a long, long time ago."

"No." Marty sadly half-smiled, "This grows on trees not far from here. I found them today." The boy's solemn too-old-for-his-age nods nearly brought tears. She turned away to shake all the pollen she could from the catkins. When that yielded too little, she tried boiling the catkins then scooped the insoluble parts out to discard. She used that liquid to cook the small daily ration of grain. The smell was aromatic, but its flavor was faint.

Since she hadn't been seeing any game to hunt during the dim hours, she limped out on the painful ankle in the middle of the day, when it was brightest. Days are longer now, she thought, wouldn't the game have to come out to eat sometime in daylight?

Light glaring off the snow from the ever-brightening sun quickly gave her a piercing headache, though she'd been squinting. Her eyes burned fiercely. That burning was so familiar she ignored it; it would quit after she got back inside the dim shelter.

She continued to go out for hours every day, to hunt, but she also picked twigs and catkins, and peeled more birch and any maple barks she could find as she passed them. She always brought wood back on the last part of her daily trek, though she towed the bark sled the whole trip. There was always the possibility she would find game to shoot, and then the sled would be necessary to haul meat. But her stubborn refusal to avoid the glaring sun caused her snow blindness to progress until, even in the morning, after hours of dim light, she was still in pain from stinging eyes that felt full of gritty sand and unpleasant, pounding headaches.

Finally she had to admit she could no longer stand to go out in full daylight. She wasn't finding more game when it was brighter anyway. Only after sunset could she stand to go out briefly to grab birch or maple twigs and bark and enough wood to last until dawn. Then at the first trace of dawn light she was back out for more wood, enough to last the day, and anything she could grab to eat, mostly a few more catkins, before the light got too bright. Any spruce trees she knew of were now too far away to reach in time.

After several days of dim light, when even looking at the fire was painful, she finally realized the sandy stinging was gone, the headache much less severe. She'd heard about snow goggles, some kind of facemask with slits to peer through that were narrow enough to hold out most of the brightness. She had no material or tools to make anything like that. Feeling desperate to get out and get food, she pulled many of the stitch loops slightly bigger in one area of her knitted scarf to look through for snow goggles. That wasn't terribly effective and it was not easy to see past the intervening strands without constantly shifting her head around, but did help some if she was still out after sunup.

Heading home in the twilight one evening, she noticed the full moon had just risen above the mountains. Its light on the snow made it seem nearly as light as an overcast day. She was tempted to try night hunting but she was already quivering with weakness and as long as she now had to sleep to regain any strength, the moon would set before the shaky weakness was gone. It was far too cold to be out just before dawn anyway, she shrugged.

The next morning Marty was pleased to notice the air was much warmer than usual. Some sort of game should be moving around. This time she set several tree snares for grouse along her wood gathering route.

Checking them the next day, she was shocked to discover one snare had caught a rusty brown squirrel. She always thought they hibernated the whole winter, and was astonished it was out, even with the air warmer. It still wasn't even close to being warm out but the deep layers of snow now looked and felt shrunken and dense.

She sadly took the squirrel home to stew, knowing Teddy's heart would break as soon as he saw it. It weighed less than half a pound, but it was better than nothing, and was already dead, so she couldn't dare waste it when they were so desperately starved. In deep thought all the way back, Marty tried to think of a way to keep from upsetting her poor little Teddy Bear.

No matter how hard she thought, or how hard she tried to hide what she brought in, Ted cried when he saw it, big, wrenching sobs that nearly tore her heart in two.

"I'm so sorry." She said while hugging the boy, trying to give a measure of comfort. "We'll do an honor ceremony like Gram told me, for this brave squirrel's spirit."

"But he was my friend!" Ted wailed, tears running down his pinched, pale face.

"Sometimes a friend may have to give his life so another friend can live. That's a great honor, a noble sacrifice." Marty turned aside and moved out through the fireside doorway. She needed a few minutes alone to figure out what to do for a ceremony, and to recall just what Gram had said about one.

After a while she returned with a handful of sprigs from the cedars just outside. She had not yet skinned or cleaned the poor little creature. She stoked the fire, which had died back during her wood-gathering and snare-checking absence, then sat both kids fairly close and bundled them warmly under the rather stiff deer hide where they could easily see what she was doing. After kneeling quietly for a moment in front of the crackling fire, she started to softly hum a lullaby whose words she never knew.

Both sober faces peering from under the hide were intent on her every move. Marty gulped and, as gently as possible, laid out the squirrel between her and the fire. In what she hoped was a reverent voice, she said, "Spirit of this brave squirrel, I wish to thank you for so valiantly giving your life to the three of us so we can live a while longer. That was a very noble sacrifice." She gently began to tube peel it then gut it.

When she was done, nearly in tears from the smallness of its body, she slipped that frail body into water in the Dutch oven, pushed into the side of the coals to boil, and put on the lid. Then she found the tiny heart, no bigger than the nail on her thumb and, humming again, dropped it into the blaze. "I send this offering back to the Spirits in thanks." Immediately smelling scorched flesh, she quickly laid cedar fronds on the blaze. As they flared into crackling, sparking life the strong incense of cedar filled their shelter, obscuring the less desirable odor.

Marty was relieved the children accepted the ceremony and actually felt as if she had done something reverent, not just a thing to mollify a broken-hearted little boy. She was suddenly aware that this honor ceremony would have to become a tradition, if they survived. The children would expect it, or something like it, at least with squirrels.

Limping out to the 'freezer' to store the meager entrails, she thought, surely we'll survive. We only have such a short time until spring.

A shadow of doubt nagged a far corner of her mind.

Even that few ounces of meat helped for one evening's meal. They were all very subdued while eating it.

Back from her early morning trek, laying half asleep though it was daylight, Marty jumped violently at hearing a cougar snarl and scream not far away. Her heart hammered as she jerked around and lunged for a rifle. Before she could reach the lever-action propped against the stone wall near the entry, she heard several dull, bumping thumps. Nearly swooning from panic, she realized the sounds were not far into the woods nearby.

Shaking badly, she fumbled into outside clothes, loaded and cocked the rifle, and snuck into the woods, terrified of the ferocious cat. But it had to be after some kind of prey animal and she was desperate enough to try to salvage some of whatever it got—when it was done feeding and left, of course!

It was galling to realize she actually anticipated scavenging off a wild animal's kill! She never thought she could ever, in her whole life, get so hungry and so desperate!

Trembling, she ducked and squirmed through the thickest, outermost trees of the forest, and was stunned to see that scant yards in, just out of sight from the fringe, little underbrush grew, leaving a park under very large trees. The snow beneath the trees, up to where the undergrowth ended, was laced with deeply worn trails. The brush's inside edge looked ragged and sparse—something had been eating it!

Reminded by a terrified bleat and a nerve-jangling crunch somewhere ahead why she was here, Marty jerked, gulped, and cautiously limped forward with the rifle aimed ahead, glancing this way and that. Her heart hammered from terror, though the sound had been a ways off, farther than those she'd heard from inside the shelter.

All over under the huge, dense trees the snow was laced with deeply worn trails, and down in one, partly covered with a sprinkle of loose snow, was a clear deer track! This is where they'd all gone! How had she failed to realize deer would also seek shelter from tree-splitting cold?

Edging deeper into the woods, alert for any sound or movement, she began to see wider hollow spots where deer had curled up to sleep. Then, in a few steps, she saw more deer beds. The snow just past there was more churned up than where she'd been, and a short ways off she saw a wide bloody swathe leading away. She noticed three other narrow, irregular furrows heading out in other directions from closer to where she stood. She limped over to peer cautiously at the wide swathe and shivered at seeing paw prints far broader than her hand; a cougar was the only creature in these mountains with paws like that. No matter how hungry she and the children became, she was not going to try and take any food away from such a large carnivore! It might eat her instead!

She sighed in discouragement and turned back toward the overhang. A flicker of movement caught her eye, almost out of sight among the shadowy trees. Inching in that direction, she followed one of the fresh furrows from the bedding area. Now her heart pounded in excitement instead of fear. The cougar would be busy with its kill, but she could also kill a deer. Even in her weakened condition, surely she could bag one that was bogged down in heavy snow!

Obviously the deer had been trying to escape through accumulated drifts, but kept sinking so deep at each leap that its body left a series of shallow dents in the snow.

Further ahead she spotted a scrawny doe bogged down in snow to its chest, its head drooping in exhaustion, its nose nearly lying on the icy crust. It was so thin and starved that ribs and hipbones easily showed through its heavy speckled grey winter coat. Its huge brown eyes were glazed with terror when it turned to look back at Marty's approach.

Huffing white fog into icy air, the starved doe struggled feebly to get away, then sagged and turned its head back, this time with a look of sorrowful resignation and a sort of pleading in its wide, brown eyes.

Marty swallowed hard against a sudden throat lump of pity and sorrow, but they absolutely had to have this meat. Vividly recalling Gram's buffalo hunt story, of them praying for the animals' spirits to allow them to kill what they needed to eat, she wondered if the squirrel ceremony last night had anything to do with her finally being able to get this much meat. Hair prickling on her neck, she stopped and looked into the doe's resigned eyes while silently praying for the deer to die for her—at this point of starvation, it was the deer's life or all three of theirs.

Shaking from the weakness of severe, prolonged hunger and overwhelming emotions, the rifle seemed almost too heavy to hold up when she raised it. Knowing all too well how it feels to starve, she really didn't want to shoot the poor emaciated thing. But they absolutely had to have this meat!

Gritting her teeth and trying her best to hold steady, Marty aimed the rifle and shot, but cried out loud at seeing a bullet-sprayed gout of snow just beyond the doe's head. The loud, sharp sound of the shot caused clumps and showers of snow to fall from branches overhead and made her cringe. She'd missed! From less than ten feet away! Her face burned in shame and tears scalded down her icy cheeks as the trapped deer again struggled in terror to get away.

Afraid it might still escape somehow, she drew the pistol and walked around to its side. Aiming only at the base of its skull where it should quickly be killed and the least meat would be ruined, she shot it and shot it, sound-loosened snow sprinkles raining down unseen all around her. Weeping in anguish at savagely causing pain by not killing with the first shot, the pistol clicked on empty as the madly thrashing doe sighed a last breath and sank limply onto the snow with sightless, open eyes glassing over. Marty sobbed in guilty relief that she finally had more than a day or so of meat, and the poor starved creature in front of her was finally beyond pain.

As soon as she could control her sobs, between hiccups, she softly murmured a heart-felt apology to it for having to take its life and thanks to it for saving three souls.

She struggled to regain self-control all the way back to camp to leave the rifle, stoke the fire, reload the pistol, and fight through peripheral brush to bring the sled to haul the carcass.

She slit the doe's throat, then felt wasteful at losing the bright red, metallic smelling blood, thinking she would need to catch it next time, though she had no idea how to fix the Blood Pudding Gram had told her about. If she ever did fix any, she huffed, it wouldn't be the first time she had to do something her own way because she knew others had done it, just not how.

Ravens suddenly appeared, croaking and flapping, working closer and closer through tangled higher branches. Where did they come from so suddenly? Marty cringed, but was determined they would get none of her kill except the already-spilled blood, the lungs, and the intestines, parts she seriously doubted were edible for humans. She could leave them that much, she reasoned, also feeling pity for the starving birds. Other frozen entrails were left to use for fish bait when ice left the stream.

She was alarmed that one raven seemed to be directing the others from a branch not far above her head. Its coarse *crawk-AWK-aaawwk* sounded and other birds moved closer, spreading a few feet out around one side of her. It was unnerving.

Marty shook her head at her own reaction, silently scolding herself for being so afraid of a few birds. Hunger must be making me crazy, she thought, turning back to the struggle to move the doe. It was a pitifully thin doe, starved down to around fifty pounds before cleaning, but she was so weak she could hardly wrench it up on top of the snow to partially gut it. Then she had to roll and slide it to get it on the sled.

Turning from fighting the limp carcass to grab the towrope, she saw several crows greedily gulping shreds of discarded tissue while a few others seemed to actually be standing guard near them to warn if she approached!

Dumb bird. Dumb bird. How many times in her life had she heard that? Shows how much whoever-said-it knew about real birds, she snorted, throwing her weight against the rope to start the sled moving toward home. Or she really was going crazy.

At camp, by the 'freezer', she skinned the doe. She was amazed at how thick the skin was and how dense the fur, despite its starved condition. No matter, she had absolutely no energy to deal with anything but heat and food right now; the hide was not important.

Cutting loose the last connection, she decided they would eat all of this animal except any parts of the digestive tract she missed in partially cleaning it. But she would save that for more bait. Also, any organs that looked remotely edible would get chopped up and go into the stew pot for tomorrow. The usual fare of crushed grain and cattail roots would be set aside for now. They were nearly gone, anyway. This meat was plenty to feed them well for many, many days. She'd been saving the flour mix for making gravy. Now was the time to start using that, too. So, for a while they would live on thickened meat stew, and hopefully regain their strength and at least some weight. Though terribly glad for the meat, she was still sad that they'd never again have flour to make biscuits. She shrugged, there's no butter to put on biscuits or bread, anyway.

Cutting the carcass into chunks she could more easily handle, Marty discovered that fragments of lead and spine chips riddled the neck meat and the hide partway down to the shoulders. She sighed in regret at the damage, but knew this time she'd pick out the bone chips and lead fragments and use the meat anyway, and all of this animal's ribs and bones would get stewed. But next time she'd use the rifle, from up closer if possible. It would save shells and meat. Not to mention sparing the poor creature any more pain than was absolutely unavoidable.

Nearly drooling over the look and smell of fresh liver while slicing it, she decided that was the best thing to end their meager starvation diet. The liver, fried briefly in a trace of rancid fat, will be an incredible taste treat, Marty thought. She cut a larger-than-normal piece for Amy, handed it to the nearly frantic girl and turned back to cut Ted's portion.

Amy crammed her mouth and gulped down a half-chewed bite then another and another so fast one was not all the way down before the next was on its way. The famished child promptly vomited up those first hasty gobbles, and wailed in dismay. Ashamed for not preventing the girl from doing that, Marty took the rest of Amy's food away and made her slowly sip on a cup of melted snow water until she cried again, this time from not getting to eat.

After watching Amy, Ted was more cautious about chewing well and slowly, but after three bites he hunched forward over stomach cramps as his body protested the rich food it was so unaccustomed to.

Unnerved and feeling mean for making Amy wail from hunger with food right there, she fed the girl a tiny bite, sternly warning her, "You chew this up good this time, and don't be in a hurry. You wasted the other food from trying to eat so fast, if you waste any more we'll all have to go hungry."

Busy feeding and watching the children, she had no chance to eat her own portion fast but, after a few small bites, Marty also felt her stomach knot and start to ache. She made the children wait a couple of hours before trying to eat another few bites, only now understanding how really starved they had become, but shocked their famished bodies would reject life-saving food. It would be necessary to ease up severity of the rationing in a less drastic way, and that what they did eat needed to be less concentrated. Still, what little portions of diced, well stewed liver and other organ meats they did eat over the next three days made them all feel miserably overstuffed and hungry at same time.

When they finally managed to eat all the chopped, stewed organs and started on the muscle meat, she found it very tough, requiring as long to cook tender as unsoaked whole grain. Now she understood what Eddie meant when he said spring feeding made meat tender. Starvation certainly made it shoe-leather tough!

The milder, warmer spell of weather ended with a moderate storm that left only a trace of new snow but put an icy crust on the old. After the storm passed, the weather was colder than it had been for that few days, but not as icy as it had been only half a moon cycle ago.

The first morning after the storm Marty was back out gathering twigs, catkins, bark to scrape the inner cambium layer from, and firewood, while also keeping an eye out for any game; it was still cold enough to freeze any extra meat. The new powder on top of the icy crust made walking any distance more treacherous than ever. After an hour or so of being mostly focused on keeping her feet under her, she noticed the new moon rising. She thought with a shiver of excitement, it was now March eleventh and they'd been here eleven months. They only had four more weeks to make it through to a full year!

But why was it still so cold, and why was there still so much snow?

She was distracted from those worries by seeing that willows and hazelnuts were also showing pollen-laden catkins. Those first hints of coming spring touched her so deeply she stood staring at them as tears of relief scalded down her cold-stung cheeks.

Back in camp, she dutifully marked the new date line and recounted the marks, recalling her naive assumption that she would use this to tell her rescuers, "I kept us alive this long." She remembered wondering if anyone knew what surviving here meant, and suddenly laughed dryly at her own lack of understanding then.

Later that night she awoke, troubled. Something was wrong with the date stick. She had eleven new moons marked, and in one more cycle they'd have been here a full year. But something was wrong with that. Too much snow was still on the ground and nothing was sprouting or budding, as it should be that close to when they'd arrived. Fully awake now, and troubled, Marty stoked the fire to see better and used a scrap of charcoal to mark on a part of the rock wall lit by flickering flames. She calculated twenty-eight days as one moon cycle, so that into three hundred sixty-five . . . equals 13! Thirteen moon cycles a year, not twelve!

Her heart fluttered panic as she realized they still had eight long, cold weeks before this valley would be like it was when they first came, and the first few edible greens began to grow. That poor starving doe would never last them that long! Totally demoralized, she crawled back into bed and fell into troubled sleep, dreaming the skeleton nightmare again.

The snow that had shrunk or melted during the warm spell before that last storm had bared mats of Kinnikinnick, and now Marty limped from one to another and frantically combed through each one for its tiny, mealy, dried-apple tasting berries. Last spring when they were in bloom a few berries had still been on the plant, so she knew they stayed on all winter. She found and picked a couple handfuls, total. Feeling like that paltry bit was a vast treasure, she split half with the delighted youngsters that night, and the rest after they ate their breakfast stew the following morning.

CHAPTER 22

After days of eating slightly thickened, lean meat stew, Marty laboriously carved away the last of the solidly frozen leg meat to stew and then tried to saw through the leg bone, but the small keyhole saw was too dull and she was still too weak. Wanting to stew out the rich, fatty marrow, she swung the big ax to smash through the long bone, but totally missed it; momentum buried the blade deep into the frozen, snowy duff beneath the giant cedar trees, barely missing the side of her foot. Huffing nervous disgust at missing the cut and nearly crippling herself, she examined the irreplaceable blade for nicks, sighed in relief at not finding any, and put it away.

Using the much safer hatchet's blunt back, she aimed more deliberately and struck with all her might midway down the leg bone. A spiral fracture shot out in both directions from the blow. Then it was easy to twist the marrow-filled pieces of bone apart and fit in the pot to enrich the stew.

Finally, with that marrow, they were able to eat calorie-rich fatty tissue. The lean meat had helped slightly with reviving their energy, but the added marrowfat helped enough to notice after only one meal. By now they could actually eat a tin cup of rich meaty stew before their touchy stomachs warned that was enough for now by starting to ache. They also could eat three times a day now, rather than only morning and evening, as had been their routine for far too long. The children's gaunt cheeks looked just the tiniest bit less sunken and their oddly swollen, rumbling bellies had actually begun to shrink, slightly.

This diet was still not enough to regain weight, but neither were they continuing to lose any. Marty thought about how long they still had to get through until fresh foods began to grow and became afraid of running out again. She limited how much she cooked each day, and each day she still had to limp around to gather wood morning and evening. Every trip out she brought back one or more kind of fresh sprigs and twigs to make tea, plus whatever edible bark she could reach to strip; getting those no longer left her shaking with exhaustion as they had, but she was still very weak.

Walking still hurt. She could never seem to get enough wood ahead to skip one trip, and for sure couldn't get a whole day's supply stocked up. Such constant use aggravated whatever injury she'd sustained from the brutal pressure between tree and solid ice that had so nearly crushed the arch of her foot and ankle, kept it painful and inflamed.

Still, reinforced more each day was her sureness that they'd live to see spring. Once spring broke and plants began to grow she had little worry for their survival; if they could live through this first learning-the-hard-way winter they could certainly make it through any other.

Finally, she used the hatchet to chop the frozen deer spine into small sections to boil off those meat scraps. She was relieved to have parts like those that she'd once spurned as not good enough; she'd even cooked the leg sinews and tendons along with the cracked leg bones. In thickening all those stews, though, she used up the last of the flour mix, then the cattail roots.

When the last of the spine had been put on the fire to be boiled clean, she started to grind more grain for thickening and became slightly frantic at realizing that only three cups of whole grain was left in the bottom of the bag. She decided then to boil the skinned skull for what nutrition it might furnish. She boiled it for nearly a full day before fishing out and discarding the bones.

Now the only food left was a scant cup of whole grain and whatever she found each day, like tea twigs, traces of pollen from catkins, and inner barks. If things got too bad they still had frozen entrails. Her stomach roiled at the thought. Even now she was not that hungry.

After another cloudy day of painful, fruitless hunting, she searching along the tangled forest's edge for moveable wood on the way home.

She was startled to see the silhouette of a chicken-sized bird on a low limb. Marty had to blink to be sure she was not imagining it, and saw bark-colored feathers barely ruffle in a slight breeze as the bird stared at her with one unblinking eye. It didn't seem to fear her! Despite the bright eye watching her, she had to wonder if it was alive.

Very slowly, heart hammering in excitement, she took a step closer, leaning lightly on the balance pole. The grouse crouched ever so slightly and closed its eye. Marty gaped. Like a young child, the bird thinks she can't see it when it can't see her!

Careful to make no sound, she aimed the sharp end of the pole precisely and jabbed forward with all her strength and weight. The grouse shot out and down from the tree, dead from such a savage blow to its breast.

Shaking and blinking back tears of relief, she vigorously plucked all the feathers right then, while it was warm and the feathers easily pulled out. If not plucked now, she would have to skin it, which would waste the skin. Every ounce of food was crucial, especially rich, fatty skin.

Several limping steps away, she jerked around to look at squabbling noises behind her, suddenly terrified some beast was after her or her catch. But it was only a dozen or so ravens pecking greedily at the bloody feather tips and speckled snow where she'd plucked the hapless grouse and cut off its head. Three of the big black birds squabbled furiously over the head. Even the ravens were starving.

Turning back toward camp, she wondered what would happen if she stalked and bagged one or two of them the way she had the grouse. But the flock numbered maybe two dozen birds; what would the others do to protect their own?

At least she hadn't cleaned the bird yet. It was easier to carry uncleaned, and she wanted to carefully check the entrails for anything possibly edible. She laid all the unwanted parts out in the lean-to to freeze where they were safe. Hopefully, later, she could also use them for bait. If hungry enough, she would still cook them. Surely that could not possibly be worse than eating grubs!

She told herself that, again and again.

That evening and night they slowly chewed and stubbornly swallowed half of the tough, resin-tasting, roasted bird, only to find their stomachs had already shrunk again. They had to eat several bites at once and wait two or three hours to eat a few more bites. Marty used the tiny wedge-shaped heart, the liver, and the chopped-up gizzard in stew thickened with inner barks for breakfast the next morning. They ate the other half of the well-boiled grouse that evening, sucking all the flavor from every single bone before dropping each one into the fire.

The next day, since the bird was all gone except for thin broth simmered from the last half of the bird, even before going for wood, Marty left the noisy sled and took her loaded rifle back into the woods, hoping at least one of the other deer remained somewhere in that dense maze. But she limped around under the dim forest canopy finding nothing but old trails for so long and so far she had to grit her teeth against crying out from the pain of walking before she could make it back to camp. She couldn't even guess where the other two or three deer had gone. Nowhere in the valley was safe from the cougar. Maybe it had eaten them, too.

For the first time, she resorted to cutting wood close enough to camp she could hurl the chunks in under the cedars to be picked up all at once. That saved considerable steps, although it also removed a small amount of their weather protection. She had deliberately left this wood for a time like this, when she hurt too much to go further—a lesson she'd learned, the hard way of course, at the knoll camp.

The following day the air felt slightly warmer, though the sky was overcast. Soon the ice would melt but, she silently chided herself, if she didn't do something to get more food now they wouldn't live to eat the first spring greens. No grain was left, so now they had nothing to eat except what she could get each day; she still wasn't willing to try cooking the frozen entrails. With the weather warming though, even those would soon thaw and start to rot. She'd really been saving them for bait. Maybe, since the air was so much warmer, the ice on the pond would be thinner and soft enough to chop through!

But that was so far to walk! Her ankle had throbbed all night from the shorter distance she'd traveled yesterday. Could she stand to walk even farther today?

Empty, rumbling bellies and whimpers from the sleeping children decided for her.

So she took fishing gear, frozen guts, a small bag, and the big axe and headed for the deepest part of the pond, limping stubbornly past the old knoll camp. She was glad for the unbroken cloud layer; at least she didn't have to wear the vision-limiting enlarged part of her knit scarf to protect her eyes from sun glare. She could not possibly go so far without getting into full sunlight without such thick clouds.

Approaching the last camp, she was puzzled about why the pointed top looked so shrunken—had there been that much more snowfall since moving to the overhang? Getting closer, she gasped in shock. The whole canopy and tent had, finally, been crushed under the relentless weight of so much accumulated snow! Her dreams warning of being crushed had been right. She'd saved their lives by moving to such a crush-proof site as the present camp; had saved them from the horrible death of her dreams, after all. She shuddered.

At the pond, she was at last able to chop a very deep hole in the ice to fish through, and used small chunks of the frozen entrails for bait.

Very quickly she caught a full dozen trout ranging in size from slightly over wrist-to-fingertips long up to fingertips-to-elbow length! Then they stopped biting. Jittery with glee while removing the hook from the last one, she realized the ice hole was already refreezing and that her damp hands had gotten dangerously numb. That was bad.

Marty gathered everything and left, only the worry about her numb fingers marring the victory she felt at catching so many fish. Limping slowly home, leaning heavily on the balance pole, she did feel a little guilty about not throwing the smallest fish back, but she and her precious babies were still too near dying of starvation for it to bother her much.

She put most of the uncleaned fish in the lean-to to freeze, cleaning and frying the two largest for a dinner that seemed almost like a feast, despite the cloying after-taste from the dab of rancid fat they were fried in. Still, it reminded her of last spring when she and Teddy had caught so many trout at once, a memory that warmed her heart.

Ted beamed his wide, gap-toothed grin, showing Marty that he remembered, too, that he'd caught almost all of them that time. Unlike that first meal of trout, this time Amy ate every scrap, no matter how tiny.

At last, for one whole day, she was able to rest that aching, now-swollen foot and ankle. To help rest it, she gathered wood only from the nearby forest.

But in the following days, thinking about how long they had to go yet, she grew scared of running out of food again and used only one big or two small fish each day. When cleaning each one, she couldn't force herself to consider discarding either the heads or guts, they might at least make more bait to replace all that she'd used to catch them; that stayed in the 'freezer'.

The sun finally burned the clouds away and made the coating of white snow on the south-facing cliffs so bright all day that even the modified scarf couldn't prevent Marty from getting another touch of snow-blindness. The brilliant sunlight, combined with a warmer-than-usual breeze, was enough to start the spring thaw. The snow's melting and shrinkage was obvious even in dim early morning light.

Despite looking through the knit-holes of her shielding scarf she noticed where the sunlight glinted off ice in cracks on the soaring rock cliffs, and saw their dark melt-water running down the face of the cliffs. That melting allowed all the ice-loosened rock to abruptly fall free, and any ice-fractured limbs to drop without warning. Either event startled Marty enough to set her pulse racing when it happened. But she welcomed this new, easily reachable wood supply.

Daily, she noticed more leaf buds starting to swell, and each new bud made her heart ache with unshed tears of relief, because with every passing day their chances of surviving this horrible winter improved.

Distantly heard in the deep wintry silence were alarming pops and rumbles as ice over the stream stretched and relaxed, cracking into great shifting chunks still held immobile by the cold, but straining, ever straining and groaning to be free to rush downstream; every pop and rumble made tears well at this sign that spring was imminent, that they only had a few short weeks left to make it through.

The slightly warmer weather condensed the snow pack so much that the bucket of snow set against the fire to melt for water felt considerably heavier. And, venturing out in twilight for fallen branches a bit further from camp, she noticed how much the snow had shrunk from what it had been only a few days earlier. That shrinkage exposed battered but still clinging rose hips and more Kinnikinnick berries. With tears of relief blurring the dim world, she picked both until she could no longer see in the evening light, then returned before sunup to gather more.

Searching for more berries and gathering birch bark and twigs one cloudy evening, Marty was shocked immobile to hear the far-away sound of gray geese honking. She looked up and finally saw them flying north in their noisy V-shape, far above the scattered clouds. They were much, much too far away for even a good shot to hit. She looked down, tears threatening, until she could gulp them away.

She sighed and glanced west as she turned to start back to camp. Another full moon hung just over the west cliffs. It must be near the end of March now, she thought with her heart thundering so hard it seemed to echo off her ribs. We'll make it. We'll make it!

Limping toward the overhang camp, sheltered only by the silk parachute canopy, she noticed a very few places where melting snow had bared light brown spots of slick mud. Travel was better on the shrunken, grainy snow than on the mud; the old snow was not as slick at this time of year. Soon she would be able to stop wearing the cumbersome snowshoes altogether. They should have been repaired weeks ago. But all the hare tubes needed for more had been painfully far away, and were now hopelessly buried under a huge mound of snow.

During that night a very warm, soft wind blew gently through the forest, whispering farewell to winter's ice. Water dripping and trickling from the nearby escarpment's face woke Marty before the sky began to lighten with impending sunrise. She slipped out of her snug sleeping bag, careful not to disturb the sleeping youngsters between her and the sheltering back wall, to go stick her head out past the edge of the canopy near the fire. She felt the wind's warmth on her face and heard distant ice crashes and rumbles in the direction of the stream. It was nearly as loud as an avalanche, and shook the ground almost as much, but this crashing rumble kept on and on.

Tears streamed unnoticed down her cheeks as she realized the stream's ice had thawed overnight and was now in the full flood of spring breakup. They'd survived until the ice thaw came! A few days more, only a few days more.

Dressing carefully, deciding not to disturb the banked fire yet, she grabbed the shorter rifle and set off along the trail below the slip-fault toward the stream. The sound grew louder and louder as she neared and the ground shook more noticeably until she was almost afraid to get within sight of the water. But curiosity kept her feet moving closer and closer, almost against her will.

Her first glimpse of the raging torrent took her breath away. Water, filled with shards and chunks of ice, surged far out of the streams banks, more than tripling its usual width. Cautious but intensely curious, she approached the maelstrom and heard deeper rumbles from the turbulent water, could feel the ground vibrate with an odd rhythm in time with the rumbles. She couldn't guess how much horrendous power that water had.

It surged over the gravelly areas that had been bare when she first saw them; now she knew what swept them so clean of vegetation. Nothing could possibly root deep enough to resist that torrent. Then she was shocked to realize the ground-shaking rumble had to be from big rocks being swept downstream by the unrelenting force of flooding, ice-choked water.

On the way back, a hint of green leaf starting to poke through the dingy, grainy snow caught her attention, stopped her in her tracks. It was near the edge of brush that lined the forest; even in summer it would be shaded most of the time. With shaking hands she squatted and carefully scooped old snow away from the plant until she could see all of it. The short leaves looked vaguely familiar but, aside from the impression it was some kind of lily, she couldn't identify it. Some lilies were deadly poison, like the Death Camas.

Her body quivered with hunger and her mouth watered. She wanted with all her being to dig it up and eat it, even unknown. But if it was poison they would all die now, with spring melt starting. No. They could last until she could identify it, until she could know if it was toxic.

Limping on back to camp, she thought deep and hard about where to go to find a patch of Glacier Lilies. They came up and bloomed through melting snow each March or April, spreading far and wide a heady aroma from their beautiful, white or bright yellow, nodding blossoms that stood out so obviously against the snow. She'd never eaten them, but they were one Gram had shown her long ago. They should be up now. Had she seen any last year?

If I can't get meat, at least I can find more vegetables, Marty thought as she stepped through the shelter door and tucked it back against the rock wall. The meadow was much too far to go, as weak as she was, but just above the fault the snow should be fairly thin. She could walk far enough to get up there and a ways along the treeless strip near the drop-off's edge. She stirred up hot coals and added dry twigs to revive the fire. Even if she didn't find any early-growing lilies, surely something should be growing by now. At least she could get another couple days' worth of spruce or birch for the teas that were so helpful in keeping them alive this long.

Limping, carefully looking out over the lower valley from not far above the fault scarp, then looking up into the upper half, she finally found a small patch of budding lilies, not the Glacier Lilies she had been looking for, but three-leaf, three-petal Trilliums. As she knelt in the half-frozen muddy slush to dig them she remembered Gram had said it took them seven years to go from seed to bloom, and now she was killing them to keep herself and her children alive. Tears streamed cold trails down her cheeks as she dug around a stem with the meat fork—the spit bar she'd used before to dig bulbs was still at the knoll camp—then scooped the icy dirt back with a bare hand, going deeper and deeper until at last she could pry out the small radish-sized bulb. It would take most of the patch of Trilliums to make even a small meal. She would not, even with them starving, dig up all the bulbs. Wiping tears away on her coat sleeve, she remembered thanking the deer for its life. Now she paused to silently thank the plants for giving theirs.

Carefully stepping down the descent at the fault's north end, she was startled to see various-sized hoof prints cut into dirty slush, some overlaid with her wide snowshoe oval. She'd walked right over them on the way up and hadn't even seen them. She huffed, would she never learn to see what was right in front of her?

That night, just before falling asleep, Marty silently asked Gram to help her get more food for her starving children, especially meat.

In hazy dream-dawn light she watched herself limp to a tree within sight of the fault's north end and step behind it to hide, then lean against it out of weakness to wait for some animal to come down the narrow passage. Waiting silently, her legs quivering with weakness and her whole body getting colder and colder, she was about to give up and go home when she faintly heard snow crunching softly near the top of the trail.

Waking suddenly, quivering for real, she understood that of course game had worn that trail down across that end of the fault, because there was no other place in the whole valley for them to move from one level to the other to feed—she knew where she could get meat!

Too excited to go back to sleep, she added wood to the fire and dipped soot-dotted water from the melted bucket to heat for tea. She broke a few small birch twigs in when the water was steaming, and set the lid on, pulling it a few inches away from the hot coals to steep. She pictured the dream again, then realized that if she took the sniper rifle she could wait far enough back not to scare anything away with her scent. The long rifle would shoot accurately almost as far as she could see clearly. But she would need a branch the right height to prop it on; even at full strength she'd had trouble holding it up steady long enough to aim accurately. She felt a new stab of remorse at not being able to shoot the starved doe right because of her trembling weakness. She didn't ever want to repeat that fiasco.

Then she sat forward and her jaw dropped: why hadn't she thought of propping the long gun over a branch before? Why had she persisted in traveling the valley looking for game when she never got anything that way? She bowed her head. Maybe hunger had made her thinking less clear, she thought; maybe it had made her mind as inadequate as her strength and energy.

Silently she thanked Gram for the dream showing her how to finally get enough to feed them. Then she pictured a big elk with regal antlers sweeping the sky, and silently asked it to please, please help her keep her children alive by giving its life for them.

Before dawn silhouetted the eastern peaks, Marty found a suitable branch on a tree in the right area from which to still-hunt. It was plenty far enough away from the descent that she felt safely out of scent range. Propping and sighting the rifle, she chambered a shell with the bolt and examined the safety to be sure it was off. The long rifle was ready to shoot with only the slightest movement to finesse the aim and pull the trigger. No large move was needed that might attract attention.

But she was cold, soon started shivering in spasms from the inactivity. Would that spoil her aim? She fretted. The dim light slowly grew until she could see fairly well, though not yet in color beyond grays and browns. She leaned her head against the rough bark of the trunk and closed her eyes for a moment. At a sudden flurry of hoof beats straight ahead, she jerked upright and her eyes flew open. She expected to see the magnificent, proudly antlered bull elk of her dream, but instead saw a scraggly-haired, pathetic looking animal without antlers skittering down the short decline.

"Please, please die for me?" she whispered, adjusted her aim slightly, and fired. Her heart fluttered madly and a pang shot through the pit of her belly as she watched the large animal lurch closer, then slowly fold down onto the mud and snow not far away.

"Thank you! Thank you!" She squealed, nearly overcome with relief. She rushed to the still creature and reached to stroke its long neck, thanking it reverently for its sacrifice. This was enough meat to last them through to when many foods would be easy to find. She didn't have to ration how much they ate anymore; that could even be all their bodies would accept! Tears dripped from her cheeks onto the coarse neck fur next to her hand. "Thank you. Thank you." She repeated.

After slitting the throat, Marty shakily peeled back the chest and belly hide to cut in and retrieve the liver and heart. Then she peeled more hide and carved much of the meat off the top hindquarter. But, even without any bone, and as starved-thin as this animal was, she still had to cut that chunk into quarters to load it on the sled. She was too tired and weak from hunger and it was too much wet, sloppy weight to get any more precious meat then, and still have strength to pull what was loaded all the way home.

She gratefully took a break to cook thin steak slices, feed the kids a bite at a time, and slowly savor her own portion. Then she rested quietly until she was no longer shaking with weakness, all the while fretting about something taking their lifesaving meat.

Finally, she felt strong enough to return to the carcass. Chasing away the persistent crows, she tried to slide it closer to a tree to hang it to finish the gutting, but the gaunt, horse-sized animal was so heavy she was unable to slide it, let alone hoist it off the ground. Realizing it was just as easy to drag it home piece by piece as to hang it here, she began to cut large chunks of meat off the partly-gutted carcass and hauled load after load to the lean-to 'freezer' to keep it safe.

Making the fourth trip for the day, she realized that so much meat would rot in this warming weather if she didn't dry all she could as soon as possible, though some would stay cold enough to keep a few days. On the return trip she figured out a good place to set up a drying rack near the overhang. But it took two more days of moving meat and marrow-filled leg bones, then cutting saplings and building the new drying rack before she could spread any slices to dry.

While the loaded rack of meat was at last drying in cool smoke, she went on top of the scarp to pick more sprigs of spruce and dig more lily bulbs just back from the brink. She was infinitely thankful that some plants were now available to gather, because eating only meat was causing constipation. The meat diet did restore her strength and energy amazingly fast, though.

Straightening up to rest an aching back, Marty looked toward the drop-off end near the stream, remembering she'd refused to let her own weakness stop her from climbing the fault's face when she first explored the valley.

Thinking of all she'd learned and accomplished since being there, she realized that, as she had gotten dizzy from looking down from the height of that first high rock she'd climbed, she now felt dizzy from looking back at the mountain of accomplishments she'd managed in one year.

Triumph surged through her as that dizziness faded to pride of accomplishment. She'd kept the skeleton dream from becoming a reality; she'd kept the two precious children, her very reason for staying alive, from dying and leaving her utterly alone.

Marty understood now that anyone who survives extreme conditions are people who have something so important to live for that they'll find a way to stay alive—she did, because she had the children she loved with all her heart and soul to keep alive. Without them she would have died from despair and loneliness long ago.

Heading back, she remembered that when she realized no one was coming for them she had vowed to get them Home, somehow.

She had kept that vow.

She had made this wilderness valley Home.